TEXAS WILDFLOWERS

FOUR-IN-ONE COLLECTION

ANITA HIGMAN

Print ISBN 978-1-61626-595-3

eBook Editions:
Adobe Digital Edition (.epub) 978-1-62029-550-2
Kindle and MobiPocket Edition (.prc) 978-1-62029-549-6

Cover design: Kirk DouPonce, DogEared Design

Published by Barbour Publishing, Inc., P.O. Box 719, Uhrichsville, Ohio 44683, www.barbourbooks.com

Our mission is to publish and distribute inspirational products offering exceptional value and biblical encouragement to the masses.

ecpa Member of the Evangelical Christian Publishers Association

Printed in the United States of America.

Dedication

To my son, Scott, and my daughter, Hillary.
You were each a miracle when you were born, and you still are.
Life has been made richer and more joyous
because you're both a part of it.
Never forget how much you are loved. . .

Acknowledgments

Praise goes to my editor, Becky Germany, at Barbour Publishing, for her expertise and support. And to Ellen Tarver, for helping to make these stories a finer read.

And much gratitude goes to my agent, Sandra Bishop, who believed in my work and who faithfully cheers me on.

The course of true love never did run smooth.
William Shakespeare

EVERYTHING'S COMING UP ROSY

Chapter 1

I'm going to kill Henry.

I stood at the back of the church, trembling beneath my wedding gown, while the guests sat poised for that one moment—that storybook moment a girl dreams of her whole life.

The ceremony was about to begin, and my groom was nowhere in sight. I crushed my gown between my fingers as my insides squeezed the life out of me. Henry, my love. Where are you? This sort of thing happened to other people. Right? Friends of friends. Strangers.

I glanced at the front door of the church for the thousandth time. The door teased and tortured me with hints of light around the edges, giving me imaginings of frantic late arrivals and apologies. And yet the door might as well have been sealed shut with nails and tar. Henry wasn't coming. *God, help me not to hate him.* He'd done the unthinkable. Henry had turned my storybook moment into make-believe.

"Rosy, we can wait a little longer," Mom whispered. "Maybe he just got delayed. You know how absentminded Henry can be." She straightened my veil and smoothed my gown. Then she took a tissue and dabbed at the perspiration on her face. Poor Mom.

Henry's best man, Ken, made his way down one of the side aisles and walked toward me as if he were carrying a thousand pounds on his back. He leaned over and said in a low voice, "Henry texted me just now."

"Yes? What is it? Where is he?"

Ken touched my shoulder. "He's not coming."

Mom gasped.

A few guests shot some nervous glances back at us.

Ken's three words, *He's not coming*, poured over me like water over an umbrella. Even though I had guessed the truth, my spirit couldn't fully absorb it. A strange hollow roar filled my head as if I were holding a seashell to my ears. A scary little dizziness buzzed around in my brain, but I refused to pass out. Henry *was not* coming. The door would never open now. Breathe, Rosy.

"This is so. . .I've never seen. . .honestly, I don't know what to say, Rosy, except I would never have agreed to be Henry's best man had I known that he was capable of. . .that he could. . ." Ken lowered his gaze. "I'm so sorry."

"But why isn't Henry coming?" I tugged on the sleeve of Ken's tux as if I were a small child tugging on her mother's apron. "Do you know? Did he say? Please tell me."

"He didn't say. But you deserve to know." Ken gave my hand a squeeze. "Listen, Henry's down in his basement if you want to ask him."

So, Henry was in his basement on our wedding day—the same place he always hid out on a Saturday. Just another day to him. The harpist played my favorite song, "Amazing Grace," but now it seemed absurd in light of my new reality.

Mocking this holy day, this promise of forever love. Mocking the lyrics of "a life of joy and peace." Why had Henry changed his mind? Did he no longer love me?

I pulled myself out of the mess in my head and turned to Mom, who'd busied herself wringing her purse strap. "I'm sorry, Mom. Tell Daddy I'm sorry, too. There'll be no wedding after all." I fingered the seed pearls on my vintage gown one last time as a bride-to-be and sighed that sigh that comes when you know your life will now waft and wander like a helium balloon bobbing aimlessly in the breeze. I would never say the vows that would make us man and wife or know the whirling joy of our reception and honeymoon or live the happily-ever-after. It was over. I removed my cathedral train and handed it to Mom. "Have Matilda make the announcement. I'm leaving."

"But, darling, don't you want to eat dinner with us? Have some of the cake, or. . ." Mom's voice faded into sad resignation. "I understand. I'll tell your sisters, but they'll be—"

"Shocked, I know. And furious with Henry." I kissed her cheek. "I love you, Mom."

"Love you, too."

I took one more glance back at the jittery guests and strode out of the church before anyone else found out what had happened. Feeling more angry than sad, I would now home in on Henry like a guided missile ready to detonate.

I crammed myself and my meringue-like gown into my MINI Cooper and sped so fast through the streets of Houston I bumped a plastic trash can along the way. How apropos. After arriving at my fiancé's house, I unstuffed myself from the car, picked up my bouquet from the car seat in case I needed something to throw at him, and then headed up the stone walkway.

I opened a small side door—the one Henry always forgot to lock—and tromped down the steps into the musty basement. Dust rose, coating my finery, but I no longer cared. The hem of my gown caught on a nail, and when the material wouldn't give way to my tugs I yanked it off, ripping the delicate fabric. "Henry?" My voice was just below a scream. "Henry!"

"Yes," came the weak reply of a mouse—maybe I *should* say rat.

Standing on the last step, I could see Henry slumped over a vial of something blue and bubbly, surrounded by brick walls and two rectangular windows, which only allowed enough light in to keep him from going as blind as one of those albino cave salamanders.

Henry looked up at me. He wore his laboratory coveralls, not his wedding tux.

I took in enough extra breaths to make myself light-headed. "What do you think you're doing? You missed our wedding! How could you do such—"

"I know."

I calmed myself. "What happened, Henry. . .to us?"

Except for the ticking of a clock, silence engulfed the cellar. I was drowning, and time was audacious enough to continue on.

"I've never been smart enough for you, have I? I know I'm clever, but not in a brainy sort of way. My parents probably didn't give me any stimulation in my crib. Or feed me enough blueberries. Or—"

"Don't be silly, Rose. You have a higher IQ than most women I know."

"What then?" I took the last step into the cellar and walked toward him.

Henry set his vial down and backed away as if I might throttle him. It *had* crossed my mind.

"I found the answer to the problem," he said, pointing to some kind of diagram on his laptop.

"Problem?"

"I did it. I finally invented an odorless spray to make the photos last even longer in your mother's scrapbooks. I'll need a patent, of course, and a way to market it. But then I might sell the idea to—"

"Henry. . .I appreciate the fact that you want to be a part of my scrapbooking family. But I needed your commitment of love today, not your odorless spray!" I lifted my bridal bouquet and smashed it against the wooden chair in front of me. The flowers fell to the floor, bruised and broken. The sight looked so pitiful I knelt down and tried to put some of the pieces back together. It was impossible, of course. A single teardrop trolled its way down my cheek. No more came out. I would save them for later, since crying in front of Henry would now seem like throwing pearls before swine.

"I'm sorry, Rose." Henry's arms made a feeble attempt to reach out to me, then they drooped back to his side. "I just don't love you *enough*."

Chapter 2

Words failed me.

And for a moment, I thought my heart might fail me, too. "An alien has come and taken my Henry."

He smiled. "You know, when I first asked you out a year ago, I couldn't believe anyone like you. . .someone so drop-dead beautiful would go out with a nerd like me. I'd never been so thankful in my life. But I guess that feeling of gratitude got confused with something much more serious."

"I see. But then I guess I have no choice but to see." I noticed one perfect white rose on the floor, so innocent looking, ready to be trampled, and it made me think of the naiveté I must have had as I fell in love.

I picked up the stray flower, walked over to Henry, and slipped it into the pocket of his coveralls. "You know, I even loved our differences. . .the way I said angel pillows, and you said cumulonimbus." I placed my hand over Henry's heart, a spot I'd often put my head for comfort. "We would have been good for each other. Perhaps you can't see that anymore. But someday, when your heart catches up with your brain, it'll be too late."

Henry made no reply, but his somber expression did at

least reveal a measure of anguish. In that flicker of sorrow, though, there was no hope for reconciliation. It was the final blow, as if I'd been dangling off the edge of a cliff, holding on, and Henry had smashed my fingers with the heel of his shoe. From that angle—looking up at him with all his power over me—he appeared to be less of a man than I'd ever imagined.

I set the engagement ring in his hand. "I forgive you, but it will take me a lifetime to forget what happened today." Then I walked up the stairs and into the light. Again, the words of "Amazing Grace" seemed to strike a chord in my spirit.

Through many dangers, toils, and snares,
I have already come;
'Tis grace hath brought me safe this far,
And grace will lead me home.

Yes, home sounded like the safest place to rest—the best place to just be.

Good-bye, Henry.

*

That evening I packed a few things, got in my MINI Cooper, and traveled back to my hometown of Galveston, back to my childhood house and to the safe confines of the bedroom I grew up in. I would vegetate in my princess canopy bed—the one with the tender rosebuds that my mom had painted on the headboard—and I would sleep for an undisclosed length of time.

I pulled up in front of my parents' old Victorian house and dragged myself toward the front door. Mom, Dad, and my three younger sisters, Lily and Violet and Heather, were waiting for me. I hadn't even made it to the door when they rushed outside to greet me.

"Group hug," Mom said.

The cozy feeling of my family was better than I remembered. I couldn't imagine why I'd ever let myself drift away from such love.

We all six huddled like that on the porch with the sounds of the late September night all around us—the beetle bugs tapping against the porch light, the occasional rumble of distant thunder, and the cool puffs of autumn air that jingled the wind chimes. Dad, who was a rugged, quiet man—also a man I admired above all others—rubbed my back in circles as my sisters made little cooing sounds to comfort me. Mom encircled all of us girls like a mother hen with her four chicks. Then she leaned toward me, touching her forehead to mine.

That's when I knew I was really home.

After a while my dad picked up my night case. "Let's get you settled, Rosy."

Heather, the second-youngest sister in the family, slipped a small scrapbook in my hands as we walked toward my room. "For when you're ready to start a new book," she whispered, "with new memories."

Violet, the sister just two years younger than me, clasped my hand and gave me her solemn nod, the one that said everything would be all right. "Good night, Rosy."

Lily, the baby in the family, gave me a hug around the waist like she always did. "Well, Rosy Posey, I'm going to make a stack of my peanut butter, chocolate chip pancakes for breakfast."

"Thanks, Lil." I couldn't imagine eating, so I just smiled. "Nighty-night."

We continued with our various good nights until everyone had been acknowledged. I eased my door shut, deposited my horrible day into the merciful hands of God, and crawled under the safe cocoon of my comforter.

But minutes later I must have asked for my troubles back, because no matter what contortions I found myself in, no matter how hard I tried to find that sweet spot, the facts of the day settled in my spirit like a triple shot of espresso. There was no putting a pretty face on it—my white-picket-fence future had burned to the ground. I tapped the heels of my hands together, which I always found calming. Why hadn't Henry at least had the decency to cancel the wedding before it was too late? My poor parents. I would pay them back for the wedding, every penny.

I turned over, flopping my arms like a rag doll. And the guests? When the wedding planner delivered the unhappy news, did they get upset? What about Grandma McBride and her heart problem? Would she be okay?

Soon, my sisters would have to answer the barrage of questions from friends and relatives. Good thing I'd had somebody to cover for me at the realty office, or I'd have a mound of queries from them, too. Did I really care what they thought? I did. And "mercy me," as Granny McBride always said, I still cared for my ex-fiancé. How could that be? Apparently, the Henry Kool-Aid I'd been drinking had made a levelheaded woman into a lovesick freak of nature. But surely the strange tonic running through my veins would wear off.

I stared at my French horn on its stand, the moonlight illuminating its golden colors and curvaceous shapes. It was an instrument I still had an affection for, but one I no longer played. I'd given it up the week I'd met Henry. He'd always hated the French horn.

Memo to myself—never fall in love again. Ever.

*

The sandman, whom I waited for patiently that night, never came. He must have been on an extended vacation. The next day or two were also iffy. I lost track of time and couldn't seem to extract myself from bed. I hated to worry everyone. I would survive my confusion and dejection, but for now I had a need to rest and reflect on what went wrong. Four meals later—my mom always gauged time by meals—my family started to take stressing over me to a new level, visiting my room almost hourly.

"Sis?" Lily knocked on my bedroom door like a neurotic woodpecker. "May I come in?"

"Sure." What day was it? Monday? Tuesday? I glanced at my clock—three. *Mercy me.* I turned over, even though it felt like I'd need a forklift just to heave my arm over to the other side of the bed.

Lily whirled into the room, carrying with her the scents of apple strudel and French roast coffee. It was a plot, since everyone said I looked too thin. "Why don't we do some beachcombing today?" She flung open the wooden shutters, letting in way too much afternoon light. "You know, just you and me and the beach. Lots of salty wind slapping our hair around and our bare toes getting tickled by the sand. Just like old times." Lily had on her usual outfit—pencil skirt and tailored blouse. She always looked like she was headed somewhere important. And I usually wanted to go with her. But not today.

A moan came out of me but no real words.

Lily slapped her palms together in excitement.

I squinted in the obscene light. "Your profession is showing." I grinned, sort of. "Honestly, I appreciate everything you're doing, Lil, but I'm afraid you'll find the seawall to be better company today."

"I'm not your counselor, I'm your sister. And I'm worried about you." She glanced at the door, looking like a guilty child. "You know, you'd feel so much better with a shower and some fresh clothes. I'll get—"

"That's okay. Not quite yet." I raised a finger. "Don't you have to go back to Amarillo? I love seeing you, but I don't want you to think you have to babysit me."

"It's no problem. We all took a couple of extra vacation days."

I heard a lilt in Lily's voice, which meant she was up to some tomfoolery. Unfortunately, I was too busy feeling sorry for myself to figure out what it might be.

My bedroom door creaked open wider.

Lily looked toward the sound and bounced on her toes like a child.

"Hi, Rosy." Standing in the doorway was Larson Brookfield. Someone I'd made friends with the very same day I'd met Henry.

"Lars?" *How unexpected.* I modestly gathered the sheet around me, even though my long beater T-shirt was as revealing and suggestive as a clown barrel with straps.

Lars grinned and took a tentative step into my bedroom. "I brought you an assortment of petits fours." He held up a white pastry box. "All your favorites. Mind if I sit down?"

Lily escaped out of the room and eased the door shut. Such a conspiracy!

"Be my guest." Larson. He wasn't your typical midthirties guy. He had unruly hair, Sasquatch feet, and goofball antics that sometimes came off as awkward as a foreclosure announcement at a housewarming party. And he always wore flannel, even in the subtropics of Galveston. Go figure. But I counted him as a good friend, and I was pleased enough to see him that I wished I'd cleaned up a bit. Well, almost.

He sat down on the bed.

"I know what you're doing here. My sisters are trying to shame me into getting out of bed. They think I'm trying to commit suicide from a lethal buildup of body odor."

He laughed. "I see you haven't lost your sense of humor in all this."

"No, but I've lost everything else." I moved a wad of sweaty hair out of my face.

"I heard. I'm sorry, Rosy."

That word *sorry*—I'd heard it a lot lately. It was an easy word to use when the trouble belonged to someone else.

Lars made a production out of opening the pastry box. He lifted one of the sweets out and studied it as if it were a jewel and not a mere pastry.

I had to admit, the intoxicating smell of ganache-covered cakes sent me into a delirium. My stomach growled loudly enough for Lars to hear the racket.

He laughed. "I hear mutiny."

Having Lars near me made me think of all the times we'd had coffee together, talking about everything and nothing, baring our souls, and enjoying the ease of friendship. And sometimes when I'd begged a little, he would make up stories just to make me laugh. But Henry had never approved of our friendship, and I had understood his concerns. So, after our engagement was announced six months ago, I broke things off with Lars.

"Want one? I bought a dozen, but I can only eat six." Lars paused with the petit four in midair, shoved the entire glazed confection into his mouth, and then closed his lips around it. It was an amusing sight, if not a little bit disgusting.

"No thanks." I scooted up on my pillow and studied him as he chewed. "You're just pretending to be cavalier and hungry. Your eyes have gone all misty."

He swallowed. "I see you haven't lost your sass either. And still the same beguiling face and Alice in Wonderland blue eyes."

I stared out the window at the autumn sky, which had suddenly darkened with rain clouds. "What? Did you say Alice in Wonderland blue eyes?"

"I just wanted to make sure you were still listening."

"Humph." I grinned, but not too much. "Tell me something."

"Anything."

"How would you describe those clouds out there?"

Lars clasped his hands behind his head and gazed toward the window. "They are islands on a dark blue sea."

"Okay. Nice. That's being creative and lyrical without being scientific." I was right—not a thing like Henry.

"I'm afraid those words came from Shelley's poetical genius, not mine," he said. "So, is this a test?"

"Isn't everything?"

He chuckled.

Hmm. At least Lars had always been an honest guy as well as attractive—in a lumberjack-James McAvoy sort of way. But unfortunately, he was still of the males species, and I wasn't feeling overly benevolent toward them at the moment. "I wish you'd tell me a story." *To make me forget about mine.*

"Maybe I will." Lars picked up another petit four from the container, placed it on a napkin, and set it right next to my fingertips. "But first, I'd like to know what it is that you want out of life."

"I don't know what I want anymore." I toyed with the delicate lace on my pillowcase, wishing that lovely things didn't have to be so fragile. "I thought I knew myself. I thought I knew my fiancé. But I didn't. I almost married a rat, Lars, and I can't see how I'll ever trust myself with love again." I arched an eyebrow as a challenge, daring him to convince me otherwise. "What do you have to say about that?"

His face lit up with rascally mischief. "Well, I could say that you're thirty-five, you've been dumped, and your biological clock is ticking louder than Big Ben. Pretty hopeless scenario. But I'm not going to say those things."

"I'm glad." I smiled, curious to see how he would dig himself out of that hole.

"I won't tell you all that because life is a mystery. You don't know what will happen tomorrow any more than you know what I'm going to say next." He winked. "But I *will* tell you a story." Lars paused, looking at me, his eyes lit with something pensive and imploring. "There was this girl in Galveston. She grew up and left her hometown for the big city to become a Realtor. Then one day she met two men. One man walked right into her life and stole her heart. But the other man. . .well, he was left wondering."

I fingered the little cake next to my hand. "And what did the other man wonder about?"

"Why he ever let that woman go."

Chapter 3

Lars really stepped out on a limb with that revelation. What could I say? The last thing on earth I wanted to do was start dating right away. "Just so we're clear, what do you mean?"

"I think you know what I mean. You were very close to marrying the wrong guy."

"You're kidding, right?" Lars had fallen in love with me? I had no idea. Although I wasn't sure I believed him. Where had that come from? It was as expected and as welcome as a sizzling meteor landing in my bedroom.

He stared at me. "Does my face look like I'm kidding?"

"How could I have known? You never mentioned it to me. I got the idea some months ago that we were good friends. Nothing more. I don't know what to say. Except that I'm busy feeling sorry for myself, and now you've come with your belated declarations and your little pastries, which look way too much like miniature wedding cakes I might add, to crash my pity party!" I turned away. "Okay. That was a selfish and thoughtless thing to say."

"Yeah, probably!"

Lily poked her head in. "Hey, what's all the hollering?"

"Nothing," Lars said. "We're just doing a little verbal

fencing. No one's been killed. . .so far. . .just maimed." He thrust his hand over his heart.

Lily drummed her fingers on the door frame and grinned. "Is Mom going to have to put you both in time-out?"

"No problem." I crossed my arms. "Lars is about to leave."

"I took several days off." He crossed his arms, too. "I'm not going anywhere, Rosy."

"Yes, you *are*."

"If I go," Lars said, "so do the cakes."

Lily rolled her eyes at us and shut the door. A little too loudly, I thought.

"Look, I do appreciate you coming by." I pulled the box of petits fours toward me when Lars glanced away. "It was very thoughtful. You always were, and apparently still are, very thoughtful. But as you can see, I'm in a foul mood, and I want to continue to be in a foul mood." I burrowed underneath the covers like the scared little moppet I'd become. "So you might want to come back when I'm human again." I closed my eyes and listened, hoping for the sound of the door opening and closing.

No door. Lars was still there. I could hear the heavy breathing of someone eating sugar-laced carbs.

I sat back up as he devoured another petit four. "Okay, you want to have it out right now. Fine. You're implying that while we were having good times as friends a year ago—wonderful times, come to think of it—you fell madly in love with me."

"Yes. You're very astute in matters of the heart."

My laugh morphed into a cackle. "Well, my parents just

spent a fortune on a wedding that never happened, so I think we can safely say I'm no good when it comes to matters of the heart."

"You give yourself no credit, Rosy."

"Why did you really come here?"

"To cheer you up and to see if I had any chance at all with you."

"Odd timing, wouldn't you say? The words, 'the wedding has been canceled' are still ringing in people's ears like a gong. . .especially *my* ears. It's so loud I'm having trouble hearing you." I smacked the covers, accidentally hitting my little cake. I looked at my icing-covered hand, groaned, and then licked the goo off my palm. "Okay, it's not bad." I sighed. "What am I going to do with you?"

"Marry me."

I took the squashed cake, put it back in the box, and then gave my bedclothes a good yank to make Lars stand up. I stared into those blue eyes of his and saw some of the sadness that I'd seen reflected in my own mirror. Since my grief hadn't rendered me totally heartless, I said, "I'm sorry for causing you pain, Lars. I just didn't know how you felt. You never said a word about it before."

"I know. I take all the blame." He scratched his head, which made his bushy hair stick up even more. "I didn't come for an apology. I didn't come here to make you feel guilty, but to speak the truth."

"And the truth is. . .as I recall. . .*you* asked for us to be no more than friends. It's what *you* wanted. I merely honored your wishes."

"You're right. I didn't want anything more when we first met. That previous relationship with Emily had gone so badly, I thought it seemed safer just to go out as friends for a while. I was a fool. What can I say?"

"Well, I was a big girl, and I did agree to the arrangement, after all. I'd always wanted a brother. I needed a friend who wasn't a sister. I mean, this house has enough female hormones to double as a womb."

"I heard that," Lily hollered from the room next door.

"I didn't mean it in a bad way, Lil."

"I know," she said.

"Love you."

"Love you, too," she hollered back.

"There's no privacy in this house," I whispered. "And so it seemed like a very good idea to have a male friend to pal around with. Little did I know. . ."

Lars lowered his gaze. "Yes, little did you know that I would start out as your friend and end up feeling a lot more. When you broke off our friendship to marry Henry, I should have told you how I felt right away. That everything had changed. I should have fought for you. But you seemed so adamant about what you wanted, I didn't think I'd have a chance. I didn't want to come between you and your joy."

He fidgeted with the lid on the pastry box. "Then when I heard about the wedding being called off, I thought. . . Listen, I had no intention of having this conversation today. I know I'm not all that socially adept, but I do know not to proclaim my love after someone has just broken up."

"But you just did." My eye started twitching. "And it

wasn't just any old breakup, Lars. We didn't just have lunch and decide to go our sad but separate ways. I was left at the altar. No, that's not true. I was left at the *back* of the church. I didn't even make it as far as the altar. I dedicated my love and life to him. . .you know, forever-and-always stuff. I loved him." My stomach growled again. I lifted the smashed cake up to my mouth. "I'm going to eat this, okay?" I pushed the petit four into my mouth just as Lars had done and chewed on the whole thing at once.

"Okay." He sat back down on the bed like he owned the place.

I sighed, not knowing if it was from Lars taking up residence again on my bed or from satisfying my hunger.

My foot peeked out from under the covers, and Lars tugged on my sock. "You have a hole in your sock."

I swallowed. "Yeah, well I have one in my heart to match it."

"I could help fill it. . .if you'll only give me a chance."

"This bit of sustenance has softened my mood, but don't take advantage of it. A year ago, you must have been brokenhearted over Emily like I'm hurting now over Henry. I'll give you that. And I won't lie and say I didn't see you as more than a friend when I said good-bye to you. In fact, when Henry said he didn't think I should have close male friends, my heart twisted in the worst way. I knew he was right. I had to give you up for the health of our marriage, but saying good-bye to you wasn't as easy as I made it look."

"Really?"

"Yes." I took a sip of water since the sweet icing had made my teeth ache. "But that was a long time ago, Lars. I moved on. I have loved. And I've truly lost. And even though it's a little bit insane to still love him, I still have feelings for Henry. It's not something one can cut off in a few hours. In fact, the pain. . .well, I think a crowbar on the foot might feel much better than what I'm feeling inside right now."

"I'm sorry, Rosy."

"I'm not myself. I'm weepy one minute and then a beast the next. Apparently, I've caused you suffering, and I don't want to hurt you any more than I have."

"I don't mind. That's the thing. I'd rather wade through these hard times with you than be back in Houston without you."

He tugged on my sock again, reminding me of the hole. It was bigger than I remembered.

"But you might be wading through these hard times with me for nothing. I don't know if I'll ever be ready for love again. For some women, they have to get right back into another relationship. Maybe to prove they're still attractive and loveable. That they didn't deserve to be somebody's castoff. But that seems as foolish to me as eating a pile of candy bars after a diabetic coma. I can't see myself giving in to it again, opening my heart with such abandon. You know, that all-consuming emotional plunge that has no safety net. At least I don't think I could. But now I barely know who *me* is. I was so sure of myself until. . .I'm just going through the motions of life right now."

"I'm willing to wait. . .with no promises from you."

"It might be years. It might be never. What do you say to that?"

Chapter 4

I say okay." Lars smiled.

"Then I say you're crazy."

"Yeah. I'm probably that, too."

I raised my hand and let it flop back on the bed like a dead mackerel. "All right, as long as you know you're crazy." But I was going to need a friend. Someone beyond my parents and my sisters. After all, I hated to saddle them with the entire burden of my recovery. And Lars had already proven himself to be the very best of friends. "This time the tables have turned. *I'll* be the one asking for nothing more than friendship, and for the same reason you had a year ago. So, do you really think you can live within the parameters of that request?"

"For as long as we both shall live?" Lars said. "I do."

I cocked my head at him.

"Okay, okay." He grinned.

"All right. Just friends then?"

He nodded.

I stuck out my hand to him. He gave it a solid shake and then released me.

"Now I'm ready for you to close those blinds and let me be," I said. "I'm planning on a few more days of moping."

"*Now* you're just being a baby."

I should pelt him with a petit four. "How dare you! You can't say that to me."

"I'm your best friend, and that's what friends do."

"They say cruel and insensitive things to each other?"

"Sometimes. And then they have to apologize," Lars said. "But *sometimes* they say things that need to be said."

"That's not fair. When I told you I had to break off our friendship because of Henry, what did you do? I'll bet you weren't all that upbeat and energetic."

"Hey, you two," Lily said from next door. "You sound just like Mom and Dad."

"I love you, Lil, but stay out of this."

"Love you, too," she hollered back.

Lars latched on to the bedpost. "Yes, I had a few too many rounds of self-pity back then. I admit it. But *I* wasn't lucky enough to have my best friend around to bring me out of it."

I took in a deep breath. "Oh. . .I see." For some reason that speech got to me more than any of his other words. It cut right through me like a knife through wedding cake, and it made me truly ache for his loss. For *his* pain and not just mine. "I'm sorry, Lars."

He nodded. "Thanks." Then he went over to my dresser, pulled out a pair of socks, and came back to the bed.

"What are you doing now?"

"What any friend would do." He pulled off my dirty white socks and replaced them with clean ones. "Doesn't that feel better?"

"A little."

Then he took a brush off the nightstand and told me to turn around so he could brush my hair.

Surprising myself, I complied. "Do I look *that* mangy?"

"Nothing a little detangling won't cure."

He had a lot of nerve to talk about mange. His wild-man locks looked as though they were too frightened to even stay on his head. But for once I didn't say what was on my mind.

Lars took sections of my long hair and ever so tenderly brushed through the matted tangles until the bristles ran smoothly through all of it. If he was trying to prove his patience and gentleness, he'd succeeded. In fact, his touch felt so warm and welcoming I leaned into it. And then something broke the spell. "What's that sound?"

Lars went over to the window and stared down at the street.

"What is it?"

"A kid. Just a little guy. . .maybe around six or seven. Not sure. Anyway, he's throwing pebbles at your window."

The whole world was against me grieving in peace. I slipped on my robe and went over to the window, limping a little, since my legs weren't in the mood to walk. I'd never seen the kid before. Cute round face with enormous dark eyes. And his shoulders seemed perpetually high, as if he were holding his breath.

"He's kind of thin."

"Yes, he is, now that you mention it."

Lars turned the latches and opened the window just as the boy was about to throw another tiny stone. "Ahoy there, mate."

The boy looked startled. "Ahoy!"

"Why are you firing on our ship? Are you a pirate?"

"Yes. . .the good kind. . .and I'm sailing around, looking for my friend."

"What's your friend's name?" Lars asked.

"Uhh. . .Charles Dickens," the boy replied.

Hmm. Odd name for a kid. I crossed my arms and battened down the hatches of my sympathies, determined not to get sucked into the conversation.

"Are you sure that's his name?" Lars asked.

"Yeah."

"Well, Charles Dickens doesn't live here," Lars said. "I'm sorry."

"Oh, okay." The boy dropped his handful of pebbles, looking bewildered and not a bit like a pirate.

"Where do you live?"

"A couple of blocks over there." He pointed up the street.

"You look hungry," Lars said to him.

"Sure. I'm *always* hungry." He bounced up and down on his toes, gesturing excitedly with his hands.

"Well, Miss McBride and I would be happy to make you an after school snack."

Chapter 5

The boy ran toward the front door.

I slapped Lars on the arm. I knew he'd invited the boy for two reasons—not only to "do unto the least of these," but to catapult me from the cozy confines of my death chamber. Nice guy. But Lars *was* a nice guy. He was the best, in fact, even on a bad day, even with his deplorable lack of social skills. Even when he hadn't a clue how to let a woman wallow properly in the emotional muck of a relationship gone bad.

Lars looked at me. "What?"

I shook my head at him, but my own mouth was about to betray me. "I thought that was sweet of you." Along with his thinness, I'd seen the dark circles under the boy's eyes, so I couldn't admonish Lars for doing what I would have done had I been in my usual frame of mind. "But we'll need permission from his parents to invite him in and feed him."

His expression was classic Lars—chin up, lips pursed, eyes twinkling with amusement. It was one of the many touching attributes that had endeared him to me in the first place. His heart was as big as Galveston Bay.

After Lars slipped out of the room, I put on jeans, T-shirt, and a vest. Then I headed down the staircase. It was kind of different not wearing one of my usual array of professional suits, but it felt freeing, too.

Apparently, the rest of the family had disappeared, so we had the place to ourselves. As I made my way toward the front of the house, I got a tightening in my belly. Ever since I was a kid, my innards had worked like a barometer of some kind, gauging the subtleties of life events and their potential for twists and surprises. Although, on the day of my wedding, I'd lost that ability completely. But I took this new twinge as a semi-pleasant warning that my life was about to take another turn. Oh well, it surely couldn't get any more dramatic than it had been over the past few days.

I joined Lars in the entryway. The boy had made good use of the doorbell, ringing it a few dozen times. "He really must be hungry. But maybe we should chat with him on the porch first."

"Good idea." Lars opened the front door.

After a few pleasant greetings we stepped out onto the porch with our guest. "So, what's your name?" Lars asked.

The boy sat down on the porch swing. "I'm Sigmund Crumby, but all my friends call me Siggy."

"Well, Siggy, before you come in, maybe we'd better make sure your parents know where you are. And make sure they don't mind you coming into a stranger's house." Lars lifted the phone from his belt and handed it to Siggy. "Why don't you just give them a quick call. It'll make us both feel better about inviting you inside and feeding you. Okay?"

"Why?" The boy looked back and forth at us as if clueless.

I fiddled with the buttons on my vest. "Because most

parents don't like their kids going into a stranger's house. It might be dangerous." It was true, but for some reason it sounded lame coming out of my mouth.

"But you're not no stranger," Siggy said. "We've said hello."

"But it's not the same—"

"I don't have any parents. And that's the truth." Siggy swung his legs as if he were running away. "I live with my aunt Marmy."

"Oh?" Lars sat down next to him.

Siggy's face wrinkled into an expression I'd only seen on weary-worn adults. "Aunt Marmy is super old."

"Is she ill?" I sat down on the other side of Siggy.

He shook his head. "She sleeps a lot. But I've got lots of friends, so it's okay."

"School friends?" Lars asked.

"Yeah, lots and lots."

I wilted a little, since he didn't appear to be telling the whole truth. "Well, it would still make me feel better if your Aunt Marmy knew where you were. What's the number, Siggy?"

He sighed, pulled a wrinkled piece of paper from his pocket, and handed it to me.

After a brief talk with Aunt Marmy, it appeared he was correct—at least about his living situation. His aunt's voice sounded as if she were elderly and tired. According to the conversation, there was no problem having Siggy stay for a snack as well as dinner and any other meals we felt so inclined to feed him.

"I guess it's okay for you to come in," I said to Siggy after I hung up.

He grinned for the first time, and it was an enchanting little smile.

I relaxed my shoulders and took in a deep breath. The air felt drier than usual for early fall. The rain clouds had run off somewhere else, and so the day was ending quite pleasantly. Considering. "Siggy, how about a peanut butter and jelly sandwich, some milk, and an apple?"

"Yes." Siggy jumped up and did a little stomping, twisting jig, nearly losing his balance.

Lars chuckled. And then I did, too. It felt good to laugh.

"Do you have any cookies?" Siggy asked. "Pirates love cookies. Cookies are like friends."

"Yes, we have cookies. Homemade, in fact." I slid off the swing and opened the front door.

Siggy wasted no time in running under my arm and into the house. Maybe he was afraid I'd change my mind.

I already knew what was at play. Lars would take Siggy under his wing. He'd been helping underprivileged kids at his church in Houston for years, and so this was only natural for him, especially with his background, growing up in foster homes. But me? I felt more comfortable with older folks. I enjoyed going to nursing homes and helping the residents put their scrapbooks together. Kids had always eluded me, giving me that funky expression that said I wasn't saying the right stuff. Or doing the right stuff. But so far, Siggy hadn't given me "the look." "Lars, you can be my assistant chef."

We got busy creating a small feast for our new friend.

Siggy set the table and helped make the sandwiches. He looked like he knew how to fend for himself in the kitchen. Perhaps he made his own meals at home, even at such a young age. I asked him to wash up, and he obeyed me, but there was nothing we could do about his clothes. His jeans and T-shirt were soiled, and there was no telling when his Aunt Marmy had last washed them. His obvious neglect was such an unhappy sight it brought mist to my eyes. I felt myself getting in too deep with his plight, and yet looking the other way seemed impossible now. Seemed as heartless as Henry.

We three sat around the kitchen table eating kid food. It tasted good, which surprised me. In the midst of our munching, Mom walked in the back door and grinned. "Hi, Larson."

"Mrs. McBride." He rose when Mom entered the room. "Good to see you."

"And who is your guest?" Mom slipped a gallon of milk from her grocery bag and put it in the fridge.

After the introductions, Mom's smile got so big, it could have rivaled a Galveston sunrise. She must have gathered that Lars had extricated me from my grotto, and she was pleased to see it. "Rosy, by the way, Carmen is having her baby tomorrow, and I'm going to stay with her at the hospital. Would you cover for us at the shop?"

"Sure, Mom," was the only answer that seemed right, even though the prospect didn't seem thrilling. "Tell Carmen I said congratulations on the baby."

"I will." Mom stood behind me and gave my shoulders a squeeze. I could feel the love in her touch, and I knew what she was saying silently—she hoped the fresh air and the new company were working like good medicine.

Mom gave me a pat and then snatched an apple from the bowl. "See you sojourners later." She caught my gaze and nodded.

I smiled back. *Yeah, I know, Mom. I will recover, even if I don't want to.*

"See you later," Siggy said to my mom. He made some odd gestures with his hands.

"And what's that?" Mom asked him.

"It means, 'Hope you are well and happy,' in the alien Zomulin tongue."

Mom made some funny gestures back to Siggy.

"What's that mean?"

"It means, 'You have a milk mustache, and I think you're a cool kid' in the ancient Mom tongue," she said.

Siggy giggled, wiped his mustache on his sleeve, and took a big bite of his oatmeal cookie.

After Mom disappeared into the back of the house, I heard a whimpering and a scratching at the porch door. "What's that?"

Siggy ran to open the screen door. "That's my dog, Zoola. She's hungry, too."

Chapter 6

The next morning I showered, put on makeup for the first time since the wedding, and headed over to my mom's little shop on the Strand—the Scrapbook Emporium. Her sign above the shop door read, "Making Memories Last." Oh well. I released a self-pitying groan at my own lack of ability to do that very thing—to marry and make memories last a lifetime.

Once inside, I flipped on all the lights and looked around the shop, getting reacquainted with the merchandise. Over the years Mom had made the store into a homey little nook, with thousands of bits of paraphernalia to chronicle one's life and loved ones. I'd pored over every corner of her shop, but today the shelves of pretty scrapbooking odds and ends seemed to mock me instead of delight me.

To keep from setting off another emotional land mine, I busied myself tidying the shop, restocking the shelves, and waiting for the stream of customers. But an hour went by and no one came in. Hmm. The sidewalks were full of people, and the other businesses appeared to be booming. So where were all the customers?

I was strolling around the shop, pondering various facets of that quandary, when I randomly picked up a scrapbook and remembered the one I'd created with photos of Henry and me living life together. Of course, mostly we just sat around reading and eating and playing video chess. We had a photo of us together at an open house—one that I'd put together for a client, but the majority of the scrapbook held photos of me pursuing Henry's life, not the other way around.

Come to think of it, Henry had been as supportive as a table with rotten legs. I hadn't been oblivious to his faults, and yet I always blew off his lack of enthusiasm in my interests. What kind of a woman had I become that I couldn't hear the distant thunder of an approaching storm?

Memo to self—throw that Henry/Rosy scrapbook into the trash can. Of course, I might cut it up and burn it first.

As I ruminated on that thought, an older woman came through the front door. A customer. Good. "May I help you?"

"Oh honey, don't you remember me? I'm Carla Gantry. You know, I'm the babysitter who potty trained you."

"Oh yeah. I'm sorry. I didn't recognize you with the hat." Also, it might have been the fifty or more pounds she'd put on.

"That's a real cute vest you got on there, hon."

"Thanks." Did she know about my engagement to Henry? I hadn't invited Carla to the wedding, so hopefully the news of the ceremony being canceled hadn't gotten to her. The last thing I felt like doing was rehashing the last few days with the woman who'd potty trained me.

"I heard your Henry stood you up at the altar."

I sat down on the stool behind the counter with a thud.

"That's what I thought. What a lying snake. No matter

how smart he was, he didn't deserve you."

"Thanks for that." I ground out a convincing smile. "Did you know Henry?"

Carla strolled around the shop, picking at every little thing. "No, I didn't get a chance to meet him. You see, I *wasn't* invited to the wedding."

"I'm sorry, but we both wanted an intimate wedding."

"No worries. I recovered from the blow." Carla gave the plume on her purple-and-red hat a few flicks with her finger.

"So, did you need any scrapbook supplies today?"

"No." Carla stared at me, her eyes bulging with cartoon animation. "I came here as an ambassador of destiny."

Why didn't that sound good?

"Listen, my nephew needs to get out more." Carla stopped her eye-bulging and went back to milling around the shop. "He needs some pretty gals around to build up his confidence. He's not very good with the women, you see. And I thought he could practice on you."

Lord, have mercy. I caught myself patting the heels of my hands together in a measured little rhythm.

"And you'd get a free lunch in the process. I heard you've been keeping to yourself, locked away in your bedroom, so this will help you get out."

How did people hear about this stuff?

"It'll do you a world of good."

I would have slipped off the chair onto the floor if my feet hadn't rescued me. "A blind date. I'm sure you mean well, but I have no intention of—"

"No, it's not like that."

I stood up as if I were fluffing my feathers to make myself look bigger and more daunting. Or at least big enough to be taken seriously. "But I don't want to date anyone right now, certainly not a stranger."

"It's not a date." Carla slapped her hand on a stack of scrapbooks. "That's what I keep trying to tell you." Her agitation level rose so quickly that two of the buttons on her blouse came undone. I wasn't sure if I should tell her. Perhaps she would notice the sudden draft.

"What is it then?"

"Honey, it's an act of mercy for my nephew. I told you, he needs to practice talking to women. Then, too, it'll help you as well. You won't be obsessing about your own troubles as much. I think you young people call that a 'win/win.'"

No, we call it a "no way." "It's a blind date, isn't it, Carla?"

"Okay, it's a blind date." Carla waved me off. "Did I tell you how cute that vest looks on you?"

"Yeah, you did."

"Look, it's too late to undo anything now. My nephew is waiting for you at the Sundowner Café as we speak. He's about your age. You'll love him. Real sweet boy. Considering."

Considering what? "I know you're trying to help, but this just won't do. I barely even made it to the shop today, because—"

"Oh, no worries. My pleasure."

Carla had ceased to listen to me. It was the same thing she'd done when I was a kid and begged her not to push that lever, since I had a fear of being flushed down the commode. "You'll have to go the café and tell him I'm not coming."

"Can't do that, hon. Can't go there right now."

"Why not?"

"Because my gout is acting up something fierce, and I've got to go on home. You can call and thank me later." She headed toward the exit and hollered back to me, "His name is Jules, by the by, and he has hair like rubies from the King of Sheba. You can't miss him. But you'd better lock up now and hurry down the street before the clock of destiny winds down."

I refrained from rolling my eyes, stamping my foot, and anything else I could do to stop the hands of destiny from going anywhere.

"Oh, and I'm so glad you're back where you belong." She held the door open with her rotund caboose. "You can't leave again, do you hear? Galveston has got 'home' written all over it for you."

Even though my stomach was growling, I wasn't about to have lunch with a man who needed to practice schmoozing women. Or with a guy who had hair like rubies from the King of Sheba. And wasn't that supposed to be the Queen of Sheba? Carla was surely the inspiration for the term "hot air."

Just before Carla stepped through the open door she added, "I know this will sound harsh, but if you don't ever marry, you're destined to grow old and die alone. Now is that what you really want, hon?"

I opened my mouth to remind her that I'd been the one to show up at the wedding ready to get married and also to tell her about her northern exposure, but she was already out the door and on the warpath again. Carla had such a way about her. She was like this giant purple-and-red tumbleweed that rolled into your life. If you didn't stand up to her, she would roll right over you. Yes, that was Carla, which was probably why I still had a slight phobia of bathrooms.

But to keep from being rude and making Jules wait for me, I locked up the shop, turned the sign over—alerting people I'd be out for a while—and then headed three shops down to the tropical themed Sundowner Café. I wouldn't be gone long. It would only be a matter of explaining everything and then gently extracting myself from this hotbed of misunderstanding and presumption. How did I get myself into such a situation? Was I wearing an invisible bull's-eye I knew nothing about?

But I had to admit, out of all of Carla's potpourri of twaddle, she did hit on a truth. Perhaps I was back where I belonged. I really didn't want to leave Galveston again. The town did have "home" written all over it. The decision to move back to Galveston solidified at that moment, but perhaps my spirit had been working on it for a long time.

A horse and buggy full of tourists passed by, taking me out of my reverie. On a more leisurely kind of day I would have enjoyed passing the time shopping in the Strand. The area was still as quaint as ever, with its old-fashioned street lanterns and awnings—a place I'd always loved. But today, right now, I was on a mission.

When I swung the door open to the café, calypso music jangled its way into my senses. My gaze scoured the place. And then there he was—the Mad Hatter's red hair—at a table for two. I had to admit I was surprised at what I saw. So, out of curiosity I walked toward him.

Chapter 7

The Mad Hatter didn't appear to be nearly as dreadful as I'd predicted, and yet I wasn't quite moved to cash in on my free lunch.

He raised his eyebrows and stood. "Hi. You must be Rosy."

"I am." I shook his hand, which was clammy, but solid.

"I'm Jules Sherwood," he said. He wore a pleasant expression, and his hair and model-perfect clothes were so right out of a catalogue that I thought there might be a photo shoot going on.

"Good to meet you." *Don't get distracted, Rosy.* "I'm afraid there's been a misunderstanding or a ruse or something."

"Yes, I know." Jules laughed. "Aunt Carla has been at it again. You don't have to stay, but if you'll indulge me for a few minutes, I think I can explain. Would you like anything? Maybe a Coke?"

"No thank you." I'd give him five. I sat down and assessed him from his aunt's perspective. Must have been a royal fib. Jules was handsome and confident-looking. He certainly didn't appear to be the sort of man who needed to practice being with women.

"My aunt Carla is an eccentric woman, but she has a good heart."

"Yes, she does." I said that in the loosest sense of the word.

"It's nice of you to say that, especially after what she just roped you into."

True. I picked at one of the buttons on my vest until the threads unraveled and it fell into my palm. *Great.* I stuck the button into my pocket. Memo to self—buy a sewing kit to stitch my life back together.

Jules took a sip from his mug. "My aunt feels it's her responsibility to help me find a wife. I don't need her assistance, but she keeps insisting. To her credit, I've met some really nice women through her, so it hasn't been a hardship. Just unusual. She's not been feeling well lately, so the word *no* doesn't come to me as easily these days."

I tried to relax my fight-or-flight stance and rested back in my chair. "I know your aunt has gout. I hope it's nothing more serious than that."

"No, but she's been slowing down over the years. So I indulge her from time to time. She's my only aunt, and one of my last living relations. Since my mother passed away a few months ago, I think Carla feels even more pressure to watch over me. . .even though I'm a grown man."

"You sound like a good nephew." Okay, I had to admit it. Jules was turning out to be a decent man. He had to be to indulge Carla the way he did. Perhaps there were a few good men left. But I still wasn't staying for lunch.

A waitress arrived at the table dressed in an explosion of bird-of-paradise colors and carrying a huge double-decker sandwich. She slid it off the tray and placed it in the middle of the table as if she didn't know who to give it to.

I looked at Jules. "You already ordered?"

"To be honest, I didn't think you'd come."

I grinned.

"Do you want an extra plate?" the waitress asked.

"No, no, that's okay. I'm about to go." The aroma of the grilled chicken tickled my nose.

"But I don't want all this sandwich anyway. Why don't you eat half before you go? It's already cut." Jules pushed the sandwich toward me like a bowl of milk to a stray alley cat.

"All right. I'll eat half."

The waitress brought over an extra plate, and I took half the sandwich, which turned out to be tastier than I thought it would be.

"It's good, right?"

I nodded with my mouth full.

"How long have you known my aunt?"

I wasn't about to tell him her claim to fame in my life. "Hmm, well, she was—"

"She was your babysitter, right?"

I swallowed. "Yes. She didn't give you any other unsavory details, did she?"

"Yes, a few. I can't lie to you. Aunt Carla has a problem holding back unnecessary information."

I groaned. Who else had she told about my potty training travails? Oh well, what did it matter? "Out of curiosity. . . what did she say?"

"That you were a willful child."

I laughed. "That's all? Did she also tell you my wedding was a few days ago?"

"No." Jules dropped some mayo on his lightly starched Ralph Lauren shirt, and unfortunately the blob completely covered the emblem of the tiny man playing polo. "My aunt failed to mention it."

"No worries, as your aunt would say. I'm not married."

Jules dipped his napkin into his water glass and wiped at his shirt, trying to undo his flub, but the effort left a huge water mess on his shirt. "So, what happened?"

"The groom didn't show." The words weren't as hard to say as I thought they'd be. I took another bite of my sandwich.

"Oh wow, that makes this situation kind of thorny," Jules said. "I assure you, if Aunt Carla had shared that little detail, I would have refused to come." He leaned toward me. "Being here must be difficult for you."

"It could be worse. You could have turned out to be a man who needed lots of practice talking to women."

A flash of unhappy surprise crossed his face. "Is that what Aunt Carla said?"

"Yeah. Pretty much."

Jules fell back in his chair. After a few seconds he burst out laughing—a real horse laugh.

My mouth wasn't full, so I laughed, too.

We were very near having a pleasant moment—even though I was absolutely certain I wasn't going to stay for dessert and coffee—when the bell jingled over the café door. I glanced behind me and wilted like the weed I suddenly knew I'd become. Of all the joints that my friend could have dropped into, it had to be this one.

Lars.

Chapter 8

Lars hadn't missed much of the action. I could tell from his expression he'd seen me giggling like a silly schoolgirl with what looked like a handsome date. *Lord, have mercy.*

Then he deliberately looked away as he walked right on by and sat down at the table right behind Jules. He faced me and left Jules oblivious to our subterfuge. I scooted my chair so that Lars wasn't in my line of vision.

Lars scooted his chair over so he could see me.

I rolled my eyes, not caring if anyone saw my gesture. But Lars was busy perusing the menu and tapping his Sasquatch feet to the beat of the calypso music while Jules was engaged in some serious mastication. *Life.*

I felt uncomfortable, even though none of the current mess was my fault. And yet—I felt sorry for Lars. I guess I could add guilt to my emotional stockpile of feelings, even though I had enough already to clog a sewer.

"I'm going to move back to Galveston." I said the words more to myself than to Jules, but the shocking disclosure didn't seem to matter to him anyway, since he appeared to be more enamored with his food than any of my charms. Feeling a strange mix of testiness, hunger, and unexplainable sadness for Lars, I took another big bite of my sandwich.

My phone rang. Just as I started to turn the thing off, Jules motioned for me to answer it. He was pretty occupied anyway, after biting off quite a large plug of meat.

I looked at the caller ID.

It was Lars and his flannel shirt calling. Quaint. I pushed the TALK button. "May I help you?" I asked with a full mouth.

"Glad you got your *appetite* back," Lars said, with just a pinch of humor and a pound of sarcasm.

I knew what he meant, and it had nothing to do with my sandwich. "I could pickle a whole crock of cucumbers with that vinegar in your voice."

"I love it when you talk in metaphors," Lars said. "Listen, you just told this guy about a life-changing decision. How come you've never—"

"Well, apparently you're the only fish who caught that worm anyway. I'm hanging up now, Mr. Snidely Whiplash."

"Oh, Snidely Whiplash, is it?" Lars said.

Jules stopped mid-bite and furrowed his handsome brows.

The jig was up.

Jules looked behind him at Lars. "Is there something going on here?"

Lars rose from his chair. "Hi. I'm Larson Brookfield, and Rosy here is a *friend* of mine."

Jules rose—not looking the least bit offended at our game—and shook his hand. "Jules Sherwood. Good to meet you. Do you want to join us?"

Sherwood and Brookfield. What a combo. Sounds like a men's pro shop.

"No. Thanks, though. Appreciate it." Lars gestured to the water stain on Jules's shirt. "Boy, somebody must have hit you with quite a bucket of water. You—"

"Gotta go." I looked at my watch. "I'm supposed to be running the shop today."

"That's what I thought." Lars gave me a *look*. "Here, I'll escort you back."

Jules reached out his hand to me. "In spite of my aunt's unusual ploys, it was nice to meet you, Rosy."

"Good to meet you as well." I shook his hand. "And thank you for the sandwich. I was hungrier than I thought."

Lars cleared his throat and held out his arm to escort me back.

What was this—Victorian England?

Jules smiled a most pleasant smile and sat back down to finish off his chips and slaw and pickle. "Bye. . .for now."

I waved, and Lars and I exited the café together. Once we were both outside I pulled free. "Was that necessary?"

"Whatever do you mean, Miss 'I-couldn't-possibly-date-anyone-right-now'?"

I tilted my head and gave *him* the *look*.

"Okay, okay," Lars said, "I know I promised I'd be just a friend to you, and so you may be wondering why I disturbed your perfectly good date. It's not what a friend would do."

"No, that's not it. I'm upset because you jumped to conclusions. He wasn't a date. I mean he was supposed to be a date, but—"

"I don't know, Rosy. Seeing you with him right now, whatever he was. . .well, just being friends with you is going to be harder than I thought it would be. When I promised friendship only. . .I suppose I grasped at anything I could get, but it's easy to see that it won't be enough. I'm a man in love. That's it. I can't undo what I feel any more than I can blot out the moon." He opened the door of the shop for me, and I walked through. But he held the door as if he weren't coming in with me.

"You're welcome to stay and visit awhile."

"I don't know, Rosy. Do you want me to?"

"Yes, I do."

He walked through the door and milled around the shop while I turned on all the lights and situated myself behind the counter, trying to look official. "By the way, I didn't set up or approve of that blind date with Jules. Somebody ambushed me. I went to the café to explain my situation, but since he thought I wasn't going to show, he'd already ordered a sandwich. He said he couldn't eat it all, so I ate half of it. What can I say? I was hungry. We had one good laugh together. That was all."

"Was it a good joke?" Lars said, and then held up his hands. "Just kidding. I just wish you could have been famished with me. I would have fed you, and then some. *And* I would have made you laugh."

"Yes, you would have. You always make me laugh. Except right now." I went to him and touched his hand. "It's just too soon, Lars."

He looked at the spot where our hands connected. "Look at that. . .our hands are having sweet fellowship."

I grinned and then pulled away so as not to torture him.

The warmth from his skin stayed with me, though, like a long summer day at the beach.

Lars picked up a scrapbook—one created especially for kids—and looked it over. "Who would be insensitive enough to send you out on a blind date right after what happened?"

"It's a long story."

"Hey, I have all the time in the world."

"Don't you have to go back to Houston soon?"

"I decided to take some time off, remember? I'm staying at a hotel in town. Spent the early morning walking along the beach. Did a lot of thinking."

It was probably too dangerous to ask him what he was pondering, so I let it go.

"Then I stopped by to see you at the house, but your dad said you were at the shop. When I got here you'd left for a bit, so I went to get a cup of coffee at the café to wait for you. And then there you were. . .having a cozy little lunch at a table for two with Jules Verne."

"Very funny. It's Jules Sherwood. And I've explained my innocence in the matter."

"I know. I just had to rub it in a little more."

Softening my voice I added, "But I admit it must have been a surprise. . .seeing me with Jules Verne and all." I grinned, hoping he would grin, too.

"It was a surprise." He brought the scrapbook up to the counter.

"I doubt it will be repeated anytime soon, since what I said still stands. I don't want to date right now. It wouldn't be wise, would it?"

"Maybe that depends on who it is."

"I like you, Lars. A lot. But who knows my heart? *I* don't even know my heart. I don't trust it. You shouldn't either."

"Then call me a fool. . .but I do trust you."

I came around to his side of the counter. "Would *you* stick your toe out in heavy traffic if it were already bleeding? Wouldn't you want to bandage it? You know, protect it for a while to let it heal?"

"Yes, for a while. But then my toe would want to live again."

"You're impossible." I sighed. "What am I going to do with you?"

"Marry me."

"I walked right into that one, didn't I?"

Chapter 9

Lars was persistent—I had to give him that. I couldn't tell if his resolve to marry me felt irritating or endearing. It was interesting and different, which made me think I'd pursued Henry too much. Maybe most of the fervor and commitment had been on my part. Why hadn't I been able to see the truth? I'd been living inside a love-bubble of my own making, and the walls were as sturdy as soap film. It was bound to pop. Hmm. *Life.* "Tell me. . . how's Siggy?"

Lars smacked his hand over his heart. "I've been eclipsed by yet another man."

I laughed. "I knew you went over to meet with his aunt. What happened?"

"Aunt Marmy is all Siggy said she was. Nice, but very tired. She's probably in her late seventies, and she's just not able to care for him very well. I told her we would take him out from time to time."

"Oh, you did. And how are you going to do that, living in Houston?"

"Well, as you know, I have my office in my apartment, and I can move anywhere I want."

"True." But I hoped Lars wasn't making plans around my

life. Too much pressure there.

"Designing homes, well, it's science embracing art, as you know, but for the last few years I've not been paying enough attention to the art. I've gotten a bit drab and conventional in my designs. But I could be inspired here, Rosy. I could do some good work."

"Does this move have anything to do with me deciding to move back to Galveston?"

"No." His head drooped to his chin. "Yes."

I grinned. "At least you're honest."

"So, wanna take a walk along the beach after work?"

"Maybe, but it's not a date."

"Not a date, and if we drink any cappuccinos or eat anything, you will pick up the check. And I'll get the most expensive items on the menu. Does that make you feel better?"

"All right. It's a date. . .that isn't a date."

He smiled.

Lars did have the best smile. It filled his whole face to the brim. Especially when he looked at me. Unfortunately, and a little late to notice, Henry had never once gazed at me that way. Perhaps it wasn't healthy to compare the two men at every turn, and yet it was only natural to do so. It made me wonder, how could I have fallen for Henry in the first place?

Lars set the scrapbook on the counter. "I want to buy this for Siggy. He might enjoy filling it up. And we can teach him how. Well, that is, if you agree to help me."

"I'd be happy to help you, Lars, but I'm paying for half the scrapbook."

"And I won't stop you."

*

When the workday was spent and the shop locked up for the day, I followed through with Lars's suggestion to take a stroll along the beach with him. Siggy came, too. Lars thought it might be a good idea if he came along. That way I wouldn't feel as much pressure, and Siggy would have someone to play with for a few minutes—something the poor kid seemed to be in dire need of.

Lars looked over Siggy's shoulder at a long ivory-colored shell he'd found.

Siggy patted the sand off. "What do you think it is?"

"I think it's a mollusk shell of some kind," Lars said. "Sorry, I'm not a shell expert. But I know it used to be somebody's home."

Siggy chuckled. "Funny kind of house." His little brows furrowed as he stared into the empty shell. "But why is it. . . nobody's ever home?"

"Good question." Lars rolled up the bottom of his jeans.

"Maybe they just needed more square footage," I said, "so they found a bigger shell."

"Spoken like a true Realtor." Lars lifted his camera and snapped a photo of me.

I tried not to run away like my sisters always did when faced with a flashing camera, so I gave him my best smile instead. Then I slipped off my flip-flops and let my toes sink into the warm sand. Nice.

"Can I keep the shell?" Siggy looked at us.

"It's your treasure," Lars said. "But then, I don't know, that shell might look mighty nice on my desk at home."

Lars grinned and loomed over Siggy as if he might consider snatching it away from him. Siggy made a run for it. Lars chased him until they were both laughing their heads off. What a sight. Beguiling, actually. Lars would no doubt make a fine father. Perhaps he'd wanted me to see this scene. Maybe it was all a ploy to make me fall in love with him.

I shook my head. *Enough, Rosy.* Someday I would have to trust again. Why not start with the present?

After the two boys calmed down, and we were all beachcombing again, Siggy said, "Why don't you two marry each other, and then I can come live with you?"

I chuckled. "Okay, Siggy, how much did Lars pay you to say that?"

"Pay me?" He gazed up at me with great interest. "Can I get money for that?"

"I'm wounded," Lars said to me. "How could you think such a thing?"

"Because it sure seemed convenient and convincing."

"I was convincing?" Siggy asked. "I know what that word means. . .it means I'm good at something.'"

"Yes, you are." I gave him a shoulder hug, and amazingly, he didn't pull away. "But Lars and I aren't dating."

"This isn't a date?" He poked at a dead jellyfish with a stick.

"No. Not really." I edged a little deeper into the water, enjoying the cool splash on my bare feet and legs.

"But why can't it be a date?"

Lord, have mercy. Siggy was not going to let this one go. The kid could really put the squeeze on a body. "Well, recently, someone I loved. . .or maybe I should say, someone I *thought* I loved, hurt me, and I need time to heal."

"Oh, heal." He looked up at me. "Like when you bash your head on something."

"Yeah. Like that." I must have hit my head pretty hard to have fallen in love with Henry.

"Okay, I get it." Siggy scratched his forehead.

"Well, and your aunt might have a lot to say about that. . . you know, if you went to live with someone else. She would miss you." After the words came out I wasn't sure they were the right ones. *Oh God, what does this child need? You know I'm clueless about kids.*

"Aunt Marmy loves me, but she's all worn out." He kicked at a pile of seaweed. "I don't think she'd mind if I found a home for myself."

"Is that why you were tapping on my window?" I asked him. "To find a home?"

Siggy didn't say anything for a while. "Yeah. I wasn't really looking for a friend named Charles Dickens. I saw that name on a book." He whipped his stick around like a sword as if he were fighting a duel, but then he threw the stick into the water. "I don't have any friends. I was just trying to find a home. And your place looked like home."

"Thanks. I've always felt that way, too, but it's not really my home anymore."

"Whose house is it then?"

"It's where my parents live. And I'll be leaving there soon. But. . .I think I'll be moving to Galveston permanently. I grew up here, and I like living by the ocean."

"I do, too," Siggy said, "except I never get to see it."

I looked over at Lars as we walked along. He smiled at me, but there was a flicker of sadness, too. I knew it was for the needy boy with us. "And, too, you just think you like us now," I said, "but once you get into your preteen years you'll think we're ogres."

"Like Shrek?"

"Yeah, only not as nice at Shrek."

Siggy laughed. "That's funny."

"Hey, bud, I think I see another mollusk shell straight ahead," Lars said.

"I'll go see." Siggy ran ahead of us to check out the shell.

"Shame on you, Lars." I gave his shirt a little jerk and stopped my ambling. "Did you send that boy off on a wild goose chase just to be alone with me?"

"I really did see another mollusk." He turned to face me.

Siggy squatted down in the sand and studied the shell.

The water eddied around my feet and ankles, teasing them, and then it receded again. "What did you want to say to me?"

"Oh, nothing in particular. I just wanted to look at you... see the sea breeze in your hair."

Okay, pretty romantic stuff for a non-date. "This is a really nice thing you're doing for Siggy. He's looking a bit healthier already."

"He'll be even healthier if he gets a chance to eat. I took some food over to his aunt Marmy. She didn't seem offended, which is good. But she looks a little on the thin side, too, so maybe they could benefit from Meals on Wheels.

I'll look into it."

"You're a good man."

"Well, it's hard to forget my youth and my own hunger." Lars threw a stone into the water, and it disappeared in the wave. "Growing up in foster homes, well, I was always needing something. . .mostly love. . .but sometimes food, too. There was a shortage of everything. It always bothers me when I see those same needs in other kids."

"Like I said. . .you're a good man."

He lifted the camera again and took a few more shots of me and Siggy as well as a few snapshots of some gulls as they swooped down to check us out.

"These photos will be perfect to help Siggy start that scrapbook," I said.

"My thoughts exactly."

"But don't we need to be careful, you know, not to get Siggy's hopes up? He thinks he can get a new home as easily as tapping on somebody's window."

"You're right. We'll take it slow. But I did promise to take him fishing next week."

Lars hadn't heard a word I'd said, but I knew him well enough to know he wouldn't make any promises he couldn't keep. And he would follow through on those promises with his whole heart. Rare gift. Even rarer man.

And then I did a risky thing. I reached out and touched Lars's hand for some sweet fellowship.

Chapter 10

Lars looked at the joining of our hands and gave mine a squeeze. "I like your hands."

"Oh, and here all this time I thought you were enamored with my Alice in Wonderland blue eyes."

"Oh, that, too. But your hands, well, they speak for themselves. I like the way you tap the heels of your hands together when you're pondering something. . .you have this beat thing going that only you can hear."

"Funny you should notice." Lars didn't miss much.

"And your hands aren't timid."

"Not timid like little lambs?" I grinned.

"No, not at all," he said. "They're as spirited and sturdy as big-horned sheep."

"Did you get that out of Song of Solomon?"

"No. *Sportsman's World Magazine.* I was—"

"You're such a romantic, Lars." I rolled my eyes, but I didn't pull my hand away.

"Hey, I haven't come to the best part yet."

"There's more?"

"Yes. The best part about your hands. They're not afraid to give." He released me.

My heart felt a tug when he let go, but I knew he was

trying not to push too hard, trying to keep things light with humor. Perhaps trying to let me move at my own pace.

"Hey, bud," Lars hollered to Siggy. "Let me see what you found. Maybe it's good enough for my treasure trove of shells at home."

Siggy held his hand behind his back. "But if I let you see it, you might steal it from me."

Lars laughed. "Well, it's not stealing if you give it to me as a gift." He caught up with the boy and ruffled his hair.

Lars was so full of meaning and so full of love it made my heart ache. How was this happening? God had indeed sent a way for me to heal, and it had come in the form of family, a dear friend, and a needy little boy named Siggy. I could never have imagined this. I looked up into the swirling clouds that were ever taking on new shapes, taking on new wonder, just like the great sea below them. *Lord, You really are too good to me.*

Watching Lars and Siggy together made me realize that I might not mind having a child or two. I was getting a bit old to start a big family, but a couple of children felt right to me. Henry hadn't wanted kids at all. He'd always said they were an impediment to progress and science. And they smelled bad. He failed to remember that his own mother was good enough not to embrace that same philosophy.

The two boys were busy whispering to each other, already thick as thieves, when I joined them. "Okay, so what did you find that's so top secret over here?"

"It's a super-good shell. And us guys decided *you* should have it." Siggy opened his hand and held it out to me.

"Me?" I accepted the gift. "And how did I get to be the lucky one?"

"Because you looked kinda lonely over there," Siggy said. "And I thought it might cheer you up."

"I looked lonely, huh?" I held the shell up to my heart. "It's a keeper for sure. I will treasure it, and every time I see it, I'll think of this fine day. But are you sure I'm not stealing it?"

"No, Uncle Lars says it's not stealing if you give it away." Siggy bounced on his toes.

"That's right. Thank you."

"Hey, you two in the mood for some supper at my house?" I felt reckless and happy. "I thought if Mom didn't have anything cooking, I'd make us some spaghetti."

"Yes, yes. I love spaghetti. I love food." Siggy did a stomping dance in the sand. "And I get to go to your house, too."

I was getting rather fond of those happy dances.

"And will you be able to come to dinner, too, Lars?" *I hope you say yes.*

"Yeah, I sure can. What time?" He dusted the sand off his jeans.

"You both can come right now if you're willing to help me. Siggy, are you sure your aunt won't mind if you stay for dinner?"

"Aunt Marmy said I could stay as long as I wanted."

"Okay." I tugged on his sleeve. "You'll get to meet all my family."

"Do you have a big family?"

"I have my parents and three sisters."

"That's big. I sure would love a big family," Siggy said. "More people to hug. . .*and* pester."

"True. I was the oldest, so I did a lot of pestering in my time."

"Hey, I have an idea. Why don't you guys put me in the middle and you can swing me up in the air. That'd be fun. Wouldn't it? I think so. And when we get to your house do you have any more of those cookies? I'd sure love some. And can my dog come, too?"

*

Later that evening, when our arms were about to fall off from swinging Siggy to the moon and back, we created our spaghetti master feast. A giant pot of it, in fact, along with Caesar salad, garlic bread, and cherry cobbler for dessert. Everyone in the McBride family had landed home from their various activities, and the whole flock and company congregated 'round the dining room table for dinner.

I cleared my throat, said a prayer over the food, and then stood to give a tiny speech. "This meal was made with great love by Lars and me and our new friend, Siggy."

"So, is this the secret recipe you're always hiding from us, Sis?" Lily asked as I sat down.

"Yes, this is it." I raised my fork full of spaghetti and shoved it in my mouth.

"Secret?" Siggy said. "We just opened a jar of sauce."

"Siggy!" I grinned. "You gave away my secret."

He took a big bite and wiped his mouth on his sleeve. "Who cares where the food comes from if it's good?"

Everyone chuckled.

"That's what I say, Siggy," Dad said. "I'm always preaching that sermon to Momma here when it's my night to cook."

A few more laughs sprang up around the table.

Dad handed Siggy the bread basket. "Glad to see a young boy with a hearty appetite. We McBrides live life through our stomachs."

"That's funny." Siggy laughed and took another slice of bread.

"By the way." I shuffled the olives around on my salad plate. "I wanted to help make the dinner tonight since you guys have been jewels taking care of me through this. . . well. . .season. I appreciate you a lot."

"You've got some of that rosy color back in your cheeks," Heather said. "It's good to see it there again."

Everyone took their turns glancing at Lars, and I knew why. Amazing what a difference a day could make—that is, in the hands of the Almighty.

"You're looking somewhat recovered, so we thought we'd mosey on back to our homes. Unless you need us," Heather said.

"No, that's fine." I raised my glass of sweet tea. "You guys are the best. And I've been thinking. . .I realized how much I miss the ocean. Since I've been here it's like we found each other again. . .like long-lost friends." I couldn't help but glance at Lars and smile. "Anyway, I've decided to find an apartment and well. . .I'm moving back here to stay. I'll expand my realty business to Galveston. What do you all think?"

My family stared at me for a moment as if trying to appraise the information, and then they cheered.

Mom's eyes got misty. "That's the best news I've had in a while. I'm so glad you're moving back to the island, dear. You always did love the sea. . .even as a little girl."

My dad nodded toward me. "Welcome home, Rosy. I hope this will encourage you other gals to follow in your big sister's footsteps and move back to Galveston. Violet, you and Lily are particularly guilty. You managed to find the farthest corners of Texas to live in. You're so far away it's almost like you live in another state. We'd love to have all of you back to the Gulf Coast."

There were collective sighs and chuckles.

"Oh well, I can dream," Dad said. "If you're not going to take my valuable advice, could you at least pass me the salad?" He grinned.

Siggy was still gobbling, not paying a lot of attention to the proceedings. I wanted to tell him to slow down—that no one was going to take his food away—but he looked so happy I didn't want to get in his way.

Mom clinked her fork against her glass. "I wanted to say, I've made a decision recently, too. This would be a good time to tell you all since you're gathered here." She stared into her salad, and then with mist in her eyes, she said, "I've decided to sell the business."

The table exploded into a noisy mass of arguments and queries.

"Now, listen up," Dad said. "I know you gals don't like the idea. The shop is so much of who your momma is. This business has been like an appendage. . .well, an extra heart, really. But you girls have your own lives. None of you wanted to inherit the business, so because I'm retired now, your momma thought it would be nice to do the same. And now, we'll have more time to travel."

Mom leaned forward and one by one caught the gaze of each of us daughters. "And the shop's business has been declining these last few months, so it seems like maybe it's a sign. . .the right time to let it go. I love what I sell, but it can't go on forever. And somebody has offered me an excellent price for my stock, so that will be good. I hope you all can rally 'round me with my decision."

Some moaning ensued, but resigned nods finally replaced the overall sadness from such a change.

Heather always said that life was forever moving on, and she was so right. I glanced at Lars and caught him staring at me.

I smiled.

He rolled a wad of spaghetti around his fork. "Since this appears to be an evening of announcements, I guess I'll make one, too."

"What is it?" Violet asked, suddenly rising out of her usual quiet mode.

He cleared his throat. "Well, as most of you know, even though I grew up in Houston, Galveston has always felt like home to me. For a long time my dream has been to take up residency here. Anyway, I've decided to take the plunge. I'm moving to Galveston."

Everyone at the table, expect for Siggy, who was still packing it in with the pasta, glanced at me and then at Lars. My family had connected all the dots—at least the ones they thought were true about us—and they set to jabbering, and grinning as brightly as a gaggle of contestants in a beauty pageant.

*

After supper Lars and I—along with a very full Siggy—settled into our family's scrapbooking room to help Siggy start his very first scrapbook. While I explained the dynamics of such a wonderful adventure, Lars downloaded and printed all the photos from the beach.

Siggy ran from one shelf and bin to another. "What is all this stuff?"

"All kinds of goodies. Stickers and punch art and paper dolls. Whatever we need to make this a really cool scrapbook."

"Sounds like girly stuff."

"No, not at all. When I say paper dolls, I'm just talking about die-cuts or pieces of paper that are in the shapes of people." I held up some samples. "See?"

"I promise this can be guy stuff, too," Lars said from across the room. "Think of it like a storybook of your life."

"Oh, okay." Siggy sat down across from me and opened up the empty scrapbook. "Well, I like stickers a lot."

I pointed to the cover. "Okay, first thing we need is a theme."

"What's that?" Siggy fingered some of the stickers that were left over from another project.

"It's what you decide this scrapbook should be about."

He slapped his hands on the table. "What about the ocean? I like it. Don't you?"

"Yes, I do." I raised my finger. "Good choice."

Lars brought the photos over from the printer and spread them out across the table.

"Hey," Siggy said. "Look at us. We're serious beach-bummers." He pointed to a picture of me. "But you look scared in this one. Like you've just seen a sea monster."

I picked up the photo. I was smiling sort of, and yet I did look worried. Or scared.

"What are you afraid of, Aunt Rosy?"

I wasn't sure if Siggy should be calling me that so soon, but he had such a look of earnestness I let it go. "I had a good time, so I don't know. Maybe I was scared that the day seemed so perfect it might all vanish. . .like the stones we tossed into the sea today." I squirmed, feeling a little vulnerable after flinging my words into the air.

"Well, I'm not going anywhere," Lars said.

"Me either." Siggy cradled his face in his hands and pursed his lips with conviction.

"By the way, buddy, this woman you see here? She's a scrapbooking guru. She knows her stuff, I'm telling you."

I gave my head a shake, smiling. "No, no, I'm only pretending. My mom is the guru. But I do have a good idea. Why don't we use the shells we collected to decorate the front of the scrapbook? What do you think?"

The boys agreed to my idea, and we all emptied our pockets onto the table like pirates with their plunder, as Siggy might say. The results were revealing and curious. Siggy and I had collected perfectly formed shells, but Lars's shells were all broken.

Siggy fingered some of Lars's offerings. "Looks like the ocean got angry with your shells."

Lars chuckled. "You're right." He picked up one of the shells and looked at it. "Maybe I think the cracked ones are more interesting to look at. Or maybe they remind me that life is still worth treasuring even if there's a chip or two."

I looked at him. "I know for a fact that wonderful things can come from broken pieces."

Lars smiled and blushed.

How much of Lars's perspective had come from his experiences in foster care? All in all, he had very few cracks, considering his loveless youth. He had come out well. God had certainly watched over his comings and goings. I was grateful to Him for that. And now perhaps God was trying to show us how to watch over Siggy's comings and goings.

"So, what is your storybook story?" Siggy asked, looking back and forth at us.

"What do you mean?" He was such a curious little boy.

"You said this is my story." Siggy patted the scrapbook. "What's yours? I don't hardly know anything about you."

Oww. Sometimes Siggy's grammar was like listening to a fork scrape across a plate. "You know *very little* about us." I sat down on one of the stools. "That's true. Maybe we could take turns talking about ourselves."

Siggy held up two fingers. "Two big things I can know."

"All right. I'll go first." I picked at the button on my shirt. "Let's see. . .I grew up playing with dollhouses, but unlike the other girls, I decided that when I grew up I wanted to help people find their real dream houses, a place to raise their families. And I think it was a good choice. I've always liked it. There, that's two." I felt I'd cheated Siggy with the last one, but it was amazing how cornered people could feel explaining their lives.

"Can I go with you to do the dream house thing?" Siggy asked me.

"Maybe someday. But I'm taking a little time off right now. You know, from what we talked about before."

"From hurting your head?"

"Yeah, I need to heal in my head and my heart."

"When will that happen?" he asked.

"I don't know, but I'm sure God knows."

"I know God. He's a friend of mine. And He's not imaginary like my friend Charles Dickens."

I grinned. "You're right. God's not imaginary, and He does make a good friend."

Siggy scratched his head, which made his hair look as turbulent as Lars's. "Maybe you could ask God to heal your head."

"That is a good idea, Siggy." I reached out and smoothed his hair. "Thanks for the reminder." I looked over at Lars, who appeared to be hanging on our every word. "Okay, it's your turn." I held up two fingers.

"Well, I design houses for a living." Lars took in a deep breath and let it out. "*And* when I was growing up I lived in foster homes."

"What's that?" Siggy asked.

"They're homes where people take care of you when you don't have a mom or dad."

Siggy folded his hands in front of him. "Did you get a lot to eat?"

"No, not really." Lars seemed to drift far away for a moment, and then he came back to us with a weak smile. "To be honest, Siggy, it always felt like there was never enough of anything."

"Your storybook sounds sad like mine." Siggy reached into his pocket and pulled out a slice of bread from dinner. "I saved this for later in case I got hungry. But you should have it. . .just in case." He offered the mangled bread to Lars.

"Thanks, buddy." Lars accepted the bread with a smile, but when I looked more closely, his eyes were rimmed in red. "Now tell us two things about Siggy."

Siggy stuck two fingers under his chin. "My parents died when I was real little. And I don't miss them 'cause I didn't know them. And number two is. . .I love bugs."

How sad about Siggy's parents. I had wondered about them. Except for his aunt he must be alone in the world. Siggy's theatrical expression made me think of the second thing he mentioned. "You mean you like creepy-crawly things?" I shivered just thinking about it.

"Yeah." Siggy pointed to my arm. "Like the one crawling on you."

Chapter 11

The next morning I woke up with a lion in my stomach. Apparently, my tummy was still making up for lost time, and it wanted food *now.* I crawled out of bed, feeling tired but without the sorrow I'd felt in the previous days. I was only tired and hungry, not exhausted and depressed. So I threw on my robe and tramped downstairs to see what was cooking.

The house appeared to be empty, but I smelled a hint of something tasty lingering in the air. "Hello? Mom? Dad? Anybody?"

Gone.

Everyone had hugged me good-bye the night before, so I knew my sisters would be on their way, but maybe I needed to say good-bye one more time. Or something. What was wrong with me now? I took a pear from the bowl, washed it off, and took a bite.

Since the coffeemaker was still on, I filled a mug, added a liberal dash of heavy whipping cream, and sat down with the paper. Hmm. The headlines. World unrest and earthquakes. Wars and rumors of wars. Same distressing news as always. I didn't want to spiral myself back down into more despair, so I shoved the paper aside and looked at the novel Mom was reading. *In Case of Rain*. Interesting title. I opened the book to the first page.

Sometimes, for no reason at all, my mind's eye conjures up a scene—there's a man, tall and sturdy in stature, who's wearing a summer suit and a straw hat—but each time the man walks toward me I can never see his face. It's always covered by the brim of his hat. Then the man disappears. I'm always stirred with queries, wondering why I would think up such a character with no identity and no connection to my life.

Then one day—an ordinary day in the park—I happen upon that same tall man with the summer suit and hat. I call out to him as if to an old friend, and this time he looks at me. His face shines with acknowledgment and wonder. With amusement and affection. How can this be? He's a stranger, and yet somehow I know—he's the man I am to marry.

I slammed the book shut. Mom placed the novel on the table for a reason. She was such a matchmaker. Or was it the stirring hand of Providence? My heartbeat revved up to a bongo-banging frenzy. Maybe I'd had too much caffeine and not enough food.

Or maybe the little story had hit home.

I picked up the pear for another bite but couldn't eat it. My gut had that funny feeling again. Change was hovering over me like a pretty butterfly, waiting for me to do something. Waiting for me to acknowledge its beauty or shoo it away. The truth was—I had fallen a little in love with Lars in those earlier months of our friendship. When Henry came through with a proposal, it seemed like my only option, but I should have waited. Knowing the confusion I'd wrestled with, I should have paused to see what might blossom with Lars. We both would have had time to grow and see if we were in the middle of something remarkable. Something not to be missed.

God, why didn't You stop me? Oh yeah, You did.

I bowed my head and thanked God for halting the wedding, even though it was at the last moment, the last hour, humiliating and expensive. Yet, it was infinitely better than marrying a man who didn't really care for me. At least nothing like the way Lars had come to treasure me.

Then I knew the source of my emptiness. Not from a hunger for breakfast. Not the quiet of the house. And certainly not from longing for Henry to come back!

I missed Lars, and I wanted to see him. That was it. So I cleaned up the table and ran upstairs to change. Lars was staying in town, that I knew, but had he mentioned where he was going today? Something about the beach house. The one he'd always dreamed of renovating and living in someday. And surely the one he'd buy now that he was moving back. Would he still be there?

I slipped on a dress, added my signature vest, and then slid into my MINI Cooper. On my way, I made a quick stop at one of the local bakeries for a box of petits fours and then sped onward. I no longer remembered the exact address of the beach house, but I had a pretty good idea of what it looked like—a two-story cottage with white chipped paint and crooked shutters. It just needed some love, Lars had said. I thought the place needed a bulldozer more than anything else, but I didn't have the heart to lessen his enthusiasm for it. Once I'd made it over to the west side of Galveston, I started to search for the house. After a few wrong turns—such is life—it didn't take too long to find the correct street and then the right house.

There it was, sitting all by its lonesome just as I remembered it. Only perhaps a little more run-down. Lars's old Mercedes sat in the driveway.

I parked, got out, and ran, my heart going into its speed-dialing mode again. When I stopped and looked up, there he was, leaning over the balcony as handsome as you please, smiling down at me, and looking like love itself.

"You can't live without me after all?" he asked.

"You're awfully sure of yourself today."

"No. I'm sure of *us*."

I made no reply but hurried up the steps to join him on the balcony. I set the pastry box down on a table and reached out to shake his hand. The formality felt silly, so I gave him a hug. I thought of several reasons to pull back, but they all dissolved into excuses that no longer mattered. Time—a sure and steady thing most hours—passed all too quickly in the sanctuary of his arms. "You know what I like about you?"

"My well-groomed hair?" Lars whispered.

"No." I grinned. "I like it that you're a man who wears flannel when no one else is wearing it."

"Doesn't say much for my character, does it?"

I eased away. "Oh, I think it does. You're not bound by

what other people do and think. You're your own man, and just like flannel, you aren't pretentious, but you're warm and safe and mostly wrinkle-free."

He chuckled. "I think you're reading more into it than there is. I just wear flannel 'cause it's cozy. But don't tell anybody I said that."

I laughed. "I'm so glad you're here." I tugged on his rolled-up sleeve.

"Me, too."

"I mean, I'm glad I didn't scare you off."

"I'm not going anywhere."

Memo to self—I love the way Lars says that to me. "You know, I drove all the way over here to tell you something."

"Well, I certainly like the way you say things with a hug."

I reached up and smoothed the wild stray hairs off his forehead. "We've been in the middle of a comedy of errors, you and me. . .and it's not a good way to live. It's all errors and no comedy. And that's what I came to say."

Lars stuffed his hands into the pockets of his jeans. "I'm just thankful that this comedy of errors didn't become a Greek tragedy. That is, if you'd married Henry."

I absorbed the truth of his statement but didn't want to linger there too long. I said nothing for the moment, but let the sounds of the ocean speak for us.

"So, how would you describe those clouds out there?" Lars asked.

"Oh well, let's see. Great gray elephants full of rumble and play. But they'll eventually go away." Nothing like a good rhyme to change the mood.

"Nice hope-filled poem." Lars clasped his hands together, almost as if in prayer. "What do you think then. . .a chance of sunshine?"

"Very good chance."

He brightened. "Well, a good weather report is always welcome news to the sailor." He rested against the railing again and looked toward the ocean. "Look at that vessel on the horizon. Maybe it's a cruise liner."

"Siggy would say it's a pirate ship."

"Yes, he just might. I need to remember to tell him that the first settlements here, well, permanent ones anyway, were built by a pirate. He'd like that bit of info."

"He would." I leaned against the railing next to Lars. "*And* America's worst natural disaster happened here. I guess that makes this beach a precarious place to live, wouldn't you say? Pirates and hurricanes?"

Lars looked at me then. "Life is full of risk."

I stared at him, taking him in, no longer bristling at his double meanings but relishing them.

"Nice dress, by the way."

"Thanks." I pointed to his red-and-black-checkered shirt. "Nice flannel."

He grinned.

"You've had your eye on this house for years, haven't you?"

"Yeah, I've asked the owners for permission to come over and dream so many times that I think they may just give it to me out of sympathy."

"What's stopping you from buying it? It's a great investment, you've got plenty of money, and it'll give you a chance to fish more. Something you love."

"I'd like to know what you think of it." Lars's tone was expectant but cautious.

"What's not to love about this house?"

"The foundation is good." He shook the railing, and the wood let out a painful moan.

We both laughed.

"And as you can see, it needs a *lot* of attention and love, which I'm more than willing to give."

"I know. It's a good house." I rested my hand over his. "I can see the potential now."

"I'm glad you can see it. It could be quite wonderful. . . someday?"

"Yes, someday, Lars." I touched his face—such a good face. I kissed him then. *Mercy me.* It felt better than any other delights and charms this old earth had to offer.

When we eased away from each other, Lars said, "I guess this kiss means I can ask you out on a real date. . .and you'll say yes?"

I chuckled. "I think you can safely say that." *And if we both feel the same way in six months you might be able to ask me something else. . .and I just might say yes.* "But I have a question. Why exactly are you so perfect, well, except for your hair?"

"I'm not. But I *am* perfect for you."

Maybe that is true. Maybe Lars is a keeper.

"And what, exactly, is wrong with my hair?"

I grinned.

"Okay, noncommittal on that one. Hmm. What's in the pastry box?"

"Something sweet. . .for us."

"So, is God healing your head like Siggy said? *And* your heart?"

"I think He is."

Lars held up his hands, his palms facing me, and without thinking I pressed my palms against his. Our fingers folded like flowers closing their petals, and we clung to each other that way. After a moment or two I could no longer tell if the heartbeat pulsing in our hands was his or mine. But such things no longer mattered.

Chapter 12

Six months later, Lars had not only purchased the house, but he'd gotten all the renovations completed. There'd been plenty of renovations in my heart, too, and Lars had turned out to be more than a friend—much more.

I decided to throw a housewarming party for him with all our friends and family, and as the evening progressed I could tell it was a hit with everyone. Lots of food. Lots of laughter. And even more love. But the air seemed charged with something else that I couldn't quite place—an energy with such hope and promise of good things to come that I caught myself holding my breath at times.

Mom came into the kitchen and hugged me. "I've never seen my Rosy so rosy."

I leaned down and touched my forehead to hers. Still felt like when I was five. Still felt like home.

"You love Larson, don't you?"

"I do, Mom. Who could have imagined how God would help me work all this out?"

Siggy ran in the kitchen and nestled himself between us. "Are you having a good time?" I asked him.

"A lotta lotta of food." He gave us a thumbs-up. "Good party, Aunt Rosy. Next time may I bring my dog?"

"Maybe. I'm glad you're having fun." I kissed the top of his head. Over the months Siggy had snuggled into our lives, and he appeared to be thriving. We weren't sure where it was leading, but we knew God had it all under control.

Lily peered around the kitchen doorway. "Rosy Posey, I think somebody has something to say to you in the living room."

"Oh?" I tried to sound a little surprised, but I knew Lars had to be up to something.

I stepped into the living room, and through a happy sea of family and friends I saw my love. Lars stood by the mantel, and next to him, of all things, was my French horn. I knew Lars loved it when I played, but surely not now. What was he up to?

I strolled over to him as he clinked his fork against his glass. Everyone got quiet. "Well, you all thought you were coming to a housewarming party put on by the illustrious Rosy McBride here, but I have a slight change of plans this evening. I'd like to turn this housewarming party into an engagement party."

A few gasps could be heard as well as giggles.

So, *that* was what he was up to.

"But I need the participation of one other person here," Lars said, "since I found out you can't marry yourself."

Everyone laughed.

"And because the love of my life just happens to be the same lady who put on this shindig, I thought maybe she could help us turn this party around."

Cheers and shouts rocked the house.

"My request?" Lars looked at me. "If Miss Rosy McBride will play us a tune on her French horn, I will take that as a yes. . .to my proposal of marriage."

He raised his glass and smiled that smile I'd grown to love.

"Well, I'm not going to give up a life with Lars simply because I'm rusty at the French horn."

Chuckles flowed through the room again, and it filled me with affection for all those who'd gathered around us. I sat down, positioned the horn on my lap, and began to play "Amazing Grace." The room went quiet and all one could hear were the strains of that age-old and beloved tune. I felt a little shaky at times, but the unbroken faith behind the song was as sure and steady as the tide waters just outside the walls. I completed the last of the tune, and the room fell quiet as if held in a holy hush.

Lars leaned down to kiss me. "I take that as a yes. So, you're ready for that all-consuming emotional plunge that has no safety net?"

"I can't believe you remembered my words." I grinned. "Yes, I am."

"You're sure I didn't twist your arm or steal your heart?" he whispered into my hair.

"It's never stealing when the other person gives it away." I smiled and set the French horn down on its stand.

Siggy jumped on my lap, and Lars and I both enfolded him with our arms and our love.

Somehow I knew. It was going to be a good year—and a very good life.

Epilogue

I had to admit, the wedding came off even better than expected. Intimate and simple, and God had provided the décor. We'd decided to have a sunset wedding on the beach, and Siggy, of course, was our ring bearer.

Our love for Siggy blossomed over the months until we all decided—with the full blessing of his aunt Marmy—to adopt him. His aunt also became a beloved member of our family. In fact, the greatest thing we learned over the months was how much we all needed each other.

*

A few weeks after Siggy became our son and we were sipping cocoa and sitting by a cozy fire at the beach house, Siggy said, "Tell us a story, Dad."

Lars frowned. "Not tonight, son."

"Really?" Siggy flailed his arms around in his usual dramatic way. "But why not?"

"Because you're going to tell Mom and me a story tonight." Lars ruffled his hair.

Funny how Siggy had thick and blustery hair just like his dad. God must have planned it that way. "Yeah, and I want a good one." I grinned at him.

Siggy snuggled down between us and took a slurpy swig of his cocoa. "Okay. Let me think." He wiped the chocolate mustache onto his sleeve and got all serious. "Got it. Once there was this pirate named Siggy, and. . ."

FOR THE LOVE OF VIOLET

Chapter 1

People are so busy being clanging cymbals they sometimes forget to enjoy nature—to listen and hear its sweet singing lullaby. The melody grows clearer every time I pass through my favorite place in all the world—the Chisos Mountains. Even now I can hear it.

I hiked up the last switchback toward the final summit on Lost Mine Trail. The late February day—the twilight of winter, as I liked to call it—felt so brisk and invigorating that I picked up my speed and jogged the rest of the way to the crest. On top I was rewarded with a majestic vista, those familiar misty peaks and piney knolls, a view of nature's finest regalia and a view I'd grown to love more every time I saw it.

I heard footsteps behind me and looked back toward the trail. Basil Skeffington—the only date I'd had in a year—trudged up to me, out of breath but looking fairly good-humored.

"Wow, you got ahead of me there." Basil dropped his backpack and collapsed on a boulder.

"Sorry, it's a habit. The closer I get to the top, the more I feel like running."

"Very few people run," he said. "If they do, they're usually in need of a defibrillator."

Cute.

"I admit, though, it's a nice place to be, Violet. I guess it's better than going out for Mexican food. Well, at least calorie-wise. So I'd say, good call."

"Thanks." I turned back to face the lovely topography. Basil. Hmm. I liked him well enough. We were close to the same age. He loved all the things I loved—God, nature, and quiet—in that order. On a rare occasion he exhibited what could pass for humor, and this could be tolerated as well as sometimes even enjoyed. Except for Basil's irregular name, he was conventional in every way, and he appeared suitable for what I needed—a man I could share this big Texas sky with. Someone who loved the desert and mountains of Big Bend as much as I did.

I breathed the cold, dry air and pondered the institution of marriage. It had always seemed like a recipe for a cluttered house and a cluttered life, but now that I was thirty-five my spirit had ripened. Or perhaps it had just finally resigned to the notion that a man might add a certain pleasantness to one's life as one grew older. A man might be good company in the evening hours—as long as he wasn't too noisy or complicated. And like a good toolbox, he might add some practical support that could come in handy.

Over the years I'd built a haven of sorts, and I treasured it. No one, unless I gave them permission to do so, would mess with my little sanctuary.

My very next step, which had been nimble since toddlerhood, caught my boot on a rock and sent me flailing toward the ground. I landed facedown in the dirt. Dust covered my mouth, my clothes, and my pride, and I sputtered and coughed. I stayed there like that, mingling with the earth, stunned at my sudden deficit in ambulatory skills, and tried to get my equilibrium back.

"Whoa, that was quite a fall." Basil took my arm and lifted me out of the dirt like a sack of potatoes.

"Yeah. . .unexpected." I slapped the dust off my pants and jacket, trying to be angry at my clothes, but they couldn't absorb the blame.

Basil whipped out his handkerchief like a nobleman and offered it to me.

"Are you sure? It's going to get dirty."

"Go right ahead."

I took the cloth, dampened it with some water from my bottle, and wiped my face. The only word that kept coming to me was *bumbling*. Good thing we had the mountaintop to ourselves or I could have humiliated myself in front of a whole group of spectators. "I don't usually trip like that."

I offered the handkerchief back to Basil, but he shook his head. "You can throw it away. The only reason I carry a handkerchief is because Mother always says men should carry a handkerchief. I've never had to use it before. . .until today." He shrugged. "Would you like a protein bar? You look like you could use one."

"Thanks. I brought my own."

"Always prepared. That's good."

I smiled.

And then Basil and I sat there on a lumpy boulder, munching on two protein bars and looking out over the natural wonders that God had placed before us. I breathed in the air that was clean enough to bottle. Basil looked as though he were meditating on something profound—perhaps a philosophical or theological issue of some kind. Then again, maybe he was merely lamenting the Mexican food he'd given up for me. "So, where do you see your life in five years?" I asked, thinking I might find out if we were on the same page and just how deep Basil's well went.

"What do you mean?" he asked blankly.

Okay, maybe Basil's well was really just a shallow pool, but at least that way you could see everything. There was never anything hiding. No mystery. No scummy little varmints lurking in the watery shadows, ready to surprise you on your tenth wedding anniversary. And lastly, surface water was drinkable. It would do just fine.

"Hmm. It tickles me that you would ask me. Nobody's ever wondered about that. . .except for Mother, of course."

Of course.

He yanked off another hunk of his protein bar as if it might pull a few teeth, gave it a few cud-like chews, and then washed it down with a noisy gulp of water.

"Well, let's see. Where do I see myself in five years?" Basil scratched his chin like he was drilling a hole. "I guess I'd like to keep on the same path I'm going. Straight ahead." He made a gesture like he was slicing the air with his arm. "Ever since high school I've been selling insurance, and I'm good at it. I make a respectable income. I have a nice house and a well-maintained car. I worship every Sunday. I'm a member in good standing at the Chamber. I don't have a dog, but I'm thinking about getting one. Well, someday when I feel the time is right, and I feel I can take on all the responsibilities that come with owning a pet. I have a good life, Violet. And I think it will continue to be good five years down the road." He let out a deep breath, as if he'd created it all and had pronounced it good.

I nodded. I could have predicted that speech, or something close to it, which was *good*. There'd be no ugly surprises like my sister Rosy had when she was left at the altar by a madman. "That's good, Basil." *Good* was apparently the word for the day. Perhaps if things were to work out between us it could be our "life" word.

"And where do you see yourself in five years, Violet?"

"Hopefully, it will be the same as the last five years. I want a simple life, like you. I'll continue running my business, and in my spare time, I'll hike and bake and help out once a month at the church." Well, behind the scenes, where I didn't have to mingle too much.

"But your life doesn't seem all that plain. I mean, your business is. . .so *exotic*." He said the word as if what I did should be hidden in a brown paper bag.

"It's pretty straightforward, actually."

"What made you think to start Romantic Images anyway? You seem more like the type of woman who would teach history at the college, not sell things to make a person's life more. . .romantic."

"Have you ever gone online to see what it is that I actually sell?"

Basil gave his head a ferocious shake.

Sure hope he didn't shake any of the *good* sense out of his head. "I assure you it's not anything you couldn't buy for your grandmother. I sell products like French milled soaps and gourmet teas and hand-crocheted throw pillows and potpourri sachets and truffles from Belgium and—"

"Oh. I see."

I stopped, since Basil didn't look all that "tickled" with my list. I put the rest of my protein bar in an airtight wrapper to keep the bears at bay and stuck it in my backpack. "You might be right about teaching, though. It might have suited me. But my father helped each of his daughters start our own businesses. He said if we had a good marketable idea, he'd put up the cash."

I took a drink from my water bottle. "As it turned out, my ideas weren't all that strong, so my sister Heather brainstormed and came up with the concept for Romantic Images. The moment she told me the idea, I knew it would work. Women are always an easy target when it comes to romance. They can't help it. It's in their DNA. And as I predicted, the company took off, and it's done so well that I was able to hire a manager to run the business for me. So, now I have more time for this. To be out here."

Basil dusted the crumbs off his coat. "Do you think you'll ever *sell* the company?"

"I don't know." Odd question. "I don't think so." Why would he ask me that? Surely he wasn't uncomfortable with my career.

"Just a thought, my dear."

I was suddenly a "dear"? Basil's expression changed from

business to something else.

"By the way, your hair is a good color." He tugged on a strand of my hair. "It's brown, so it doesn't clash with your brown eyes."

Well, I can certainly live on that compliment for years. Surely that wasn't Basil's idea of getting amorous?

"This might be a good time for me to kiss you," he said. "There's no one here to see us."

"A kiss?" Right now?

"I mean, I know it's our first date and all, so if you don't want to kiss me, I completely understand."

He sounded like he was talking himself out of it. "It's fine if you want to kiss me." I hadn't gone out on a date in so long I'd almost forgotten what a kiss felt like. It might be good to try it again. It'd be like getting a refresher course at a community college.

He motioned toward my cheek. "Well, you still have a little dirt on your face."

"Oh?" I took the damp handkerchief and wiped my face again.

"Yes. Good. Much better." He wiped his hands on his pants. "Are you ready?"

"I'm ready." There was so much deliberation surrounding the kiss, I thought maybe we were still waiting on the jury to come back with a vote. Or maybe we were waiting on Basil's mother to signal him from the sidelines somewhere.

But all in all, it felt like a pretty good time for a kiss. It was, after all, a date. And we were having a good time together. We'd had no arguments. Plenty of pleasant conversation that flowed as easily as the Rio Grande. And Basil and I certainly weren't strangers, since we'd gotten to know each other through church.

He closed his eyes and leaned toward me. He had bits of protein bar left on his chin, which made him look a little like a child in his high chair waiting for his momma to clean him up. I could see his mother doing that very thing, and I almost laughed. Good thing I had self-control, because the laughter would have ruined a perfectly good kiss, which still hadn't happened yet. But it was getting closer by the second. His breath smelled of the mint flavor from his protein bar. Not bad.

I leaned closer to his mouth, anticipating a good kiss.

I left my eyes open for our affectionate little enterprise, because I wanted to see things as they really were. I could hear his breathing, which was sure and steady, just like Basil. Just like Basil. *Just like Basil.* Would I be saying those words if we married and grew old together? It was just like Basil to take out the trash every day? Just like Basil to buy extra insurance coverage? Just like Basil to hold an umbrella over me if it rained? Hmm. The words could grow on me like a trumpet vine on a porch trellis.

Anyway, the kiss could be described as a good one. Just the right pressure. Dry, which was always a plus. And sincere.

Basil pulled away and looked at me. "That was a good kiss, Violet."

"Thank you. I thought so, too."

"Good." He smiled like a man who had the assurance that one more scene of his life had gone well—like a drill sergeant giving him the nod that his bedsheet was tucked perfectly or the barrel of his gun was clean enough to pass inspection.

Overall, the kiss was far better than kissing one's own hand, but, of course, not anything like the flamboyant and impassioned kisses portrayed in books and movies. Because my personality could be likened to the character Charlotte in *Pride and Prejudice*, I never entertained any stormy fantasies about love. After all, boats never capsized on a calm sea.

Basil was certainly nice enough to look at. His lips were thin and even, like window blinds, and they coordinated with the rest of his face, which was accented with angles and points. Not a bad face when all the odd pieces were put together. Some would say he was handsome, in fact, especially if you didn't have your contacts in. I wondered how many of the women in his insurance office had tried to have the lips of Basil Skeffington touch their own. Hard to postulate on that one.

Basil busied himself staring at his fingernails. Not a very mannish thing to do, I had to admit, especially with all the gorgeous scenery he could be looking at. I guess a woman had to ask herself—could she marry a man who insisted on getting a weekly manicure?

I pulled the binoculars out of my backpack to have a closer look at the deer I'd spotted on one of the grassy knolls below.

"What do you see? Anything interesting?"

"A deer." I pointed. "Down there." I handed him my binoculars.

Basil readjusted the lenses and had a look. "Too bad. I didn't get a good look. It took off. There must be something around that spooked him."

"I wonder what—" Terror, the kind you only see in movies, had never been in my repertoire of emotions, but it decided to show up anyway. "Basil," I whispered. "Don't move. Remain calm."

"Why?"

"There's a mountain lion at ten o'clock coming toward us."

Chapter 2

Ever so slowly, Basil rose from the boulder.

"Don't run away," I whispered, trying not to move my lips. "It will only make him want to attack us."

"Right."

I glanced at the mountain lion again, but this time I felt mesmerized, unable to move my gaze. The huge cat appeared yellow-gold in the sunlight, every muscle tensed within his angular body, his eyes piercing though us. I felt as awestruck with his magnificence as I was terrified by his stare. "He's watching us, but he's no longer moving toward us." Droplets of sweat formed on my face in spite of the winter chill. Could he smell our dread? I felt drenched in it.

Without bending over we picked up our backpacks from the rock.

Step by cautious step, we backed away from the lion, and with great care, we inched toward the trail. Fortunately, the lion wasn't blocking our path down the mountain, which I counted as one of God's great mercies.

Basil stumbled on a rock but recovered.

The lion's tongue swiped over his mouth. Not a good sign.

The next few seconds I prayed more than I breathed.

We were steadily distancing ourselves from the animal, but mountain lions were unpredictable, and the beast could certainly make up the distance in seconds if he chose to, or he could track us down the trail if he were hungry enough. What would it feel like to be torn apart or eaten by a mountain lion? The contents of my stomach churned as I imagined the unimaginable. *Calm yourself, Violet.* I reminded myself that mountain lion attacks were rare in the park.

Suddenly, the mountain lion turned as if bored and padded in the other direction to haunt some other part of the park. He must have thought there was easier prey elsewhere. In all my years of hiking, I'd never had a mountain lion come close. Perhaps the smaller animals he preyed on had diminished in the area, or maybe he'd seen us as a threat. I would never know the answers, but when the animal turned to go, I felt aware of our freedom and so profoundly mindful of my relief I bent down with my hands on my knees to catch my breath.

"You all right?"

"Yeah. We'd better go."

Basil and I hiked back and forth down the switchbacks almost at a trotting pace. Neither one of us made fun of the other's speedy descent. We both understood what could have happened and that things could have gone badly for us.

I glanced up toward the heavens and nodded. "Thank You, Father."

*

Later, in front of my house, sitting in my car, and after yet another discussion surrounding our wildlife encounter, Basil walked me to the door. "Quite a day. Quite a day. I'll be talking about this at the office for years. Won't you?"

I wasn't sure I even wanted to think about it again, let alone let it eat up the rest of my life. "I don't know. Maybe I just need a cup of chamomile tea. I'd like to get back to normal."

Basil reached out to me as if he were going to touch my face, but then he let his hand fall back down. "Good idea, Violet. Go have your tea."

Again I could see us as old folks. The two of us in our rockers and Basil saying, "Go have your tea, Violet." It sounded like home, come to think it. It reminded me of my family and growing up in Galveston.

I placed the key into the lock, and with one more goodbye, Basil lumbered toward his car. He didn't bother asking for another kiss. Guess he thought we'd reached our quota for the day. Or maybe he'd had the romance scared right out of him by the lion. My legs still had a shimmy at times when I thought of those wild eyes staring at me. Almost laughing at me.

I showered off the grime and some of the memory, changed into my everyday clothes, and headed to the kitchen to make my tea. A sound like a gunshot startled me. What was *that*? I put the teakettle on the lit burner, walked into the entry, and opened the front door.

Right away, I admonished myself for not looking through the peephole. A stranger stood on my welcome mat. "May I help you?" I rarely had stray visitors, since I lived way outside of Alpine and since everyone who knew me was aware of my hermit-like tendencies.

The man fixed his gaze on me. He looked a bit older than I was, and his gray eyes were so intense he could set off a match without striking it.

"You're much younger than I imagined. Just a kid really," he said. "Your hair is short, and you're dressed like a man."

I glanced down at my very cool Ralph Lauren tie—for women. "Excuse me? And how do I know you?"

"I know you from your website, Romantic Images. I guess your professional photo makes you look older and more casual."

"I'm not a kid. I'm thirty-five. . .not that it's any of your business. Who are you?" This guy scared me more than the mountain lion.

The stranger laughed.

I was one irritated foot tap away from shutting the door in his face.

He held up his hands. "I'm really sorry. I've offended you right off, and I didn't mean to. Sometimes my enthusiasm gets ahead of my manners, like a longhorn at a tea party."

Did he expect me to laugh?

"I'm Morgan Jones. . .at your service." The man reached out his hand.

I crossed my arms so I wouldn't be tempted to shake his hand. "I'm sorry, but you're a stranger to me."

The man who claimed to be Morgan Jones drew back in surprise. "Well, I introduced myself."

I narrowed my eyes. "Are you connected in any way to that terrible noise I heard? It sounded like gunfire."

He pointed his thumb toward the pickup truck parked in the front of my house. "Oh, it's my jalopy. She backfires. Indigestion. Sorry. She's addicted to jalapeños."

That was so *not funny.* I frowned. "How may I help you? If you're selling something, I'm not—"

"No, not at all."

That's what they all say, right?

"The thing is. . .I'm a huge fan of yours, and I've come all the way from Tulsa to hire you as a consultant."

"If you'd read my website carefully enough, you'd know I'm not a consultant. My company is like a clearinghouse. We sell products online that offer our customers a way to live romantically. I'm sorry you drove so far to be turned away, but I can't help you." I started to shut the door.

Morgan didn't place his foot in the doorway, but his expression—one of imploring guilelessness—was as powerful as any iron crowbar. Or at least what appeared to be guilelessness. He'd probably been practicing that earnest expression in the car, and I was being duped by a flimflam man.

"But I'm willing to pay you a great deal of money to instruct me." Mr. Jones straightened his shoulders and raised his chin, but it came off more innocent than confrontational.

I opened the door wider. "Teach you to do what?"

He shrugged. "To live romantically, of course."

"I've never heard a man say such a thing. Most of my customers are women."

"Well, I'm a man who would love to romance a woman. . . to do it properly, to have that unique life-approach. And you're the perfect woman to teach me that frame of mind."

I wanted to laugh, but then I remembered how much the price of online advertising had gone up, and then suddenly Morgan Jones didn't sound quite as loony as before. At least his clothes weren't as dreadful as his vehicle. He had kind of an Eddie Bauer thing going. Not bad.

The whistle on my teakettle blew, demanding my attention. I ran to the kitchen to remove it from the burner, and when I turned around with the boiling water, Morgan Jones was standing right next to me. The scream I let out could have frightened off an entire ecosystem.

He stumbled toward me and jostled my arm, which made the boiling water splash onto his hand. He stepped back in obvious pain.

So, there we were—two people in the kitchen, one flustered and one blistered. "Why did you follow me in? You scared me to death. What were you thinking?" I set the kettle back on the stove.

"I came in because you waved me in." He didn't yell, but I could tell he was toying with the idea.

"I did *not* wave you in." I raised my voice a notch, but I admit, I was starting to feel sorry about his burned hand.

Morgan made a motioning wave with his uninjured hand. "Like this."

"You misunderstood. That was an exasperated wave. Can't you tell the difference? I don't invite strange men into my home."

"I introduced myself," Morgan said. "So I'm not a stranger."

"But you *are* strange."

"Yes. I guess I am. Which means I will require your

services even more." Then he laughed. Not the maniacal laughter of a crazy person, but the contagious laughter of someone who loved life and was anxious to make merry.

I was *not* in the mood to make merry, however, and I would not get dragged into his folderol. And yet surely I was a Christian with some heart left. "Are you injured badly?" seemed like the only thing to ask.

"I've survived worse."

I got a glimpse of his hand then, and it was redder than a patch of Indian paintbrush. Since I didn't want to get sued, I pulled a chair out from the table and said, "Sit."

Amazingly, Morgan eased off his jacket and obeyed.

"I'll get something to put on that burn." As I rummaged around in my bathroom medicine cabinet, knocking things around, I told myself a thousand times how foolish I'd been for leaving the door open for a stranger to come traipsing in. He could be a killer on the loose for all I knew. And yet his gray eyes, which had a hint of sadness in them, didn't show any signs of malice. In fact, he had a benevolent countenance—sort of round and friendly looking without being fat. Morgan was like a character actor, hired because he was unique, not because of his good looks. Odd sort of woolgathering, as my mother would call it.

I found the burn cream, cotton pads, and bandages and headed back toward the kitchen. Perhaps Morgan really had misread my gesture as a friendly wave. Could the mishap be my fault after all?

Morgan wasn't in his chair when I arrived. He stood by my French doors, staring at a fly that bounced against the glass trying to get out. He reached for the handle.

"What are you doing?"

Morgan opened the door just enough to let the fly become a fugitive and then shut it again.

So, he's a fly-hugger. "Why don't you sit at the table and let me tend to your hand." We sat down, and without hesitation he rested his hand on the table for my treatment. But then, I was the one at a disadvantage, not him, since I was a single woman with a strange man in my home. What would Basil think? And his mother? They'd probably light the town on fire with a blaze of speculations. Somehow, the thought was funnier than it was worrisome.

In the meantime, I had someone in my home with a burn that required medical attention. But after I was finished he'd need to do the proper thing and leave. I put some cream onto a cotton pad and dabbed it onto his burn. He was a grown man and could certainly dab the goo on himself, and yet I felt sorry for him. "Does it hurt?" He didn't wince, but I knew it couldn't be pleasant.

"No. I'll heal. . .eventually."

I looked up at him just in time to see the sparkle in his eyes. He was also one of those—a kidder. As a rule, I detested teasing in any form.

While I opened a bandage, he occupied himself staring at me, absorbing me as if I were some kind of rare nutrient that would bring him sustenance. *I must be losing it.* The thing was, I had no idea if he would find anything in me worth absorbing. And that bothered me. Why it concerned me, I had no idea.

Morgan placed his hand over mine, stopping my fidgeting with the Band-Aid. "Thanks for the burn cream, but I don't need the bandage."

"Why not?"

"Because wounds heal better if you leave them exposed to some air and light. You know, open and not wrapped up tightly." He rested back in his chair, his head angled with a bit too much confidence.

I released him to his lecturing mind-brambles and set the bandage on the table.

Instead of giving me the traditional thank-you, Morgan stood. He went to the stove, took two mugs from their hangers on the wall, and poured hot water from the kettle into them. He set one in front of me and took the other one for himself. After he settled himself again—a bit too comfortably, I thought—he pulled from his pocket a couple of packages that I recognized immediately.

"That's the jasmine tea I sell online. . .the one that blooms in the cup."

He opened one of the packages and dropped the leafy-looking ball into his mug.

Almost like magic, the tea leaves slowly opened in the hot water. Inside were tiny flowers. "This tea is special," I said. "It's from the Fujian Province in China. But I've never tasted one before. May I?"

Morgan handed me the other packet. I opened it and dropped the green ball into my cup. Little by little it unfolded and bloomed like some enchanted garden. No wonder the tea was such a big hit with my customers. I breathed in the aromatic scent of jasmine. “Thank you.” *This is nice. Unexpected.*

My shoulders relaxed a bit. But still, I reminded myself, the audacity of Morgan to make himself at home in my kitchen so quickly and easily was not to be tolerated. I wanted to stand up and order him out of my house. But I didn’t. Something stopped me. And it wasn’t the promise of cash as a potential customer. It was something else that I couldn’t define. I simply wondered what he’d do next and what he’d say next. But, of course, after my curiosity was satisfied, I would order him out of my house.

Chapter 3

Morgan said nothing for a moment as he sipped his tea. Then he fingered the violets in the center of my table. "I'd be a butterfly born in a bower, where roses and lilies and violets meet." The words flowed off his tongue as if they were always right there. He plucked one of the violets from my plant and twirled it around in his fingers.

"So, are you a poet?"

"No, those words are from Thomas Haynes Bayly."

"My brother-in-law, Larson, loves poetry, but I never latched on to it. And it's odd you would choose that quote. My sisters' names are Rosy and Lily. And I have a younger sister named Heather." Morgan had turned me into a chatty little nitwit.

"Your mom must love flowers."

"Yes."

Morgan seemed to know more about me than I was comfortable with. "Why have you really come here?"

"For the very reason I told you. But if I'm to be a client, you should know more about me."

"I think the operative word here is 'if.' I never said I would help you."

"Okay. *If* I became a client." Morgan reached around to the back of the chair and stuck the tiny violet into the lapel of his tweed jacket. "I've been single all my life, but I don't want to be. I'd like to know more about the art of romance. I seem to be lacking something with women. Something that has eluded me all these years."

I picked up my mug and finally took a sip of the jasmine tea. Pretty heady stuff. I couldn't believe I'd never tried my own product. "I think you'll be wasting your money."

"Well, I see it as an investment in my future. I want a wife. I want to marry. . .raise a family. And I'm convinced you have the piece that's missing from my puzzle."

Hmm. I hated to walk away from income, and yet his request seemed crazy. "I don't know why you've never been successful at dating or why you're not married. Maybe you'd benefit more from my sister's expertise. Lily is a family counselor."

I could tell I hadn't convinced him yet. What more could I say? "Look, I don't know if I'll take you on as a client, but I will give you one free tip while you're here. Don't come strolling into a woman's house. . .a woman you don't even know, and start taking over her kitchen. Pouring your own tea and plucking her posies. She won't want to kiss you. She'll want to chase you with a cleaver."

Morgan laughed then—a big, blustering laugh. Like a kid holding his belly and rolling on the floor with abandon. It nearly shattered the glass in my china cabinet. Never had there been such noise in my kitchen. Enough! I blinked back the tension building in my gut. "It wasn't really *that* funny."

"Yes, it was."

I frowned.

"By the way." Morgan rubbed the top of his head as he gazed around the room. "I like the way your house is designed, but I noticed it's kind of barren, and so is your yard. No color. No life. Why is that? I'm curious. Even Amish homes have more character. I assumed everything you touched would be overflowing with charm."

Had he not heard a word I'd just said about pushy behavior? No wonder he didn't have a girlfriend. "Try not to choke on that foot in your mouth."

Morgan laughed. "But you *are* funny. You really are."

"No one has called me funny since high school, and that was just a misprint in the yearbook."

Morgan grinned. "I wasn't trying to be rude. I was just asking an honest question. That's the kind of person I am."

Irritation rose up in me again. "Well then, you're the kind of person who's going to lead a very lonely life, Morgan Jones." Why was I getting so riled up? *Calm down, Violet. Easy does it.*

"One last question." He took a sip of his tea. "I'm very familiar with your merchandise, and it doesn't appear that you use any of it. Why is that? Where are all the candles and dried flowers and hand-painted teacups and—"

"Earlier you said that sometimes your enthusiasm gets ahead of your manners. Well, that's impossible," I said.

"Why's that?"

"Because you *have* no manners."

He laughed. "Good one."

I waited for an apology, but none came. Maybe I was annoyed because he'd found me out. Perhaps he'd exposed me as the real flimflam person in the room, and it infuriated me. But I would give him an honest answer before I gave him the boot. "I don't use the products I sell, okay? Of course it's okay. And I don't feel right taking your money. I mean, I could always use more income, even though my business is doing well. Still, I'm not going to take you on as a client. I can't really teach you anything about romance."

"Why not?"

"The truth is, Morgan Jones. . ."

"Yes?"

"My company may be inspiring and ingenuous at selling products to make life more romantic, but the truth is. . .Violet McBride doesn't have a romantic bone in her body."

Chapter 4

I don't believe you." Morgan leaned forward and perched on the edge of his chair.

Easy does it, Violet. Two times in one day I'd had to explain my business's existence. "My sister thought of the idea for Romantic Images, not me. But I knew all my froufrou products would be as irresistible to the female psyche as honey is to a bear. Women can't seem to help themselves. But I'm not most women. I don't have a lot of wistful notions. So, I don't need a lot of sentimental paraphernalia or feminine stuffings or dainty enhancements for the home. However, I knew the overall concept would do well. And I thought if my company became successful enough, which it has, then I could hire someone else to run the business. Then I'd have more time for *this*." I motioned around me, feeling silly, since I'd just given Basil the very same spiel.

"What is *this*?" he asked.

"Well, the mountains and desert out here, of course." Who could ask such a question?

Morgan slapped his hand on the table as if convinced. "That's one proof right there that you are a romantic at heart."

"It doesn't prove anything."

"Of course it does. Generally, single women don't move

way out here to be around this rugged kind of nature. Most folks would consider you to be on the outer fringes of the earth. And that you are someone with a spirit of adventure… a dreamy idealist. You must have a great passion for it to make that kind of sacrifice. And to have so much passion for a place, well, it must mean you're secretly a romantic."

"I think you're reading too much into it. And I haven't sacrificed anything to be out here. . .except that I don't get to see my family as often as I would like. But I do love it." I moved my pot of violets closer to me. "It's home."

"And why is it home?"

"Because. . .well. Well, that's kind of personal. . .and you're a—"

"A stranger?"

"Another free tip. When you take a woman out on a date, don't start pelting her with a million personal questions. Act interested, but don't pelt. Deer are more likely to come out into the meadow if there's no gunfire."

"Is that what this is?"

"You mean gunfire?"

"No, a date." Morgan splayed his hand on the table.

"No, this is not a date."

"Okay. Got it. And no pelting." He gave me a thumbs-up. "Okay, so do you mind if I ask you one more question?"

I rolled my eyes. "One more." Basil wouldn't have put me through such an inquisition, such nonsense.

"If it's not too personal. . .why is it that you love these mountains and the desert so much? I really want to know."

My hands fluttered around as if they could help me come

up with the right words. "It's bursting with that same color and life and character you talked about. And on a deeper level, the desert is full of music. It has its own poetry, unwritten, yet more poignant and powerful than a library full of verse. . . because they're whispers from the master poet." I placed my hand over my heart.

"That's the sort of thing I'm talking about. You *are* a romantic. I read your blog. Those entries are stirring and literary and full of beauty."

I would have to set the record straight. Again. "Just now I got carried away. I always do when I talk about my home here. But I didn't write a single one of those pieces you've read. Not one."

Morgan appeared taken aback by my words. Some part of me was glad to shoot down his false impression of me, but another part felt disappointed to disappoint him. I really wish I *had* written those blog entries.

"Who wrote them?" He took a slurp of his tea.

"A freelance writer I hired. Her name is Gertrude Brown. She's very good. That's why I hired her. She does all that romantic hyperbole really well. So the woman you came all the way from Tulsa to meet, the woman whom you thought was a true romantic, who could give you the key to unlock that mystical thing called a woman's heart, well it's just plain old me. . .a hardworking businesswoman." I tapped my unmanicured fingers on the table.

"You're more than that. . .even if you don't believe it." Morgan drank down the rest of his tea, stood, put his mug in the sink, and turned back to me. "I can see it in your eyes.

They don't call them windows to the soul for nothing. It's all right there. The effervescent creativity. The fury of feeling. The thirst to imagine things beyond our mortal grasp. The passion of wonder."

You sure it's not your flare for farce? "I'm afraid you're not being logical. This has become the Theater of the Absurd."

"Great response! You *are* Romantic Images. Why are you hiding behind a veil? Playing the part of the shrinking violet? A part that isn't really you?"

"Who do you think you are, barging into my home without an invitation and talking to me thusly?" *Thusly? Did I really just say that?* "You don't even know me. I'm not hiding behind anything." This time I stood to be heard. "Why can't you accept it? I have no passion!"

Morgan eyed me. "Oh, really?" He smiled like a doctor who was a little too self-assured about his diagnosis.

"You tricked me into raising my voice."

Morgan leaned against my cabinetry, looking far too leisurely for my taste. "You could have asked me to leave, and I would have," he said.

I couldn't take anymore. I was done being the lion whisperer for the day—whether in animal or human form. And I'd had enough roaring from Morgan Jones. I raised my finger and pointed to my front door. "Thank you for that excellent suggestion. I'm asking you politely to leave my house." I shook my finger for emphasis. "Right now. Please."

Morgan didn't blink.

I took in a deep breath and exhaled. I hardly ever raised my voice. This crazy, infuriating, raucous stranger had unraveled my perfectly spun life in less than thirty minutes.

Morgan took his jacket from the back of the chair and slipped it on. "I'm still interested in hiring you if you're interested in teaching me how to live romantically."

His audacity was without limits. But an idea occurred to me, making me feel reckless and a bit smug myself. "All right, under one condition." I pulled a tablet of paper out of a drawer and scribbled a figure on the top sheet—an outrageous amount of money—tore it off the pad, and then slid the paper over to him. "My price per day." I knew the amount would send him packing for good.

He studied the price. "I agree to your terms. I'll be here at seven a.m. sharp."

He had trumped my self-satisfied grin with his own.

Chapter 5

After the initial shock wave of disbelief surged through me I realized I'd have to keep a verbal mallet handy—the guy had a lot of kinks to work out. But Morgan would tire of me once he realized he was wasting his money on a woman who had nothing to teach him. Then he could go off and torture his way through another crowd of women. "All right then," I said. "Let's do it."

Morgan nodded, sauntered toward the front door, and like a hapless pup, I followed. "I assume your fees don't include breakfast," he said.

"What?" I gathered my wits, which had scattered across the floor like a bag full of pebbles. "No, my fee does *not* include breakfast."

"That's fine, I'll bring my own. And a little something for you as well. Do you take cream and sugar in your coffee?" Once he'd made it to the front door, he turned to look at me.

"No, I like it black. Straight up. No frills. Nothing to smooth it out or sweeten it up. I don't like anyone manipulating or trying to *fix* my coffee." Or my life. "Are we clear?" I narrowed my eyes.

He merely smiled.

And then he left my abode. Like the Cat in the Hat,

Morgan Jones swept up his mess and strolled out just the way he'd come in—dripping in cheeky flamboyance.

He climbed into his rattletrap and cruised off without a care, but not without burping one more cannonball backfire—a royal *kabang*—which was augmented by a flame out the tailpipe that could singe the fur right off a mountain lion. And then that was it; the man chugged down the road in a cloud of Texas dust and out of my sight. Which was a good place to be. I shut the door. Loudly.

Well, that was rich.

What a character. If someone had made him up, no one would believe it. But I would put up with Morgan's annoying irregularities so I could supplement my online advertising. And I would do it for Angelica, the woman who managed my company. She'd done a great job so far, and rewarding her with a Christmas bonus later in the year would bring me great satisfaction.

I looked at the clock on the wall. Dinnertime. Where had the afternoon gone? I headed to the kitchen but stopped to gaze at the walls. Were they really that bare and pale? It had been easy to leave them as is, with the builder's generic paint—a milky white. Except for a few pictures, my walls did look a little sparse. And the house suddenly felt a little empty, too. Humph. I'd been happy until Morgan Jones rambled in. Well, he *barged* his way in.

I opened my pantry and stared at my shelves of canned soups. I had bought them because they were easy and nutritious, but I had grown weary of them. Someday it might be nice to dine on something more substantial. Since there was nothing else to be eaten at the moment, though, I opened yet another can, gave it a dash of cayenne pepper to give it some gusto, and then sat down to eat my vegetable beef soup. Alone as always.

Something caught my eye—something hidden on the other side of my potted violet. A candle tin. I recognized it immediately as one of the scented candles I sold online through Romantic Images. It had been imported from the Pays de Digne in France, which was one of the regions of Provence famous for their lush and aromatic lavender fields. Morgan must have deposited it there while I was busy pulling the writing tablet out of the drawer. What was he up to? Surely he wasn't trying to romance *me*.

I lit the candle and watched it flicker and sputter as I ate my soup. The scent of lavender calmed me, and I caught myself breathing it in. I had smelled the candle tins once before, tested them, but I'd never bothered to bring any of them home. I hadn't wanted my home to become a warehouse of product. Didn't want the clutter. But right now, at this moment, this one candle from Provence seemed like company.

After I ate the last bite of soup, I wiped my mouth with my napkin and then brushed my fingers over my lips. Since I wasn't big on wearing lipstick, they were a part of my body I spent little time thinking about. But those lips, *my* lips, had been kissed today by Basil. We'd come together in a kissing ritual that was as old as Adam and Eve, and our little assembly had been congenial. Granted, kissing Basil wasn't the most enticing experience, but it hadn't been disagreeable.

Although.

If I were going to be brutally honest with myself, Basil's kiss had reminded me of a science experiment from my junior high days. The teacher had promised us that a particular beaker was going to foam and hiss, and even though we waited and waited, with mounting anticipation, nothing happened. The whole class had groaned with disappointment. They'd expected fireworks of some kind. At the very least a vinegar-and-soda kind of fizzing. I ran my fingers along my lips again. That was how Basil's kiss had been. . .disappointing. Perhaps he'd felt that way, too.

I touched the pot of violets on my table and remembered Morgan's expression as he left. At the time I'd wanted to stomp on his toe, but now I wasn't so inclined to do that. Morgan was quirky and maddening, but he was also interesting. Not in a romantic way, but he did intrigue me. I certainly wasn't in the mood to live inside the pages of a romance novel, and yet my own parents' love story had been quite the drama—passionate and stormy. And now they could boast of having been happily married for decades.

Lord, I know You work in mystifying ways, but please tell me You haven't sent Morgan for reasons other than business. The thought of amorous stirrings connected to Morgan made me want to wash my mouth out with soap. Besides, I'd already resigned myself to the possibility of marrying Basil.

However.

Basil Skeffington hadn't mentioned ever going out again or even calling me. Was it over before it began? Funny how I hadn't noticed those deficiencies before, but now they were as gaping as Juniper Canyon.

I blew out the candle in one huffy blow and scrubbed my soup bowl out in the sink until my hands were red. I would check in with Angelica for our usual evening phone conference and then go to bed. But first, I needed to take care of the grumbling in my stomach as well as the heartburn. I seldom had tummy issues. Had it come from the seasoning I wasn't accustomed to? More likely, it was a spice called Morgan Jones. I popped a couple of antacids and marched upstairs to my office.

God, help me. Morning would come way too soon.

Chapter 6

Still half-dreaming of candle flames scaring away mountain lions and thinking I'd heard gunshots, I roused from a profound sleep. Hmm. Curious thing to think. Oh no. Gunshot? Backfire? Morgan. What time was it?

I sprang up like a prairie dog popping out of its hole and checked my alarm clock. Seven. I'd forgotten to set my alarm. What had happened to me? I'd never been one to oversleep.

I grabbed some clothes from my closet and bounced around the room, trying to get my foot into a pant leg and then a top on so my head wasn't through an armhole. I managed to get it all on correctly just as the doorbell rang. What in the world would I teach Morgan today? I didn't even have an inkling.

I glanced into the entry mirror, gaped at my disheveled appearance, and then opened the front door.

"Good morning, Violet." Morgan held up a large sack and a cardboard caddy with two steaming coffees.

"Hi. Please come in." Okay, that coffee smelled good. Not a terrible start.

He didn't move. "Are you inviting me in this time? Just want to be clear."

"Affirmative." I opened the door wider. "How's your hand?"

"I'm making progress."

We set up the mini-feast on my kitchen table, and I had to admit, it did look good and smelled even better. I was hungry, and my stomach was calm. I just hoped I could keep it that way. "Thank you for bringing breakfast."

"You're welcome."

I took a cautious sip of the brew. Mmm. Hazelnut. One of my favorites. How could he have known? Morgan certainly looked rested, and with the exception of a five-o-clock shadow, he appeared well groomed. But why was he dressed for the mountains? "Going for a hike today?"

"Maybe. So, where's your tie?" he asked.

"My tie? Oh, that." I waved him off. "I don't always dress that way. . .like a *man*."

"I thought it was cute."

I stopped midbite. "If we're to have a professional relationship, you'll need to refrain from using inflammatory remarks like that."

"Like cute? I can't say cute?"

"No. Now, if we were on a date it would be okay. But this isn't a date."

"Right." Morgan crumbled his slices of bacon all over his scrambled eggs.

"I can see where our discussions are going, and I don't want these sessions to become lessons in how to attract, date, or talk to women. I don't feel comfortable with that. I'm not a dating coach or life coach or whatever. It's not my area. I can explain ways our company tries to help people seek a more romantic way to live with our products. But that's about it. I know it's not good business to say this. . .but I still have my doubts I can help you."

He took a slurpy sip of his coffee. "Mmm. That's good, isn't it? Listen, why don't you let me decide if it's worth the money at the end of the week?"

"A week? You're kidding. Shouldn't take me more than a couple of days to—"

"How about we take it one day at a time? All right?" He rested back in his seat, looking too comfy and snug in my kitchen again.

A clock chimed in the living room. I tapped my fingers.

I thought about his proposition, this tweak of his, and because it made the noose feel a little looser, I nodded. "All right."

Morgan worked on his croissant, and I worked on mine amidst our first bout of silence. The quiet that nudged its way between us wasn't as awkward as I thought it would be. He seemed to be pondering life, and so we left out the words and just enjoyed the food. I did notice, however, that while I ate my croissant meticulously from one side to the other with a fork, he picked his up and randomly devoured it, skipping here and there until it was no more than a lick on his fingers.

Morgan broke the silence by saying, "I have an idea. Instead of you worrying about what to teach me, why don't you just let me ask you questions?"

"That would make it easier on me." Why was this

guy being so nice today? Or had we just gotten off on the wrong foot yesterday? Perhaps I could make a little friendly conversation. "What is that stuff you stirred in your coffee?"

"Honey."

I should have guessed. "Yeah, but it doesn't pour. You scooped it out of your little jar."

"That's because it's raw and unheated."

"I've never liked the taste of honey. It's so sweet it tastes almost bitter to me."

"Oh, you'll like this." Morgan took the full spoon from the jar and lifted it to my lips.

Without thinking I opened my mouth and let him feed me the raw honey. It wasn't very professional to allow such an intimate connection, but my mouth was suddenly too full of the creamy goo to verbally slap his hand. Oh wow, that did play on the tongue with some delightful notes. A little chamber music for the palate. "It's good."

"It's more than good. I can see it in your eyes."

I laughed. I'd need to wear sunglasses with this guy. He was too watchful. I placed my hand over my mouth so Morgan couldn't see me licking my lips. "By the way, thank you for the candle. But please don't bring me any more gifts. It's just not—"

"Yes, I know. It's inappropriate."

"Right." I drank down the last of my coffee.

"You know, I got to thinking that you might feel more comfortable in your domain today rather than staying here at the house."

"What do you mean?"

"You said you loved being in the mountains. Maybe we could take a hike in the park. I read that it's 800,000 acres, so I guess we've got a lot of area to cover."

I grinned. "Are you sure? You're paying me a lot of money just to be a hiker's guide."

"Well, as I see it, I'll get two for the price of one. Someone to teach me about living romantically and someone to tell me all about Big Bend National Park."

"Okay. It's your money. But you're going to need more than a tweed jacket. It'll warm up today, but right now it's in the upper thirties."

"I'm ready. I have some gear in the pickup."

Guess he'd planned the whole day while I slept. We cleaned up the table, and this time, I didn't mind as much that Morgan invaded my workspace. I changed into my hiking clothes, gathered up all my usual gear, and locked up the house.

"We can take my pickup." Morgan pointed to his rolling scrap heap in the driveway.

"No offense, but your pickup isn't going to make it one yard beyond where it's sitting right now unless we give it a good push." Preferably toward the junkyard.

He patted the hood. "Oh, she's fine. . .just needs a little tune-up."

"You sure she doesn't need a salvage yard?"

Morgan laughed as he tossed our gear in the back. He opened the door for me, and against my better judgment, I climbed inside. He was still a semi-stranger to me, so that was a serious demerit.

When I got inside, I didn't get too comfortable. His vehicle smelled like an oily rag and the windshield surely had thirty years of grime. How could he even see?

After he slid behind the wheel, he looked at me. "You're an outdoor girl. You're used to dirt, so what's the problem with a little dust?"

"I don't mind God's dirt. It's people dirt I'm fidgety with."

"Wow," he said. "I'm sure a psychoanalyst would have a heyday with *that* remark."

"Excuse me?"

"Come on now, don't get your boots tied into a knot so early in the morning." He offered me a disarming smile as we sputtered and backfired our way down the road.

"Fine, but I have another tip even though I *don't* give dating advice. You're way too chummy and direct in your conversation way too soon. It's just not appropriate for a date."

"Well then, it's a good thing this *isn't* a date." He grinned.

Remain calm, Violet. Don't let him get to you. "Why don't we get down to business? You were wanting to ask me some questions."

"I don't have any queries at present."

"The Window Trail would be a good hike today." I didn't bother telling Morgan about the encounter with the mountain lion on Lost Mine Trail. I was afraid he'd insist on checking it out right away.

He pushed a button, turning on his CD player. I assumed it would fire up with some wailing country song about a drunken derelict and his gambling dog, but he surprised me with Bach—"Jesu, Joy of Man's Desiring," one of my favorites. I never knew from one moment to the next how Morgan would affect me. Such a tug-of-war with the emotions. Once again, I thought of my parents when they first met. Same lightning and thunder. Same gentle rain. All together.

Maybe I was in trouble.

After our drive into Big Bend, Morgan insisted on stopping at the park headquarters before we hit the trail. Apparently, he was a man who liked brochures and maps and things. Once inside, I milled around, waiting for him to gather his materials. An older Hispanic woman, who seemed to be hearing impaired, was having trouble communicating with the ranger.

Much to my astonishment, Morgan walked up to the counter and started signing back and forth with the woman. She looked greatly relieved to meet someone who knew sign language and could translate for her. After a few moments of signing back and forth Morgan explained her question to the park ranger. When all was resolved the woman got teary-eyed and gave Morgan a hug.

In the meantime I stood mesmerized by it all. Morgan got his materials from a very grateful park ranger, and we left. "That was impressive," I said to him as we made our way back to his pickup. "Where did you learn sign language?"

After we got back inside his truck Morgan said, "I have a niece who's deaf, so I wanted to know how to communicate with her beyond just the usual. I wanted her to know that I loved her enough to learn *her* language."

"Admirable." And it was. Truly.

He made no more comment on the subject. If he were trying to impress me, he had. What he did for his niece went beyond a good deed—it was sacrificial. What kind of a man was Morgan? So many new layers to discover. And those hands of his that signed so well—the ones I had barely noticed before—were now an object of study. They were beefy, usable hands, the way they clasped the steering wheel, but they were emotive, too, enhancing whatever came out of his mouth. Basil had good hands, too, but they were smooth and a bit anemic, if hands could have that quality. They were without real life. Had I really strived so hard for simplicity that I forgot about soul?

"What is it?" Morgan asked me as if he could read my mind. "Are you okay?"

"What? Yes. I'm fine." In the midst of my distraction I wanted to frown at him, to chide him for being too intimate, and yet he'd never reached out his hand to me—it still clung to the steering wheel. He'd stirred me so deeply with his look, it felt as though he'd physically touched me. "Please tell me, what exactly do you do for a living? You've never said."

"Oh, odds and ends. Sometimes I'm a reader for several publishing houses. And I do research for Hugo Averill."

"You're kidding." I gave him a good long look. "Do you mean *the* Hugo Averill?" I tried to keep my voice steady. "The author?"

Chapter 7

Morgan nodded. "Yes, that's the one."

Everything within me wanted to start chattering nonstop about how I was a big fan of Hugo Averill and how I'd always wanted to meet him at a book signing. And how I always thought he was a great author because of his beautiful prose and his meticulous attention to detail and his obvious penchant for research. To think that *penchant* was sitting right next to me. Imagine. "That's so. . .interesting. I've read all of Hugo Averill's work. His literary style is masterful. It's absorbing and enchanting, almost fairy-tale–like." Guess I was working myself into a flighty blather.

Morgan went back to assessing me.

"You're going to run us into the gully if you don't stop staring at me."

"I know what you're thinking. That there might be more to old Morgan than you originally thought. Maybe not always a walking faux pas. Am I right?"

"You're far too honest." This time I grinned at him.

"I know."

But it's growing on me.

"You know, when I first arrived, I wasn't kidding when I

told you I was a fan of your work. I like it that all the things you sell online have one thing in common. They're things meant to soften the rough edges in life. To bring a smile after a long day at work. To make home feel more like, well, home. There's real value in that."

"If you know so much about my work, why do you need me at all?"

He glanced over at me with the oddest expression. It was as if he knew me, and it made me shiver. I was always in a quandary around this man. And my stomach was playing funny games again, too. Best to diffuse the moment. "You haven't asked me any questions. I'm starting to feel guilty for charging you a fortune. Maybe instead of paying me, you should put the money down on a new pickup truck." I couldn't believe I was giving away the money, but with each moment I spent with Morgan, I no longer felt right accepting it.

"But I don't need a new pickup truck."

It was my turn to laugh, and I did. "Are you kidding? Most people would have traded this thing in ten years ago."

"But I'm not most people."

Ya think?

"Honestly, when I need a new pickup, I'll get one. But right now this is what I want to do with my money. I'm here with you as my guide. . .and I'm discovering. . .gathering. . . and changing.

"But I haven't really *done* anything."

"All right," he said. "Have it your way. What are we doing today then? Is this a date?" His tone held a trace of hope.

Lord, please tell me what I'm doing here. Perhaps one way off the treadmill was to give in to the moment. A new concept for me. It felt ill-advised, but it also felt more appealing than living a prosaic and predictable kind of nonexistence—a Basil way of life. Where having tea was a directive, not a celebration. And we'd rock away our lives until there was nothing left but two worn-out chairs and a small pile of regrets. That kind of life suddenly felt like no life at all. "Okay. All right. Let's call this a date." I winced. "But does that mean I have to be nice to you?"

Morgan laughed.

Then I laughed. The moment felt jolting, like staring into the eyes of a mountain lion, but the shock also felt energizing, as if someone had plugged my life into a wall outlet, and I was glowing.

*

After Morgan and I parked, we slipped on our coats and backpacks and began our long descent into the canyon. The air felt nippy and fragrant and dry, just the way I liked it. But we were still a few weeks shy of spring. Soon the desert, which was now a hundred shades of ivory and amber, would be awash with flowers. Morgan would surely love to see the desert in full bloom. "You look like you've hiked before. You have all the gear."

"It's all new," Morgan said. "I've only hiked a couple of times in my life. I've mostly just read about it."

Finally, I'd found something that Morgan wasn't proficient at. "Do you think you'll like it?"

"I think I'll love it."

After we'd hiked for a while, Morgan pointed to a bird's

nest that had fallen to the ground. "I wonder if the wind brought it down."

"Maybe. We do get some strong winds through here." I leaned over to inspect the nest. "It's not too often that I get to see one of these up close. Such an engineering marvel." But of course the bird's home was empty, which made it look a bit forlorn. "When I see a nest I always think of mothers and how protective they are."

"It would be easy to feel that way about you. . .protective."

That was a kind thing to say. "And what would you want to protect me from, Morgan Jones?"

"Yourself," he said.

All the sweet, cold air drained from my lungs. *Calm yourself, Violet.* I felt a bout of bluntness coming on, and fortunately, I'd been studying with the master of candor. "I'd like to know who made you my savior."

"Well, I was just—"

"I know what this is about. It's like I've been written into one of Hugo Averill's books. His novels are all about the profound changes that his characters make in their lives. Is that what you think I need? Am I some kind of experiment? Like Frankenstein's monster?"

"I'm not Doctor Frankenstein," Morgan said. "I'm just a guy who can't talk to women."

Okay, that came off sort of sincere, but I wasn't going to let him off the hook so easily. "You know—"

"I came here, begging you to change me. So, I'm asking you. . .what's wrong with a little change?" He rubbed the top of his head. "As long as we're alive we're going to need it whether we like it or not. Change is as much a part of life as breathing."

Hmm. Not a bad speech overall. But I needed a moment to think, so I picked up the nest and set it on a cluster of pine tree branches. "I don't know." I turned back to face him. "It feels like we're on some kind of funky ride here. You banter with me and schmooze me and romance me. You make me crazy, and I wonder why I even came."

"You're a big girl," Morgan said, smiling. "You're here because you want to be here. . .with me."

I shivered, not because of the cold but because what he said was true. In spite of everything, I did want to be here. And I wanted to be here with him. *God, help me.* "But I mean, are you really that clueless about how exasperating you can be sometimes?"

"That's why I need your expertise."

"Well, you need *something* all right, but it might be a well-placed and therapeutic stomp on your toe."

He chuckled. "Maybe you're not used to your friends being direct with you. My friends are brutally honest, and I want them to be."

I hiked on down the trail without him and listened to the even cadence of my boots crunching on the gravelly trail. "I don't have that many *real* friends. I'm kind of a loner."

Morgan caught up with me. "I'm sorry."

"Don't be. I like it that way." Or at least I thought I did. "To be *honest*. . .friends can be more trouble than they're worth sometimes." The few friends I'd known in high school had taught me that lesson all too well.

"True. Hey, new subject. Tell me, what did you mean when you said that the desert had a kind of music? I'd love to know."

We hiked a bit more, and finally I said, "Let's stop and listen to the quiet for a minute."

As the swishing of our walking stopped, the silence wrapped around us like a heavy quilt.

"You're right. No planes. No cars. No human noises." Morgan looked around. "It's almost eerie, if you're used to the city."

"But if you listen beyond the initial stillness, the canyon will come to life."

We paused again, and after a few moments we could hear the rustling of a small animal in the thicket. The echoing cry of a bird soaring high above the canyon. The leaves prattling in a sudden breeze. The burbling of water through mossy crevices. "It's like all of nature is crying out to the glory of God. Like it's saying, 'How beautiful is Thy name in all the earth.' Eventually the sounds harmonize together. . .it reminds me of Beethoven's *Pastoral Symphony.*"

"Or Vivaldi's *Four Seasons,*" Morgan said.

"Yes, that's it." I raised my hands. "Exactly. They must have been truly inspired by God's natural world to compose those works." I sat down on a dead tree branch that had weathered to a silvery gray. "And away from the lights and the busyness and clamor of the city, you can breathe out here. You can hear God better out here. At least *I* can."

Morgan sat down next to me. "And what is God saying to you?"

"That He loves me. He loves everyone. That He's the greatest lover that this world has ever known or ever will know."

"Amen."

I smiled. But what I didn't tell Morgan was that God hadn't been as talkative as usual lately, and for me that usually meant some kind of change was coming. I hated change. Who wanted to break out of one's shell? The inside of the egg was such a cozy place to be. "I guess some people don't bother coming way out here, because they think Big Bend is just an arid and lifeless place, but they haven't experienced the magic. When it's time, the Chihuahuan Desert comes to life with such exotic beauty, it leaves you breathless. And the Chisos Mountain can claim every hue imaginable. Some of these colors, well, I think the only other place you can find them is in heaven." I took a swig from my water bottle and grinned. "Sorry, I get carried away."

"I don't want to be the cause of a writer losing her livelihood, but you don't need Gertrude to write those blogs. You've got a flair. . .the heart of a true romantic. I know you don't want to hear it, but it's true."

"Actually, it would save me a lot of money if I wrote them myself, and it would give me something to do. Angelica is such a good manager of my company, some days I have to hunt around for things to keep myself busy."

"Why did you insist earlier that you weren't a romantic at heart?" Morgan's tone came off gentler now, more soothing than bold, and I didn't mind answering him.

"I've always believed it. I don't know why." I picked up a

leaf and stroked it along my cheek. "Maybe I *do* know why. When I was in the sixth grade, I had a crush on a boy. He liked me, too. His name was Elton. Anyway, I sketched a picture of us together. I did it in charcoal, and I thought it was pretty good. . .for a sixth grader. The teacher, Miss Nightingale, saw it and carried it to the front of the class. I thought she was going to single me out and tell everyone how much she loved my drawing."

I crushed the leaf in my hand. "She singled me out, all right. She pinned the picture to the bulletin board and told the class what a dreamy-eyed little boy-chaser I was for scribbling such a picture. Everyone laughed. I scooted down in my seat and never resurfaced. Anyway, Elton was mortified. I could never look him in the eye again. Somehow, in that one moment Miss Nightingale locked away that artistic and romantic side of me. I never could quite get it back. . .even when I tried." I looked at Morgan. "Now you know my tale of woe and what has made Miss Violet McBride into such a tragic figure of humanity." I said the words almost flippantly, but they held a heaviness that couldn't be lightened.

"It *was* tragic if it turned you away from what God intended."

"I suppose. Maybe my teacher was secretly bitter because she'd never fallen in love. It's sad and strange, isn't it. . .how people can change the course of our lives with just a handful of words, whether good or bad? Mold us into things we weren't meant to be or maybe even escort us right to our destinies."

"How true. People have an awesome responsibility with

their words. And speaking of destinies, I found out that the century plant here in the park only gets one chance to bloom in its lifetime. If it misses that one chance, well. . ."

"Yes, I knew that." *And I catch your full meaning.* "But how did you know?"

He smiled. "That's why I love brochures." He hovered close to me. Like guys do in the movies when they're thinking about a kiss. Like he found the woman he was with to be irresistible. Imagine me, irresistible?

"Violet?"

"Yes, Morgan?"

"I didn't want to mention this earlier, but I keep hearing a rustling sound, and I'm pretty sure there's something a lot bigger than a bird in the brush."

"This isn't funny." I rose from the branch. "Morgan, if you're pulling my leg, I will never forgive you. Do you hear me?"

He tugged on my coat sleeve, wanting me to sit beside him again.

I was too annoyed with him to be scared, but when I remembered the mountain lion's sharp teeth from the day before, I eased back down on the rock and listened.

Chapter 8

There was indeed a rustling in the brush. We stared at each other for a second, and then Morgan started singing "Home on the Range." To say he erupted might be a more apt description. Then he changed the lyrics to, "where the bears and the mountain lions play." He belted it out as my eyes went buggy with the noise. He had a wailing style and a tin ear, and the decibel level was enough to scare off anything—man or beast—within a ten-mile radius. While he sang he yanked a can of bear mace out of his backpack and crouched like 007 sporting a handgun.

At that point there was nothing left to do but laugh. Almost as loudly as his singing. After a few moments I gave him a push and said, "Please stop. I can't breathe."

"Okay."

"I think whatever hid in the brush is gone now." I took a quick glance around, just to make certain. "We have a lot of animals around here besides bears and mountain lions. It could have been a gray fox or a javelina, or a—"

"You're hurt."

"What?"

"You cut yourself on something."

I looked at my hand, and the side of my palm was

bleeding. "Maybe I scratched it on a prickly pear cacti."

Morgan whipped a first aid kit from his backpack.

"You're ready for everything, aren't you?"

"Hey, I saw the movie *127 Hours*. You can't hike the same after that. I have everything in this backpack but an emergency room and a doctor."

I sat still as he cleaned my cut. "This seems familiar." Maybe some people were good at patching each other up.

He gingerly pressed a Band-Aid over my wound and released me.

"Thanks."

"Anytime." This time he gave me a wink, and we both rose to continue down the canyon.

He zipped up his backpack and walked in front of me, which was fine, since I wanted to spend some time observing him. And to spend some time wondering why I felt so disappointed when a rustling in the bushes had interrupted the possibility of a kiss. How could humans go from anger to annoyance to amorous leanings within the span of an hour? Or minutes even? We were such pendulums of emotion, swinging wildly from side to side. *Lord, we are an odd bunch down here, aren't we, roaming these winding trails? We can't see very far down the road. Can't even figure out what we're about. How to live or how to love.*

*

After another hour of hiking through the canyon and pondering and occasionally chatting, we got to the end of our trail. "Well, here it is," I said. "What do you think?"

"Wow, this Window Trail was definitely worth the hike."

The canyon had narrowed, and we were surrounded on both sides by rock walls that seemed to reach up to the sky. In front of us the canyon opened to a great fissure in the stone, an oblong porthole that gave its visitors a window-view to the scenery below.

We moved cautiously on the slippery rock toward the rim, which had a sheer drop-off of a couple hundred feet. I shivered at the distance, as I always did. We took in the big sky and the colorful, jagged spires of the Chisos Mountains.

"I never tire of seeing this," I whispered.

After we reveled in the view for a few moments, we backed away from the edge and sat down on a log to enjoy the view at a safer distance. "So, are you hungry?" Morgan asked.

"I am." We opened our backpacks. "What did you bring for lunch?"

"Lemon pound cake."

I kept myself from rolling my eyes, reminding myself that everyone had different tastes in hiking foods. I wanted to say, "Are you kidding? All that sugar is going to give you a wild rush, and then your glucose is going to plummet like a boulder off this cliff." But I just stared at his cake as he ate it and wished I had no concern for practical things.

Morgan held up the chunk of cake not too far from my mouth. "Want a bite?"

"No, I'd better not." He stared at my organic "tree bark" protein bar made from all natural ingredients, meant to offer optimal energy, but which could dishearten even the most indifferent palate.

Bite by luxurious bite Morgan worked on consuming his huge hunk of pound cake. "So why don't you want a bite?" He asked this as if ignorant of the consequences of eating so many empty calories on a hike.

"Because it's cake. That's not a lunch or even a decent snack for a serious hiker. It's too frivolous, insensible, self-indulgent, and. . .well, I don't know. I ran out of adjectives. You have everything else in that backpack of yours. Why not proper food?"

Morgan looked puzzled over my drama and said, "I do have plenty of protein bars in my pack, but right now I felt this moment was too unique and beautiful for just a protein bar. This moment deserves cake."

"You always have such a nice twist on things, don't you?"

"I try. It's the investigative part of me. I can always see more than one side to a thing."

"Sounds more like debate than research." I tore off a large piece of my protein bar and popped it in my mouth. "But you can't always have what you want, Morgan Jones," I said with my mouth full.

"Is that so?" He was teasing now, but there was something else there, a seriousness that creased his brow.

I stood. "You're a child. I hope you know that." I sighed. "And if I stay around you for five more minutes I'm going to need a bottle of antacids."

He rose with the last bite of cake still in his hand. I tried not to stare at it. The cake did look buttery. So creamy, in fact, it refused to fall apart. I swallowed my tree bark.

Morgan lifted what was left of the cake to my lips, and

before I could stop myself I took a bite and then another. In fact, I nearly bit his finger, I was so ravenous for something sweet. The cake melted on my tongue. . .oh my. . .just like I'd imagined it.

"How is it?"

"Good." I munched. "No, it's wonderful."

"You like me, don't you? I can see it in your eyes," he said.

"Yeah, I do. Just a little."

"Only a little?" He took a step closer to me.

"Okay. . .more than a little." I licked the cake residue off my fingers. "But I have no idea why, logically speaking."

"Life is funny that way," he said with a grin.

Life was indeed funny that way. It was like this winding trail—a beautiful and wild thing—you just never knew what was around the next bend. "Okay, so what do we do now?"

"About us? Guess you'll have to buy a bottle of antacids."

I laughed.

"Yesterday you said my behavior wasn't supposed to be inflammatory or I'd be in some trouble with you." He whispered, "So, does kissing fall into the category of inflammatory behavior?"

"I'm sure it does." His warm breath tickled my ear. "But surely we can make an exception."

He moved closer to me. "Well then, let's enjoy our exception."

Yes, why don't we?

He leaned down and kissed me, and the connection closed us off from the rest of the world. We luxuriated in our cocoon of profound delights. Yes, I was busy kissing Morgan

Jones, and nothing in my life had ever felt so good. *Oh, the difference a day can make.*

When we parted, we grinned at each other. And I knew why. The kiss had been more than a pretty view—it'd been a whole vista. Not just the opening of a bloom, but the desert in springtime. I chuckled inside. It was the hokiest thought I'd ever had. And perhaps the most honest.

Morgan sat down on a boulder. "Tell me. . .about your family." He looked at me. "What are they like?"

"Well, my parents are pretty wonderful. And I have three amazing sisters. Even though I live way out here, we're all close. Most of the time that means texting and Skype. But we've made it work."

"So, you had a good home life?"

I sat down next to him as I considered my answer. "Yes, I did. I had the very best family. Still do. We're very close."

"I know that kind of upbringing would have made a difference in your life." Morgan said the words to me but seemed a zillion miles away.

"It really does make all the difference. . .to be surrounded by that kind of love. You know, I haven't thought about it in a long time, but I remember one of the girls I grew up with, Haley McKinney, wasn't surrounded by that kind of love. And she, well. . ."

"What happened?"

"Well, after Haley's father passed away, her mother became so career-obsessed that she was rarely around when Haley needed her. One day Haley didn't show up for class. Everyone was pretty worried about her, because she'd been acting so strangely. They found her the next day. She'd taken her own life by driving into Galveston Bay. The tragedy was, Haley's mother finally showed up, but it was for her daughter's funeral." I shook my head, remembering the wild array of emotions I'd felt toward Haley's mother at the time. When I snapped out of my daydream, I asked Morgan, "Did you grow up in a good home?"

"I did, yes," he said. "With a lot of loving attention. And I feel very fortunate. Every kid deserves that. . .what we had." His shoulders sagged a bit.

"You okay?"

"Yes. You've influenced me. . .what you said. . .to make a decision."

"Oh?" I was afraid to ask any more questions. Surely it wasn't a proposal. We were getting along much better, but a declaration like that would be laughable. "Is this good news or not so good?"

"It's good news." But Morgan's voice didn't sound as upbeat as his words.

"What is it?"

He stuffed his hands into his coat pockets. "Well, I have this. . ."

I put my hands over my ears. Childish, I know. "I don't want to hear anything that is going to spoil this wonderful day. Please tell me everything is going to be okay."

"I don't know," he said. "But these words, no matter how hard they are to say. . .must be said."

"Oh dear." That sounded so heavy. So final.

Morgan looked at me for a long time.

Feeling silly for covering my ears, I lowered my hands. As much as the kiss had taken us to one summit, I felt that the next few words would push us right off the cliff.

Chapter 9

All the playfulness and light had gone out of Morgan's eyes. "I will take this in stages."

"Oh?"

"First the easy part. Everything I've told you is true. . . about why I came, all of it. I really did want to improve my chances of finding a wife. Because it's not been easy, as I said. My parents didn't meet until later in life, and I seem to have inherited that problem of losing one's way, romantically speaking. But I'd also hoped something might develop between us while I was here. And if we hit it off, then whatever I learned from you, well, I planned to use on Violet McBride."

That made me smile. "But how could you have gotten such a hope from looking at my website?"

"I loved your face, Violet. You looked. . .intriguing to me. I wanted to take a chance and come out here. I couldn't tell you that part yesterday, because I wasn't sure how it would work out."

"Are you sure you weren't just enamored with those blog posts? I mean they—"

"No, that doesn't matter. I *saw* Violet." Morgan gestured the last words in sign language. "And your face, your eyes, moved me enough to drive out here." He grinned. "And now, well, I see your wonder. The amusement. The mischief. The drama that you were trying to hide. All of it. And I've started to fall in love with you. Just you. Not some phantom named Gertrude."

I breathed again, since I think I'd been holding my breath for some time. "What you've told me isn't terrible news. I think it's charming. And you did it all on your own. You didn't need help from me to romance a woman. . .even if that woman was me. So, why did you make it seem as though you had unhappy news?"

"Because there's more."

"Oh?" I sat down next to him on the rock for support.

"I told you I have a niece who's deaf. Her name is Amber. But here's the awful part. Amber's parents were killed in a car accident several months ago."

"Oh, I'm so sorry." I latched my finger onto the edge of his pocket.

"Yes, we all are. Anyway, Amber is almost thirteen, and she has no one else to take care of her. No family, except for my parents. And they're not in the best of shape, being older now, to take on a teenager who has Amber's particular needs. If I don't take her in, well, bottom line, she'll have to go into foster care. I've prayed about it. What to do. But you were the turning point. Right now."

"I was?" I didn't know if I wanted to hold that kind of power.

"When you talked about the importance of family. . .how it made all the difference in your life to be among people who really loved you. Well, I've put off this decision too long. I know what I have to do now. You made me see it more clearly. I'm going to adopt Amber. If left to the foster care system, she might never know the right way to go. She might drop out of school. Or maybe no one in the foster family will know sign language or bother taking her to church."

Morgan removed his hand from his coat pocket and grasped my hand as if I might run away. "I hesitated over the decision these months because I thought I'd be a terrible parent. I don't know a thing about raising teenage girls. And, too, I knew my hope for marrying someday could get put on hold for a long time. Very few women want a ready-made family. But now I know what I have to do, even if it's inconvenient. I must take care of her. And I *want* to. It's the right thing to do. Amber wouldn't be opposed to it, and it's what my sister and brother-in-law would have wanted."

I made no move to let go of his hand. "That is a heavy load for you."

After a few moments, Morgan said, "And it will be a heavy load for the woman I marry, since Amber needs a mom. Not just a dad. She misses her mother terribly, and she's taken this loss very hard. So, if I were to ever marry, my wife will need to be a mom to a young woman who is not only having some emotional issues beyond the usual teenage angst but a mom to someone who is deaf. I won't lie to you. I'm going to be on a rough road here with Amber. I just have to know that if you and I were to get more serious. . .well, do you think it's a road you could deal with?"

During Morgan's speech I tried to remain calm, but with

each new part of the story I realized that I couldn't imagine myself in such a family situation. Life as I knew it would be torn apart. What would that feel like—that kind of ragged uncertainty and upheaval? I could feel myself backing away, wanting to run for cover. "I don't know, Morgan. Even though I love my family, I've never felt a strong desire to have any children of my own. My sister Rosy and her husband adopted a little boy, and that's fine for them. But I'm not my sister."

Morgan let go of my hand, and the warmth drained out of it.

Calm yourself, Violet. Easy does it. But no longer did my pep talks work. I felt myself on a roller coaster—going down at full speed. "We just met. I mean, I like you. I really do. But this. . .this is frightening for someone who never intended to. . .I mean, I live a quiet life. You know that. It was one of the reasons I moved out here. I don't. . ." What could I say? It was impossible. "Morgan, even if we fell in love, I could never be the woman you want. I could never be the mother Amber needs. And I know it wouldn't be right if I force this. I would only be pretending. Going through the motions of being her mother. It wouldn't be fair to any of us." I had closed the door. *Oh God, what have I done?*

"I understand. You just. . ." Morgan's voice broke. "It's all right."

As we sat in the shadows of the canyon, the chilly air settled into my bones and my spirit. "I'm so sorry, Morgan. Please forgive me. We just got started, and I had hoped for. . ." My words ceased because of my tears.

He pulled me into his arms. "Shhh. I don't blame you."

"I admire you for what you're doing for Amber. I didn't say that before. . .but I do. I think you're a hero."

"I shouldn't be called a hero for doing the right thing. I hadn't even figured out what I *should* do until you said what you did."

So strange—wasn't it—that I would be the one, the person who would unknowingly bring an end to what might have been a beginning?

"I have to tell you. . .I feel unprepared for the task. Even. . ."

"But you love Amber. You already know sign language. Those two things alone are so much. It already shows your commitment to her." I looked at him until I caught his gaze. "I barely know you. . .and yet I am so proud of you." I had just talked myself out of happiness. Some darker, self-seeking part of me wanted things as they were before Morgan's revelation, and yet if he walked away from Amber, he wouldn't be as appealing. He wouldn't be Morgan.

"But I guess we can't have everything in life. That's just what you said."

I winced.

"But it is true." His voice had lost its vibrancy, its subtleties of joy and animation.

We'd come to an end. Morgan and I could no longer move forward. Good-bye would be the only option. . .at least it would be for me. And yet the thought of good-bye already seemed so very hard. How could I have come to know and care about this man so quickly? I had no idea how it happened in such a short period of time, but it was as true as the blooming of the desert in the springtime. I cared about Morgan Jones. Whether it would have turned into love would never be known.

A small group of hikers made their presence known in the narrow canyon. There was no reason to prolong our misery. Time to go. "I guess you'd better take me home now."

Chapter 10

We hiked back to the pickup, sober in thought and steeped in unhappiness. There was no teasing. No laughter. No squabbles. And there were certainly no kisses. Just quiet. I had always loved the quiet. It had always been my watchword. My refuge in a world that seemed obsessed with noise. But now the silence around us was thunderous. Unbearable. I shoved my hands into my pockets, since they'd gone cold.

Once we got back to the house, Morgan walked me to the door. I couldn't imagine how the discomfort of the hour could be any worse until I saw Basil drive up. So not good. I felt certain of one thing—life had a big hammer, and it wasn't afraid to use it.

Morgan stayed put, without saying anything, but he watched as Basil moseyed up the path and greeted me.

"Hello, Violet." Basil tossed a few squirmy glances toward Morgan.

"Hi, Basil." I fumbled with my house keys, knowing I should invite them both in, but also knowing it would be the most awkward thing I'd ever endure. "Let me introduce you two." I made the proper introductions, which felt painful enough, but then I did what I dreaded—I invited them inside with the words, "Would you both like to come in for a few minutes?"

Basil nodded. "Sure, maybe a cup of tea would be good."

"Sure," Morgan said. "Thanks." The fire I'd seen in him earlier had been doused to an ember. It was hard to witness, since I'd been the one with the water hose.

"So how is it that you two know each other?" Basil asked Morgan as we walked through the entryway and into my kitchen.

"Morgan is a fan of my company," I said, trying to keep things honest, but casual. "He wanted to meet me." I tapped my fingers against my arm, wishing I could speed up the seconds.

"Really? What for?" Basil sat down with his stomach smashed against the table so tightly he looked as though he were about to start banging a fork and spoon on the table, demanding service.

Morgan didn't sit down. He ignored Basil's question and said to me, "I'm glad I came. It was good to meet you, Violet. It's been a real privilege." The words came out of his mouth with sweetness but also with an unnatural formality.

His expression of loss undid me. "Thank you, Morgan." Tears burned my eyes. I set a full teakettle on the stove and turned on the burner.

Morgan turned back to Basil. "So, what do you do?"

Basil puffed his chest out. "Insurance. Yeah. It's a good business. Lucrative. Steady. It's good work."

"That's a fine thing if you want to get married someday," Morgan said.

"Married? Well, that part is just. . .well, what's the right word?"

Yes, what is the right word, Basil? I piled a few cookies on a plate.

"Hopeful. Yes, that's always a good word." Basil glanced at me, looking uneasy, as if he were sitting on a cactus and not my kitchen chair.

"Hopeful, eh?" Morgan asked. "You two are dating then?"

"Yes. . .well, not really. We just had a date yesterday. *First* date, really." Basil eyed the cookies, so I set the plate down in front of him.

Morgan backed away. "Well, let me just say that Violet is one of the finest women I've ever met. She'd make you a happy man."

Basil choked, but there was nothing to strangle on, except for Morgan's nuptial declaration.

Morgan looked so strained I thought he might disintegrate right there. And what was he doing with all the matrimonial maneuverings anyway?

Basil looked at Morgan, blinking and squirming with what looked like intense curiosity. He seemed about to say something but instead stuffed his mouth full of cookies.

"I don't think I'll stay after all," Morgan said. "You guys look like you could use some alone time. Am I right, Basil?"

"Time alone?" Bits of cookie crumbs puffed out of Basil's mouth. "Right. Sure. Why not?" He fumbled with his tea bag until it fell on the floor.

While Basil made a full-scale production out of the retrieval of his tea bag, I gazed at him, glad to be given a fresh vantage point. Basil was a kind and stable guy, and yet when it came to the important things in life—those things that might require passion—he was destined to exist in a monotone, colorless vacuum, oblivious that there was another world just beyond the one he'd constructed. One that was vibrant and pulsating with life. Not the best way to live, or to love.

Morgan rolled his eyes at Basil and then turned toward me. "I have one request, Violet. Just one. If you'll indulge me."

"Yes? What is it?" There was so much more to say. *Don't leave yet.*

Morgan motioned toward the front door. "I just want to say good-bye to you. . .in private."

"Yes, of course." Why in the world was Morgan trying to marry me off to Basil? Perhaps his intentions were noble—but it made me want to kick him—well, and then kiss him.

"Good-bye, Basil," Morgan said. "Good to meet you."

Basil offered him a little wave from the floor.

Morgan gave up on shaking hands with Basil and walked me to the front door. Trudging seemed closer to the correct verb, but then I was dragging my feet as well. I wanted to give Morgan more than a good-bye—some sort of promise or hope—but couldn't. It would be too unfair to both of us. It would only cause more sorrow down the road.

The moment we both stood on the other side of the front door, Morgan took me into his arms. "Well, I guess this is good-bye."

"I guess it is." *But I don't want it to be.* "I wish you well. I wish Amber well, too." I wanted to ask him to stay in touch, to e-mail me from time to time, or a lot, to let me know how things were going with his soon-to-be daughter, but I thought this might be too much torment. It would be less upsetting to let go now and not look back. "Take good care of yourself, Morgan."

"I'll try. You will remember me, won't you? From time to time?" He cupped my chin in his palm.

"Impossible to forget you."

Just when I thought Morgan would kiss me good-bye, he instead surprised me by letting me go. He took off, walking down the path with a reckless kind of pace and then climbed into his hideous excuse for a pickup. I would miss that truck. Well, maybe not the truck.

Basil joined me on the porch, holding up the tea bag as if it were a prized catch. He was oblivious to my misery, as he was to most things in life. I shuddered to think that I had toyed with the idea of marrying him.

The enlightenment I'd been given in twenty-four hours was a gift and a curse, though, since now I could feel the heartache of what I was walking away from—the possibility of love. I thought of the century plant—had God given me my one chance to bloom, and I'd missed it?

I gazed at Basil, who stood smiling at me. It was a *good* smile—to use *his* word. But with Morgan I got a glimpse through a veil that was secret and unfathomable. Something wonderful. And I got the truth of what I'd become—I'd sought to live a simple life, but it had turned out to be a selfish life. My sister Rosy had never been all that good with kids either, and yet God had blessed her and Larson with their adopted son, Siggy. Even though the idea of being a mom made Rosy nervous at first, motherhood was growing on her. Perhaps it would grow on me as well.

"Come drink your tea, Violet," was all that came out of Basil's mouth.

"You know what, Basil? I don't think I will. There is more for me. . .out there." I pointed to Morgan's pickup, which was creeping down the road. "I'm not totally sure what I'm doing, but I know I've got to try. That part I'm certain about. And somewhere out there God has more for you. I don't want to live a lie. I thought I could make a perfect and quiet place for myself. . .and maybe even share it with you. . .but that kind of life would have been a desert with no spring."

"Violet McBride, what has come over you?" Basil asked.

I patted Basil on the chest, right over the spot where I thought his heart must be, and I told him honestly, "I don't know what has come over me. But the thing is. . .I'm willing to find out. Now, if you'll excuse me, I have some serious running to do."

I took off down the road, chasing after that rust bucket as fast as my legs would carry me. "Morgan! Wait!" I waved my arms and screamed so loudly I frightened myself. I wasn't used to hollering so much.

Suddenly the truck halted. Morgan jumped out of the vehicle and ran toward me. I waved again and then stumbled on my shoestring, falling facedown in the dirt.

Morgan picked me up. "That must have hurt. You okay?"

"I am now," I said, sputtering. Well, looks like I'd officially become a klutz—but I didn't care.

Morgan bundled me into his arms, dust and all.

I clung to him and said, "I guess Miss Nightingale was right after all."

"How could that be?"

"I really *am* a boy chaser."

Morgan laughed. "What you may not know is, I stopped my pickup before I saw you."

I eased out of his arms. "You did?"

"I'm not the kind of person who can let you marry a. . .a Basil."

"I'm glad you're not that kind of person. In fact, I can't tell you how glad I am." I buried my face in his coat to keep the tears from flowing. We held each other for a moment, delighting in each other, even though I knew we'd have to talk about the hard stuff sooner or later. I raised my head. "If God is trying to give us a gift, I don't want to be caught tossing it away."

"But how do you feel about Amber?" he asked.

"If we take 'us' to another step, and that step leads to an altar, well then, I will trust God with my future. Our future. I can't trust me, but I can always trust Him."

He smiled. "Just so you know, I would never take you away from your mountains and desert. I can work anywhere. All I need is a computer. And Amber would love it here. Not only that, but she'd love you as well."

"Really? Morgan, how can all of this be? I mean, I've just met you, and yet I feel as though I've known you all my life. It's such a movie line. Right?"

"Never discount the power of a well-placed cliché."

I grinned. "So, did Hugo Averill say that?"

"No, I did. And so what does the heroine in your movie say next?"

"Let's see. She says, 'I know the perfect stocking stuffer you could buy me at Christmastime.'"

"Antacids?"

I laughed. "And my gift back to you could be for your mouth—a big roll of duct tape to remind you how lovely the quiet can be sometimes."

"Well, now," Morgan said, "it'll be hard to engage in any inflammatory behavior if I have duct tape over my mouth."

"Speaking of inflammatory behavior, do you think we could. . ."

"Anything for the love of Violet." He grinned.

In that moment all went quiet as Morgan melted into one of those heavy-lidded, sultry gazes that comes right before the boy kisses the girl.

When Morgan and I completed our joyful journey, he pulled back and said, "Delicious kiss, even though you taste a little like mud." He licked his lips. "But you also taste like pound cake."

"I guess life is always a little of both."

And then, well, Morgan kissed me again, and I was more than happy to let him to do so.

Epilogue

That summer, Amber and I painted a few of my white walls a vibrant green. And we planted every kind of flower we could find at the local nursery. We wanted a celebration of color, a shout of beauty that would turn the heads of all who walked through our neighborhood. And we had good reason for jubilant hearts. Not only had Morgan and I fallen in love and married, but we'd widened our circle of love to include Amber.

Months later I did learn sign language, although my poor brain had to really stretch to accomplish such a feat. I managed it, though, so I could communicate with and argue with and delight in Amber Jones—who turned out to be a creative and noisy and affectionate teenager. And with each passing month she became dearer to us than we could have ever imagined.

Funny about life. It is indeed a winding trail, a beautiful and wild thing. You just never know what's around the next bend.

FORGET ME NOT LILY

Chapter 1

After a long hard day at my counseling service, there are three things I do to decompress. One—I smash my face into some peonies and breathe. Two—I tell Andy about my day. Andy is a goldfish and has nothing to say, so he makes a good listener. And three—if my day has been particularly wretched, I work on the hole I'm digging in my backyard. Someday soon, though, I'm afraid that hole will become the proverbial six feet deep, and all the dirt will fall right on top of me.

Just a thought.

At the moment, I was fine. Sort of. Rita Mackenzie—a middle-aged client of mine—sat knitting and shaking her head over my latest bit of counsel. Rita's greatest fear was falling in love, and I was in over my head as usual, clueless how to advise her, since most of the world hunted, hounded, and hurtled to get the very thing Rita hid from. I love the calming effects of alliteration.

Rita stopped clacking her knitting needles. "So, you're saying I need a male friend? Are you sure that's necessary? By the way, do you *really* have your degree? I mean, you look young enough to be my daughter. . .if I *had* a daughter."

"A male friend would be an easy first step for you. And

then men wouldn't look so scary. And yes, Rita, I know I look young, but I'm twenty-seven, and my degree is hanging on the wall right behind me." I grinned.

"I know you're trying to look older by wearing that pencil skirt and by putting your hair in a bun, but it doesn't help." Rita raised her hand. "Okay, okay. Because I'm such a nice person, I'll take your questionable advice."

I clicked my pen a few times. Rita could be so exasperating.

"Will I see you next week?" She adjusted the hibiscus in her hair, a silk adornment she never left home without. Pretty flower, but it was always hard to know what to look at—Rita or the flower with the stamen that wagged when she talked.

"Sure, same time then." I walked her out of my office and into the tiny reception area, which was empty at the moment. I'd sent Uriah, my receptionist, home early for the weekend, and there were no more clients scheduled for the day.

Rita stopped to gaze at the shadowbox on my wall and tapped on the glass with her knitting needle. "You like mementoes. No doubt these are dried flowers from a long-lost love."

"Not really." I gazed at the box, remembering that lovely and puzzling part of my youth. "This shadowbox was made by a boy I knew in school. . .a long time ago."

"Quaint."

"Actually, it was, Rita. He also gave me three pink peonies from his mother's garden. I didn't know that was my favorite flower until he gave them to me. After they dried I put them inside the shadowbox for keeps."

"Yes, but these things are mere shadows of living. . .not

living." Rita took on the ethereal glow of a mystic sage and tapped on the glass with her kitting needle again, as if it were the staff of Gandalf.

Yes, Rita was always a jack-in-the-box full of surprises. Never a dull moment. I lingered there, musing, while she walked a few steps to the front door.

"I know I'll probably be at that party you're having on Saturday night, but I still need to know if you'll be leaving your cell phone on all weekend. You will, right?" She latched on to the door handle until her knuckles went white.

Rita also had separation issues. "I will leave my cell phone on at all times."

"Sometimes you go to Palo Duro Canyon, and you're so far out of range I can't get in touch with you."

"Just leave me a message, and I'll call you back." I went to her and patted her shoulder. "I promise."

"But what if I start to fall in love, and I need advice right then? Amarillo is just teeming with single men, especially in early September. It's the twilight of summer, you know. This time of year you can fall in love just by breathing the air." Her eyes brightened.

Where did she come up with that stuff? Sometimes, though, Rita was just pulling my leg. She'd say something outrageous and try to get me to go along with her. Then she'd snicker. Did I mention that counseling could be a rather peeving profession? Provoking and piquing as well.

"Who will talk me through it if it starts to happen?" she whispered.

"Trust me," I said. "I've been trying to fall in love for the past ten years, and it's not nearly as easy as people think." It was a new kind of treatment I'd been working on—blunt therapy. The idea hatched from being around my new brother-in-law, Morgan Jones.

"Really? You've been trying to fall in love for that long and can't?" Rita looked at me like I'd just laid an egg.

"Yep, that's right."

"But don't you *ever* go out on a date?" she said, making me wonder why I'd brought it up.

"Sure. I go on a date sometimes. Well, not that often." I rolled my eyes. "Okay, hardly ever."

"So, what happens when you *do* go out?" Rita seemed mesmerized by my every word.

"Well, there's never a spark. Not for me and not for the guy. All the dates I've been on have been sputtering duds. . . like firecrackers that fizzle on the Fourth."

"That is sooo sad." Rita squeezed out a tear. "You need a hug today, don't you?"

"Sure, I can always use a hug." Maybe I was too open in sharing personal information with my clients.

Rita picked up one of the stuffed bears I kept around for the children and placed the animal's arms around me, pretending it was giving me a hug. "It's the definition of irony, isn't it?"

"What's that, Rita?"

"Well, I have a phobia of falling in love, and yet I've fallen in love three times. And here *you* are. . .really struggling to fall in love and you can't, even when you try." Her laugh escalated into quite the cackle. Rita and I would also need to work on social skills.

I nodded. "Yes, Rita. That is a perfect example of irony." A face full of peonies to breathe in sounded good about now. *Lord, give me extra patience.*

Rita seemed pleased with my reply. So much so that she didn't say any more about my out-of-range cell phone problems. She walked out the front door a little more buoyant than when she'd come in.

I sighed and glanced in the gold mirror that decorated the reception area. I set my long hair free from its bun and wondered why I still looked so young. I was the baby in the McBride family of sisters, but I was old enough to no longer be referred to as a child. That term seemed to haunt me everywhere. I wondered if that's why I became closest to Rosy, my oldest sister. Was I trying to distance myself from that baby status? Give myself some clout?

I turned my attention toward the fish tank in the reception area and said, "Andy, you look like you've had a long day, too." I touched my fingers to the fish tank. "Hey there, you're looking a little drifty, kind of sideways. You're not going to die on me, are you? Like your brother, Amos, did?"

I gazed into Andy's pretend pond, at the mermaid castle with the bubbles floating to the surface, and at the plastic seaweed and the pretty-colored marbles that decorated his watery world. He just stared at me. Before he'd gone all sideways, Andy looked so purpose-filled, the way he darted around, with places to go and fish to meet. But really, he was fooling himself—because his other fish friend was just his own reflection, and he was swimming in never-ending circles. Hmm.

Ever so slowly I eased open the bottom drawer of the receptionist's desk and glanced down at Uriah's private stash. He only bought the good stuff. Just a little something to take the edge off. I reached down, opened the bag, and grabbed a big handful of cheese puffs. I stuffed them in my mouth all at once. Oh yeah. Sooo cheesy, sooo good.

I turned back to Andy. "How is it I became a counselor anyway? My life feels as real as your plastic seaweed. I don't even know what I'm doing. Rita will probably recover simply because my life looks so much bleaker than hers. The contrast will transform her into a grateful and happy woman. I don't think that's how this counseling thing is supposed to work."

Isn't life grand?

"I've wanted to help people ever since the seventh grade. And now, after college and all these years later, I wouldn't even be able to counsel you, Andy. That is, if fish needed advice."

I stuffed my mouth full of cheese puffs again. I even had to pull my lip over the last one just to fit it in. Guess I was out of control.

Something, or somebody, stirred behind me. I whirled around and saw a man, about my age, standing in the doorway. From the look on his puzzled face, he must have heard my sad and sorry monologue—directed at a fish.

I swallowed stiffly with a slow, simpering sigh, searching for some of alliteration's soporific relief. None came. "May I help you?"

Chapter 2

"I have felt that very same way," the stranger said, smiling.

"What way? You mean you heard some of that?" *Please say no.* My face felt like it had been popped into a toaster oven. "You probably shouldn't creep up on people like that. You'll hear secrets."

He took a step or two into the room. "But I like secrets."

I tilted my head at him. "People always like secrets the most when they're not the ones giving them away."

"By the way, I'm Rubin McCall."

I reached out my hand to him. "Lily McBride."

We shook hands, and sparks flew between us, zapping us both. Not from any chemistry between us, but from the carpet's static electricity. We laughed.

"Sorry." I spilled another little laugh all over him. "I think I zapped you."

"Well, it could be said that *I* zapped *you*."

I liked him immediately. He had a pleasant expression lighting his face—a look as though he'd weathered life well, with a kind heart and a helping of good humor. The man was a young Tom Hanks lookalike for sure and just as fresh-faced and sweet looking.

"So, how much did you hear just now. . .for real?" I asked,

still feeling twitchy that a stranger had just gotten a play-by-play of my inner thoughts.

"Honest answer?"

"I don't know." I chuckled. "Maybe."

"I heard enough to know you're not too happy with the way your life is going."

I glanced away. Hmm. Some people were good at the piano or volleyball or texting. *Lord, why do I have to be so good at humiliating myself?*

"It was a good little talk, actually. . .humble and self-effacing and. . .real."

My spirit softened a little. "Even though I was talking to a fish?"

"Fish make good listeners."

"That's what I've always said," I whispered. "I would ask you if you came by to inquire about counseling sessions, but after the speech you overheard, I'm sure I botched any chance of you wanting to use my services."

"On the contrary. I was moved by what you said. And I did come by to schedule a counseling session." He pointed to his mouth. "By the way, you have this little orange mustache right there."

"Oh great." I slapped the powdered cheese off my mouth.

"No problem." He grinned. "I keep a stash of cheese puffs in my office, too."

"Well, they're not really mine, but. . ."

"That's what I always say, too. . .Lily."

Rubin said my name as if he'd always known me. "My receptionist has gone home for the weekend. Would you like to take a seat?"

I sat down at Uriah's desk and Rubin took the chair across from me. "I've hesitated in getting counseling, but I'll give it a try."

"Why do you hesitate?" I tapped my pen on the schedule book. "Do you want counseling?"

Rubin leaned back in his chair. "My boss told me that if I wanted to continue working, I'd need to get some counseling. I don't agree, but I want my job. So, here I am. I work in this building, so at least I don't have to go out of my way for our appointments."

"Oh, I see. What seems to be the problem?" I hoped it wasn't anything too. . .abnormal.

"Well, my fiancée left me for another man. It was six months ago, but Charlie. . .that's my boss, claims I'm not over it. And that it's distracting me from my work."

Hmm. Sad tale. Made me think of my oldest sister, Rosy, and how she was left at the altar a couple of years ago. "I'm sorry to hear that. That must have been hard on you."

"It wasn't easy at the time."

"And what do you do?"

He ran his fingers in little circles on the knees of his jeans. "I'm a graphic artist."

"Really? I've never met one of you. . .before. . .now." *Serene is the word, Lily. Don't try to knock him out with your brilliance all at once.* I rolled my eyes. "Well, you know what I mean."

"And I've never gone to a counselor before. Hope I don't say anything too fruitcakey."

I laughed. "Is your boss right? Are you distracted at work

because of what your fiancée did to you?"

"I did grieve for a while, but then I got over it once I realized it would have been a mistake to marry her. I think God has someone better in mind for me." He leaned toward me. "Someone a little more. . .genuine."

"Oh, I see." Fascinating case. And the flirting wasn't bad either. "So, you don't really think you need my services, but you're going to do it just to keep your job?"

Rubin raised his finger in the air. "That's pretty close."

"But that seems silly, doesn't it? What will we talk about?"

"We can talk about *you* if you want to."

I gave him a skeptical look.

"Okay. To honor my boss and your profession, I will talk about my past. I will talk about the breakup. You never know, I might still have some angst down in there somewhere. Nothing wrong with cleaning out the basement. It'll make room for more stuff. Better things. New people," Rubin said velvet-like.

My face went back to the toaster oven. "All right." I looked at the schedule. "How about later next week. Thursday afternoon?"

"How about right now? My workday is over, and it's only"—he looked at his watch—"three thirty."

"Oh. Now?" No sense in glancing at the schedule. I knew I was out of clients for the day. "All right. That would be fine. Are you familiar with my fees?"

"I am, from your website. They're fair enough." He rose, and with lanky and easy movements, strolled over to the fish tank and looked inside.

"Well, okay then. Follow me." My office was only a few feet away, so that came off pretty goofy. But whatever. He didn't seem to register my silliness and got in step behind me.

"Nice office. Says a lot about your personality."

"Oh yeah? Like what?"

"The shelves of used paperbacks tell me you're a real reader and not someone who just decorates with fancy hardbound books. The basket of stuffed animals says you're caring. And the framed pictures reveal your love of beauty and art."

I shrugged. "What can I say? I'm a Renaissance woman." Oh great. Now I'd been caught flirting, too. *Reel yourself in, Lily. You can't swim in these waters.*

Rubin sat on the overstuffed couch and bounced a little on its cushy pillows. "So, what happens. . .exactly? I've never been to a counseling session before."

"I will ask you some more questions, and if you feel comfortable answering them, you may. And then we'll see where it goes. How does that sound?" I sat down and clicked my pen.

He shrugged. "Reasonable."

"Okay." I waited for him to get settled, but then I realized I was the one who was lacking focus. I was the one who was stalling. I clicked my pen again and doodled on my pad. How could I counsel a guy who was so cute and who was looking right at me the whole time? I couldn't think. I couldn't do anything but sweat. "Uhhh. . .okay. . .you said your fiancée broke up with you six months ago?"

"Yes, that's right."

"How did you feel when she first told you?" Rubin was surely going to laugh, since that question was so clinical and cliché.

But Rubin didn't laugh at all. Instead he said, "I thought I was lost. Ally was. . .well, she was like this wonderful story you're told as a kid." He grinned. "There's always this maiden who needs saving. I don't know, maybe every boy grows up thinking he's supposed to live that story. Anyway, I met Ally at the single's group at my church. She'd just been in and out of a series of bad relationships. She had this sweet and vulnerable way about her. She was always in need of rescuing, and I was always good at taking care of her. We became so comfortable in those roles we decided to get married."

Rubin looked around the room and then landed on me again. "Then some months later, Ally told me she'd met someone else. And that was it, our engagement was over. I was hurt by it, but after some time I came to see we were really like two kids playing dress up in the attic. Having a good time but not nearly understanding what the real thing was like or what we were about."

By the time Rubin was finished, I was entranced by his story. I wished I hadn't agreed to counsel him. If he were to ask me out on a date, I couldn't go, because it wouldn't be professional. On the other hand if I'd said no to counseling him, he would have walked out, never to return. Hmm. What had he been saying?

"Are you okay?"

"Am I okay?" *Let's see.* "Yeah, I'm fine." I waved my hand. "Please continue."

"But I was finished."

"Oh. So, you feel that your breakup was a blessing."

"Yes."

"I have to be honest here. You sound fine to me. You've dealt with this situation in a healthy manner. Looked at the past with wisdom and hopefully forgiveness. And you've carried on with your life. I mean, is that true? Have you been able to move on?"

"Move on? What do mean, exactly?" He rose and meandered around my office, studying my eclectic array of knickknacks.

"You've dealt with the past. But have you started to date again?" I leaned toward him, so far I nearly toppled out of my chair.

Rubin winced a little. "Not much. Rarely, actually."

"Oh? Well, it sounds like you're willing to move on. You just haven't had a—"

"Do you sail?" Rubin pointed to one of my many sailboat models.

"No."

"Ahh. You know, an awful lot of what you have in your office has to do with flying or sailing or gliding away. I get the impression either you want to escape from your life or you just need a vacation."

"Well, we could all use a vacation." No sense in handing him my whole purse full of eccentricities right away. I smiled. "Do you like to sail?"

"I do. My dream is to buy a boat someday. Sail off into the blue." He grinned.

"Sounds like a seamless kind of day."

"Seamless? Interesting word choice."

I chuckled. "It's a word I grew up with, since my mother loves to sew. But I've always thought life was like a garment full of seams. They're always coming unraveled. Just as soon as one gets sewn up tightly then another one comes undone. Sometimes I wish life could be seamless, even if only for a day."

"I guess that's how you make your living. . .helping people stitch up their bulging and frayed holes."

I laughed. "Well, I try to." *Think fast, Lily.* How could I spend time with this guy socially but still be considered a professional? "By the way, maybe I can help you a little with meeting some new people. I'm having a party at my house for my clients on Saturday. . .tomorrow evening. The RSVPs are already back, but you're welcome to come. They're all nice people. I mean, they're not nuts or anything." I groaned at the amateurish sound of my words. "I mean, they just need a little help. . .like we all do."

"I've never heard of a counselor doing that. . .having a party for clients. Is that common in your profession?"

"I don't think so, but then I'm not all that conventional."

"I could tell that. . .the minute I read the name of your service."

"Actually, Rent-a-Friend was my sister Rosy's idea. But it fits me. I didn't want anything that sounded too clinical or detached or. . .stuffy."

"I think it sounds warm and friendly," Rubin said. "And I'd love to come to your party."

Serene is the word, Lily. "That's nice. I'm glad you can attend." I scribbled my address down on a card and handed it to him, hoping he didn't see the tremor in my hand. "I live just outside of Amarillo. My party is tomorrow evening at seven o'clock."

Rubin shuffled his shoe on the floor. "Is it all right if I bring a friend?"

A friend? Did Rubin mean a girlfriend? But I thought he said he rarely went out. Hmm. Maybe I encouraged him a little too much to move on with his life. Oh boy, disappointment already. I melted a little then, but not like butter on hot rolls. More like the blubbering of a tire losing its air after hitting a nail. "Sure. That would be fine. A friend."

"Great. My friend doesn't get out much, so this would be a good thing. Thanks. By the way, your fish, I think you called him Andy. I didn't say anything earlier, but I noticed that. . .well, he's passed on."

Chapter 3

Saturday evening came, and my party arrived with a flurry of success. My guests flooded my bungalow and then poured out onto my patio to enjoy the late summer evening, which was breezy cool and desert dry. The catered fajitas sizzled, and the salsa music energized the crowd. A dozen tiki lamps and the glow that comes from people enjoying each other's company lit the event, but no human torches could compare to the millions of stars that lit my backyard. I stared up at the night sky. The stars were spangled and splendid, like diamonds flung on a bolt of black velvet. Beautiful. And even though my clients had to deal with various emotional issues, I was proud of the way they were interacting and having a good time together.

But Rubin and his "friend" hadn't shown up, and the party was already starting to wind down. My disappointment was palpable, but I wasn't about to show any visible signs on my face and be the one who couldn't rise above her issues.

Rita walked up to me on the patio. "You're upset about something. I can tell. So glad you decided to ditch that pencil skirt for something a little more stylish. A wooly green dress. Hmm. Not too passé. So, tell me, what's got your Freudian slip in a knot?"

"Good one, Rita." I stopped mashing my knuckles together. "Well, it's not that big of a deal, but one of the guests I invited hasn't arrived."

"A guy?" She adjusted her hibiscus flower. She'd changed the color to black for evening.

"Yeah, it's a guy."

"Well, there're some people who've just arrived. Marley's been answering the door. You know he's a control freak." Rita said all this through a mouthful of chocolate cake.

I winced at her reference to one of my clients as a freak, but let it go.

She handed me her plate of half-eaten cake. "You need this more than I do. You're skin and bones."

"Thanks, Rita."

She gyrated around me, wiggling her hips and shaking her finger in the air to the salsa music. *Okay, pretty scary.* As I turned to go inside to welcome the new guests, Rubin drifted out onto my patio like a tropical breeze, dressed in dark khakis and a pale blue shirt. *And* he carried a glass bowl, which contained a perky little goldfish. "For you," he said.

"Now that was thoughtful." I set the plate down so Rubin could hand me the fishbowl.

Rita boogied over to us. "Oh, isn't he a cutie," she said, tapping on the glass.

I gingerly eased the bowl away from her. "He's adorable. I'm already in love. I think I'll name him Methuselah. You know, to encourage him to live a long life."

"Good idea," Rubin said.

Rita rolled her eyes at me.

"Sorry to be a little late," Rubin said. "Charlie, my boss, had an errand to run on the way here."

"Charlie?" His boss? Hmm. So, he didn't have a girlfriend after all. "How sweet of you to bring your boss." What a relief. Maybe life really was grand.

"Yeah. Charlie and I went to the same college. We have some history together, so sometimes we still hang out."

"Are you hungry?"

"Those fajitas look good," he said. "Did you grill them?"

"I'm afraid it's all catered. But I did make the phone call."

He laughed.

And then Rita laughed. She was standing close enough to Rubin to be his shadow. For someone who had a love phobia and felt panic around men, she certainly had a unique way of fleeing from her fears. Or maybe she'd finally read that book I'd given her on behavior modification.

I introduced them to each other and prayed Rita would run along. And just like that, she shuffled off. *Thanks, Lord.*

"Would you join me?" Rubin pulled out a chair for me. "I hear the hostess never gets to sit down."

"Everybody seems to be having a good time, so I have a few minutes." Methuselah and I sat down at the table with Rubin.

"Nice house. The whole Southwest thing with the adobe fireplace inside and out."

"And does it say a lot about me?"

"It does. It says you've got good taste, but you also appreciate what's functional. And best of all, you can see the stars way out here. You must have an appreciation for stargazing."

"I do. I used the inheritance from my grandparents to buy this place. It's pure magic out here, but mostly it's about the stars. I'm glad you noticed. I have a telescope if you want to look more closely."

"I'd like that," Rubin said. "To get a little closer." His eyes twinkled—how merry.

I accepted his playful offer and upped the bid with my own rosy smile. The logs in my outdoor fireplace popped and sputtered. I always loved the sound of a nice, hot, crackling fire.

Rita breezed over to us with two glasses of iced tea, nearly pouring them all over us. "You two look like you need to cool off." She deposited the glasses on the table and then scuttled off before I could give her a piercing look. "Thanks, Rita," I hollered after her.

"You're welcome. I've got your back," she yelled in response.

Rubin didn't seem the least bit offended by Rita's manner or her insinuations. Nice guy.

"By the way, I like your hair that way," he said.

"You mean washed?"

He laughed again.

Little did he know that I, his counselor, had curled my hair to perfection with the hope that I would hear Rubin, my client, say those very words. I was dancing on thin ice, even though it was only September. Maybe Rita had been right about the twilight of summer after all—a time of the year when you can fall in love just by breathing the air. Ridiculous, of course. And yet. I tried not to look rapturous, but I was officially over the moon. *I am dreaming. And if anybody even thinks about waking me up, he or she is going to get quite the vicious tongue-lashing.* "Where were we?"

"I think we were talking about the stars," Rubin said. "Speaking of stars. . .did I just see Ormond Euler go by? Isn't he from that local talk show?"

I nodded. "Yeah. I have an eclectic group of clients."

"Hey, great party. Lily," somebody called over to me.

I found the source of the compliment and waved. "Thanks, Ed."

Rubin looked as though he was about to say something, but was immediately interrupted by a woman who whirled over to him. He rose from his chair, and she circled her arm through his as if they were a couple. She was dressed in a black fitted sweater-dress and had a face and figure that some women out there would kill for. Not me, of course. But some women would. Out there. Somewhere. Who was she, anyway, and why did she have a grip on Rubin's arm like she'd just been rescued from a burning building?

Rubin looked at this mysterious stranger as if he knew her. As if they had a history. "Lily, I want you to meet someone. This is Charlie, my friend, who also happens to be my boss."

Chapter 4

I shot out of my chair on wobbly legs, nearly falling on Rubin. He caught me, and with swift and gentle hands, righted me to a full standing position.

"You okay?" he asked.

"Yes, thank you." I reached out my hand to Charlie. "Well, it's so. . .delightful to meet you, Charlie. I didn't realize you were a woman."

They both laughed.

I swallowed what felt like a pinecone. "That didn't come out quite right. I meant—"

"I know what you meant." Charlie splayed her hands, which showed off her ruby nail polish. "I get that a lot. People hear of me, and then when they meet me they're confused for a second."

"It's a pretty name. Very chic and spunky." And you smell like freshly crushed lilacs. Hard to compete with that.

"Thank you." Charlie shrugged in that way all young and attractive women do when they succumb to the knowledge that they must cope with more than their fair share of physical beauty. All the right adjectives in all the right places—captivatingly curvaceous, charmingly colorful, and creamy. Hmm. No amount of alliteration was going to work in this case. Still, she was a pleasant woman. Surely she had lots of redeeming qualities. At least, that was what women like me told ourselves.

"I heard that Rubin here has been using your services," Charlie said to me.

"Yes, that's true." I couldn't do much more than acknowledge her statement without breaking counselor-patient confidentiality.

"While I'm here I wanted to talk to you about the possibility of getting some counseling for myself," she said.

"Really?" I tried not to sound too shocked. Maybe that was why Rubin brought Charlie.

"Yes. Rent-a-Friend and all that. Clever marketing concept, by the way. Bet you get lots of takers. So, how does your counseling service connect online? I'm curious." Charlie used her hands to emphasize her words.

She was so expressive with her hands and face I felt like a block of wood standing next to her. "Well, I have a counseling service in my office and on online. It's mostly just for extra support for my clients when they need it."

"Intriguing." She raised a doe-soft eyebrow. "Of course, no one can rent or *buy* a friend, can they? I mean, if you have to pay someone, then it's not friendship. Is it?"

"True. But I'd like to think that my clients can call me when they're in trouble, and that they know I truly care about their needs."

Charlie took a step toward me. "And you think other counselors don't care?"

"I can't speak for others, but years ago I went through

some grief counseling when my aunt died. I never felt like the counselor really cared about me as a person. It was like she was saying what she learned in her textbooks. She had all the lingo down, but she was just going through the motions. I decided I'd like to provide something more. I may not have all the jargon down, but I care for each person's needs and I pray for my clients every day."

"Well, you're pretty convincing," Charlie said. "I'll give you that."

"She's very good," Rubin said to Charlie. "I highly recommend her."

"Well, you two have talked me into it. How can I make an appointment?"

"Just call my office. Uriah, my receptionist, will get you set up." What a unique turn of events. But all I could think about was whether or not Rubin was dating his boss.

"Thanks. Well, time for dinner." Charlie went back inside like a swan gliding on the surface of a lake. And most importantly, the swan didn't even bother looking back at Rubin.

Well, maybe Charlie *wasn't* dating Rubin after all. But the hope of going out with him was only a pipe dream anyway. By midnight my golden coach would poof back into a pumpkin, and I would never even have had a chance to go to the ball. Bottom line. Rubin was my client, and it would be monstrously unprofessional to date him.

"Once again, back to the stars." Rubin leaned toward me, his eyes showing plainly that he was enjoying my company.

Slight addendum to the monstrous thing. Even though

nothing could happen between us, no one could stop me from enjoying the way Rubin looked at me—with hope. The spell was broken when my cell phone buzzed to life.

"Are you on call?" Rubin asked.

"I always seem to be." I held up my hand. "Just give me one sec." I saw that the call was from Rita. What could she possibly need? "Rita?" I stepped over by the bushes so that our call would be private.

"Hi," Rita said. "I think it's happening again. The love thing."

"Really? You mean, you're falling in love right here at my party?" I tried to remove the exasperation from my voice. No easy task.

"Yes, it's that man you introduced me to," Rita said. "That guy. . .Rubin McCall."

Rita might have forgotten to bring her knitting, but those needles of hers were pressing precariously against my heart.

Chapter 5

I cared about Rita's journey toward good mental health—I really did—but sometimes she pushed the envelope, making *me* a bit daft. Later that evening she told me that she wasn't really falling for Rubin. Her phone call at the party was meant to be a little joke. I tried to smile about it, but I'm guessing it didn't look too convincing. More like the grin you get when your finger meets the full force of a hammer.

Along with the irritation I felt toward Rita, I couldn't help but wish that Rubin could have stayed longer. Our tête-à-tête had ended too quickly. But a good hostess is always thinking about *all* of her guests, not just the one she was rhapsodizing over. So, after the party, and after everyone had gone home, I went out back in my yard to dig that hole a little deeper.

*

Back at the office on Monday I poured myself an extra-large stein of morning caffeine and walked into my little reception area.

"Good morning, Miss McBride." Uriah closed his fantasy novel.

"Morning, Uriah. You know, you really can call me Lily."

"I know. But I think you deserve the distinction that a title brings. It adds a nice decorum to the office. Don't you think?" He restacked a bunch of papers that were already neat and tidy. "That was a great party you had on Saturday. I'm sorry I was only able to make it toward the end. But it was good, wholesome fun."

I smiled at him over my cup. "Glad you enjoyed it."

Uriah tucked his hand under his double chin and looked at me beguilingly over his horn-rimmed glasses. He must have gotten his glasses from his grandfather, since the style had gone out decades ago. The lenses were thick enough to use as coasters. And his suits looked like he'd fished them out of a cardboard box at a garagc salc. Pcrhaps I needed to give him a raise so he could buy some new glasses. "Uriah, do I pay you enough?"

"What? Of course. You're most generous." He patted his moustache.

"Okay. Just wanted to make sure." I felt lucky to have Uriah as my receptionist. My clients loved his gentle manner, and because he was middle-aged, he added a certain stability to my office. Sometimes, though, when I'd caught him gazing at me between all his tidying rituals, I thought maybe he was looking at me with amorous intentions. But it had only been in my imagination, because the one time I confronted him about it he was so mortified he swallowed his gum. "Who do we have this morning?"

"A new client named Charlie Henderson. A woman. She should be here any minute."

So, Charlie hadn't changed her mind. Life was always a grab bag.

Uriah took the pencil from behind his ear and tapped it on the schedule book. "And then, looking at your notes from Friday, you have another appointment with a client named Rubin McCall."

"Yes, that's right. You know, you really can put scheduling on the computer so you don't have to erase things all the time."

"I know. It's just that I'm old school."

The front door swung open, and Charlie walked through the door. "Well, here I am. I followed through with my promise. To use your services."

"I appreciate your confidence in me. You're right on time. We can go back to my office."

"Very good." Charlie followed me inside, and I shut the door.

She got cozy on the couch, making a fortress with the pillows all around her, while I got situated in the swivel chair next to her.

She picked up a box of tissues, fiddled with it, and then set it back down as if she couldn't make up her mind whether she was going to cry or not. "I have a confession to make," she said.

"Oh?" *Already?* I hadn't even gotten us warmed up yet.

"Rubin is using your services because of me." She put up her hand. "Wait, before you reply. That's not my confession. He told me that you know the truth about why he's here. . . that I insisted he come because he lacked focus at work. And that's all true. I really do think he needs to talk to someone about his fiancée's rejection. But what he doesn't know is. . . the reason I hoped he would get over that ordeal with his fiancée is because. . .well, I'm in love with Rubin McCall."

Chapter 6

Awk-ward!

In fact, my brain sort of shut down for a sec. Maybe Charlie had been talking to Rita and together they were trying to pull off the mother of all pranks. Just a thought. Most likely not. I could see the love in Charlie's misty eyes—she really did love Rubin. *God, You're going to need to give me an extra helping of wisdom on this one.* I wrote something on my pad, but it was as legible as crayon scribbles.

Charlie pulled out a tissue and dabbed the corners of her eyes. "So, you can see my problem. I think the reason Rubin doesn't ask me out is because he's still hurting. I'm hoping you can help him get through this. And then maybe you could put a good word in for me. You know, kind of encourage him along for me."

Talk about plopping me between two stones and then giving me the squeeze. "I can't do that, Charlie."

"Why not?"

"Because I'd be breaking some kind of professional code. It could be perceived as trickery and manipulation."

"No, it's called *love.*" She blew her nose into a tissue with the daintiest foghorn sound imaginable and then set it on the coffee table.

"I'm sorry I can't help," I said, softening my voice.

"But you call yourself a *friend.* It's even in your logo. And friends help each other out."

"Real friends don't resort to subterfuge. I wish I could help you. To be in love and feel helpless must be very hard for you." I wanted to reach out to her, but my chair was too far away.

"Love can be such a mess if all the little puzzle pieces don't fall into place," Charlie said. "When there's one piece missing it's like the whole universe comes apart. That's the way it feels."

She stuck her lip out in a way that made me think she was used to puckering her full red lips and getting her way.

"I've always loved Rubin. I wanted to marry him in college, but he just saw me as a friend. I was the one who got him hired as a graphic artist here. I did that for love, too, but he never knew it. I keep waiting for him to feel the way I do. I'm beginning to think it'll never happen."

"Maybe it's meant to happen, but just not with Rubin." Talk about a moral dilemma. Was I discouraging Charlie from pursuing Rubin because she needed to move on? Or was I discouraging her because I wanted to date Rubin? *Oh God, help me. I'm getting in deeper by the minute.* "Is there anything else you want to talk about in our sessions. . .something besides Rubin?"

"If you can't help me, at least tell me this one thing." Charlie gathered her hands over her heart in a little bouquet. "What can I do to win Rubin?"

"I don't know the answer to that. I'm sorry. But aren't

guys lining up to date you?"

"Yes, but none of them are Rubin."

"Oh." I had a feeling Charlie was going to say that. It would be how I would feel if I fell in love with him.

Her little hand bouquet came undone. "My heart is breaking, Lily, and I don't know what to do."

Tears tingled in my eyes—well, burned actually. Counselors weren't supposed to get so emotional. "I'm really sorry. Let me ask you this. Do you believe in God? Have you prayed about it? Have you asked the Lord who He wants you to marry?"

"God and I used to be close, but we haven't been communicating too well ever since my mom died."

"When was that?"

"Three years ago."

"Do you want to talk about it?"

"No." Charlie plucked another tissue from the box. "Yes, maybe, I do."

"That's fine."

"My father died when I was little, so it was always just Mom and me. She raised me by herself. Worked a job. Took good care of me. Everything."

"Sounds like a good and loving mom."

Charlie nodded. "Oh, she was. My mother was the best. She lived every day to the fullest. . .but mostly for other people. Maybe some people looking on thought she lived an ordinary life, a simple life. But it was the selfless way she lived that made her extraordinary."

"What happened to her?"

"She came down with early-onset Alzheimer's. She lived with me for a while, but she became. . .well, difficult to handle. She didn't know who I was some of the time. She'd forget things, like not turning off the stove or locking up the house. One day she wandered off, and a neighbor had to bring her home. It was unbearable to see her deteriorate. She'd always been the strong one. The wise one. The one close to God. And some days when I was with her, she didn't even know her own name. Anyway, I was busy with my career and was on the rise at work. . .being groomed for promotion. I couldn't take the pressure of both Mom's condition and my job."

Charlie paused for a moment, and I gave her time to go on at her own pace.

Finally, she said, "I put her in a nursing home. It sounds so simple. It's what everybody does. Don't they? But it shouldn't have happened to my mother. Not Mom. Not the woman who sacrificed everything for me."

She pulled out a wad of tissues and tore them all into bits, letting the white paper fall all around her. "My mother only survived two months in that terrible, nightmarish place. People screaming at night because they were either out of their minds or frightened. Who knows if my mother ever got fed properly? The place smelled like urine and death, and the times I was there people had bedsores because there was no one to tend to them. They called it a 'luxury health care facility for your loved ones.' What a lie I swallowed. . . willingly."

Charlie seemed to drift into a daydream for a moment.

"My mom had to endure that awful place while I was busy building my career. I abandoned her when she needed me the most." She gathered all the bits of tissue, covered her face with the pieces, and wept.

I couldn't stay removed from her pain any longer. I knelt down next to her and wept with her.

When her gasping sobs had calmed, she chuckled through her tears. "Are you supposed to do that?"

I looked at her, a bit puzzled and a little bleary-eyed from my own tears. "What do you mean?"

"I've never heard of a counselor crying with her patient."

"No, I'm probably not supposed to. But I see how hard life is on people, and it touches me."

"Life *is* hard." Charlie wiped her eyes and blew her nose.

I got up off the floor, sat back down in my chair, and waited for her to continue.

"I have to tell you something else. It's kind of strange, but I'm sure you've heard of everything by now, so I'll just tell you. Ever since Mom died, I've had this pressure on my diaphragm. More of a tightening that comes and goes. But each time it comes, it's more strangling. Like someone is trying to kill me. I can hardly breathe sometimes."

"Have you been to the doctor?"

"I've been to lots of doctors, and I've had more tests run than I can count." She shrugged. "They claim it's in my head."

"Maybe it's in your heart." I said this before I even had a chance to think it through.

"What do you mean?"

"Well, if you forgive yourself for what happened to your

mom, the tightening might go away."

"Forgive myself?" Charlie huffed with disgust. "I don't deserve it."

"None of us deserve anything good, do we? We're here every day by the very mercy of God. He gives us breath, life, blessings. And what do we do with all the goodness? We soil it and trample on it and then walk away. Even the greatest among all of us are sinners. . .even my mom and even yours."

"I'll need to think about this."

"Sure. Will you pray about it, too?"

"I'll try." She picked at loose threads on her sleeve. "God has been distant for a long time, but I get the feeling I was the one who moved away. Not Him." She glanced around the floor. "Look at this tissue mess I made."

"I'll clean it up. No problem."

Charlie puckered her lips and gave her head a little shake. "Weep with those who weep." Her eyes got misty again. "Even my close friends didn't do that with me when Mom died."

"I always think it's an honor that people tell me what's bothering them, and a privilege to weep with them."

Charlie held the back of her hand over her mouth. "Thank you."

"You're welcome."

She rose to go, and I led her to the door.

"Do you think I should come again?" she asked.

"I'll leave that up to you."

"Thanks." She walked out the door, and I spent a few minutes picking up all the bits of tissue. Maybe I wasn't such a lost cause as a counselor. I put the tissues in the trash, cleaned up my face from my own tears, and peeked around the corner into the reception area.

Rubin sat in a chair, fiddling with a magazine. He looked as though he had a lot on his mind the way he was beating the tar out of it, bouncing it on his leg.

"Rubin? Have you been waiting long?"

"I just got here."

"Come on in."

He got himself settled on the couch while I sat behind my desk, wondering what we were going to talk about. Unless he wasn't telling me something, Rubin appeared to be recovered from the breakup with his fiancée. Perhaps he'd promised Charlie that he'd come in for more than one session.

"I enjoyed your party on Saturday."

"I'm glad." Rubin was so beguiling, it was hard to concentrate.

He tapped his foot on the floor, looking more nervous and boyish than ever. "I felt like everybody there, though, was doing their best to keep us from chatting. But I know you had other guests to take care of."

"I suppose parties aren't the best places for quiet talks."

He leaned toward me. "Listen, I think it's pretty obvious that I'd like to ask you out. I haven't been able to hide it very well." He tossed the magazine aside. "Lily, would you go out to dinner with me. . .sometime soon?"

I wrote something on my pad, but hieroglyphics would have been easier to read.

"Are you ignoring me?" He grinned. "The air is getting a little sticky in here."

If hearts could get tangled, well, mine was twisting like a grapevine with both joy and misery. Poor Charlie would weep all over again if she knew Rubin had just asked me out. "I can't go out with you while I'm your counselor. It's just not the professional thing to do. You know, to date one's client. I'm sorry."

Rubin rose from the couch. "Then you're fired."

Chapter 7

Really? I'm fired?" That came out with a surprising little squeak. I clicked my pen.

"That's right." Rubin frowned, but it was laced in mirth.

Okay, I get it. Was I supposed to play along? "Well, I'm sorry to hear it. . .that is, when anyone is that displeased with my services. But I wish you the very best, Mr. McCall." I attempted a somber look.

"Okay, good." Rubin wiped his hands on his jeans. "Now that you're no longer my counselor, will you go out with me?"

I grinned. It had been so simple. And now it would become *that* complicated. What did the rule books say now? What would Charlie think? She would surely find out, and it would be devastating to her. And yet, I'd never met a man with sparklers. Was I to deny the light spraying all around us?

Rubin shuffled his feet and looked at me, smiling. "This pause of yours is unnerving."

"I'm sorry." I licked my lips. "I don't mean to make this complicated. But do you think. . .just for now. . .we could go out as friends?" The words physically hurt to say them.

"Friends? I have lots of friends. Good ones. I was hoping for a bit more than friendship."

"I understand." I rose from behind my desk, but I really wanted to hide underneath it. "I wish I were at liberty to explain myself. If you can be patient with me for a little while, things may change. But for now, for this first excursion of ours, wherever we go, could we go as friends?"

Rubin fingered the little ceramic kite on my desk. "All right. I'll go out with you any way I can. But you have to know that the whole time we're out, I'll be praying."

"And what will you be praying for?"

"That you'll want the date to be. . .more."

"I see. I give you permission to pray as much as you want." No matter how much we talked of friendship, I was still going to have to deal with the guilt of spending time with a man who was the heartthrob of a woman who was now under my care. Not the best scenario for carefree dating.

"Great. How about this afternoon after work?"

I ran my fingers back and forth along the edge of the desk. "Maybe."

"Do you like to hike Palo Duro Canyon?"

"My sister Violet loves hiking. She lives down in the Big Bend area. I'm more of a walker and sitter than a hiker."

"I can deal with that. How about a picnic at Palo Duro? I know a perfect spot for. . .contemplating our friendship."

I smiled. "Okay."

"I'll pick you up at your house at six?"

"Six it is."

Rubin and I bantered a few more minutes, and then he left so we could both get back to some real work. But keeping a clear head the rest of the day was going to be mental hopscotch.

I peered around the corner to get the latest from Uriah, but the poor man was holding his head in his hands, looking pitiful. "Are you all right?"

"Sure." His shaggy eyebrows furrowed a bit. "No, not really."

I walked over to him. "You look ill. Do you need to go home?"

"I'm not ill, Miss McBride." His shoulders drooped. "It's just that I've been wanting to talk about something."

"Sure, what is it? Would you feel more comfortable in my office?"

"No, it's nothing like that. I just. . .well, it's just that there's this woman I want to ask out." His face broke out into a sweat.

"Bravo. That's a good thing. Isn't it?" I wanted to hug him, but I touched the back of his chair instead. "Did you meet someone at my party?" I was pleased for Uriah, since he seemed to be a bit of a recluse. "If it's not too personal, may I ask who it is?"

"Well, to be honest, the woman I want to ask out. . .is you, Miss McBride."

Chapter 8

Me?" *Oh my. What have I done now?* So, Uriah's affectionate glances weren't in my imagination. I glanced at the clock. "I have a few minutes before my next client, so maybe we should discuss this. First, let me say that I have the upmost respect for you. But I also have to—"

"Please." Uriah held up his hand. "Please, don't say any more. Just let me finish."

"Okay." He'd never spoken so assertively, so I felt it was a good time to pull up a chair next to him and sit down.

He wiped his forehead with a handkerchief. "I've wanted to go out with you ever since I came to work here three months ago. You are the kindest, dearest woman I've ever met. You treat all your clients with such care. Like they were those little porcelain dolls you can buy off the Home Shopping Network." He looked up at me, wild-eyed. "I mean, I don't buy those dolls, but you know what I mean. Don't you?" He dabbed at his face again.

I placed my hand on his arm. "It's all right. I know what you mean. It was a sweet thing to say."

"Oh, okay. Thank you."

I removed my hand. Even though I wanted to lessen

Uriah's anxiety, I also hated to burden him with false hopes.

"Well, I've put a lot of reflection into this, and I think I would make an excellent date. I would take you to a reasonably priced café, and I'd amuse you with my jokes. I learned a lot of them from a VHS tape I have at home. We wouldn't talk about the clients, though, because that wouldn't be right. But I can see it all, the whole evening, in my mind's eye. . .that we would have an exceptional evening together." Uriah skimmed his fingers along the edge of the desk. "So, what do you think?"

Mist stung my eyes. *Well, isn't this going to be splendid?* Another notch was going to get carved in the tree of dating heartbreaks, and I was the one holding the knife.

He handed me a tissue. "Please, put me out of my misery."

"First of all, I apologize if—"

"You're not at fault in any way. I just thought a date with you. . .with us. . .would be a thrilling way to spend a few hours of our lives."

"That was beautifully said, Uriah. But I see you as a kind friend. And I need friends. This world never seems to have enough of them." I sighed at the situation, at life in general. "You're a good man. You're the best receptionist I've ever had. My clients love you because you have so many fine qualities. You really care about them, and it shows."

"So is that a final no?"

"I'm sorry. I don't have those kinds of feelings for you, but I wish I did. If I could choose without feelings, then I would choose you." Was that what I really wanted to say?

"I know you meant for that to make me feel better, but in

all honesty, it made me feel like a bucket of dirt." He spit out a chuckle as if that were the last thing he'd expected to come out of his mouth.

He was suddenly so amused, I got tickled, too.

Then we both laughed, so hard in fact, tears came streaming down our faces. Uriah had to take off his bulky glasses and wipe his eyes. When he looked at me, I gasped. "You have green eyes." Emerald-green eyes. The kind some girl was going to get charmed by if she were ever given the chance.

"Yes, I've had green eyes ever since I was born." He smiled and then frowned. "I mean, they're not contacts. Well, and why would they be? I wear glasses. Sorry. I'm still a little nervous, so I'm not making any sense."

"I understand." Perhaps I'd never noticed Uriah's eyes before, since he was always looking away from me. "It's rather forward of me to say this, but you have striking eyes. Maybe you should consider getting contacts, so women can see what they've been missing."

He looked away. "I don't know. Well, maybe. People have told me that before, and I didn't listen."

"But you'll listen to me?"

"Yes."

"Good."

Uriah rubbed the bridge of his nose, but he didn't put his glasses back on. "By the way. . .is it okay if I still work here? I like my job, and I promise I won't ask you out again."

"I want you to stay. This place wouldn't be the same without you."

"Thank you, Lily."

I smiled. Before I could say any more on the topic, Rita showed up at the door for her counseling appointment wearing a dress so splashy it looked like a rainbow with a hemorrhage. "Hi."

"Hellooo there." Rita locked her gaze on Uriah and didn't let go. "Uriah?"

"Yes?"

"You're certainly looking. . .well today."

"Thank you." He smoothed his pencil moustache. "And you look as pretty as a big blown-up bouquet of. . .of. . .party balloons."

I breathed again, but my left eye went into a wee spasm. I recovered after a few blinks.

Rita placed her hand over her mouth and her cheeks pinked like freshly sliced watermelon. Amazingly, she didn't seem offended by Uriah's awkward compliment.

"Do you want to come in, Rita?"

She nodded, scurried into my office, and took a seat in the swivel chair.

I sat on the couch this time, pad and pen in hand.

"Do you believe in love at first sight?" Rita blurted out.

I clicked my pen and thought for a moment. "Yes, I suppose I do, in certain cases."

"I think I've fallen in love with Uriah. . .even though I've seen him a number of times."

"Uriah is a fine Christian man. He would make a considerate and generous husband." I took a few notes and then let my pen wander over the page.

"Do you really think so?" Rita craned her neck to look at my pad. "What are you scribbling over there? I want to see."

"Just notes to remind me of our discussion. And also I'm doing a bit of doodling."

"And what are you doodling?"

"Angels." I showed her my pad. "I draw angels."

"Quaint. Why do you do that?"

The client/counselor relationship was getting muddy again. If Rita kept this up she'd probably be sending *me* a bill. "I'm not sure. Angels are a comfort to draw, I suppose."

"Very interesting. And how long have you been doing this?"

Since forever. "Since I was twelve or thirteen, I guess. Never thought about that, really. But I will." Maybe for Rita, coming to someone younger for guidance made her feel like she was losing control of her life. So maybe it was okay to let her take the helm for a moment as a reminder of her worth, that we are all on a journey toward freedom. "Thanks for the insight. Now back to you, Rita. I saw the way you and Uriah looked at each other."

"You know, he's so shy that I don't think I ever *saw* him."

Hmm. I wondered if Uriah was shy because his mother gave him that awful name. Rather cruel of her. "It's his eyes... isn't it?"

"They are the rawest kind of green." Rita shivered. "And he has such an artless smile. Doesn't he? And today his suit had the slightest hint of mothballs. Reminds me of home and my mother." She sighed. "Amazing that I didn't see it all before." She pulled a daisy out of the tiny vase on the coffee table. "But I don't like to think about it, because all these feelings are so erratic. So full of elation and panic all at the same time. It's the best of emotions, but it's also the worst." She plucked each petal off the daisy and let them fall to the carpet.

I was going to need to hire a maid. "Let me ask you this, Rita. What is the worst possible scenario for you? If your greatest fear is to fall in love, what is the worst thing that can happen?"

"Well, there are so many things that can go wrong."

"But for now, give me the worst."

"Well, that I would get left at the altar. That I would be embarrassed in front of all my friends and relatives. Especially the ones who are convinced I'll never marry. It would be unbearable, Lily."

"Actually, that very thing happened to my sister Rosy."

"It did?" Rita's hand slapped her heart. "What happened to her? Did she grieve uncontrollably? Have a panic attack? Did the stress give her a life-threatening illness?"

"No, but it was hard on her. She did some moping and sleeping. And praying. But she recovered. Now she's happily married to a great guy."

"Really?" Rita dropped the naked daisy stem on the coffee table, took her knitting out of her basket, and started clacking away. "By the way, I'm sorry I teased you at your party. Telling you that I was falling in love with Rubin. I knew you liked him, so I was trying to help, actually. You see, when you have something that you think you might want, but you don't really know for sure, well, sometimes clarity comes when someone threatens to take it away. That was my gift to you." She grinned.

"Well, thanks for the clarity." *I think.* I clicked my pen, and between my clicking and her clacking we had quite the nervous little ensemble going. "Was it *that* obvious I liked Rubin?"

"You see?" Rita said. "It's not so nice to be the one caught with your feelings out there."

"You're right. It makes me feel. . .vulnerable. And that can be scary." I took a few notes. "So, what are you going to do about your feelings for Uriah?"

"I might ask him if he'd like a cup of coffee after work and then go home and have a panic attack."

"But Uriah likes you. I can tell. Just ask him. I think it's a wonderful idea."

"Oh yeah? Well, women do ask men out now. We're no longer living in the days of corsets. We have the vote, after all." She snapped her needles together.

"That's the spirit." I raised my pen. "You're absolutely right."

She let out a breath. "It does feel good to be here. You've helped me a lot. I mean, I'm still scared, but I'm not paralyzed."

"Good. It helps to know that everyone is a little scared in matters of the heart."

"Even you, Lily?"

"Even me." Especially me. I glanced at some earlier notes. "The first time you were here you mentioned that your father left your family when you were fifteen. Are you ready to talk about that now?"

"Maybe, a little." Rita put her knitting down and began the story of her youth.

*

Later, after Rita left my office, every pore in my body tried not to eavesdrop at the door to hear what was going on between her and Uriah. But I didn't quite live up to my usual ethical standards. I smashed my ear against the wooden door until it ached. No discernable words. Hmm. I tried holding a water glass against the door. I'd seen that done on TV, but it didn't seem to help. Something was definitely going on, though, and I think it was good stuff. I heard a giggle and something like a clearing of the throat. Maybe that was a yes.

Hmm. Were they going to meet for coffee? Would they date and fall in love? Marry and all of that? Could happen. But then, perhaps I was getting ahead of myself. Yes, I was in a good mood—glad that Uriah would have a date at last and pleased that Rita was taking a decisive step toward her recovery. And I might also be a little bit happy that I had a friendship date coming up with a really nice guy.

The rest of the day breezed by like a summer kite let out on a string. There weren't any serious problems I had to deal with. Mostly simple stuff like OCD, hypochondria, a couple of anger issues, and a woman who was a recovering shopaholic. Nothing too dire. I sent Uriah home early, locked up, and thought immediately of Rubin.

The temptation to have a quick look at the suite of offices where he worked was overwhelming. It would be so easy. He was just on the other end of the building, on the same floor. All I had to do was mosey over there and glance in the window. But what if Charlie saw me? Wouldn't she wonder what was going on? Too dangerous. And yet, maybe I was being overly cautious. Curiosity got the better of my clear judgment, and before I could talk myself out of such uncharacteristically clandestine behavior, I strolled—zoomed really—down the long hallway, looked for the right number, and glanced into the office of Graphics Unlimited.

The second I looked through the double glass doors, I saw Rubin inside. He was chatting with a woman—a strawberry-blond Barbie beauty—as he was walking her to the door. *Not a good time, Lily.*

I turned to go, but as I stirred, Rubin looked up. I didn't wait to find out if he saw me as I fast-walked and then ran down the hallway. One, two, three, four. . .if I counted, surely I'd be safe by ten. Five, six, seven, eight. Almost around the corner.

"Lily, is that you?" Rubin's voice boomed down the hallway like mighty thunder speaking from the clouds. I shook. I had been caught spying, looking for him! Pressing my nose against the glass. Pining for him. What must he think of me? That was one refresher class I'd never need to take—How to Embarrass Yourself 101.

Because I wasn't familiar with that side of the building and I was freaking out, I walked full force into a clear glass wall. My body took the jolt as if I'd been beaten with a mallet. I bounced back and my head did a buzzy thing. In that nanosecond I considered passing out—since I could then miss some of the humiliation that was coming. *Just a thought.* Unfortunately, one can never pass out at will. I rubbed my head and recovered just as Rubin and the pageant queen approached.

Chapter 9

Rubin touched my elbow, making me even less steady. "That was quite a blow. Are you all right, Lily?"

I'm a little dizzy, and I taste blood, but other than that. "Yeah, I'll be okay. I can be pretty silly at times. I was just fleeing the scene, kind of embarrassed." He looked at me with a new expression, as if he'd just awakened from a dream. What was that? I tapped my knuckles together. Bad habit I'd picked up from Heather.

"You mean you were embarrassed that you came to visit me?" Rubin asked. "I couldn't be more pleased that you did." He turned to the woman. "Lily, I want you to meet Ally."

While he finished up the introductions, it dawned on me through my fuzzy brain that it was *the* Ally I was being introduced to—his former fiancée—the one who'd broken off the engagement. "It's nice to meet you," is what I think I said. It may have come off like a mouthful of marbles.

"Nice to meet you, too." Ally lifted a big satchel up on her shoulder. "Well, I'd better get back to work. I've got a modeling job I need to get to."

"Modeling?" Guess I didn't really need to look puzzled, since her windswept beauty reeked of model splendor—

everything she touched surely spun itself into gold. Had Rubin dated every last debutante in Amarillo?

Ally shrugged with sweet resignation. "Yeah, I model on the side for extra money. Which is good, because I like to buy. . .you know. . .lots of stuff."

Rubin looked at me, but I avoided his eyes and said to Ally, "Well, you're certainly beautiful enough to be a model."

"Thanks. Most women are envious." Her tone was matter-of-fact, with a tinge of bemusement.

"I'm not," I said. "I wouldn't even know what to do with such beauty. I'd probably just squander it."

Rubin laughed.

Ally rocked her head to the side as if to ponder such a statement. "That's a heavy thought."

I smiled.

"Well, you all take care." She gave us a tiny baby wave by her face. And then that was it. She sashayed down the hallway with her enormous bag of whatever models carry, looking like life was busy meeting her every desire. I just hoped that desire no longer included Rubin.

"You came to see me." Rubin stroked his jawline.

"I wanted to see where you worked. I've never been to this side of the building before. I guess you must use the west elevator."

"I do."

"So, that was Ally, your former fiancée? She's very beautiful. With an emphasis on *very*."

"No, with an emphasis on *former*. The only reason she stopped by was to bring me this." He pulled a ring out of his pocket. "She'd never given it back to me, so she dropped it by the office."

"That was the right thing for her to do."

"Yes, but she should have given it back six months ago and not waited until she was engaged again."

"Oh, she's engaged?" I tried not to sound elated, but I was. Although, perhaps it wasn't a good time to toss confetti.

"She's engaged to a model. He suits her perfectly. And by the way." He touched my elbow again. "You *are* beautiful, and you've not squandered it. You don't have to be a model for people to enjoy the view of an attractive woman."

"Oh, well, that's quite a compliment. I'll live on that for at least. . .a lifetime."

Rubin laughed. "I like that."

"What?"

"Your unassuming nature. It's charming."

"It is?" If Rubin didn't stop complimenting me I'd have to wrestle him down to the floor and kiss him.

"I'm looking forward to sharing the canyon with you this evening. But for now, how about a tour of where I work?"

"I'd love it."

Rubin opened the door, and then I remembered Charlie—his boss. How many different ways could I live the word *panic*?

Chapter 10

Later that day I stared into my bathroom mirror, contemplating life and love. I grabbed a bar of Dove soap off the holder and scrawled the letters *M-E-S-S* across the glass. Good vivid word choice. I was hoping God would wash it off later.

The doorbell rang. Ah yes, the man behind my front door. Unfortunately, he would only be a friend. Perhaps someday—when Charlie was no longer my client and when I was assured she'd be okay—I would move forward. But until that day, I was at least glad Charlie hadn't seen Rubin and me together when he gave me the grand tour of his office. Not much consolation, but tender mercies nevertheless.

I opened the front door to a man whom I liked a lot but could only dream about. "Hi there."

Rubin fell back and grabbed the door frame with his fingers. "Do you always look this incredible for a picnic?"

"It's just jeans and a T-shirt." He appeared hardy, handsome, and happily holding my attention. And he had the scent of rain on him, like just before a good storm. "You don't look bad yourself."

"Thanks."

I pulled my stare away from him and locked up. We

headed toward his SUV and traveled toward Palo Duro Canyon on 127. All the way, we talked and laughed and got to know each other better. And everything I learned—I liked.

"Back in high school," Rubin said, "I was at the canyon with a group of my friends, and we made this huge campfire. We told some scary stories, roasted our way through way too many bags of marshmallows. And we sang. . .loudly and obnoxiously, I might add. It was pretty juvenile, but a lot of fun."

"Sounds wonderful to me." I wish I'd been a part of it. "I grew up in Galveston, and so I had more of a beach experience. But since I've been here I've enjoyed the canyon. I'm always so stunned by its colors and the mysterious-looking formations."

"Sort of an alien landscape."

"Right. There's something familiar about it, and yet so much of it seems like the great unknown."

Within minutes we were inside that beautiful alien landscape called Palo Doro Canyon. After parking, we set up our picnic paraphernalia on a great spot that overlooked the canyon.

I lowered myself onto the quilt and gazed out over the vista, toward the Lighthouse formation. The canyon's arid landscape came to life with cottonwood, juniper, and mesquite, but it was the stone pinnacles adorned in rings of color that always made me pause and stare. They reminded me of guards, watching over the chasm. It was easy to see why it was called the "Grand Canyon of Texas." I broke our silence. "I'd love to know why you became a graphic artist."

"I was always scribbling as a kid. It's just in my blood, I guess." He pulled out a couple of sodas from the basket and handed me one.

I popped the top and took a sip. I ran my fingers across a thick patch of Indian blankets and let their beauty seep into my spirit. "I started to say that this is my favorite time of the year here, just before autumn, but then, every season is my favorite."

"Mine, too." Rubin pointed toward the west. "Isn't that a roadrunner over there?"

"Where?"

"He's already gone. Sorry. Guess that's why they call them roadrunners."

"I'm just glad it wasn't a diamondback." I studied him as I munched on a couple of grapes. "I'm curious. How many girls have you brought here for a sunset picnic?" Maybe that was way too personal. "You don't have to answer that."

"I don't mind. Two."

"Hmm, they must have been really special."

"I brought Ally one time and my mom on Mother's Day."

Okay, so was this guy charming, or what? And boyishly handsome. There had to be something wrong with him. Maybe he lived with his aunt Tallulah. Or he was a hoarder of used toothbrushes. A kleptomaniac, maybe? A fear of postage stamps, of mouse tails, stale coffee. Of course everybody had a fear of that last one. But the list of possibilities was pretty much endless. I know—I graduated and made my income off that list. But I hoped Rubin was all he seemed, just a really nice guy. I held up my finger. "One good secret."

"A secret?" Rubin took a bite of his sandwich. "Okay, here's a big one. My one claim to fame is that I can play 'Jingle Bells' on my teeth."

I chuckled. "Really?"

"Yeah. Learned that valuable skill in the second grade."

"Weird and cute. . .but that's not the kind of secret I meant."

"Okay, so you like the dark stuff. Let's see. Something dastardly."

"Now we're talking."

"I once stole a therapeutic pillow from a medical supply store. It was for my dad. He'd just had surgery, and I didn't have enough money in my piggy bank. I thought the pillow might make him heal faster. Don't ask me what I was thinking. I have no idea. Maybe I thought my mom was poor, but she wasn't."

"That story is sad but sweet."

"That I was a thief?"

"That you were that worried about your dad. So, did he recover?"

"He did. But then a few years later he died of lung cancer. . .just couldn't give up the smokes."

"I'm so sorry, Rubin. Truly."

"Me, too, since it was preventable. Sometimes I resented the fact that he couldn't give them up. Made me feel that he loved the cigarettes more than he loved me. If it hadn't been for those little white sticks filling his lungs with chemicals, he'd still be around, making me laugh."

"Must have been so hard."

"It really was. He was my hero. When he died, everything changed. I no longer believed in myself. I became this goofy little kid with very few friends."

"So you weren't Mr. Popular?" I took another bite of my chicken salad.

"No. I was a pudgy kid with acne issues."

"I don't believe you. That's really hard to imagine."

"I've got photos to prove it." He chuckled. "I'll show them to you sometime. But listen to me. I've unloaded on you like a dump truck. I'll bet all your friends start doing that to you. You know, telling you way too much, because you're a counselor."

"Sometimes. But I don't mind."

"I heard when you were talking to your pet fish, you mentioned to him that you felt inadequate. Why is that? I can't imagine why you feel that way."

"When I was in college I missed some of my psychology classes—a lot of classes, actually—because my roommate was ill. I took care of her some of the time, and well, since I missed so much school, I barely graduated. So I never felt I got all the material nailed down. I've been able to get by, though. People still come to see me. But I guess you could call me 'shrink-light.'"

Rubin grinned. "Taking care of your roommate says a lot about your character. Most people wouldn't mind their counselors having a lot less head knowledge if they could have a counselor with your kind of heart."

"But please don't put me too high on a pedestal. The fall will kill me. My roommate recuperated, but my grades never did. I was always grateful for her recovery, but sometimes I resented the fact that she exaggerated her illnesses. At times she could be a bit of a hypochondriac. I never confronted her about it, and I see that as a mistake now. I've made a lot of them over the years."

"Me, too. May I be a member of your club?"

"You may, and I'll waive the membership fee."

He laughed. "It must be hard to listen to everyone's problems all day, every day. Do you end up taking work home with you?" He pointed to his heart. "I mean right here."

"In a way, it is hard to let go at home and have a relaxing evening when I know some of my clients are still suffering. Mostly I just get concerned that I'm not helping enough. Not doing enough."

Rubin took a drink of his soda. "Charlie bragged on you… said you were amazing."

"That's good to hear." I opened a bag of chips.

"As you know, Charlie and I go way back, but there's nothing there but friendship. A long time ago I think she wanted more between us, but that's long gone. She doesn't feel that way anymore. At least I hope she doesn't. But then again, she's been acting kind of funny lately." He looked at me and chuckled. "Sorry, I'm just kind of rambling here. It's not always easy for guys to know what women are thinking."

"Well, you've hit on a real nugget of truth there." I'd had a feeling our chat might head toward Charlie. I kept munching, hoping the conversation wouldn't stay parked at that station but would move on down the line.

"By the way, are my prayers working?" Rubin asked.

"Prayers?" What was he talking about? Had I missed something? "What prayers?"

"I've been praying you'd want to be more than friends."

"Oh, that." At least we'd moved on from Charlie. "I don't know." Rubin angled himself a little closer to me. He looked so endearing, I longed to reach up and touch his cheek, but that kind of contact would send all the wrong signals. At least all the wrong ones for friendship. "Things are not the way they seem."

"Please let me see inside your thoughts."

"That might be a very dangerous place to be right now." I smiled. "Impossible to share."

"I'm not thinking of the word *impossible*. I'm thinking more, *irresistible*."

Rubin was going to kiss me, and I knew I wouldn't push him away. *God, forgive me if this is somehow wrong.* "Do I hear thunder?"

"Yes. It's my heart." He grinned.

"That was so corny, but sweet."

"Okay, you don't impress easily. I'll give it another try." He came a little closer. "The sunset has put a golden glow on your skin."

"For real?"

"For real. Right here." He kissed my forehead. "And right here." He kissed my cheeks. "And right here." Then he ever so slowly leaned down to my mouth. Oh my. If kisses could reach a higher plain, then our kiss touched heights unknown. If it was hokey to think it, I didn't care. The moment was ours, and it was sublime. And yet, the thought of Charlie, my concern for her, stole my joy. I pulled away.

"Is everything all right?" He touched my cheek with the back of his hand.

"It was a great kiss, Rubin. If it were in a chick flick, women would go away thinking they'd really gotten their money's worth."

He smiled. "I guess this means we're more than just friends now."

"Well, I've never known friends to kiss with such. . .gusto."

He gave the tip of my nose a playful touch.

Why did that gesture seem so familiar?

"When we talked of secrets earlier. . .well, I do have another. Do you believe in love at first sight?" he asked, fidgeting with the quilt.

"Someone else asked me that recently."

"Oh?" He stroked his finger along his jawline. "But do you believe in it?"

"Yes, honestly, I do. Are you trying to tell me something?"

"I don't know. But I will say this. . .I'm very grateful that Charlie insisted that I get counseling with you."

"So am I." *Dear Rubin, so am I.* And yet this was so heartbreaking for Charlie.

He turned toward the setting sun. "Look at the sky's colors against the canyon. Grand and humbling. It's like a window to heaven. Like God wants us to see just a little of His home to keep our hearts from fainting down here. To give us hope."

The artist in him was seeping out, and it made me smile. "It does look like hope. That was beautifully said, Rubin."

The rocky gorge and formations were always colorful, but the setting sun lit the canyon on fire. And the clouds, wispy and luminous, were like sails ready to put the world out to sea. So miraculous—this vast space of shapes and hues—one of God's finest moments of creation.

"Too bad we can't take it home. Put it in a shadowbox."

Shadowbox. Interesting word choice. A tender memory trembled inside me.

"Are you cold? Do you need your sweater?"

"No, that's not it." I reached up and touched his cheek, but my attention was suddenly drawn away from Rubin by the sound of shuffling feet.

We turned toward the noise. A woman marched toward us—a woman who looked a lot like Charlie. That was because the woman *was* Charlie!

Chapter 11

Feeling like a shamefaced child with my hand in the cookie jar, I backed away from Rubin, leaped off the quilt, and stumbled backward. "Charlie?"

Rubin got up slowly, looking more confused than angry over Charlie's sudden appearance.

As Charlie approached my heart sped up and my brain flooded with questions. What would she think of me? And how in the world did she know where to find us? The look in her eyes made me think she might like to take off one of her stilettoes and use it to give us the thrashing of a lifetime.

"Charlie? What's going on?" Rubin asked. "Is everything all right?"

Charlie planted her feet. "Not really. We need to talk."

"Privately?"

"No, I need to say this in front of both of you." Charlie shoved the hair out of her face with vengeance.

Rubin took a few steps toward her. "It must be important to come way out here. How did you find us?"

"Easy." She shrugged. "You wrote it on your day-planner. And then I drove all the roads out here until I found your SUV."

"Why would you snoop around in my day-planner?" Rubin asked. "What's this all about, really?"

"Very simple. I'm on a quest. . .for the truth."

"About what?" Rubin asked.

Charlie turned her fiery gaze on me. "Why are you here, Lily, when you know how I feel? You betrayed me. No wonder you look so guilty. You *are* guilty."

"What are you talking about?" Rubin asked. "Please, tell me."

"Lily knows what it's about."

"Well, can you enlighten me, Charlie?" Rubin lifted his arms in an imploring gesture. "I have no idea what's going on."

I stepped forward, knowing now was the time to speak up. "I'm truly sorry, Charlie. I never meant for—"

"No more." Charlie glared at me. "I trusted you with the story of my life, with all the scary stuff I don't tell anybody. And this is how you repay me?" She drew her fingers into fists. "All that counseling. . .was it just stuff they taught you to say? And when you cried along with me, was it playacting?"

"No. I assure you it wasn't." I stuffed my hands into my pockets then yanked them back out again. "I meant everything I said. And in spite of what you've seen here, I still mean all of it. I promise."

"Right. Is that why you said the words, 'maybe Rubin isn't meant for you'? You had your sights on him, didn't you, Lily?" Charlie took a step toward me, her eyes wild with wrath. "I see it clearly. How can you deny it?"

Oh God, how can I make her see the truth? Or maybe Charlie *did* speak the truth. "To be honest, I worried about that later. I was hoping that I'd said the words for all the right reasons. I want to be honorable in all I do, but I *am* human."

"You said you were my friend." Charlie's chin quivered.

"That's what your ad boasts. Even your billboard. I've seen it. Who could miss it? But I can tell you this. No matter how honorable you claim to be or want to be, no friend would do this. You knew that I was in love with Rubin, have always been, and then what do you do? You go out with him, and I find you in an intimate embrace. There's no form of friendship, professional or otherwise, that would allow for that kind of behavior, Lily."

My hands trembled, so I wrapped them around my waist. "I have wronged you in the most egregious way. I'm stunned, no, disgusted, at my own lack of discipline."

"Words. Too many, too late." She waved me off. "How appropriate that you chose this place for your tryst. Your character, Lily, is as empty as this canyon."

I scraped my knuckles back and forth against each other, but I didn't respond. How could I? She was right.

Rubin walked up to Charlie and put his arm around her. "I've never seen you like this. I don't—"

Charlie pushed him away. "I'm a woman in love. I have been since college. Didn't you even notice?"

"I did. We talked about it some time ago. It got resolved. I thought you'd moved on. At least I'd always hoped you'd moved on."

"I haven't been dating," Charlie said. "I never got married. It was because I was waiting on you, Rubin." Her hands shot up and then slapped to her legs.

Rubin rubbed his neck. "But six months ago I was engaged to Ally. Didn't that tell you we were never going to be a couple?"

"When you became engaged it was the worst day of my life." Charlie clawed at her arms with her fingernails. "And then when you broke up. . .I saw it as a sign that we were meant to be together. Don't you see?"

Rubin looked down at the ground for a moment and then back at Charlie. "You're a wonderful woman, Charlie. You've been a good friend to me all these years, and you make an excellent boss. I wish you'd told me. You should have come to me with this earlier. We could have worked it out."

"You mean you would have married me?"

"No, I mean I would have set you free, and you could have moved on. You would have a husband and family by now. You shouldn't have waited for me, Charlie. I'm not the best husband for you. There's someone better out there for you." He touched her sleeve.

She reached out to his hand. "But I would have had enough love for both of us."

"Charlie, listen to the sound of that. No one person can take on that kind of burden. That's not good enough for either of us. As your good friend I want the best for you, and I'm not the best. You need somebody who'll love you, really love you, for all the wonderful things you are." He took her hands in his. "This is your friend talking here, Charlie. Please know that if I could, I would have surely fallen in love with you."

I backed away, feeling like I was spying on a very intimate conversation. *Lord, please help them work this out.*

Rubin released Charlie's hands. "Just so you know, Lily wanted this picnic to be a friendship kind of outing. She insisted on it. I'm the one who badgered her into making it something more. It's my fault. . .not hers."

Charlie looked at me with such sad eyes. My heart ached for her. *Oh God, please help her.*

She turned back to Rubin. "My dear friend, your services are no longer needed at Graphics Unlimited."

Rubin shook his head as if he'd not heard her correctly. "You're firing me?"

"Yes. To use your own words, you could say, I'm setting you free, so you can move on. You can clear out your office tomorrow morning. Please know, that if I could keep you on, I would. But be comforted, Rubin. There's a better job out there for you." She blew him a kiss, turned her back on us, and began her march toward the parking lot.

Misery would now be the operative word for the day. The pretty colors of the canyon—which minutes before had been vibrant in the last rays of the sun—were now diminished. The moon had come up clear and bright, beaming at us like a long-lost friend, but the perfect evening was no more.

I expected Rubin to call after Charlie, to stop her, but he fell as silent as the stones around us as he watched her go.

Oh God, what have I done? I was not what I had hoped to become. I felt as though I stood on the rim of a precipice, waiting to fall. But then perhaps I'd already fallen, and the final blow was seconds away.

After a few uncertain moments Rubin turned to me and said, "I guess I'd better take you home."

"I'm so sorry, Rubin, that you lost your friend and your job over me. I'm sorry about everything."

"Don't be. It's not your fault. It's mine alone." He looked as though he wanted to reach out to me. "If I'd been paying more attention, I would have known this was coming. I should have seen it. I shouldn't have let Charlie suffer like this all these years, waiting for me. I was a fool to let this happen."

"I'm so sorry." I rubbed my hands along my arms, feeling the chill that was settling over the canyon. "What will you do for a job?"

"That part is easy. I've been promised a job at a couple of other places. . .that is, if I ever chose to leave. I think in some way I felt an obligation to stay at Graphics Unlimited because of the history I had with Charlie. You know, old college chums sticking together and all that. It's time for me to go anyway. I just wish it could have happened in a hundred other ways but this one."

I wanted to say so many things, but words—or perhaps *my* words right now—seemed as valuable as used gum. Rubin's reply to Charlie had been appropriate and brotherly. But Charlie didn't want a brother—she wanted Rubin. For always. And what was wrong with that? *God, why is love so complicated and painful that people have to seek help to deal with it?* Life could be a tangled heap of emotions, just like a basket full of snakes. And my livelihood was all about what was inside that basket. What a twisted way to make a living.

Was it time for a new profession? But I had no other talents. Some people had multiple gifts, but I never did excel at very many things. I could talk to people, and I could dig holes. Not too impressive.

Rubin and I looked at each other and sighed in resignation at the impossible moment.

"We haven't come to the end of this," Rubin said. "Not at all."

But in spite of his hopeful words, the consensus was in—sometimes life really wasn't so grand.

*

After Rubin dropped me off at home, I turned on all the outside lights and dug in my backyard until my arms ached and my hair was splattered with wet dirt. Someday, if I ever got my act together, I'd hire a crew to finish making this hole into the prettiest lagoon pool anyone had ever seen. And it would come in handy on starry, starry nights. Just a romantic thought. I could at least dream, couldn't I?

I placed the tarp back over the opening, shut off the backyard lights, then dropped on my bed, mud and all. I think Nathaniel Hawthorne wrote, "Life is made up of marble and mud." Yes, well, tonight I had mud in my hair and more sadly, I had feet of clay.

Steady and serene, Lily. No sense in flying off to the moon in a spaceship of worry and regret. I felt like Skyping my mom, telling her all my travails, but I knew she was busy traveling with Daddy right now. And yet something had to be done. It wasn't enough to just tell myself to remain calm. Self-talk just wasn't going to cut it. What I needed more than anything was a heart-to-heart with God. *Lord, I'm at the end of my own resources. I need intervention. You are the real Counselor. I could sure use a visitation tonight. For Charlie. For Rubin. And for me.*

Before I got to work the next day I knew what I had to do. I needed to make certain Charlie was going to be okay. But when I arrived she was already there waiting, making quiet chitchat with Uriah.

Chapter 12

Charlie saw me and said, "May we talk in your office...just woman to woman?"

Poor Charlie. She looked like she hadn't slept all night. "Sure. Come on in. I have time."

When she'd gotten seated on the couch, I sat across from her in my swivel chair.

She hugged one of the stuffed animals that had been sitting on the cushion. "I got some clarity last night. I felt you should know."

Just what I'd hoped for—prayed for.

We sat for a while in silence and then she said, "There were guys I had wanted to date through the years, but couldn't admit that to myself. I see now I was obsessed about Rubin, and I confused that consuming fixation with love. I lost track of my real feelings. I lost track of a lot of things, including friends...well, I see that now. Not sure why I didn't recognize it before. It seems really in my face right now. But last night was a productive night. A night of revelation. Of moving forward. Even though I don't think I got five minutes' sleep."

She placed the stuffed bear on the coffee table. "I've been stagnant for a very long time. And even though I came pretty close to hating you yesterday, I'm grateful for what happened.

It was the only way I was going to break free. I'm relieved to finally move on."

"Those are great words to hear, Charlie, and not because I had some interest in Rubin. Listen, if there are guys you wanted to date, maybe you still can."

She looked puzzled. "Do you mean call them up?"

"Well, you said they were interested. Maybe you could ask them out for a cup of coffee after work. And women ask guys out all the time these days. It's no longer the days of corsets. We have the vote, after all." *Sometimes recycled advice is the best.*

"Hmm. Maybe."

"What's the worst that can happen?"

Charlie chuckled. "They could say no. That would be pretty painful."

"Yeah, it would. A lot of things relating to falling in love are painful. As you know."

"I guess I ruined it between you and Rubin. Listen, if you can make it work. . .go for it. I won't be throwing you two any parties, but I won't hunt you down again either."

I smiled. "Thanks, Charlie."

"I don't wish him ill. I'd hate for you to think that. But I just can't work with him anymore. I'll give him a good recommendation. All of this will be fine. . .someday." She tried on a smile, and it fit her face well enough.

"That must have been hard to say."

"Yeah. But not quite as bad as I thought it would be." She took a piece of bubble gum from the glass bowl on the table, unwrapped it, and popped it in her mouth. "This used to ruin my teeth as a kid, but I've missed these little guys." She rose to go. "Well, take care of yourself, Lily McBride."

"You, too. Drop in anytime to let me know how you're doing. I'm always here."

"I know where to find you. By the way, those skirts aren't a good look for you."

"You're the second person who's said that."

Charlie smiled. "I wouldn't doubt it." She took another piece of bubble gum from the bowl and strolled out of my office. I thought she might turn around to say more, but she didn't. Good-bye, Charlie.

I glanced up toward the heavens and gave God a thumbs-up. "Thanks," I whispered with all my heart.

*

When the workday was finally over, and all the clients were seen and cared for, I locked the door to Rent-a-Friend. For some reason I couldn't quite move from that spot. Suddenly feeling overly tired, I leaned my head against the door. I'd given it my all to keep focused on my clients instead of the fact that I might have lost my chances with Rubin, but now that the workday was over, I felt the sadness building in my spirit. The only bright spot was the golden glow of the afternoon sun spilling through the window. Made me think of Rubin. Several tears fell and then a familiar voice said softly, "Lily. Don't cry. Please."

I turned toward the voice—Rubin.

He took a handkerchief out of his pocket and dabbed my cheeks, soaking up the tears.

I wanted to say so many things to him, but started with, "I thought maybe you'd been chased away for good. But then I was thinking I don't deserve to go out with you after what I pulled. I mean, here I am. . .a counselor determined to wreck the mental health and joy of a precious client. Not exactly how I envisioned my professional life."

"That's not true at all. I talked to Charlie after she came to see you. She's going to be okay. And we reconciled. . .as friends. But we both agreed it's wise for me to move on." He touched my cheek. "I can't see how you're at fault. I'm the one who manipulated you into a kiss."

I chuckled. "I didn't feel all that manipulated. I wanted to kiss you as badly as you wanted to kiss me."

"That is so good to hear."

"I think you're right about Charlie. She'll be okay."

"I'm glad." Rubin grinned. "It'll be all right for us to go out now. So, what do you think?"

"Okay. But what are you hiding behind your back?"

He brought his arm up, showing me a bouquet of pink peonies. "For you."

I pressed my face into them and breathed. Bliss. "How did you know they're my favorite?"

"Let's go to the atrium. The one here in the building. I have a story to tell you. And one I hope you love."

He took my hand and we strolled—with a sense of urgency—toward the center of the building. He opened the glass doors for me, and we went inside. Immediately we were surrounded by tropical trees and flowers and warm light streaming in from the glass ceiling like pale ribbons. It was a restful place, where people came to eat their lunches. But right now, with Rubin, it was paradise.

When we were situated on one of the stone benches, Rubin offered me a sly grin.

"What were you going to tell me? You are such a mystery." I held the peonies close to my face to enjoy the pleasure of their company along with Rubin's.

"A long time ago there was this boy who gave you peonies."

"That's true." Rita must have told him at the party. "Those flowers are in a shadowbox, and it's hanging on my office wall."

"I wonder how I could have missed it," he said. "So that shadowbox full of flowers means something to you?"

"It means a lot to me. A boy named Austin made it for me a long time ago, and then he disappeared. I don't know what became of him."

"You cared about him?" Rubin asked.

"Yes."

"Well, I can tell you that the boy forgot the girl's name, but he never ever forgot the girl."

"But how could you have known. . ." My voice died away. Rubin's eyes were so familiar. Who was he really?

He reached around my shoulders. I thought he was going to hug me, but instead he moved my hair away from my shoulders and touched my back in two spots. "Did you know you have something invisible right here and right here?"

My skin grew warm from his touch. "What do you mean?" I'd heard those words before. And his touch was so familiar.

"You have wings. . .hidden there," Rubin said, "because

you're really an angel."

My mind reeled. That phrase was from somewhere—my youth? "Where did you hear that?"

"I didn't hear it from anyone," he said. "I'm the one who said it to you. . .fifteen years ago."

"But the kid, the boy who said it to me, was different."

"I looked very different back then." He chuckled. "I was this chubby little kid with acne who sat right behind you in school."

I really studied his features. I saw it then, as if a veil had been lifted from my eyes. "It's you? Really? But your name. Wasn't it Austin?"

"Austin is my middle name. I'm Rubin Austin McCall, but back then I was going by Austin. Every time we moved I switched my first and middle names."

"Austin. . .Rubin. . .I can't believe it! I'm so glad to see you again." I gave him a good long hug. *So glad to have you back in my life.*

We lingered together for a moment in each other's arms. When I eased away I said, "That's why you seemed familiar to me. Your easy laugh and smile. Especially your touch. In class you were always bumping up against me. Like a puppy wanting to play."

Rubin chuckled. "I think I was more pesky than playful back then. I tried anything and everything to get your attention."

"Come to think of it. . .that's true."

"One time I got my pen caught in your hair because I was twirling it around your pretty brown curls."

I shook my finger at him. "I still remember that."

"But it was a blessing to sit behind you. I got to study you. That's how I knew about your angel wings."

His smile warmed me all the way through. "So that's why I've been drawing angels."

"You have?"

"Yes, while my clients are talking I take notes, but I also sketch these little angels around the words. I've been doing that for a long time. Ever since I knew you. I hadn't made the connection until now."

"I'm so glad you did." Rubin leaned toward me but didn't kiss me.

"I wish you could have stayed longer in Galveston. We could have grown up together."

"Wouldn't that have been something? But as you know, we were only there for about six months. Before that we lived in Dallas, Midland, and Austin. Fortunately, after Mom moved me to Amarillo, we stayed put, and I was able to graduate here and go to college."

"Do you remember meeting my parents?"

"I do. Your mom was into scrapbooking, and your dad was into reading nautical books. As I recall, you had a Norman Rockwell kind of family."

"You think so? We fight some, but yeah, maybe it is, come to think of it. I'm sure my sisters would remember you from school. They'll be glad we met up again. But I feel silly that I didn't recognize you right away."

"The reason you couldn't remember me was because I was *that* fat."

"It was probably just a little leftover baby fat."

"At twelve? That's kind, but untrue." He grinned. "By the way, I think if a kid can fall in love, I did with you."

"But why?" I shrugged. "I was just a silly little girl with quirky habits."

"That's not at all what I remember."

I placed my hand next to his on the bench. "And what is it you remember?"

"I was the new kid in school, and almost no one wanted to sit with me, let alone talk to me. I looked like a genuine outcast. Maybe they thought they'd taint their school careers if they talked to me. They were probably right."

"Kids can be so cruel."

"Yeah, they can." He edged his hand over mine and grinned. "But you weren't. In fact, Lily, you changed my life."

"How?" It was hard to concentrate on anything but Rubin's hand, the one holding mine. They fit so well together, like two warm candles softening and fusing together.

"My dad had always been my best friend. It was the hardest time in my life, trying to cope with losing him. I almost went under."

"What about your mom?"

"We're pretty close now, but we weren't back then," he said. "Anyway, those months at that school were the hardest in my life, but you made it easier. You gave me a life injection, and it made me want to try again."

"Are you sure that was me? Sounds like a fairy tale."

"No fairy tale. I lived it. After my father died you were my only friend."

"Really?" I squeezed his hand. "I was so sorry when you moved away."

"My last day at school there in Galveston was terrible, knowing I'd never see you again. Knowing I'd be moving to the other side of the state. But the confidence you gave me enabled me to start exercising and lose some of the pudge. I didn't become a jock, but I did lose enough that I was no longer harassed. I joined a chess club. Got involved. I was never a leader type, and I didn't date a lot, but you gave me enough courage that I made a few friends along the way. You got me through the roughest spot in my life. You were my brown-eyed angel." He touched the back of his hand against my cheek. "It's no wonder you went into counseling. You had the gift right from the beginning."

I rested my head on his shoulder. "You will never know how important those words are to me. I've been considering giving up."

"Promise me you won't ever do that. You're too talented to walk away."

The words trickled through me. "I promise." He held me for a moment, and then I pulled back. "Hey, you know. . .you never did say good-bye back then."

"I'm sorry about that. My mom had some trouble after Dad died. She had to work for the first time in her life. It was pretty hard on her. When she finally got a good job, we had to leave. We were living in an apartment at the time, so when we moved we did it quickly. I regretted not telling you good-bye, but then I thought in the long run it would be easier. It was a foolish thing on my part. I should have told you what happened and where I was going."

"It's all right. God saw fit to bring us back together."

"I never forgot you, Lily, even though your name escaped me over the years. But I always wondered what happened to you, and I prayed you'd have a great life. I thought it would be nice if our paths crossed again, but this is nicer than I imagined." He shook his head. "Little did we know that God had put us in the same building. Amazing."

"Rubin?"

"Yes, Lily?"

"When did you first realize who I was?"

"Right from the beginning you seemed familiar to me, but I didn't know it was you until the incident in the hallway when you came to my office."

"Oh, you mean when I slammed into that glass wall?"

"When you were a kid you used to have trouble with tripping and falling like that. You know, when you got flustered."

"Ohhh." I shook my head and covered my face with my hands. "I can't believe that was the tipping point for you."

Rubin gently removed my hands from my face. "I thought it was adorable then, and I still do. But I'm sad you keep getting hurt." He brushed his lips over my hand and then let me go.

"Why didn't you tell me right then who you were?"

"Well, at first I was too pleasantly stunned, and then later I'd planned to surprise you by telling you at the picnic."

I took in another heady sniff of my peonies, and for some reason, visions of lagoon pools under a starry, starry night danced in my head. Perhaps someday Rubin would love a dip in a backyard pool under the stars.

He looked out at what seemed to be a faraway place. "I hoped you hadn't forgotten me, and yet I wanted the new impression of me to overshadow the old. . .just in case. . .well, in case your memories of me weren't all that sweet."

"Oh, but they were as sweet as any memories could be."

"That's good to hear. Very good." He took a deep whiff of my flowers. "These peonies. They're unique. It's like you can't see the end of the petals. They want to go on forever."

"Yes, and why not?" I looked at those lips of his, and knew what they felt like against mine. I didn't want to rush the moment, but I hoped to know the pleasure of his kiss again very soon.

Rubin picked up one of the fallen petals and stroked it along the contours of my face. I leaned into the delight of his touch. Yes, the moment was a splendidly sumptuous and shining serendipity sent straight from heaven. *Oh God, how wonderful is this?* Austin/Rubin was back in my life and all grown up. "So do you think you could tell me one more time where my invisible wings are?"

"That can be arranged." He reached around and touched my back, along both my shoulder blades.

Rubin's arms were around me, which was where I wanted them to be.

"I'm so glad I'm not twelve anymore. . .because now I can do this," he said.

This time, Rubin's lean had connotations. His lips found mine and together we created a kiss so soaring and carefree that we sailed off into the blue together, and I don't think we had any intentions of coming back for some time.

After all, it was the twilight of summer. . .

Epilogue

Mr. and Mrs. Joseph McBride
are happy to announce the joining of their daughter,
Miss Lily Larkspur McBride,
in holy matrimony
to Mr. Rubin Austin McCall.

Please celebrate their marriage with us
on February 14th
at 12:00 noon
Christ's Church Cathedral
Lavendale, Texas

Reception in the atrium following the ceremony.

What is life without the radiance of love?
J.C.F. Von Schiller

DREAMING OF HEATHER

Chapter 1

My finger hovered over the computer key. If I pressed the SEND button my life would forever change. No more livelihood. No more trips to the spa or lavish business lunches.

But—no more sleepless nights.

I glanced over at the endoscopic photo of my ulcer. Why had I'd allowed myself to get so stressed, to the point that my body was staging a rebellion? All from taking the road heavily traveled. I thought of Mom and Dad, their love, their earnestness in all things right and good, and then smashed the SEND key. There was no turning back now. I was a raft over the falls.

I'd officially resigned. I never wanted to go back to sales, ever, ever, ever again. At least not for a company that expected me to make false claims to the customers as well as make promises they couldn't—or wouldn't—keep. "Deal enhancements," they called them. I called them lies. Fortunately, I'd never had to resort to their shady methods, but it had come to a head—either succumb or resign. At least my honor was left intact. I just wish integrity could pay the bills.

I closed my laptop and breathed deeply—maybe for the first time in years. There really was enough oxygen. Who knew? I raised my hands. I was free. I giggled, even though giggling wasn't my thing.

I walked onto the porch, letting the screen door bang shut. It felt particularly satisfying today, that crisp smack of wood hitting wood. I leaned over the railing to gaze at the rain-swollen current. April was always a promising month in Horseshoe Bayou, my little corner of Southeast Texas. The air was pregnant with scents—the aroma of new life. The cypress trees with their gangly trunks sprouted feathery plumes, just to impress the willows. The grasses came up in festive tufts, and critters of all denominations sang hymns in the twilight—as my sweet neighbor, Evelyn, used to say.

A dragonfly buzzed by me, heading toward the cattails. He must love the water, too, the way it curled around the bend, going places beyond our small world. Streams had always fascinated me—the way they were ever shifting. Even my bog, which could be sluggish, never stayed the same, since it was always moving, ever changing.

I took a whiff of my potted rosemary on the porch and then gave my wind chimes a swing, adding some merry sounds to the music in my head. Quitting my job gave me a jolt of liberty and joy—more than I'd expected. And it gave me a dose of something else. *Truth serum.* That was it, and this strange new "elixir of candor" now pumped through me, seeping into every tissue. Yes, that was the deficiency in my friends and colleagues. I had enough stories to fill volumes of all the times I'd seen them offer carefully massaged half truths rather than what people needed and wanted to hear. And it wasn't just a problem in the workplace; it was everywhere.

In the midst of my awakening—my epiphany, really—I realized it would become my calling to give the general populace what they longed for—good old-fashioned honesty. I was meant to show people the importance of being earnest. Whether they wanted to hear about it or not!

From here on out I would live more honestly. Speak more openly. And people would find that in the end they craved it—that rare brew called truth—more than caffeine in the morning. My resolve made me think of my brother-in-law, Morgan Jones, who would now consider me a kindred spirit.

And my first experiment could be on the man coming up the footpath—my brand-new neighbor. I'd seen him from a distance several times and waved, but we'd yet to do any formal intros. He had a purposeful stride, a glow of tenacity, and he was dressed in a tuxedo. Strange attire for late afternoon. And what was he humming? Was that Mozart?

When he arrived at my back porch, he lit up like headlights on high beam. "Hello there. I'm Evan Finch."

"Hi." I went around to the side steps of my porch to greet him. "Heather McBride. Welcome to the neighborhood."

"Thanks." He reached his hand over the railing, and I

offered him a firm shake. "I wasn't sure about the protocol. I mean, there aren't any fences in our neighborhood, but I wasn't sure if it was kosher to just walk up to your back porch like this."

"You're perfectly fine." He certainly was. Our hands lingered. Then we parted. *Evan.* Nice name. Good solid face up close—a nose that had decent angles, a strong chin with lift without being haughty, and a charismatic ambiance in his brown eyes that could keep a girl a little off balance. Not bad. Dark hair down to his collar? *Hmm.* Different, but at least it was ultra-groomed. Neither one of us said any more. In fact, I lost track of the seconds. "I think somebody had better blink or say something. We're having a staring match."

He laughed. "I guess we are."

I leaned on the railing for support. What was it about men and tuxedoes? They never failed to look dashing, as if there was a white horse waiting for them in the wings somewhere. "Do you always wear a tux to meet your neighbors?"

"No, but I'm thrilled you brought that up." He gestured as if quieting a round of applause. "I'm in a bit of a bind, and I know this might be way too forward of me, bad etiquette and all, but I was wondering if you'd like to go to a wedding with me. Today."

"You're kidding. Right now?" I glanced down at my wrinkled denim jumper. Guess my departure from business suits was a wanton leap.

"Yeah, right now." He glanced at his watch. "Actually,

it starts in just under two hours, but the chapel's only ten minutes away. Listen, I know it's last minute, but I thought—"

"Wait a minute. How do you know I'm not married?"

"Well, since there aren't any fences, our lives are a little exposed. . .and well, I happened to notice that you're always alone on your back porch. *And* you only have one car." He held up his hands as if in self-defense.

"Good detective work. You must watch *NCIS*. I had no idea I was being watched so carefully or I wouldn't have come out on the porch all those times wearing my jammies." Of course, they were always long T-shirts like my sister Rosy wore, too, but still. . .

He grinned. "I tried not to stare. . .if that gives me any points."

"I'll have to think about it."

"Listen, I know coming over like this is unorthodox. I mean, we don't know each other at all."

"I *do* know something about you." I came down the steps to get a better look at him. "You inherited your house from your aunt Evelyn when she passed away several months ago. A hard loss, by the way. I knew Evelyn. She was a great and godly woman. And she mentioned you from time to time. . . said you were a fine Christian man. And then she would always wink, like she was hoping we'd meet." I couldn't believe I'd said the last part, but speaking more openly felt like tender shoots bursting through the earth in the springtime. I was sprouting more courage by the minute.

"That sounds just like Aunt Evelyn." Evan chuckled

softly as if he were remembering pleasant and amusing things about her.

"Before I consider your idea, I have a question for you."

"Okay. Anything. . .well, almost." He grinned again.

"Your request is so last minute that your real date must have cancelled on you. So, I'm the *second* choice. Right?" I slipped my hands into my kangaroo pockets. "Just keeping it real."

Evan dropped his chin to his chest and then looked up at me. "Okay, that's true. Look, I understand if you don't—"

"I would love to go with you." I blurted this out, startling myself. My hands flopped around in my pockets excitedly like fish in a bucket.

"Really? You'll go?"

"All I have to do is slip on a fancy dress."

Evan placed his palms together and then touched his fingers to his lips. "It's a joyous day when things go your way."

"Did you actually just say that?"

Evan chuckled. "It's something my dad used to say. Listen, before you get all dressed up, I have something I need to tell you."

"Oh? Revelations already?"

"Just one. I promise. You see, out of a large family of aunts and uncles, I'm the only offspring, and so when I bring a living, breathing date, they are. . .expectant."

"*Expectant* is never a good word on a first date." I wrapped my arm around one of the cedar posts.

"True. But because I'm the only one of my generation,

there's an abnormal amount of focus on me. And because I'm thirty-six, well, they're all in this panic mode, matrimonially speaking. I feel you have a right to know what to expect."

"Well, I still say yes to your request."

"Yes!" Evan held his arms up as if addressing an invisible crowd.

Unique guy.

"I promise I'll keep my aunts in line. They won't push us for a wedding date or anything. . .at least not today."

I laughed. "My family is getting a little pushy, too, since all my sisters are married now." *And because I'm thirty-one and counting.* I waved him onto the porch. "Please come 'have a sit' on my porch, as your aunt Evelyn would say, and I'll get dressed as fast as I can."

While Evan got comfortable on my porch swing, I ran inside to do my best at making myself presentable for a spring wedding. I refreshed my makeup, including two kissable coats of premium lip gloss, a bit of gold eye shadow on my lids to bring out the gold in my brown eyes, and then touched up my short hair with a curling iron. I did a pretend kiss in front of the mirror, which was something I'd never done in my life. Guess I felt a little off balance, being out of work and all, and a little excited to have a date with some potential.

I slipped on my yellow finery, plopped on a matching shammay straw bonnet, and slid on some lace gloves for good measure. Done. I gave myself a ta-da moment in front of my full-length mirror. Hmm. Not too shabby for a last-minute effort. But was the hat stylish or absurd? Who knew? I headed to the porch.

Evan rose when I squeaked open the screen door.

"Here I am."

"Look at you. The sun is rising with you in that hat and dress."

"Thanks."

"Really. You look beautiful."

I batted my eyelashes. "I'm wearing a ton of makeup."

He laughed.

Feeling self-conscious at Evan's close study of me, I rummaged through the contents of my beaded bag.

"Do you have everything you need in there?" Evan pretended to peer into the bag with me. "A man should never take lightly the contents of a woman's purse."

"How true." I grinned and snapped my purse shut. "Actually, I have a first aid kit in here in case you injure me on the dance floor."

Evan laughed again. I took some mental notes—he had a great laugh, without being wheezy or snorty or too bombastic. And a good laugh is always well received in my family.

"Are you ready?" he asked in a soft but stirring voice.

The sun passed behind a cloud about then, darkening the bayou and the light in his eyes. It was a good thing I didn't believe in foreboding signs. "Yes. I'm ready," I said with confidence.

I locked up the house, and Evan led me to his driveway.

His hand rested at the small of my back, guiding me. Men are clueless about how that simple gesture can stir up a storm of emotions. But then, perhaps it's solely dependent on who the man is.

I slid into Evan's Lexus convertible and we cruised in style toward what he called the "Little Chapel in the Woods." He turned and smiled at me. "Thanks again for being my date this evening."

"You're welcome." I fiddled with the buttons by the window. "It'll take my mind off the thing I just did."

"The thing you just did? Whatever it was, it sounds illegal."

I laughed. "Maybe all careers in sales should be illegal. I just quit my job. It was in oilfield equipment. . .sales."

Evan pulled out of our subdivision and into heavy oncoming traffic like a salmon headed upstream. "So, do you have a backup plan?"

"No, there's the rub, or I should say, there's the poorhouse. No plan. I left suddenly. . .for ethical reasons."

"Really?"

I picked at the loose beads on my purse. "They wanted me to stretch the truth about their products."

"Oh, I see."

"They paid me very well, but in the end they left me no word choice but good-bye. I hope I never make that mistake again. In fact, it makes me want to run from anything that smacks of dishonesty or anything that feels like an embellishment. I no longer think we should ever arm-twist or manipulate people. Don't you think?" Wow, it felt good to say that. I took off my hat, since it was making my head sweat. "So what do you do for a living?"

Evan took a deep breath and then said, "I'm a motivational speaker."

Chapter 2

What were the chances of that? Evan glanced over at me, and I knew he was gauging my reaction. But I refused to wear a mask of delight over his not-so-exhilarating news. "Motivational speaker?" *One of those?*

"You look like you're about to say, 'So, you're one of *those*?' I promise you I'm not just a man with a toothy grin who arm-twists and manipulates people with clever platitudes."

"What *are* you then?"

He swerved, getting out of the way of a squirrel on the road.

I tugged off my lace gloves, which were getting as itchy as day-old mosquito bites. "I don't mean to be confrontational. I'm just curious about *that* kind of profession."

"You make it sound like I'm a gangster." He chuckled at his own joke, but it lacked some of his initial vitality.

Gangster, indeed. Little did Evan know that my best friend, Lucy, had been engaged to a motivational speaker. Turned out he was full of deceit, false teachings, and a penchant for seedy behaviors. Of course, Lucy had never been good at picking boyfriends, and Evan was innocent until proven guilty, but I was going to keep a watchful eye on him.

"To answer your question, I'm a man trying to honor his father's legacy."

"Legacy. Finch. Of course." Why hadn't I figured that out? "You're Martin Finch's son? Wow, your father's a pretty famous guy." Best to keep the conversation light.

"*Was* a pretty famous guy." He glanced at me, his expression strained. "My father passed away last year."

"I'm sorry to hear that. I had no idea." Guess I should have known. My spirit melted. "I'm sure you miss him."

"He was an amazing man. He not only believed everything he ever said, he lived it."

"And you?"

"I'm a man of doubts at times. . .about my job. . .but I'll get there."

I guess even motivational speakers weren't up all the time. Hmm. Maybe Evan's doubts made him seem more human, more approachable.

He pulled up in the parking lot of the chapel and cut the engine. "By the way, I never mentioned who was getting married today."

"Is it a friend of yours or a relative?"

"Her name is Julie Stravinsky. She's a friend of my family. Because none of my aunts and uncles had any kids and because Julie was a close neighbor of theirs, well, my aunts sort of adopted her."

"Your aunts must be very kindhearted." In fact, I had to

admit, they sounded like the McBrides.

"You'll like them if you can survive the smothering. When I tease them about it they remind me that the word *smothering* proudly contains the word *mothering*."

I chuckled as Evan came around to the passenger side. He helped me out, and like a gentleman, he held out his arm to me. "Shall we?"

It might be nice to put my concerns aside for a little while and make the best of the evening, especially since his aunt Evelyn had spoken so highly of him. I circled my arm through his, and together we strolled on a stone footpath through a canopy of piney woods. The chapel was just ahead in the clearing. Pretty place to be married. I filed that bit of info away for future reference should I have need someday. *Lord, will I ever have the need?* Maybe not, if I kept concentrating on the faults of every guy I went out with.

"You must be a spontaneous person," Evan said. "You know, coming with me at the last minute like this."

"To be honest, I stepped out of my comfort zone to do this. I usually don't breathe unless my day-planner gives me permission."

He laughed.

"I don't need my day-planner right now, though. I've decided to take some time off. See who I am. . .you know, who's been hiding under all that sales training and stress."

"Sounds like a season of reflection."

"That's what I'm excited about *and* afraid of." Evan's arm felt sturdy enough for both of us, so I relaxed.

The path through the woods opened up to a meadow, and on a rounded hill sat the Tuscany-style stone chapel with heavy oak doors. "It's beautiful, Evan. Look at those arches. Are those flying buttresses?"

He leaned close and said, "You'll have to watch your language in the chapel."

I gave his arm a shake and grinned. "To think this place was here all along and I never knew it. Something so close, and yet it might as well have been a million miles away."

"It *is* beautiful." He looked at me with brown eyes amiable enough to warm up a cold muffin.

Get a grip, Heather. It was impossible to miss his meaning. This guy had enough charm to hypnotize a basket full of cobras or a harem full of women. "So will your mother be here, too?"

"No, I'm sorry to say that my mother texted me and said she was too tired to come."

"I'm sorry to hear that, too." We continued to chat as we followed a decorative sign with a golden arrow—apparently we were in need of guidance—which led us away from the chapel and off to another stone building.

When we arrived at the front door, Evan inhaled like he was about to dive underwater. "You want to talk pressure? Okay, here we go. Get ready for the gauntlet."

I stiffened. "Gauntlet?"

"Of aunts." He opened the door, and within seconds we were milling around in a marble-floored entry hall amidst classical music, throngs of people, and bolts of swishing chiffon.

A woman who seemed to have several different hairdos going all at once approached us in a gust of delight. "Evan, you're finally here. We were getting wor-ried," she singsonged as she turned to me. "And who do we have here? What a pretty thing, and a yellow hat, too. You look like a butterfly about to take off. But don't go too far. We want to know every little detail about you." She winked at Evan and hummed a few bars of "Here Comes the Bride."

Before Evan could respond, another woman dashed over to us, wearing an eruption of periwinkle taffeta, and said, "Evan, you must bring your new girl over for supper sometime. I can tell she's a peach."

More of the aunts gathered around us—bubbling and sparkling as if they were flutes overflowing with Pellegrino—and so Evan made a formal introduction. I was greeted and hugged and loved on until my dress was crushed and my heart was melted. Even though they were as subtle as a barrel full of nutmeg when the recipe called for a dash, it was easy to see why Evan was so fond of his aunts.

Then Evan led me around the room, introducing me to a host of his friends. What a crowd. They all adored Evan. There was a considerable amount of enthusiasm over me as well. In fact, I think I heard the words *Heather Finch* erupt from someone's lips. Guess they were trying the name on for size.

Evan cupped my elbow and steered me to a quiet corner, away from the undulating crowd. "Pretty intense, huh?" he said. "You should see them when I *don't* come with a date.

They're much worse." He eased down on one of the gilded benches that lined the entry hall.

"Ohhh. I get it now." I sat next to him. "I'm the decoy."

"Exactly." He fingered the long ribbon from my dress that lay curled on the bench. "But you're the prettiest decoy I've ever seen. And you smell like roses." He smiled, and the expression could have been labeled a classic. It could almost make me forget about my misgivings concerning his livelihood. After all, I'd never once heard them speak, father or son. I glanced at a clock on the wall. "Isn't it time for the wedding?" The laughter that had surrounded us had been replaced with whispers. Not a good sign.

"The ushers should be moving the guests inside by now." He looked around the room. "Something's not right." He went over to talk to a couple of his friends. One of the young men said something in his ear. Several people frowned and shook their heads. Looks of distress and exasperation trickled through the crowd.

What was going on? Was someone ill? Evan sat back down next to me, looking perplexed. I knew what had happened before he even said the words.

Somebody has cold feet.

Chapter 3

"What's wrong?" I touched Evan's sleeve.

"Julie's in the bridal room. She's having second thoughts."

"Oh my." I really didn't want to be right. "She must be so scared with all of us out here, trying to hurry her up."

Evan rested his elbows on his knees. "The family asked me to talk to Julie since she doesn't seem to respond to her family or her closest friends. She has the door locked, and she won't let anyone in." He stared at his hands and then at me. "But I don't know what to say to her."

"But you're the obvious choice. I mean you talk for a living. Right? You say positive and convincing things all the time. It's bound to work." I fiddled with the ruching on my dress, nearly tearing it.

"But I haven't been close to Julie since we were kids." He looked at me with a questioning stare. "Anyway, I told the family *you'd* talk to her."

I shot up off the bench. "You did what?" I lowered my voice. "I've never been in love. I've never had a daughter. Or counseled anyone. I'm totally incompetent when it comes to this sort of thing. It would be just as easy for me to dock a ship. I mean, we're talking cataclysmic damage here."

"Come on now." Evan pulled me back down on the bench. "They thought it would be a good idea, because you're a stranger. She'll be more likely to listen to you. You know, a neutral party."

"I highly doubt Julie would listen to me. But even if she did, I don't know if I'd want her to. I don't want this kind of responsibility. I mean, if I talk her into it, which is surely what the family wants me to do, then what if it's the wrong choice for her? What if this is God trying to tell her that this is the biggest mistake of her life? I see trouble either way." I was sweating now. I took a tissue out of my purse and wiped my face. But it didn't help much. At the rate I was perspiring, I'd need a roll of paper towels. "My sister Lily is a counselor. She'd be perfect, but not me."

A host of people stared at me now, including a young man in a tux who was wringing his hands. Must be the groom.

A woman who looked like she might be the bride's mom came over to me. "I'm Josephine, Julie's mother. I guess Evan has explained to you what's happened, but if you feel uncomfortable with our request, we understand. It's just that my daughter has locked the door, and she doesn't seem to want to speak to anyone she knows. Not even Roger. . .or me. Maybe she'd talk to you. I know this must be upsetting, but I assure you that we don't expect you to have all the right words. You could just listen to her. Be there for her. Do you think you could do this for us?"

The woman's expression, bordering on frantic, was so

beseeching I couldn't find it in my heart to say no to her, but I wasn't going to sugarcoat my feelings or make any guarantees. "I wouldn't feel right about talking her into a lifelong commitment just to appease the guests or just because a lot of money is on the line."

"I understand. We just want our daughter to be happy. We know it can't be about the money. So, please, just listen to her."

"Okay. I'll do it." I rose off the bench.

The woman's shoulders relaxed in what looked like pure relief. "Thank you." She gave me a hug. "I'll take you to her."

With a sea of eyes on me, Josephine led me down a hallway. When I looked back at Evan, he mouthed the words, "Thank you."

I wanted to respond, but my face had gone numb. And my poor stomach. Who knew what was going on in there? Deep breath.

Josephine led me to an ornate door with a cherub adorning the top of the molding. I stood there staring at the angel, trying to gather my wits. When I turned around, Josephine was gone. Left to fend for myself here in this long darkened hallway. How would I react to my newfound philosophy under such enormous pressure? There was an emergency exit at the other end of the hallway—the little red light winked at me, giving me permission to make a run for it. So easy to run and hide. *Oh Lord, what can I say to the young woman behind this door?*

I tapped ever so lightly on the door. "Hi. Heather McBride

here. I'm a stranger." *That sounded lame.* "They thought you might like to talk to someone who's a disinterested party. I mean, I'm not uninterested in your plight, but I'm someone who doesn't have an agenda. I'm not going to try to talk you into anything. Okay? I've just come to listen. Are you there?"

Nothing.

I banged my knuckles together. What now? My mind deserted me and became a barren land with a few miserable cacti. "I'd feel pretty stupid if I found out I was talking to an empty room." My voice had a tremor I couldn't control.

"I'm here," came the words from behind the door.

"Well, do you want to let me in? I mean, it's okay if you don't want to let me in, but it's going to be hard with this wood between us. I'll have to holler."

After a heartbeat or two I heard a tiny *click*.

Chapter 4

Good. An open door. *Thank You, Lord.* I let myself in. The bridal room was dimly lit, and elevator music wafted around the space, making it seem more like a funeral parlor than a bridal chamber. The bride stood in front of a full-length mirror, with no expression on her delicate features, except for an occasional sigh accompanied by a hiccupping sob. Her eyes were puffy-red, and mascara had drizzled here and there where she'd dabbed her tissue.

"I let you in just now because you sound more scared than me," she said.

"I *am* scared. . .spitless."

"You look like it. Kind of pasty, like you're going to pass out. Maybe you'd better put your head between your knees."

"Isn't that for nosebleeds?"

Julie grinned. "Maybe."

Well, at least I got her to break a smile. "Look, I've never been trained in counseling, so I might be useless to you. And I've never been in love, so I'm not qualified in that respect either. But I can listen to you. . .that is, if you have anything to say." I stole a few glances around the room. It was fairy-tale luxurious, trimmed in gold and velvet like Cinderella's coach. *Oh Lord, how did I get here?* I sat down with snail-like slowness. When my posterior had made sufficient contact with the seat, I straightened and smoothed my dress.

"Why are you moving like that?" Julie asked.

"You look frightened. I don't want to scare you off."

"Oh. I'm Julie, by the way. But I guess you knew that. I'd shake your hand but mine's covered in snot."

"No problem." I chuckled and handed her a box of tissues off the bench. She didn't look more than twenty-one. Pretty young for marriage. But then again, who was I to say?

Julie blew her nose. "You're a stranger, so what are you doing at the wedding?"

"Evan brought me."

"Evan Finch?"

"Yeah."

"He's a great guy," Julie said. "You should marry him."

"Well, let's concentrate on one wedding at a time."

She sat on a bench across from me, her elegant gown billowing around her. She gave her dress a punch, letting the air out. "I know a lot of money has been spent today. My dad keeps saying 'twenty thousand dollars' like every five minutes. If I don't go through with this, a lot of people are going to be mad. . .and hurt. I can hear it now. They'll all call this day tragic."

"But it would be much more disastrous if you married a man you didn't love."

Julie sprang from her seat. "But I *do* love Roger. And he loves me. . .so much so I can't believe it."

"Then why aren't you out there marrying him?" I raised my voice a notch.

Julie picked at a thread on her lovely gown, and one of the beads fell off. I prayed it wasn't one of those threads that could take apart the whole gown, releasing seed pearls like raindrops flooding the room. "Mendacity," she mumbled.

"Did you just say mendacity?"

"Yeah." She wiped her nose. "Have you ever seen *Cat on a Hot Tin Roof*?"

"Sure. It's a play. Tennessee Williams. Won the Pulitzer Prize for Drama. Why?" Where was this conversation headed? Were we going to cover famous plays now?

"Because *mendacity* is the word that pops into my head when I think about my sister. While I was getting ready in here I overheard what was being said in the ladies' room next door."

"And what did you hear?" I leaned forward, ready for some serious answers.

"My sister told someone that she filed for divorce. She hasn't even told our family she was having problems in her marriage. They must have been pretending all these years." Julie looked at me. "Even if you were a counselor, Heather, I'm not sure what you could say to that."

I took off my hat, set it on the floor, and dabbed at the sweat trickling from my scalp. "What you've said is pretty heavy, I admit. And I'm very sorry for your sister. But what does that have to do with you and the man you love. . .right here and now?"

Julie frowned. "It has everything to do with it. When they first started out, I know they adored each other. I'm certain of it. Then they lived a lie. And now they're divorcing. If they can't make it, how will Roger and I ever last a lifetime?"

"Are your parents divorced?" I was grasping at straws now. *Lord, help me.*

"No. And they still love each other after thirty years."

"That sounds pretty impressive. So it can be done. You've seen it firsthand. You can't control people, Julie, or circumstances, or much of anything in this life. In fact, everything imaginable will try to break you and Roger apart over the years. People, temptation, pride. You name it. There are no guarantees, but if you put God at the center of your marriage and pray together, you'll have a fighting chance. You'll have the best chance."

Julie nodded as she fiddled with the delicate chiffon folds in her dress, first scrunching them and then smoothing them out. "I can't tell if you're trying to talk me into it or out of it."

"Neither. Although, if you told me you had doubts about your love, then I'd say walk away. Run, in fact. But just remember, this day isn't about your sister's divorce. . .it's about the love and vows between Julie and Roger."

Julie walked over to the mirror again, adjusted her pearl cap sleeves, and gave herself a serious look. "You're right. It's about us. No one else."

Someone tapped at the door, startling us both. Oh dear. The vultures were gathering. "I'd better get that. It's all right.

It'll just take a sec." I hurried to the door and opened it a crack.

Evan stood there, wide-eyed and a little pasty himself. "Everything okay in there?"

"Yeah. Why?"

"I think Josephine is about to pass out."

"Really? Give me five minutes, Evan. I think it's going to be okay."

"Has anyone ever told you that you look cute when you're petrified?"

I grinned and eased the door shut.

"Okay, Julie, I'm back."

She placed her palm against the oval mirror. "You know, the first time I saw Roger I was at a coffee shop. I was at a table by the window, and for some reason I put my hand on the glass—just thinking, I guess. And he came up to the window from the outside and put his hand up to mine on the other side of the glass. And you know what I thought of?" She lifted her hand from the mirror.

"No, what?" My foot started tapping without my permission. I had to hold my leg to get it to stop. I hoped Julie could make up her mind soon. I could imagine everyone waiting out there, preparing for a meltdown. I felt the pressure like a water heater about to blow.

Julie turned back toward me. "I thought how much I wanted that stranger on the other side of the glass. . .with me. You know, to get to know who he was. What he was all about. Now, here I am. Roger's on the same side of the glass with me." Her hand flew to her mouth. "Oh dear."

"Oh dear? What's the matter?"

"I guess I lost my focus, Heather. I somehow forgot what Roger and I had. . .what we still have. Well, that is if I didn't mess things up with him." She said in a panic, "Oh, what will he think of me, hiding in here like a pouting child? Please tell me I haven't messed this up. Did he seem angry?"

"No. . .just very concerned about you."

She sighed. "That is sooo Roger. A lot of men would be angry or hurt. . .but that's how rare and wonderful he is." Julie came to me, took my hands in hers, and lifted me from the bench. "Thank you for helping me see I was about to make a terrible mistake by turning him down." She hugged me and then pulled back. "Do you think he'll still want to marry me after I've embarrassed him in front of his family and friends?"

"I do."

She smiled.

Billy Joel's song, "Just the Way You Are," wafted through the overhead speakers. Julie's hands waved like swans taking flight. "That's our song. Can you believe it? It's like a sign." She jumped up and down, laughing and singing along with Billy.

To keep with the festive mood I jumped up and down with her. When we were played out I looked down. Then Julie looked down. My hat was stomped to death—flat as a tortilla.

"Oh, I'm so sorry about your hat." She fanned her hands in distress again.

I picked it up. The hat had lost all its poise. "I should pay you. I think I secretly hated this hat." I gave it some good wrist action, making it sail across the room.

Julie giggled. "Please go tell everybody out there. . .let the wedding begin!" She took her veil off its stand and fluffed it.

"Are you sure you're not doing this out of pressure?" I caught her gaze.

"No pressure." She shook her fingers as if conducting an orchestra. "Just love."

I gave her another hug. "All right then. I'll send your mother in so you can get cleaned up a bit."

"Hurry, please."

"Okay, okay." I went over to the door and opened it.

"Heather?"

"Yes?"

"Thank you."

"You're welcome."

"But go, go, go." Julie shooed me. "We're already running late!"

"Got it." I left the room and speed-walked toward the entry hall. The guests were huddled together like a school of fish, and they sort of swam toward me as one entity. The man who I guessed to be Roger broke away from the group and rushed up to me.

I gave Roger a smile and a nod. Then, not wanting to torture the family with more delays, I repeated Julie's words to the crowd. "She said, 'Let the wedding begin'!"

The guests cheered, and someone even tossed their rice in the air. I felt like I was inside some strange enchantment. I felt a little giddy, too.

But where was Evan? I didn't see him anywhere in the crowd.

Chapter 5

Julie's mother touched my arm and gave me a squeeze. Her eyes misted over, and I could see the gratitude in her face. "Julie wants to clean up a bit," I said to her. Before I could say any more, Josephine ran down the hallway toward the bridal room.

Roger gave me an enthusiastic bear hug. "Thank you. Thank you. Thank you. Can I buy you anything? Flowers? A day at the spa? A new car?"

Chuckles trickled through the guests.

"What did she say?" Roger whispered to me.

"Julie loves you very much," I said. "She'll explain everything to you later. All is well."

"I'm just so happy everything's okay." Roger drifted off into the crowd, looking bleary-eyed with joy. A man lit from the inside, a man in love. People patted him on the back and gave him friendly hugs and slaps.

I felt a tug on my arm—Evan.

He pulled me aside. "What in the world did you say in there?"

"Right now it's a blur. Where were you?"

"I stood right back here," Evan said, "praying for you."

Nice. My opinion of him was gaining momentum. "Thanks. You know, they both really do love each other. Julie just lost her way for a bit."

"You are inimitable, aren't you?" He smiled at me, and I almost turned away from the attention. But not quite.

"Well, I *am* getting inimitably hungry. All this stress has made me ravenous."

He grinned. "I hear they've planned quite a wedding feast after the ceremony, so I think your hunger will be taken care of soon."

I realized that my hair must look as matted as a seal pup's. "Off the subject, do I have hat hair?"

"No, why? Hey, what happened to your hat?"

"Wedding casualty. No problem. I hated that hat."

"I did, too."

My lips made a little *O*.

"I hated it because it covered up your beautiful hair." Evan gave his head a shake.

I laughed.

"I mean that. By the way, the bride's family is missing an usher, so they've asked me to fill in. Do you mind waiting for me while I seat some people?"

"Not at all. Go ahead." He escorted me into the foyer of the chapel, and I waited while he ushered some of the family and friends to their seats in the sanctuary. It was nice to bury myself in the corner for a while and unwind after such a wild ride with the bride. I took in a few deep breaths. It was impossible not to wonder how things would have gone if

I hadn't resigned from my job and gotten in touch with my candid side. Perhaps I would have tried too hard to talk Julie into marrying Roger and she would have felt manipulated. Maybe she would have called it off, and there would be no wedding at all. How many times over the years had I just said what others expected me to say? Parroted what they wanted to hear?

Well, no more.

Someone coughed behind me, and I turned toward the sound. A middle-aged, tuxedo-clad gentleman stood near me, lighting a cigar.

The nerve of the guy, wanting to puff on a smelly cigar in the church, at a wedding. "You can't smoke in the chapel," I said to him.

"I'm going to smoke, and no one's going to stop me." The man's face and neck flushed red.

I stuck out my foot and tapped my size-eight shoe against the marble floor. "That's inappropriate as well as noxious."

"So?" He shrugged.

Without thinking, I reached over, yanked the cigar out of his mouth, opened the chapel door, and tossed the burning mess onto the concrete steps like it was a ticking bomb. "Thank you for not smoking in the church," I said, trying not to glare at him for his rudeness.

"I know who you are," the man said. "You think you own the day since you talked Julie into marrying my son."

I studied him then—his clenched jaw, his ruffled hair—and I felt a pang of sorrow for Julie, that she'd have to endure such a cranky father-in-law. "So Roger is your son?"

"He is indeed. Roger is all I have left. I lost my wife six months ago, and he's our only. . ." The man yanked a handkerchief out of his pocket and wiped his eyes. "Have you ever had a child, Miss Whoever-You-Are?"

"No, I haven't."

"Then you can't understand. Roger was always the brightest part of our lives. . .our treasure."

"But after the wedding Roger can still be the brightest part of your life. And with Julie and possibly some grandchildren in the future, you'll have even more treasures," I said as quietly as I could so no one would overhear us.

"My wife didn't like Roger's pick for a wife. She always said that Julie wasn't good enough for our son. We're all graduates from Harvard, and Julie didn't even get her high school diploma. When she was pulling out of the wedding, I thought it was an answer to my prayers. And then you showed up with your emotional bandages and turned it all around again."

My stomach went as sour as his expression. "I'm very sorry for your loss. I really am. But they do love each other. And Julie seems like a lovely girl. Perhaps you could help her get her diploma. If you don't embrace Julie, you might lose your son. Surely you don't want to grow old alone. . .not to have your family around you."

"I'm honoring my wife's wishes by opposing the wedding," he said.

"But in a few minutes the wedding will begin. . .with

or without your approval. Roger and Julie will go on living and loving without you. Wouldn't you rather be on the inner circle of that love than on the outside, looking in? I can't imagine that your wife would want this kind of life for you."

"Who *are* you anyway?" the man asked.

"I'm Heather—"

"I don't mean your name. I just can't imagine who you *think* you are. God? Is that what you think? You've meddled with my affairs, changed the course of our lives, and now you're lecturing me on how I should live and feel." He spat out his words.

I wanted to throttle him as much as I wanted to offer him a hug. "I'm sorry. I only meant to help."

The man shook his head at me. He lumbered away from the sanctuary, down a narrow hallway, and away from the happy day.

I shook my head, shocked over the harshness of his words, and my words. But more than anything I felt distressed that I'd added to the suffering of another person—to a heartbroken widower. *Oh God, what have I done? Please be with this man. Show him extra mercy because of my interference. Bring him peace and a way out of his misery, that he might embrace his new family. A new life.*

Evan came up to me in a hurry. "Sorry you had to wait so long. There were more guests than I thought. We can be seated now. Are you ready? You look a little pale."

I stumbled a bit and Evan caught me. "You okay?"

Chapter 6

I tried to straighten my shoulders, but I felt withered on the inside like a flower tossed into the fire. "I'll be all right."

"Do you need me to take you home?"

"I just want to sit down." I attempted a smile. "Would you please escort me into the sanctuary?"

He offered his arm. "I'd be happy to."

The chapel's interior was gaspingly lovely—a cathedral ceiling, clear glass windows overlooking a small woods, and a rough-hewn cross at the front. The beauty of it felt so inspiring I thought the walls and the woods might break out into the "Hallelujah Chorus." The peace surrounding the place and the worshipful moment eased my anxious thoughts.

After we were seated, the bridal march began, the audience swooned appropriately, and the ceremony commenced. Evan glanced over at me from time to time with concern while the minister talked to the couple and to the audience with reverent and joy-filled words.

The couple appeared to be drenched in a sunburst of happiness. I was not at all sorry for what I'd said to Julie. How could I be? And yet my spirit ached for the father who was grieving, who had said good-bye to his wife and could not seem to say good-bye again so soon. *Lord, help him to see that this doesn't have to mean good-bye.* And there was a lesson in it for me as well—not everyone feels blessed when presented with the truth. Some people feel persecuted, not liberated.

*

Thirty minutes later we shared a splendid meal—minus the slightly tough chicken—and participated in all the festivities that surround a wedding. Then we watched as the blissful couple rode off into the sunset in a white stretch limo. The only sad part was that I never did see Roger's father again. Whether he showed up later I would never know. I just prayed he would recover from his anguish and anger and join his new family before it was too late.

Evan drove us home, and since there were still lingering rays of evening light, I invited him to enjoy the last of the glow with me on the porch. We chatted for a while, and rocked for a while, and listened to the black-bellied whistling ducks overhead. I never got tired of hearing them. While listening to Evan talk about his life, my original fears of his vocation began to dissipate.

I rose from the rocking chair, snapped off a sprig of my rosemary plant, and headed down to the bayou. Evan followed close behind. I went right to the edge, amazed that the water was still so high and murky from the early morning showers. Still moving and gurgling like an unsettled stomach.

I pinched the fronds on the rosemary, releasing its scent into the moist breeze.

Like the Spanish moss swaying all around us, my thoughts drifted back to the wedding. In the midst of my reverie, my body suddenly lost its stability and lifted off the ground.

Evan had gathered me up in his arms and was running toward the porch. "Evan, what is it?"

At first I thought he was being playful, but the alarm in his eyes and the tension in his arms told me to panic. "Evan!"

"It'll be all right."

Once we were on the porch he turned and looked toward the bayou.

"Please tell me what's wrong." I smoothed out my dress as best I could.

"The high waters brought in an unwelcome guest," he said, out of breath.

"You mean a snake? I've dealt with a few of those."

"No. An alligator."

I'd never been a baby about such things, but I tightened my grip around Evan's neck anyway. "Where did he go? Maybe we'd better call the fire department. Or the zoo. Or the army."

Evan laughed. "Yeah, and they might just say, 'Well, you live in Southeast Texas.'"

"Should we go inside? Haven't gators been known to climb porch steps?"

"I think we're fine up here. He's gone on downstream now."

The scary moment, which was enough to keep me

secured in Evan's arms, turned into something different as we looked into each other's eyes—a summons as old as paradise. "Except for the gator thingy. . .I enjoyed today." *Not the most starry-eyed words, Heather.*

"I enjoyed today, too."

"I guess you can put me down now." But I didn't loosen my grip around his neck.

"You still smell like roses. Heady and soft. . ."

The moment heated up like two eggs tossed on a hot summer sidewalk. *Maybe if you put me down a kiss would be more manageable.* "Aren't your arms aching? I'm not *that* petite. In fact, I need to go on a diet. A gym membership might—"

Evan kissed me—perhaps to taste my lips, but most likely to stop the flood of unnecessary information flowing out of my mouth. The kiss was a magnum opus, and we were just getting started. My wind chimes rang with approval. But then, maybe I was still under the spell of the tux. The only disappointing thing about the kiss was that it ended too soon.

"I guess you can put me down now."

"I will, if you promise not to be mad when I tell you something."

"Okay. I promise. I guess." I frowned. "Wait a minute. What is it?"

"I was just kidding about the alligator." Evan looked like he was holding something back—a laugh.

"What?" I wiggled my legs to make him put me down.

He released me as he laughed.

"Are you kidding me? I can't believe it." I planted my hands on my hips for dramatic effect. "You made it up just so you could pick me up and kiss me?"

"Yeah, that about summarizes it."

"That is sooo juvenile." I gave him a punch.

Chapter 7

"Yeah, but it worked." Evan placed his hands over his heart. "I was tempted beyond my endurance."

I gave him a droll little stare. "Excuse me?"

"Well, in that yellow dress you were like this Southern glass of lemonade on a hot day. And I had to have a taste."

"You're full of baloney. The cheap kind full of nostrils and hooves."

He laughed again.

I looked at him. "All right. It was kind of funny." I pointed my finger at him. "But don't do it again."

"Actually, I saw a log floating downstream, and for a second I did think it was an alligator."

"Nice try. You should have just kissed me. I had such a good time, there was no need for your little *ploy*."

"So, are you going to invite me in? Perhaps offer me a cup of coffee, which I'll refuse because it's so late?"

I rolled my eyes at him as I opened the door. We stepped inside my oversized living room.

Evan looked around, making himself at home. "What's the décor? I like it."

"I call it rustic elegance. I designed the rock fireplace myself."

"A real working fireplace. No gas logs for you. I like that," he said. "I'm sure it's plenty cozy in the wintertime."

"It is whenever the temperature dips below eighty degrees."

Evan grinned and touched one of my favorite scrapbooks on the mantel—the one covered in antique keys. "My mother was into this. Still is. Do you scrapbook?"

"Some. My mom had a scrapbooking shop on the Strand in Galveston, but she finally sold the business. We girls got some of the best merchandise before she sold everything."

"I see." He went over to the wall and studied some of the photographs that were matted and framed and lit with halogen lights. "These are amazing. Is that your signature?"

"It is. I dabble in photography. I don't know what I'm doing, but I love it."

He looked at me. "No way. This isn't a hobby. These could hang in a gallery."

"Thanks. That's nice to hear." He'd chocked up some points for his interest in my hobby. Most guys would already be yawning as big as overfed lions.

"I'm just being honest. I have a friend who opened a gallery in Round Top, and he's doing very well with his watercolors. Why not consider a career change to photography?"

Nice thought, but I didn't have enough confidence in my hobby to make it a career. *End of topic.* "Are you planning on staying in the neighborhood?"

"Okay, I guess you're shy about talking about your talent. In answer to your question, I think I *will* stay. . .for now. I like living out here away from the city. . .far from the madding crowd."

"Well, I know the house was an inheritance from your aunt. But you probably already had a house or an apartment when she gave it to you. Right?" I sat on my overstuffed couch, hoping Evan would follow me.

"I did have an apartment in Houston, but I let it go. With my career, I can live pretty much anywhere. And I do like my house, although I never envisioned living right next to a bayou. . .kind of swampy and dusky. But I have to say, it's nice to have a real home to come to after traveling. And Beaumont isn't too far away to get to an airport. So there's a lot to love about this place." He gazed at me. "The reason my aunt gave me the house was to encourage me to settle down. She thought it would be easier for me to snag a wife if I had a place like this. Good prenuptial PR I guess." He let out a little chortle.

"What's so funny?"

He sat down next to me "I think your frankness is rubbing off on me. I wouldn't normally have said anything like that."

"My honesty can be endearing stuff if I'm not using it to club somebody over the head."

He chuckled.

"And just for the record, your aunt was right about the house. Women have a need for security. Even if they don't think it's what they're after. They're hardwired that way." I picked up a throw pillow and held it close.

"And is it the way *you're* wired, too?" he asked.

"Yes. So much so, that I didn't give my profession enough thought. My father offered to help each of us girls to get set up in a business. I'm the only one who didn't take him up on it. Maybe I should have, but I just went for whatever would make money. I wanted the security of a home, but I wanted to do it on my own. Be independent. Just in case I never married. I didn't want to feel the pressure to marry just to gain some security."

"And was it a good trade-off. . .this decision you made?"

"I don't know." I flicked and fiddled with the tassels on the pillow. "What about your career?" Good time to talk to about his business. Flush any last covey of quail out of the bush.

"I like what I do, but my presentations still need some tweaking." He settled back against the cushions.

My new assessment still held; he wasn't just some smiley lecturer spewing positive-thinking tripe. I rested back on the couch and let my stomach relax. "Maybe they're in your father's style, and you just need your own voice."

"So you no longer think I'm schmoozing my audiences?"

"I've never heard you speak. But now that I'm getting to know you, I think you seem. . . satisfactory."

He laughed. "Not quite the most glowing endorsement, but it'll do for now. I guess I'd better go. I have a speech tomorrow, and I have to get up early. I had a wonderful time."

"I did, too. I guess we've already said that."

"Oh, it never hurts the mood to hear it again." He drifted toward me.

Then Evan took the throw pillow out of my grasp, tossed it across the room, and moved closer to me. "Isn't that what you're supposed to do with throw pillows?" He reached up and fingered my dangly earring. "Amethyst?"

"My birthstone. Purple. Good. Color." I was no longer making sense. I guess the anticipation of a good kiss can do that—make the blood drain from one's brains, causing a regression to "see Spot run."

Evan's steady breathing picked up its pace suddenly, which harmonized well with my ka-banging heartbeat. I wanted desperately to touch his hair, but it looked so perfect I thought my fingers might cause a breach in protocol and set off some kind of alarm.

"Your skin is so soft." he whispered.

"It's the chemical peel."

"Uh-huh." He leaned over to my ear and whispered, "I'm not buying it."

"And the one-hundred-dollar moisturizer I keep on the shelf in my—"

Evan ignored my ramblings, which I'd been hoping for, and made some serious contact with my lips.

Oh yeah. A more dreamy-eyed woman might say that the world did indeed spin for a reason. She might even say—in a moment of weakness—that his kiss was warm Godiva melting over a scoop of Ben & Jerry's. But just as I was revving up for a sugar high, my cell phone came to life on the coffee table. We both startled. "Sorry, let me shut it off." No, better yet, let me get my sledgehammer.

"Maybe you should answer that. It might be important."

Whoever was texting me was officially scratched off my Christmas list. I picked up the phone. "It's a text from my friend Lucy. She says she has a surprise for me." I sighed. "Hope it's not what I think it is."

"You expect a problem?" Evan leaned back on the couch.

"Well, I think her boyfriend is about to propose, so that might be what she's talking about."

"And is he a good guy?" Evan asked.

"No, I'm afraid he's not."

"That's too bad then. I hope it works out well for her."

He rose to leave, and I suddenly hated cell phones more than the vacant promises of nonfat, decaf lattes.

"Perhaps your friend's surprise is something else. . .a new hat for you to hate."

I laughed. "Good positive spin. You're living up to your reputation."

"Sorry. Can't turn it off totally when I leave the stage. Hey, listen, I do a lot of Saturday speaking gigs, and tomorrow I'll be at the Hotel Gabriel doing a seminar for the Albright Business Women's Association. It'll take most of the day, but you could come toward the end. Say, five, and then I could take you to dinner. Would you be my guest?"

"I would love to see what you do." See the other side of Evan Finch. I walked him to the door, hoping we were going to start up where we'd left off. But he stepped out onto the front step and said, "Well then, good night. I'll look forward to tomorrow."

"I will, too. Good night."

I closed the door, put on my softy PJs, and sat on the bed, smiling all the way down to my bunny slippers. But my romantic sighs were soon replaced with worries over my lack of employment. Before I tucked myself in I padded to my computer. How had my resignation affected the world? Were they horrified? Did my boss regret all the unethical pressures he'd placed on me? Did my coworkers hear the news that I'd left? Would any of them miss me?

A trickle of e-mails had indeed come in, but nothing earth-shattering. Yes, fellow employees had gotten the news, and there were a few sad good-byes. My boss, Lex Luthor—okay, that wasn't *really* his name—mentioned the company's regret over my notice. He wished me well, but the e-mail was just a note of closure, with no hint of apologies or fanfare surrounding my departure. Sigh.

Was that what I'd expected? Maybe. The company would move on without me, like all the bayous flowing toward the Gulf. They would survive just fine. They would find others to fib in my place—people happy to have a job, any job, in a sluggish economy. Hmm. Not the best thoughts for a good night's sleep. But even with the roller-coaster ride that the day had put me on, I still fell into a drifty mode—dreaming of alligators and tuxedoes. And of Evan.

*

On Saturday morning I woke up, groggy, thinking that a black-bellied whistling duck was pecking on my head.

I rubbed my eyes and realized the tapping was somebody knocking on the front door. I looked at the alarm. After nine. I'd lost my business edge in less than twenty-four hours.

Whoever it was knocked again. Could it be my parents? Maybe they'd driven in from Galveston for a surprise visit. I did a quick-change routine into my denim jumper and T-shirt and went to the door. The peephole revealed Lucy and her boyfriend, Buddy. *Oh no.* Anything but that.

I smiled on, opening the door and offering my usual bear hug to Lucy. Buddy got my side-hug version only. "Hi. Come on in. I got your text." I wanted to spill everything to my friend—that I'd quit my job and I'd met an interesting man named Evan Finch—but it was sooo not the right time.

Our threesome settled in the living room, but it took Buddy quite a while to situate his hulking frame on my couch. I would have offered them something to drink, but that meant Buddy would stay longer. Uh, no.

I cleared my throat, and yet they remained silent. Buddy glanced around the room, twiddling his thumbs while Lucy looked as though she might burst.

"Luce, you said you had a surprise for me."

"Well," she began, "I thought it would be nice for Buddy and me to tell each of our friends in person rather than just call. So, let me tell you our good—"

"Our news," Buddy finished. "I'm sure Heather has other things to do, and she might want the short version."

Lucy wilted a bit but recovered. "Why don't you tell her, darling?" She lounged on his arm like it was a pillow.

"I'm trying, honey bunches. Just give me a chance." Buddy pulled his T-shirt down to cover some semi-revolting exposure. Then he turned to me with his nose high, as if he were Prince William asking for Kate's hand in marriage. "We're gettin' hitched," he said, with no flourish whatsoever. "Anyway, uhh, that's our news."

What was I going to say? I couldn't stand the guy. What a bedeviling mess!

Lucy held out her hand, showing off her ring.

"The stone is gigantic." *Wow, Buddy—big fake diamond, small brain.*

Lucy bounced on the couch, her flouncy dress bobbing with her. "And I want you to be my maid of honor." She looked at me with her puppy dog eyes. "Please say you're happy for me. . .for us. Please, please, please."

"Give her a chance, Lucy Goosy." Buddy oiled us with a big ol' Texas bubba grin, and my opinion of him—although dangerously low—plummeted into the basement.

To speak the truth now would be one of the hardest things I'd ever had to do. But I cared about Lucy's happiness. I cared enough to say what no one else would say.

Chapter 8

"I feel honored that you would choose me to be your maid of honor, but. . ." I stopped, thinking about how my next words should come out. How my word choice might change the direction and flow of their lives from here on out. It was way too much responsibility for one person.

Lucy clapped her hands together. "Oh, this makes me so happy. I can't tell you what that does for me, having my best—"

"Snookums, I think your friend isn't quite finished." Buddy glared at me. "You were saying?"

"You're right. I'm not finished." I looked away from Buddy and focused on Lucy. But staring into her hopeful eyes was torturous.

"Oh? Well, what were you wanting to say, Heather?"

"I know your mom died some years ago, Luce, and she would want to be here for this. To talk to you. Guide you. Give you advice."

"What kind of advice?" Lucy's eyes were as innocent as a lamb's being led to slaughter.

"Well, assess your situation, and weigh all the issues, and—"

"This isn't a business proposition," Buddy said. "It's a marriage."

I never knew anyone with so many auxiliary noises. Buddy had this talent for making assorted mumbly sounds after he finished talking, like when a car engine keeps rattling after you've turned it off. Very annoying. *Concentrate, Heather.*

"You are so sweet to always watch over me," Lucy said to me. "You've not only been a good friend, you've been like a big sister. But I'm—"

"Look," Buddy said to me, "if there's something you want to say to my fiancée, just spit it out."

"You're my best friend, Luce." I blinked back the mist in my eyes. "I care a great deal about you. . .and that's why I can't be in your wedding."

Lucy's eyebrows came together in a puzzled frown. "But what do you mean?"

"To be in the wedding party would put my stamp of approval on this marriage. And I can't. I don't think Buddy is worthy of you. Lucy, you are good and kind and respectful, but I haven't seen these qualities in Buddy. I just want you to marry someone who will know what a jewel you are."

Buddy rose off the couch, his body rigid, his eyes blazing.

I ignored his dragon routine and kept my attention on Lucy. "And if you'll notice, Luce, you've barely been able to finish a sentence since you've been here. If Buddy acts that way now, while he's on his best dating behavior, what will he be like after you're married?"

"Buddy's just excited about the wedding," Lucy said,

"That's why he keeps—"

"How dare you," Buddy said. "Lucy came here with good news, and you've trampled all over it like it was garbage." His stomach rumbled.

Lucy started to cry.

I went over to the couch and pulled her into my arms. "I'm so sorry for hurting you. I just don't see it the same way you do. You're making excuses for him. And I want so much more for you."

Lucy eased away from me. "I'm getting older, Heather. I'm thirty-four. I may never be proposed to again. Buddy is right about that. I don't want to be an old maid. I want to have a family."

"Let's go, Lucy," Buddy said. "We have lots of other friends and family who'll be happy for us. And my sister *wants* to be in the wedding." He raised his chin, which made his jowls do unsavory things.

Lucy stood next to Buddy. It was a scary sight, his large body hovering over her delicate frame like a storm cloud. Why couldn't she see it? She'd done it again—chosen a man who was far below her in every possible way.

They walked to the door, and I let them out. "You'll never know how sorry I am." I gave her another hug and whispered, "But I care about you too much not to speak my mind."

Buddy took her by the arm, and Lucy started to weep softly again as they walked toward his car.

I wanted to holler for her to come back, but what would I say? *Buddy, I can't wait for you to marry my best friend so you can smash her tender spirit with that Stone Age hammer you call a mouth?* I shut the front door. Was that twinge my ulcer gaining momentum? I leaned against the door and couldn't seem to move. *Lord, this feels horrible.* The truth no longer felt honorable. It felt cruel. I could have—should have—done better.

After I stood there for a while, pondering the clumsy moving parts of my mouth and the dull matter residing inside my head, I realized that truth was still right and good but could be swallowed more easily when dipped in compassion and sprinkled with gentleness. Two qualities that might have been sorely lacking in my diatribe. I still hadn't changed my view of Buddy—how could I?—but I knew I could have done a better job in sharing my concerns. I could have talked to Lucy in private. I could have found a better way to speak my mind without it turning into such an emotionally charged episode. Was my newly found need for utter straightforwardness turning me into a jerk?

I'd botched it big-time, and I might have lost my best friend forever.

The bell rang again. This time I opened the door to Evan. He was dressed in a handsomely tailored suit, looking optimistic and fresh, like he was ready to speak words of encouragement to a receptive and needy audience—like he could change the world.

He gave me a sunburst smile and I burst into tears.

Chapter 9

Evan reached out to me. "Heather, what's wrong?"

When I didn't answer, he stepped over the threshold and took me into his arms—even though he was fit for a presidential ball, and I'd just slunk out of bed into a soiled denim jumper. Apparently, I had no shame.

I stayed right there in his arms and breathed him in as he made soothing sounds to me. I had no idea what the protocol was after one date, but being near him felt comforting and right.

After a while he said, "Do you want to talk about it?"

"Maybe. Do you have a minute. . .or a month?" I tried to chuckle, but it came out sputtery.

"I have a few minutes. What's on your mind?"

We sat down in the living room and I told him my sad little story and how I'd wielded honesty like a machete instead of a torch of freedom. He didn't say anything for a moment.

"Okay, did you just need a listening ear, or did you want me to give you some advice?"

"That's nice of you to ask. Most people dump advice even when nobody asks for it. But yes, what do you think I should I do?"

"Maybe a letter of apology, not for the concerns you had about Buddy—they were valid—but for the way you presented it. I don't mean e-mail or text, but a real letter. Carries a lot more weight. Has a more serious, thought-out feel to it. And you could add something about your friendship, that you hope it can continue."

I touched his sleeve. "Your advice is good, and I'll take it."

"Good. I know this must be hard right now, having things uncertain between you both, but I promise it'll be all right. Maybe not immediately, but in God's good timing, He'll work this for good." Evan kissed my hand and then looked up at me. "I hope you'll still be able to come this evening."

"I will." I reached up and fingered his hair. Just couldn't resist. It wasn't as gelled as I thought it would be. "I love your hair. It's longer than mine, but it's also shinier. What's your secret?"

"I eat a lot of corn chips."

I laughed. "I've never gone out with anyone who looked so well-groomed. Most of my dates would look like bums next to you."

He grinned. "I hope I don't come off shallow."

"On most men it would be. . .but not on you for some reason. By the way, why did you stop by?"

"I'm not sure." Evan looked at me then, a serious attentiveness marking his features. "But there's an English proverb that says, 'A good beginning makes a good ending.'"

*

After a day filled with letter-writing—I kept tearing up drafts of my apology to Lucy—as well as hours of talking to God about my job-less horizon, I gathered enough energy to make it to Evan's speaking engagement in Beaumont. When I arrived at the Hotel Gabriel, I made inquiries at the front desk and then headed up the escalator to the main ballroom. It was quite a large hotel and more than a little posh.

Just outside a room, in front of two closed doors, sat an easel holding Evan's photograph, alongside a perky woman behind an official-looking table. She was obviously the gatekeeper.

"May I help you?" the young woman asked, brandishing a Chanel smile. The name tag on the lapel of her suit read SUZANNE.

"I know I'm arriving at the last of Evan's speech, but I just want to sneak in the back."

"I'm sorry. There's no 'sneaking' without a badge, and the badge is two hundred dollars."

"You're kidding. That much?"

The "thou-shalt-not-pass" gatekeeper chuckled. "Everyone who comes to one of Mr. Finch's seminars leaves feeling it was more than worth the money. I'm sorry you've missed the whole day. He's doing the wrap-up now."

"But you don't understand."

"Yes?"

"I'm Evan's date."

"Oh?" Suzanne ran her French-manicured fingernail

down a master list and then turned an interesting lobster-tail hue, which color-coordinated with her dress, I might add. "I'm so sorry. You must be Ms. McBride," she warbled.

"Yes, that would be me."

She stood and handed me a badge. "You won't tell Mr. Finch about my error, will you? I need this job, and I just love all the traveling. It's like this position—Mr. Finch's assistant—is tailor-made for me."

"No, Suzanne, I won't mention it to him."

"Thank you sooo much. It's just that Mr. Finch is like this American icon. People are always searching for heroes, and well, we have one in our midst today. Don't we? He's a great man, and I feel so honored to be here."

That's it. It's official. Somebody's infatuated with the boss. But I kept my thoughts to myself for a change.

The woman cringed. "I've gone on too much about him, haven't I?"

"Not if I were just an attendee. But since I'm his date. . . yeah, maybe you did." Couldn't help saying that. She had a thing for *Mr. Finch*. And she did ask.

"Sorry," she said. "Please don't—"

"I know. Don't tell Mr. Finch." I made a gesture like I was zipping my lips. "By the way, you have a big gob of spinach stuck. . .right there." I pointed to my teeth.

The woman, horror struck, grabbed a mirror and a tissue out of her purse. "Thank you so much."

"You're so welcome." I walked toward the double doors, smiling like a cat with a mouse tail wiggling in its teeth. *God, forgive me.* That honest moment was enjoyed a bit too much.

But I was also left with a nagging feeling. What was the advisability of a single Christian man choosing to travel with such an attractive assistant—and one who thought he was as dazzling as the rhinestones around her neck? What were the traveling arrangements like? And the temptations? For now, I set my concerns aside and went to the doors. I placed my hand on the handle then paused. I knew that whatever was on the other side of that door was going to change my life. I felt it in my spirit as strong as Turkish coffee. I acknowledged the internal caution and opened the door.

There was no way I could have ever been prepared for what I saw inside.

Chapter 10

The room—which made me think of the Palace of Versailles—was a huge ballroom dripping in chandeliers and gilded boiseries. My best guess was about five hundred women filled the room. A quick calculation money-wise—at two hundred dollars a pop—told me Evan was doing very well with his speaking engagements. But it wasn't the money that impressed me as much as the hush in the room. Every face tilted expectantly toward Evan or toward the two huge screens on either side of him that gave us the close-up version of his face. Every breath seemed to be frozen in time, as if the whole of the audience waited for permission to move, to exhale.

Who was this man up on stage? Perhaps Evan and Mr. Finch were two different people. I dropped my badge and scrambled for it on the floor. After getting a couple of dirty looks from some attendees in the back, I sat down on the last row and tuned in to his speech.

"Life can be brutal," Evan was saying. "The only way to live is to embrace God as your deliverer *and* as your intimate friend. Christ is unfailing in His devotion to you. He not only longs to spend an eternity with you, He wants to live with you now. . .in joy. . .as surely as you are breathing. You are His keepsakes, His daughters, and like a loving father, He wants so very much for you. But more than earthly gifts that pass away. He wants to touch your eyes so you can see life in a new way. He wants to press His hand to your heart and let it beat to a new rhythm. He wants to cup your face in His mighty but tender hands and say, 'You are more precious to Me than a thousand sunsets, a million stars in the heavenlies, and all the crowns of kings throughout the ages.' When you experience this, embrace this new way. . .His way. . .anything is possible."

He gripped the podium. "Perhaps because of life's hardships, you have sealed off part of your life—like a heavy stone rolled in front of a tomb. . .the part of you that can believe in a fresh start, in hope, in blessings, in redemption and love. You no longer have faith in the goodness of a loving Creator. You no longer believe you can leap into your Daddy's arms, and He will catch you."

There were a few sniffles in the crowd.

"The enemy," Evan went on to say, "makes us forget these truths. At times, I have forgotten, too. We all need reminders of what is important. . .what is everlasting. Reminders that the stone blocking our hearts wasn't meant to stay. It was meant to be rolled away. . .to let the light in, the grace, the forgiveness of Christ. To let the joy of eternity begin now!" He raised his voice to a feverish pitch.

Evan placed his palms together. "If we humans enjoy giving, especially if we have shiny new credit cards to break in. . ."

Chuckles trickled through the audience.

"Then how much more will our Father in heaven give good gifts—His light, grace, forgiveness, peace, and joy to those who ask Him?" He took the mike from the podium and walked to the edge of the stage. "As you leave today I want you to think about this. Ask yourself, 'Am I ready to receive?'" He gestured as if he were conducting. "Say it with me. . .am I ready to receive?"

The audience echoed back to him, "Am I ready to receive?"

"Say it like you mean it," Evan called back.

Everyone shouted in unison, "Am I ready to receive?"

After the booming replies reverberated around the room, all went silent again. Evan said, "The answer to that question must be resolved in the secret places of your heart." He lowered his voice, but the passion remained. "I pray your answer will be 'yes' to God and to flying free!" He raised his arm and then unfurled his fingers as if they were the wings of a bird taking flight. His gesture, graceful and emotive, matched the glitzy logo of a bird just behind him.

The spotlight intensified, and the crowd moved as one, rising in a roaring ovation. Cameras flashed. Evan bowed slightly and then rose with a glorious smile. He raised his forefinger in the air and shook it toward the heavens, which brought another round of applause.

I simply had not been prepared for what I'd witnessed. I couldn't have imagined the powerful and passionate way Evan could work a crowd. Even though the words had been simple, his delivery had been majestic—the way he clutched and caressed the podium, the way he murmured and sighed and thundered and romanced the audience until they were transfixed, until each person became a little wad of Play-Doh in his hands.

Music exploded around us—probably the theme music for the conference—and the crowd became energized again, heading toward the corner of the room where tables were set up with paraphernalia, with Evan at the helm of it all.

I stood in line with the other women, just wanting to watch the spectacle and think for a moment. If I began to care for Evan on a deeper level—and if I chose to put myself under the influence of his persuasions—how would I ever know if he was being honest or if he was just manipulating me with his engaging smile and silver tongue? Good, haunting questions that had no immediate answers.

I moved up in line. My greatest concerns about Evan were no longer relevant. He was using biblical principles to support his talks rather than pumping his audiences up with a lot of hot air from the prosperity gospel. And yet the idea of dating a showman kind of guy like Evan seemed, well, unnerving.

The local media homed in on Evan like locusts on a ripe cornfield, pointing their cameras at him and snapping photos. He didn't even seem to notice. He must be used to the attention.

Women were busy fawning all over him as they bought his wares and asked him to pose with them in photos. They didn't seem to care that their admiration was really flirtation with a little hero-worship thrown in. Or a lot. Just like his assistant, Suzanne, out in the hallway. That part made me sad and a bit perturbed at Evan for allowing it. Or was I merely jealous?

I moved up in line again. Two women were talking behind me, and it was impossible not to hear them.

"I went to college with Evan," one of them said.

"Really? Ohhh. What was he like? Tell me more," the other woman said.

"Mmm. There was always something dazzling about Evan Finch. . .even then. He was president of the student council, and everybody loved him. Well, the guys were usually annoyed with him, because their girlfriends would swoon over him when he walked by. Used to drive my boyfriend crazy, too. In fact, we broke up because of Evan. . .just because I couldn't keep my thoughts to myself."

Oh, you mean, like right now? I shifted my purse and shuffled my feet, feeling more uncomfortable by the minute. Unfortunately, though, I was intrigued by the dialogue. Kind of like not being able to take your eyes off a car wreck.

The other woman spoke up again, "I read in an article that Evan dates around, but he's not serious about anyone. Not yet, anyway."

"Okay then. Fair game. Maybe he'll ask one of us to dinner."

They giggled.

I drooped in my pretty new pantsuit like a rain-drenched petunia. It wasn't from the lack of air-conditioning. It just wasn't how I'd imagined the evening going.

The line moved faster suddenly, and when a large woman stepped away with her armful of DVDs and T-shirts, I stood smack-dab in front of Evan.

Another assistant handed him a DVD from a huge stack, and then Evan looked up and saw me.

Chapter 11

Heather, I'm so glad you're here." Evan rose and smiled at me. If smiles were money, his was a cool million. "I thought you'd changed your mind. You didn't have to wait in line." He came around the table and escorted me to a seat right next to him. "Here, this is where you're supposed to be."

He gave my hand a squeeze under the table. "Do you mind waiting until I can get through this line?"

"No, it's fine." *But we might need to talk later. Really talk.*

"Thanks." He went back to his adoring crowd, and in the meantime a few perplexed looks were shot my way. Perhaps the ladies wondered if I was competition. At the moment I wasn't sure what I was.

When the line of attendees was gone and everyone was satisfied—except for the women who were hoping for a dinner date with Evan—he turned to me and said, "You deserve to eat anywhere you'd like for having to wait so long. I don't usually have such a long line."

"I'm okay. I thought it was intriguing to watch."

He didn't look the least bit convinced. "What happened to honest Heather?"

I chuckled. "I'm still right here."

"Good. I wouldn't want you any other way."

I hoped he meant that, since I had a lot to say. Later.

Evan introduced me to the rest of his entourage—a mellow woman in charge of his DVD and T-shirt sales, a small, round sound dude, and his manager, Winnie, who came off like a warrior Viking. Someone who could keep Mr. Finch's schedule rowing forward no matter the weather. Interesting crew.

Evan took my hand. "Let's get out of here. Where do you want to go?"

"Can we go someplace we can talk for a while?"

"Sure we can. I know just the place." He led me downstairs to a quiet spot near an indoor stream and waterfall. "Is this all right?"

"Perfect." On closer inspection I noticed Evan had changed into yet another suit since I'd seen him earlier that morning. It appeared to be tailor-made and quite expensive. "Do you ever get casual?"

He laughed. "Not often. People always expect me to dress up."

"And do you *always* give the people what they want?"

"That's a loaded question, isn't it?"

"Probably."

"Got it." We sat down on the love seat. "I don't want to put words in your mouth, but I think I know what you want to talk about."

"You do?" I looked at my hands for a moment, wanting a

brief respite from those startling eyes of his.

"You're going to say that I'm no longer the person you thought I was. And you don't think you can see yourself in a more serious relationship with someone who does what I do."

"Maybe, but I'm trying to keep an open mind about it." *I am. Because I like you.*

"I generally get this talk after about the sixth or seventh date, after the novelty of what I do wears off. When women no longer feel as though they're with a celebrity but with an average guy whose job includes a lot of travel and being around crowds of women." He leaned toward me. "But because you're so honest and unmoved by theatrics and notoriety, you're cutting right to the chase. I'm impressed by that. So much so I'm hoping. . .no praying, you don't walk out on me right now."

"I'm still here." I gripped the couch and glanced upward. Two women were staring down at us from an upper level of the hotel, and they certainly weren't gawking at me. "But you have to admit, it's a lot to take in." I went on, trying to get my focus back. "I mean, I knew what you did for a living, and I had envisioned it. . .some. But I just wasn't ready for this level of popularity, the adoration."

"That's laying it on pretty thick. I just—"

A young woman—pretty as a spring garden in full bloom—rushed up to Evan and without even asking his permission handed him a DVD. He signed the cover and gave it back to her. "Thanks for coming today."

"Oh, you were wonderful, Mr. Finch. Because of you I can finally imagine. . .freedom." She opened her fingers like a bird in flight as Evan had done on stage and then winked at him. With a flick of her long hair she sashayed off as if a bit tipsy from being in his presence.

I leaned my head to the side, gazing at him. "I rest my case."

Chapter 12

Evan placed his palms together and touched his fingers to his lips. "I admit it. Some of the women do get a little worked up. But I don't pay much attention to that part of it anymore. Neither did my father. He was considered handsome and charismatic by the ladies, but he ignored their flirtations. He felt he had a calling on his life, and no one was going to stop him. When he handed the business to me he gave me some advice. He said we can't control other people, but we can control our reactions. He was faithful to my mother all his days, and I intend to do the same for my wife, whoever she may turn out to be."

"That's a beautiful speech, Evan. Very moving. And I admire your father for what he did and didn't do. But temptation is a wily beast, and it can take on many forms. The enemy is always checking the chain, forever testing, looking for that one weak link until he finds it. . .and breaks it."

"I agree it can be hard at times. I'm not completely immune to the flirtation. But I've made a decision, just like my father did. I want to be able to look in the hotel mirror at the end of a seminar and be able to like myself. And when I have a wife someday, I want to be able to go home and look her in the eyes without guilt or remorse." He took off his suit jacket, shook it out, and folded it across his lap. "You may not know this, but I give seminars for men as well as women. And some of the time, it's a mixed crowd. Meaning that the intensity isn't always at this level. I did this deliberately, you know."

"Did what?"

"I wanted you to see the worst scenario first. I like you—a lot already—and I was afraid to get my hopes up just to have this happen. This conversation. This disappointment."

"You know, for somebody who's a motivational speaker, you can be quite negative."

"What do you mean?"

I smiled. "I haven't gone anywhere, have I?"

A waitress came over, and we both ordered a Perrier with lime. We weren't even seated in the open restaurant area, and yet the woman seemed happy to wait on us. Then I noticed her wistful gaze directed at Evan.

"By the way," she said, "we're honored to have you in our hotel for your seminar, Mr. Finch. I hope it went well today."

"It did, thank you. Appreciate the kind words." When the woman left, Evan scooted closer to me. "So, you like me, in spite of what I do?"

"Yes. But I'm sure we'll have more of these conversations. Your lifestyle will take some getting used to."

He rested his arm on the back of the couch, almost touching me. "I think you have something that could make this work between us."

"What is that?"

"Honesty."

Hmm. I really wanted to tell Evan about Suzanne's crush, and for him to be watchful, but it didn't feel right to put her job in jeopardy, so I let it go. "I will say this. . .you should be aware of your surroundings. . .concerning women."

"Sounds like I'm being stalked by wild animals."

"Yes, actually." I raised a brow. "Look over your shoulder from time to time. And a bit of armor wouldn't hurt. . .biblical armor."

"I take my faith seriously," Evan said. "I'm not spouting words up there that I don't believe. . .that I don't live."

"I believe you. And God has indeed given you quite a gift. You could mesmerize people just by reading a grocery list."

He chuckled.

"I mean, right now you come off like this regular kind of guy, but up on stage it's like something else takes over. This magnetic, larger-than-life, beguilement thing happens that seems to sweep women off their feet."

"Maybe *you* should be my booking agent." He laughed.

"This isn't funny. . .Mr. Finch."

"Okay, I got it, Ms. McBride."

We couldn't seem to hold on to our seriousness, and our scowls morphed into grins.

The waitress popped back over and handed us our drinks.

After she walked away Evan said to me, "I know what you're saying is serious and important, but will you at least have dinner with me this evening? You can talk about my dysfunctional profession all you want to. I promise. But please say yes."

I took a sip of my water. "Are you sure you're not used to getting exactly what you want all the time?"

"I'm sure of it," Evan said. "I would be married if I got everything I wanted. I'd hoped to have a family by now, but no one will have me. Which is another reason my relatives are getting nervous. They've even suggested I give up the business so I can settle down. What do you think? Should I walk away from it all? Everything my father built?"

"You'll never hear it from me. That's between you and God."

He took something out of his pocket, unwrapped it, and slipped it into his mouth. "I keep thinking there's something *else* I'm never going to hear from you. You claim I can mesmerize a whole audience, but evidentially I can't even charm one of them long enough to go out to dinner with me."

Chapter 13

"What are you eating?"

"Herbal lozenge. Tool of the trade." He looked at me. "You're sneaky. You keep changing the subject."

"Okay. All right." I raised my hands in surrender. "I'll have dinner with you."

"Yes!" Evan leaped off the couch, lifted me into his arms, and twirled me around. "You've made me a very happy man."

It did feel good to be in his arms. I was falling a little for him in spite of my misgivings. I loosened his tie. "Better." I smiled. "But why me, Evan?"

"Because you're different." He released me. "To me you're this charming cottage with many rooms. Enough rooms to explore for a lifetime. *That's* why."

"Oh. It is hard to argue with such sound logic."

He chuckled. "Does everyone in your family have a good sense of humor?"

"In my family, you'd be in trouble if you didn't."

Evan sat back down, reached for his sparkling water, and made a little twister with his straw. "Any new thoughts about your job?"

"You mean my *lack* of one." I plopped back down on the couch and sighed. "No new thoughts. If I'm a house with many rooms, I think the rooms are empty right now."

"Are those the sighs of regrets I hear?"

"No, not at all. But where I go from here is still unclear. As I mentioned, I'll take some time off. Pray more than I ever have in my life. Panic a little, too."

"You sure you don't want to be a photographer?" he asked.

"It would bring me a lot of joy. But in spite of what you or Lucy says, I don't think I have what it takes to do it full-time."

Evan took a long swig of his Perrier and then set it down with an exaggerated gesture. "You know what? You talk a good talk about truth and how other people should accept it. No. . .you *demand* they accept it. And yet you can't even deal with the truth about yourself. That God Almighty has given you a talent—one He expects you to use. A talent you've chosen to hide under a bushel."

"You don't know me well enough to say that."

"Sorry to disagree," he said, highlighting each word. "But I think I *do* know you well enough to say it. And you know what else? You're not a bayou kind of woman. I can see you in a sunlit meadow. . .surrounded by bluebonnets. In an artsy community like Round Top, selling your work in a gallery there. Perhaps your very own gallery."

I was gathering up my verbal ammo to level Evan's pontification when a middle-aged woman came weaving over, carrying a glass of orange juice. A very *tall* glass of juice that sloshed as she walked toward us. The woman planted herself right in front of Evan and stared at him, her face pinched and red.

Evan pulled out his marker, ready to autograph something. "Yes? How may I help you?"

"You're Mr. Finch," was all she said.

"Yes, that's right."

The woman tossed her orange juice all over Evan's suit and then dropped the empty glass on the floor.

Evan gasped, and I sat stunned, not knowing what to say or do.

"What seems to be the problem, ma'am?" Evan rose and shook off some of the liquid, looking more perplexed than outraged.

"I went to one of your workshops several weeks ago. I took your advice and listened to my husband. Loved him. Stayed with him. Gave him one more chance. And he rewarded me by beating me up again. This time I could barely call 911. Your advice almost cost me my life, Mr. Finch."

"That grieves me to hear it. I'm so sorry. I wish you'd called my office. I would have talked to you."

"Well, I was kind of busy holding on to my life. But I did call later and your secretary woman. . .her name was Suzanne something. . .anyway, she wouldn't let me talk to you."

"Well, that just won't do. Do you mind telling me your name?"

"Bev Livingston."

"As far as I remember I never got your message. And my assistant will be reprimanded for this." Evan rubbed his chin.

"You know, I do remember you, Ms. Livingston. You had a very sad look on your face that day."

"I'm not sure how you could remember that."

"In our breakout session, did you mention that your husband had a history of violence?"

She lowered her gaze. "No."

"The reason I ask is because if I'd known your husband had this kind of background with abuse, I wouldn't have encouraged you to stay."

Her face flamed red. "So, you're saying this is *my* fault?" she yelled.

"Not at all," Evan said. "It's your husband's fault, and he belongs in jail."

"He *is* in jail. But now I'm going to need assistance. And some help with my kids. I don't know what I'm going to do."

"Once again, I'm sorry. Here's my card with my personal cell phone number." Evan handed her a business card. "I can connect you with the right people to help you and your children. I'll do whatever I can to make this right."

The woman held on to the card so tightly with both hands it almost tore in two. "Thank you."

"No problem."

The waitress came over to us. "Is everything okay, Mr. Finch? Should I call security?"

"No, not at all. Everything is fine."

"Okay." The waitress picked up the glass and walked away, looking unconvinced.

The woman turned to go, and when she was out of sight,

Evan's shoulders collapsed along with his smile. "I think I know what it feels like to be an old man." He squeezed the orange juice out of his tie.

"You handled that situation very graciously." Such patience and humility. That scene was like a hundred snapshots of Evan. Pretty revealing stuff about his character, and none of the images were left wanting.

"Do you think so? Thanks. To hear you say those words, well, it softens the blow. . .a little anyway."

"Does this sort of thing happen often?" I asked in my gentlest voice. "You know, people who get upset with you?"

He sat back down on the couch and stared straight ahead. "Not too often, but I hear stories you might not even believe. People come up to me during the breaks and tell me everything. Secrets they wouldn't even tell their spouses. They come to the seminars so needy and hurting." His voice was gravelly. "If I can point even one person to the true Comforter and Deliverer, then I have succeeded. Even if I botch it from time to time or if some people misunderstand me." He looked at me then, his jaw tightening. "But I hope Mrs. Livingston's husband stays in jail for a *very* long time."

"Me, too." I wasn't sure what else to say. Evan had lost his patina—his effervescent glow, the one that must come from the joy of helping people. And perhaps a little from the adulation and attention. He was human, after all. *And* he was back to being the Evan I'd met, a simpler guy. I had to admit, I liked him the regular way, even though it was sad to see him discouraged. I disliked myself for only being able to relate to the shorter Evan, the one who wasn't standing tall at that podium under the spotlight. Perhaps I was a one-dimensional person—only interested in men who were ordinary—because I was ordinary. As close as I felt to my sisters, I always thought I was the generic one on the McBride shelf of hand-painted cups. I was the scrapbook that never got full of photos. Of memories. Of life. I was Heather Ann—without the *E*. No more, no less. My sisters were the extraordinary ones with interesting careers, doing what they loved. I was the odd sister out, who had chosen sales and who was full of regrets. But then, perhaps lots of folks had the same kind of vision of themselves, which was why they flocked to seminars offering a way to see beyond their own skewed viewpoint.

In the meantime, I did something that took me one more step away from the old Heather—I took Evan's hand, unfolded his fingers, and placed my hand inside his.

"My fingers are all gooey from the juice," Evan said, his voice still heavy with emotion.

"I don't mind the stickiness." Then I reached up and kissed him on the cheek.

He let out a deep breath, and his body seemed to relax against the cushions.

The waterfall gurgled and splashed next to us, as it pooled and meandered through the hotel. But it was only a fake stream, going nowhere. Pretty, but without life. Before, I might have been tempted to describe Evan that way, but I felt there was more to discover about him. Much more.

Since the guest traffic through the hotel seemed to be less now and the moment felt more private, I rested my head on Evan's shoulder. We stayed that way for the longest time, quiet and content. We were a good fit, like a slipcover over a pillow, and we both knew it. I could not deny the joy and the growing affection between us, but only God knew if this connection was meant for a lifetime.

Chapter 14

When Monday morning arrived I woke up early, thinking about my Nikon. And then Evan. In that order. As I ate my breakfast, suddenly everything looked in need of being captured in more permanent images. The angles, the shadows, the design, and the grouping of objects—all of it came to life like dormant seeds after a good soaker. The camera and I became friends again, and there was a joy and freedom in it that I'd forgotten. Life was no longer about satisfying a list of customers, but satisfying my artistic eye. And so, for a few hours I forgot I was jobless. I forgot about everything. I was at play, and in my heart it felt like some kind of homecoming.

After hours of blissful creating, I took a lunch break. Just as I was biting into my tuna on rye the doorbell rang. I opened the door to a young woman with spiky red hair, a rose tattoo, and a bit of sass in her grin. She stood on the welcome mat with an enormous bouquet of bridal pink roses.

The girl yanked out her ear buds. "You Heather McBride?"

"That's me."

"Then these beauties are for you, eh." She handed the vase to me. "Cool, eh?"

"Yes, they're beautiful. Are you from Canada?"

"Naw, it's just that each day I pretend I'm from a different country. Keeps the job from sucking me dry. Know what I mean?"

"Sort of." I retrieved a ten out of my pocketbook and handed it to her. "Thanks."

The girl looked at it. "Sure. Say, I happened to notice the name on the invoice. Are these roses from Evan Finch, that speaker dude on TV?"

"Yes, that's him."

"Pretty cool. You must stay inflated all the time being around a guy like Finch. Yeah, an air pump for the soul. I'd be a florist today and not a delivery girl if Finch were *my* boyfriend. You know, somebody to believe in me. You're lucky."

"He's not really my boyfriend. We've only gone out a couple of times, but Evan is a good man."

"Oh yeah? I mean, a lot of people who get a little fame going, well, they go crazy with it. You know, they basically become self-absorbed jerks."

"Well, from what I've seen so far, Evan Finch is no jerk."

"Yeah, I could tell. He looks kind of flashy, but he has a real kind of smile." The girl nodded in a big way. "Cool."

I couldn't keep from staring at her tattoo. How could anyone make such a senseless decision? Should I speak up? "Listen, I know we're strangers and all that, but I just have to say something about your tattoo in case your mother hasn't warned you yet. It's always a bad idea. They're unhealthy, unsightly, and you'll regret it later in your life."

"Oh yeah?" The girl stumbled backward like I'd hit her. "Well, Evan Finch says that truth is like a laser, capable of great healing or harm. Just now, I think your words weren't under the heading of healing. Capiche?" She saluted me and then walked away. "Oh, and just so ya know. . .my mother is dead," she hollered over her shoulder.

"I'm sorry. 'Bye. Thanks." God help me. I got too pushy—again. "I really am sorry," I hollered, but she'd already climbed into her delivery truck. *Yes, indeed, I'm a sorry human being.*

I shut the door, pondering my Christlike love—or what was left of it. Was it more important to set the record straight or just to love? I'd been given a chance to inspire this young woman to pursue her dream as a florist, and yet what did I do? Instead of seeing her potential and encouraging her, I was blinded by her tattoo, blinded by my own judgmental attitudes. Hmm. When does a sense of rightness turn into self-righteousness? I lacked balance. Was that Evan's secret? For now, it would remain a paradox, playing hide-and-seek with me.

Willing to let the mystery go for the moment, I took a deep whiff of the roses and slipped the card from the bouquet. The note read, *You were right, Heather. Warmly, Evan.* Now what did *that* mean? Right about what? Well, if he had some bad news, he wouldn't have sent flowers. But then, maybe he thought the roses would soften the blow of something disappointing. This circular argument was going to drive me nuts, so I put on some makeup, clean jeans, and a frilly top, and marched over to Evan's front door.

I rang the bell and waited. What was that sound inside? I placed my ear to the door. Opera? And sour notes? Somebody was belting out a song from Puccini's *Madama Butterfly*. Really? After an eternity Evan came to the door pajama clad, five o'clock shadowed, and with his hair looking like a lump of seaweed—floating all the wrong way. It was enlightening and downright entertaining to see him so disheveled.

"Morning. What a pleasant surprise." He opened the door wider.

"Was that you singing selections from *Madama Butterfly*?"

"No, just a really bad CD." He grinned. "You look pretty."

"You do, too. In your Superman PJs." I puckered my mouth, tying not to howl with laughter. That was it. It was official—Evan was adorable.

He looked at his attire. "Gag gift from one of my aunts. I didn't have any clean clothes, so. . .well, did you come to thank me for the flowers?"

"Yes, sort of. Looks like I woke you up, though." Wouldn't Evan have a housekeeper to keep him in clean clothes?

"I've been awake for a while. Come on in. The coffee just finished brewing."

I followed him inside.

He grabbed a robe off a chair. "I'm not considered human until I've had my caffeine."

And a little opera. I grinned and glanced around. "I like your décor."

"It's perfect if you like doilies and floral wallpaper." He

slipped on his robe. "But I appreciate my aunt's generosity, so I don't really mind." He looked back at me with a sleepy grin. "It'll eventually get manified. It just needs a big screen TV and a gun cabinet on the wall."

I chuckled. "Do you always sleep until ten?"

"I do when I don't have to speak."

"Oh." I followed him to the kitchen, which was more of the same décor—antique lace meets bluebonnet charm.

The coffee smelled good—Gorilla robust good. While he poured I rummaged around in his pantry for some sugar. None could be found, but several super-size bags of corn chips lined the pantry shelves. "Wow, you have this bachelor thing going with corn chips."

"Well, they're just so versatile." He reached around me and pulled out a sugar bowl next to my hand. "Corn chips are the foundation to many kinds of sixty-second meals. Can of beans over a bed of chips. Jar of queso poured over a bed of chips. Can of—"

"I get the general idea. I think you need to hire a cook."

"No, I just need a wife." He set a carton of cream on the table. "Hope this hasn't soured. . .too much."

I grinned, but said nothing about the cream or his need for a wife. When we'd settled at the kitchen table with our coffee, I finally got to the real reason I'd barged in. "So, what did the message on your card mean? It seemed more like a message from the FBI not FTD."

Evan laughed. "Yes, yes. As soon as I hung up the phone with the florist, I thought maybe my message on the note wasn't quite right. But I knew it would get your attention."

"It did get my attention." I took a swig of the coffee and cringed. It was stout enough to arm wrestle me to the floor. But I swallowed it anyway and said, "It's hard to imagine you coming up with the wrong words. . .you're the master communicator."

"No, my *father* was the master communicator. I'm just a portfolio of speeches that I can deliver with panache." He ran his fingers along the edge of the table. "Big difference."

My, my. Yet another facet of Evan Finch. "That sounds kind of pathetic, and I think you might be the least pathetic person I know."

"I've always lived in my father's shadow. Even more so, now that he's in heaven," Evan said. "But I don't mind that spot, being in his shadow. He was a *great* man."

"And you're not?"

He winced when he took a sip from his coffee mug and then stood and spit it into the sink. "How can you drink that? It's liquid tarmac."

I laughed. "*Now* who's changing the subject?"

Evan poured my coffee into the sink. "By the way, my note with the flowers was an apology."

"But what do you need to apologize for? You—"

He put up his hand. "Let me finish. Please. You were right when you told me to be aware of my surroundings. . . concerning women. You know, to look over my shoulder from time to time. Well, I guess I wasn't paying attention."

"What do you mean?" Did I really want to know? I braced

myself for unhappy tidings.

"Suzanne, my assistant. . .apparently she has feelings for me." Evan placed his palms together and touched them to his lips.

"Oh?"

"After I took you home she dropped by here, claiming she didn't understand a research assignment I'd given her for a new speech." He shook his head. "Anyway, I invited her in. I'd never had a problem before with that sort of thing, so I didn't think too much about it. But it's a big ugly problem now. Suzanne, well. . .let's just say she made her intentions known to me. I had to practically throw her out."

Chapter 15

And did she go?" My voice shimmied.

"Yes. She was angry, though. She thought I knew about her feelings. She thought I was okay with it. I guess I've been giving off all the wrong signals and didn't even know it. Anyway, it's time for some new policies. I need to screen my help better, ask more questions. Get references. And I shouldn't ever be alone with my female employees."

"Sounds like a good solid plan." Part of Evan was this savvy businessman, and another part came off as naive as a Hobbit.

He sat back down and took my hands in his. "We have a good start here. You and me. And I don't want to do anything to mess that up."

I placed my hand on his cheek. "You haven't. I admire the way you handled the situation. Your father would have been proud of you." I must have said something wonderful, because the kiss that ensued was pretty memorable stuff. To conserve energy and keep our transformers from blowing, I finally disengaged and whispered, "I got my Nikon out this morning."

"Will you take my picture?" he asked.

"I'm sure you've had your picture taken thousands of times."

"Yes, but I've never been photographed by the illustrious Heather McBride."

"All right, I might do it. But you'll have to look more natural."

"Done. So, you'll photograph me for my new brochures? I don't want to hire anyone else. It has to be you."

"We'll see. Are you sure you're not just charming me with your charisma?"

He fingered the ruffles at my wrist. "Is it working?"

I smiled.

*

Over the next three months, spring gave way to midsummer as easily as a petal gliding down the creek, and Evan and I enjoyed some, shall we say, *pleasant developments*, in our relationship. We argued a little, we laughed a lot.

And we fell in love.

I just couldn't help it. Evan met my family. They came to love him, too, and he fell into step with the McBride ways and wonders. I met Evan's mother, who was a sweet delight and a lot like Evan. Mrs. Finch seemed to enjoy and appreciate my direct approach to life, so I counted all of it as another tender mercy from God. Life was good.

On this day, I smiled at Evan, who twitched with the most mischievous grin. He was in the process of taking me on a surprise day-trip vacation. The final destination, however, was still unknown to me.

"I have to know what you're up to." Even though I was riding on a cushy leather seat with adjustable lumbar support, I still fidgeted. "I'm terrible at waiting on surprises. Have some mercy on me."

Evan took one hand off the steering wheel and touched my cheek. "So, are you one of those people who opens your gifts before Christmas and then wraps them back up again?"

"Of course. But I don't usually bother to wrap them back up."

"Shocking." He laughed. "Well, today, this one thing is out of your control."

Hmm. Guess I was going to have to sit tight and exercise some patience. A few minutes later we entered the city limits of Round Top, and it dawned on me what he'd cooked up. He probably wanted to take me to an art show, to encourage me in my photography. There was no doubt about it—Evan Finch was as sweet a man as God had ever made.

He parked near Bybee Square, which was a cluster of elegant boutiques, galleries, and eateries. The last time I'd perused the shops was on a girls' day out with Lucy. We'd had the best day, shopping and laughing and just being girls. I'd missed her over the months, but was glad to hear her voice when she finally phoned a few days ago. She called to tell me I'd been right about Buddy and that she'd called off the wedding. I hadn't wanted to be right about him, and yet I was rejoicing over her freedom and her chance to find a man who really deserved her. She invited me to her house for lunch, and I knew our reunion would be like old times.

"We're here." Evan reached over, placed his hand over mine, and gave it a squeeze. "So, Heather, are you ready to receive?" he asked in his larger-than-life stage voice.

I grinned. "I'm ready."

But instead of taking me into one of the bustling stores, Evan escorted me to one of the shops that appeared to be empty. I looked in the window, already feeling the Texas heat on my back and anxious to feel some air-conditioning. "This place is closed. What's up?"

"Patience, Ms. McBride." He lifted a key from his pocket and slipped it into the lock.

"But how could. . ." I let my words go, since I knew Evan would just shush me again.

He opened the door and turned to me.

"What's this all about, Evan?" Because the surprise seemed to be grander than I imagined, I was glad I'd dressed in something besides denim. And I was equally glad to see Evan in a more casual khaki look. Our clothes must have gone to a weekend symposium together and come back forever changed.

"Well, your surprise is in three pieces." He clasped his hands together. "This is part one." He took me by the hand and led me inside.

"Sounds wonderful." I looked around the shop, which appeared to be spacious and well designed. "What is this place?" Oh no, he didn't. Did he? "Evan?"

He opened his arms like he was going to embrace the world. "It's the Heather McBride Gallery. I rented this space for you." He lifted the key, dangling it in the air.

"You did what?" My head spun.

"You have a real talent, and you're the only one who doesn't know it."

"I've rarely shown my work to anyone, so I don't know how that last part can be true."

"*You* haven't," Evan said, "but I have. Remember those pieces you gave me when we first started dating?"

"Is it possible to feel elated and furious at the same time?"

"Maybe, yeah," he said.

I bashed my poor knuckles together until Evan reached over and gently prevented the onslaught.

"Listen," he said. "I've shown your work to some people who're in the know. Gallery owners. People in the business. And they agree with me. You've got a great talent."

"I can't believe you did that. Even though this has to be the most amazing gift anyone has ever given me. . .I can't accept it. I just can't." I could feel my stomach pumping acid.

"But why not? You never found the job you wanted. You're in limbo, and I know it's eating at you. This is a gift from God and from me. . .and you won't accept it? You won't *receive* it?" He caught my gaze, his expression full of bright animation.

"Are you being Evan now, or am I being schmoozed by Mr. Finch?"

"Ouch." He placed the shiny key on the front counter, but it took a moment before he let go of it.

I'd gone too far. The pained look in his eyes tore at my heart. I took in a long, slow breath. How could the Almighty put up with me? When would I ever learn to balance truth and love? Surely now was the time. I reached up and kissed his cheek, the spot I loved to kiss—my spot. "I'm sorry, my darling. That was cruel. Please, will you forgive me?"

Evan didn't hesitate to wrap me in his arms. "Because you've been photographing almost everything in sight for three months, I thought this gallery would bring you joy, not tears."

"Part of it is joy. I love the fact that you care about me so much to do a thing like this." Mist filled my eyes and came out as a single tear. "But I'd have to move here to Round Top, and—"

"Not necessarily. We can always hire someone to run the shop. But that's secondary. I can tell something else is wrong." Evan wiped away my tear with his thumb. "What part of this is making you want to cry?"

I patted his cheek and eased away from him. What would it feel like to run a shop that featured my work? I stood behind the counter and ran my finger through the dust, creating a flower design. "My reluctance is connected to a photography class I took years ago." I murmured this before I even knew where my thoughts were going.

He stepped closer. "What happened?"

"Sometimes people have more cruel words than they know what to do with, so they fling them around until they hit something. Maybe that's what I did to you a moment ago." I winced at the thought.

"I assure you, I'm fully recovered." He smiled. "But you're right, some people can be brutal."

"Yes." I said nothing for a moment as memories of cameras and childhood dreams came back to me.

"Talk to me."

"Well, I was just thinking about the past. You know, ever since I was a kid, I've loved taking pictures. When I was little, my dad bought me my first camera. . .a Kodak. I thought I was the great Ansel Adams with that thing." I chuckled. "Over the years my interest never let up, so after college I took a professional-level class. At the end of a pretty intense three months, the instructor pulled me aside, shook his head, and said two words to me. 'Give up.' That's all. I was too devastated to even ask him any more questions. I just went home and put my camera way up high on a closet shelf. Every time I wanted to bring it down, those two words would mock me. Eventually the camera came off the shelf, but I never again entertained the idea of doing it professionally. Just couldn't imagine it."

I brushed my bangs out of my eyes. "As ridiculous as it sounds, those two words still haunt me, even though I've never been the kind of person to feel sorry for myself for long. I usually snap back, but in this one thing. . ." I looked at Evan, at the depth of caring in those dark brown eyes of his, and smiled. "You know, for a guy who talks for a living, you really are a good listener."

"Thanks." He leaned on the counter and took me in with his gaze. "I'm so sorry that happened to you."

"Me, too."

"But what you have to ask yourself is. . .are you going to allow those two carelessly said words to cripple you for the rest of your life, or will you allow God to wipe them away? He's given you this talent, this yearning. He wants to give you the desires of your heart. . .if you'll let Him." Evan reached out to me but didn't touch my hands. "What does your heart tell you?"

"It's time, Heather." I know, Lord. I looked around the room, imagining my work on the walls, imagining the people milling around and being inspired by the way I saw the world, and I knew what my answer would be. "My heart is whispering 'yes.' No, it's *screaming* 'yes.'"

The tears came, and Evan was good enough to let me cry on his shoulder. Such a great place to be. "Thank you for the shop." *But I won't move to Round Top without you.*

After a moment or two, Evan asked, "Do you think you're ready for your second surprise?"

I blew my nose in his handkerchief. "I'm ready. What is it?"

He flicked on a long-nosed lighter and lit several candles, which sat here and there on gallery shelves.

What's going on?

Then he turned on a halogen light in the corner, and it

illuminated something across the room. Something nesting in a black velvet box, which sat on a golden pedestal. How could I have missed seeing that?

Chapter 16

Evan?"

"Yes?"

"What wonderful thing have you done now?" I followed him across the room, and we stood in front of the open box, which held the most exquisite heart-shaped diamond ring I'd ever seen. "I will not cry. I will not cry. I will not cry."

"You can if you want to, but I hope they're happy tears."

"The happiest."

Evan took the ring out of the box. "I'm in a bind, you see, and I know this might be way too forward of me, bad etiquette and all, but I was wondering if you'd like to go to a wedding with me."

I grinned, remembering Evan's first words to me. Apparently, he'd remembered them, too. "And who's the lucky couple?"

"I'm hoping it'll be us." He held up the ring. "You know, Thoreau said, 'There is no remedy for love but to love more.' And it's been the easiest thing I've ever done, Heather. I love you more every day. Every hour." He grinned. "With this ring, I offer my life. . .my love. That is, if you'll have me. If you'll attend this wedding with me and become my wife."

"Yes, I'd love to go with you. . .and become your wife."

"Really?"

"All I have to do is slip on a fancy dress," I said. "I love you, Evan Finch."

"Then this is a very good day." Evan started to slip the ring on my finger and then paused. "But wait. I have to know one thing first."

"What?"

"Do you know how to cook with corn chips?"

I laughed. "No."

"Good. Glad that's settled."

He got the ring halfway on my finger before I stopped him. "Oh, but I have something to say, too."

"Really? What is it?"

"As soon as we get married, I'm going to wash that gel right out of your hair."

"Promise?"

"I do." I helped him get the ring all snug on my finger. "Beautiful."

"I kept the receipt in case you hated it."

I laughed. "Not on your life." I turned my hand back and forth under the lights. The diamonds not only winked at me, they put on their own laser-light show. *Sweet.* And then amidst the candlelight we shared a kiss that sealed our little love covenant in style.

When we came up to breathe again, I said, "I guess we've made progress. You no longer have to resort to scaring me with alligators to steal a kiss from me."

Evan chuckled. "It is a less complicated way to live." He raised his eyebrows and spread his arms. "And now, are you ready for part three?"

"There's no *way* to top all of this."

Evan pointed to the light where the box sat. There was a sheet of paper under the velvet container.

"For me?"

"Yes."

I picked it up and skimmed along, reading the page until I realized what Evan was up to. It was a press release. "Oh no. You can't let go of your father's business. All that he worked for—what you both worked for."

"I'm willing to. It's all in the press release."

"But the changes you've made—those new policies—they fix the problems you had."

"True, but it's so much more than that," Evan said. "Even if I cut back on my traveling, it would get old after a while. Maybe not right away, but over time I'm afraid it would make you weary, Heather. There would be too many good-byes."

"But your mother did just fine with this same kind of life, didn't she?"

"Yes, but that's different."

"How can it be different?"

"She ended up growing a tough hide. I don't want to force you into that kind of life."

"I already have a tough hide. It was the one and only good thing that came from working in sales. See?" I took his hand and let it glide along my arm.

"Your skin is as soft as a baby's whisper." He kissed my arm and lingered there.

I pulled away. "Seriously, you're not getting out of this. Until God tells you to, I'm not releasing you from this amazing life your family has created."

"Why? Give me one good reason why."

For once, I'm going to get it right. "I can give you a dozen good reasons. For one thing, you are Evan Finch, and you inspire and challenge people. You make them better. You show them Christ. Over the past three months people have been coming up to me, telling me what your ministry means to them, how it's made all the difference in their lives. One woman said she'd lost her husband and was thinking of taking her own life. After your seminar she's now running a homeless shelter in downtown Houston. You and God did that. He's given you this amazing gift, Evan, and from the sound of it, you're going to throw it back in His face? If you do that, then you're not the man I thought you were."

He looked at me, startled. "You really do want me to continue?"

"I believe in you, just like you believe in me." I took his face in my hands, getting his full attention. "And I trust you around all that estrogen."

He chuckled. One at a time and with exquisite slowness, he kissed the palms of my hands. "All right then."

"So, please tell me your manager hasn't sent this press release to the media. Not yet, please?"

"Winnie was going to send out the press release this afternoon, just as soon as you approved it."

Without hesitation I tore the press release into pieces, tossed the bits into the air, and watched them flutter around us like confetti. "Well, Mr. Finch, it's not approved."

"I'm so glad I found you."

"Are you sure it wasn't *I* who found you?" I shook my finger at him.

Evan caught my hand and grinned.

"So. . .no more doubts about your speaking, then?"

"Not with you standing next to me."

I wrapped my arms around him and squeezed. "You know, I *was* a bayou person, but my life needed some. . .alterations. And I'm so glad you were one of them."

He pushed me back and kissed my nose.

"I love Round Top, Evan. . .the bright meadows and the fields of bluebonnets. Why don't we move here? Live here full time?"

"Raise our family here." Evan let his finger trace the contours of my face. I closed my eyes for a moment, taking in the warm and stirring sensations of his affection, of his love.

When I opened my eyes to smile into his, Evan said, "And maybe we'll have children who'll grow up to be artists."

"Or perhaps they'll be great speakers. . .like their father." The words flowed right out of me, and they couldn't have been more earnest.

Evan and I had both shifted here and there over the months—in big ways that took us by surprise and in small ways we barely noticed. But it was indeed change just the same. I doubt I will ever live on the bayou again, but I'll always be fascinated with the movement of water—the way the meandering currents travel to places unknown to me. The way they shift, never staying the same, always moving, ever changing.

Just like life.

1
윤미경

"LET ME SEE, LITTLE GIRL...
"THE ELDER, WOL-HA, HAS GIVEN YOU TWO RED STRINGS.
?
"IN THE FUTURE, YOU WILL HAVE TWO LOVES."
COME HERE AT ONCE!
SOAH! HOW MANY TIMES HAVE I TOLD YOU NOT TO RUN AROUND BY YOURSELF?
WHO SAID THAT?

IS THAT CHILD THE BRIDE OF THE WATER GOD?
I HEARD THAT THE SHAMAN MUNYEO-NIM* CHOSE HER AFTER RECEIVING A REVELATION.
SHE IS *SO YOUNG,* POOR THING...
IT CAN'T BE HELPED. THE DROUGHT HAS ALREADY BEEN GOING ON FOR TOO MANY YEARS. OUR WELL DRIED UP A LONG TIME AGO.
WE DON'T EVEN HAVE WATER TO DRINK, LET ALONE FARM WITH!
WE *MUST* OFFER A BRIDE TO APPEASE THE ANGRY WATER GOD.
SOMEBODY *MUST BE SACRIFICED* FOR THE GREATER GOOD.
BUT STILL...
...IT'S SUPPOSEDELY A GOD...
...BUT WHO KNOWS IF IT'S A MONSTER OR NOT.

***NIM:** KOREAN HONORIFIC, SIMILAR TO "SIR" OR "MA'AM."

PLEASE DON'T BLAME US TOO MUCH. WE DIDN'T WANT TO DO THIS, BUT...
...BUT SOAH, IT'S SO FORTUNATE FOR ALL OF US THAT YOU'RE GOING.
WE ALL TREMEN-DOUSLY APPRECIATE YOU.
NOW WE CAN ALL *LIVE* THANKS TO YOU.
LIES...
"IT STILL DOESN'T MATTER IF ALL THIS SUPERSTITION IS A LIE... IF ONLY IT WOULD RAIN..."
"LUCKILY, SHE IS NOT OUR DAUGHTER."
"WE ARE NOT TO BE BLAMED. YOU WERE JUST UNLUCKY.
"IF IT'S NOT ME, THEN IT DOESN'T MATTER WHO IT IS."
"AFTER ALL, SOMEBODY HAD TO BE SACRIFICED."

I DON'T CARE WHAT HAPPENS TO THE VILLAGE.
BUT...
SOAH, YOU'RE GETTING MARRIED? YOU LOOK SO PRETTY...
I WANT TO BE A PRETTY BRIDE ONE DAY, TOO...
SOAH...
SOAH...
!
...BUT...
FSHHHAAP

...HABAEK...
...PLEASE...

...PLEASE...
...PLEASE GIVE US RAIN!
FSHHHAAA

쏴아－
SPSHHH
쏴…
SPSH

SPLOOSH
THIS IS...

...THE LAND OF SUGUK?
VOON

바스락
SHFF
FSHHHAAA
오
KOOM
오
KOOM
오
KOOM

?!
WELCOME.
I AM YUK-OH. I AM IN CHARGE OF THE PALACE.
PLEASE FOLLOW ME.
I WILL GUIDE YOU.
GUIDE YOU TO WHERE HABAEK-NIM IS...

PLEASE WAIT HERE FOR A MOMENT.

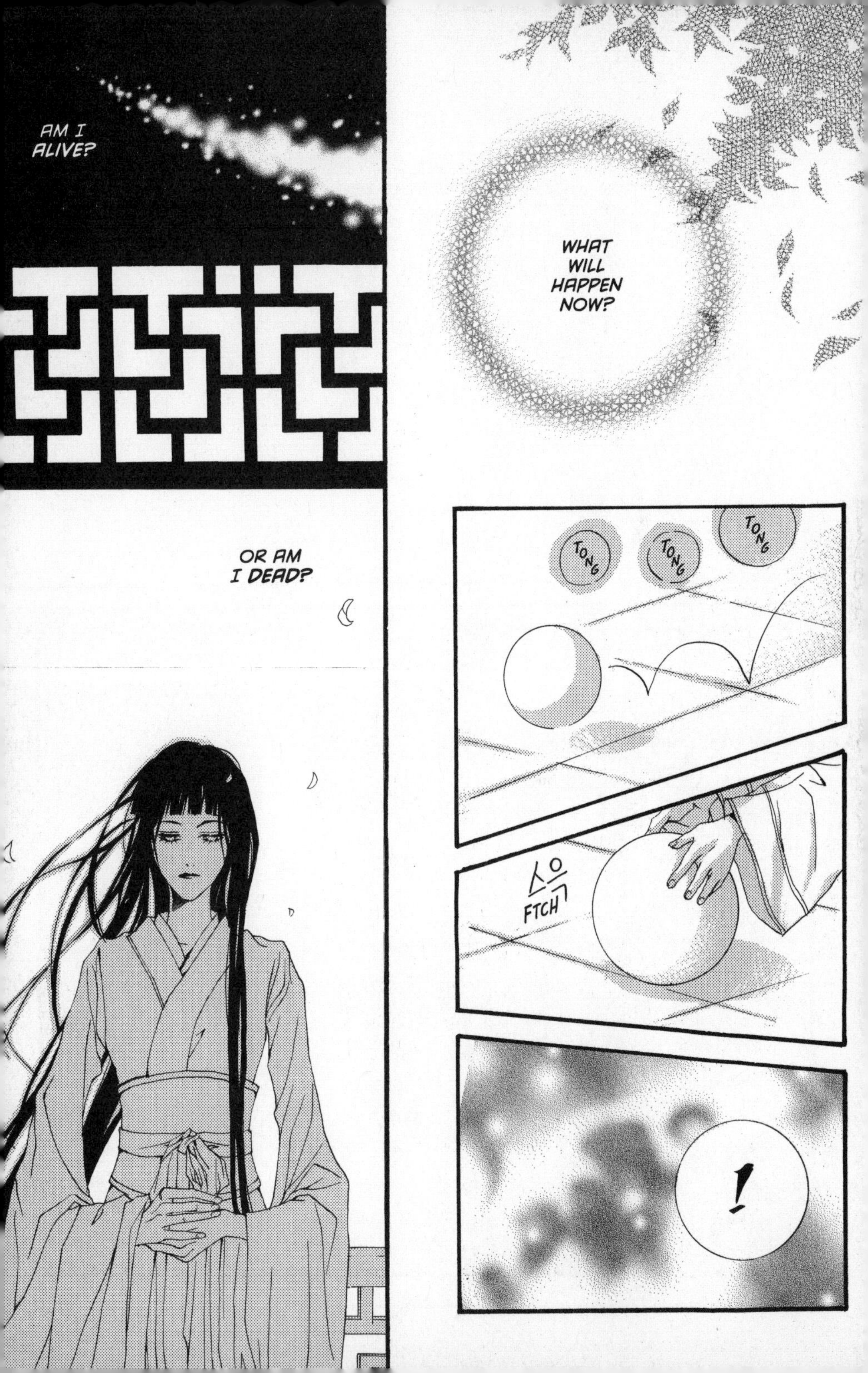
AM I ALIVE?
OR AM I DEAD?
WHAT WILL HAPPEN NOW?
TONG
TONG
TONG
스으
FTCH
!

A CHILD?
CLOSE TO MY SISTER'S AGE...
HELLO, LITTLE ONE. DO YOU LIVE HERE?

훽
WSHH
쿼쳐쳐
AWW!
COMPLETELY IGNORED...
저벅
TOK
저벅
TOK

쏴아아...
SHWAA WSHAA
PERFECT...
COMPLETELY LOST. I SHOULD'VE JUST WAITED.

IS THAT HABAEK?
TA-THUMP
TA-THUMP
THEY SAY ONCE YOU SEE HIM, YOU NEVER FORGET HIM.
I HEARD HE'S A TERRIFYING *MONSTER.*
YES, I ALSO HEARD HE *EATS PEOPLE!*
TA-THUMP
TA-THUMP
TA-THUMP
TA-THUMP
TA-THUMP
TA-THUMP
TA-THUMP

THU-THUMP
THU-THUMP
THU-THUMP
THU-THUMP

THAT MAN IS...
...MY HUSBAND...
!
SHFF
HERE YOU ARE. I'VE BEEN LOOKING FOR YOU FOR QUITE A WHILE.
HWK
WHAT'S THE MATTER, SOAH-NIM?

THE GOD, THIS BEING, IS BEAUTIFUL...
...THAT'S WHAT I WAS THINKING...
HABAEK-NIM IS HERE.
THU-THUMP
KAKUNGG
THU-THUMP
끼이익
SQUEEE
THU-THUMP

AH HAH...
...YUK-OH...
I BROUGHT SOAH-NIM.
THU-THUMP
THU-THUMP
THU-THUMP
THU-THUMP THU-THUMP
......

SOAH-NIM!
AH... YES?
PLEASE MEET HIM. BEFORE YOU IS *HUYE* DAE-JANG-GUN-NIM...
NOD
...AND...
WSH
!
...HERE IS...

...HABAEK-
NIM,
THE WATER
GOD.

...THE WORLD OF A GOD... HUMANS CAN NEVER UNDERSTAND...
...THAT'S WHAT I WAS THINKING...
NOBODY WOULD BELIEVE ME IF I SAID THE HABAEK THEY WERE SO AFRAID OF IS ACTUALLY JUST A CHILD...
...BUT IT'S BETTER THAN HIM BEING A TERRIFYING MONSTER...
THANKS. YOU'RE A LOT MANLIER THAN I AM--AND HANDSOME AS WELL.
LITTLE JERK...
I'M SURPRISED. I DIDN'T KNOW YOU WOULD LOOK SO CUTE, HABAEK.

BTAMM
KFWUMP
HYAA!
UWAA!
DON'T PAY ATTENTION TO US AT ALL. JUST KEEP DOING WHAT YOU'VE BEEN DOING.
BUT WHAT WERE YOU DOING, ANYWAY?
I'M JUDONG.
PLEASE JUST CALL ME YOHEE.
I'M MURAH, THE GODDESS...
...SHE IS MU-SAN-SHIN-NYEO.
HEY, YOU'RE CUTE.
CAN HE DO THAT?
WHAT-EVER.

DON'T BE SO MEAN-- AND BE GOOD TO HER THIS TIME, HABAEK.
SHE'S AWAY FROM HER FAMILY. HAVE PITY ON HER.
IT'S NONE OF YOUR BUSINESS!
SHE ACTS LIKE SHE DOESN'T CARE...
...BUT TO BE HONEST, SHE'S BEEN DESERTED.
......

MURAH--
THAT THING--
BECAUSE OF
HER BIG
MOUTH...
DON'T YOU MISS THEM? YOUR FAMILY...?
NO, I DON'T MISS THEM AT ALL.
SEE, MURAH DIDN'T KNOW ANYTHING. SHE JUST TALKED LIKE SHE DID.
TCH! HUMANS ARE--I CLEARLY SAID TO OFFER THE MOST BEAUTIFUL WOMAN...NOT ONLY FIVE YEARS, I WON'T LET IT RAIN FOR FIVE HUNDRED YEARS.
?

HFF...
HFF...
A STORMY DAY IS ENDING...

...MOMMY...
......

YOU ARE
A LIAR,
LADY.

콰아아…
FSHHHAAA
벌떡
WOOSH
RIGHT... THIS IS *NOT HOME*...
콰아아…
FSHHHAAA

AN UNFAMILIAR ROOM...
STRANGERS...
I THINK I DREAMT SOMETHING LAST NIGHT... BUT I DON'T REMEMBER...
DID YOU SLEEP WELL, HABAEK?
YOU...

WHAT DO YOU THINK I AM?
HUH? YOU DIDN'T BUTTON UP RIGHT.
슥슥
BUTTON BUTTON
I'M NOT A CHILD!
"SOAH-NIM, PLEASE LET ME KNOW IF YOU NEED ANYTHING."
THE GRAND-FATHERLY BUTLER LOOKS LIKE A GOOD MAN.
A BUTLER?! GRAND-FATHER?!
ALTHOUGH HABAEK IS ALWAYS GRUMBLING AT ME, THERE'S SOMETHING CUTE ABOUT HIM, TOO...

멈칫
PAUSE
I FORGOT...
...I SHOULD'VE WARNED HER NOT TO GO NEAR THE OLD PALACE.
WELL...SHE'S ALREADY BEEN HERE A WHILE... SHE'LL BE FINE...
......
I GOT LOST AGAIN... AND WHY DO I KEEP SEEING THESE OLD PALACE BUILDINGS?

CHKREEE

WHO IS IT? THIS PALACE ISN'T OPEN TO JUST ANYONE...
허둥
UMM...
지둥
UHH...
OOPS... I'M SORRY! I DON'T KNOW MY WAY AROUND VERY WELL...
AH...!
HABAEK'S *BRIDE!* RIGHT?

IT'S NICE MEETING YOU. I'M *TAE-EUL-JIN-IN.* I'M A DOCTOR AND AN INVENTOR.
I'M *SOAH.*
ARE YOU IN ANY KIND OF DISCOMFORT OR HAVE ANY ILLNESS? A COLD? ATHELETE'S FOOT?
TELL ME ANY-THING.
NO! I'M FINE.
THEN I WILL WRITE YOU A SCROLL.
SHK SHK
IT IS A SCROLL OF *WISH FUL-FILLMENT.*
......
IT MAY NOT LOOK NICE, BUT ITS EFFECT IS *POWERFUL.*
I'M SORRY. I DON'T HAVE ANYTHING TO WISH FOR.
I USED TO WISH FOR *RAIN,* BUT IT'S AL-READY BEEN *GRANT-ED.*
HUH?
I DON'T THINK IT RAINED YE DID IT?

HABAEK!
IS IT TRUE?
WHY ARE YOU MAKING ALL THIS FUSS AND NOISE?
IS IT TRUE? YOU DIDN'T MAKE IT RAIN?!
IF IT DOESN'T RAIN AGAIN, MORE PEOPLE WILL DIE.
WE ALL TRUSTED YOU...
MAYBE IT'S A SPORT TO YOU, BUT TO US... TO PEOPLE... OUR LIVES DEPEND ON IT.
WHY ARE YOU PLAYING WITH PEOPLE'S LIVES? YOU TREAT LIFE LIKE IT'S SOME KIND OF GAME!

IT'S JUST CAUSE AND EFFECT.
NATURE GIVES BACK AS MUCH AS IT RECEIVES.
THE TRULY SELFISH BEINGS ARE HUMANS, DON'T YOU THINK?
AS LONG AS THEY'RE SAFE, THEY DON'T CARE WHAT HAPPENS TO OTHERS.
"IF WE OFFER A SACRIFICE, WE CAN LIVE! JUST ONE..."
"JUST ONE..."
YOU MUST KNOW THAT BETTER THAN I DO, NO?
AND...
TINK
달그락
...DON'T YOU THINK YOU'RE MISUNDER-STANDING SOMETHING?

YOU'D BETTER KNOW *YOUR PLACE* NOW.
화
BLUSH
휙
HWIK
......
탁 탁
TAK TAK
탁 탁
TAK TAK
IT WAS MY **ILLUSION.** I WAS DECEIVED BY HIS LOOKS...
...AND FORGOT THAT HE WAS AN **ILL-TEMPERED** GOD...

탁
GRAB
휙
HWIK
WHAT ?!
AH... *HUYE*... I'M SORRY.
WHAT'S THE MATTER?
NOTHIN
REALL

살랑
RUSTLE
살랑
RUSTLE
IF YOU HAVE A PROBLEM, TELL ME.
I'LL HELP YOU... *ANYTIME.*
쏴아아아..
SHWAA WSHAA
THANK YOU...

BUT I'M NOT RUNNING AWAY *YET.* I'LL DO *THE BEST* I CAN.
SOAH'S SO DIFFERENT FROM THE OTHER ONE...
..."LET'S RUN AWAY...
"...LET'S RUN AWAY TOGETHER, HUYE," SHE USED TO SAY...

WHY ARE YOU BEING SO *MEAN* TO HER, HABAEK?
IT'S *NOT* LIKE YOU DON'T LIKE HER...
......
휘이이이
FWOOOO
NO MATTER WHAT...

...WHAT-EVER IS GOING ON HERE...
...I LIKE *THIS WORLD.*
FWOOOO
THE EARTH IS UGLY AND ALL DRIED UP BECAUSE OF *DROUGHT,* AND WAR IS RAGING AMONG THE HUMANS. THEY'RE FIGHTING AND KILLING EACH OTHER, BUT THE MOON REMAINS THE SAME...IT'S *STILL BEAUTIFUL.*
IT'S NOT *ME*-- IT'S HUMANS WHO STRANGLE *THEMSELVES.*
HUMANS POLLUTE WATER, AND...
...THEY EVENTUALLY KILL *NOT ONLY* THEMSELVES, BUT OTHER BEINGS AS WELL.
IN THE END, EVERYTHING WILL BE DESTROYED.

BUT STILL, ARE YOU GOING TO LEAVE THE CUTE BRIDE SAD AND ALONE LIKE THAT?

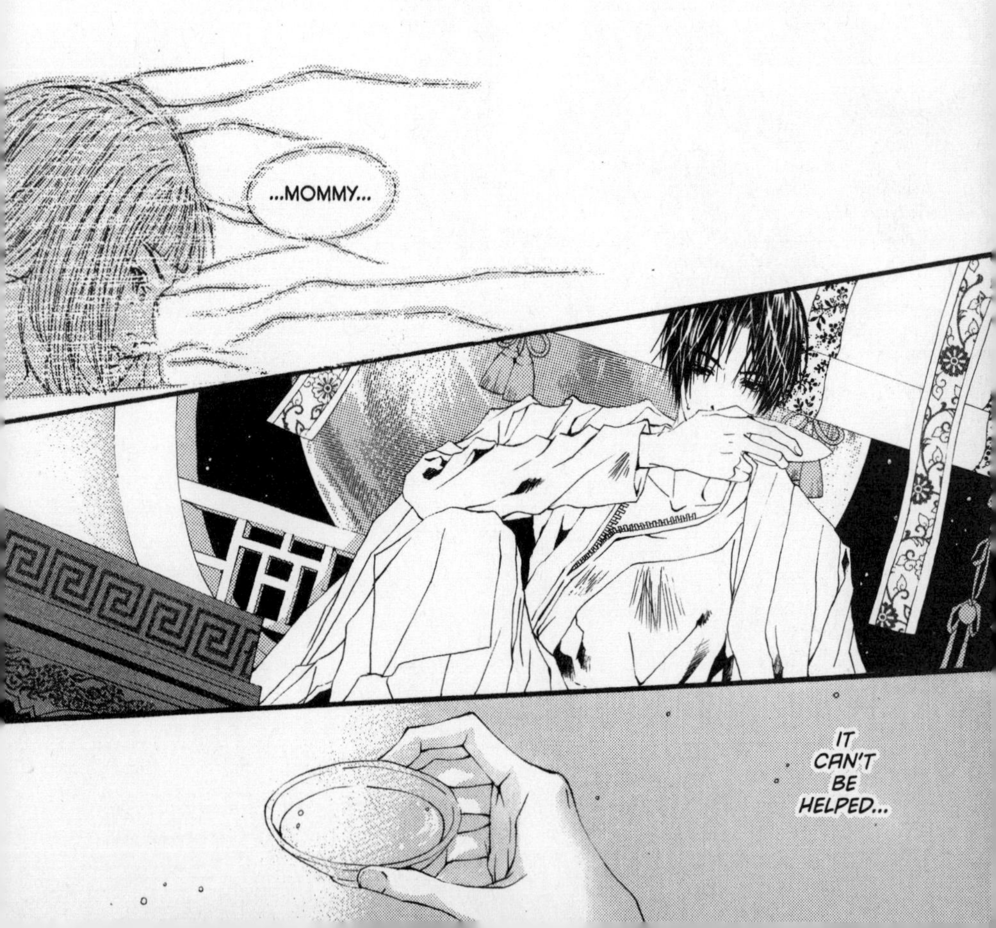
...MOMMY...
IT CAN'T BE HELPED...

SPSHH
...IT'S JUST THE WAY IT IS. A GOD IS ALWAYS DECEIVED BY HUMANS BUT FORGIVES THEM IN THE END.

HUH?
PLIP
PLIP
SPSH..
PLIP
IT'S RAINING !!
RAIN!
FSHAAAA

PERHAPS SOME OF THEM RECALLED SOAH, WHO SACRIFICED HERSELF TO BECOME THE BRIDE OF HABAEK.
IN THE YEARS TO COME, IT WILL PASS INTO LEGEND...

...A LEGEND OF A GIRL WHO SAVED HER ENTIRE VILLAGE...
...BY SACRIFICING HERSELF TO APPEASE THE RUTHLESS WATER GOD, HABAEK...

I HEARD THAT HABAEK GAVE *RAIN?*
WHAT GOT INTO HIM ALL OF A SUDDEN...?
......
BY THE WAY...
...DON'T YOU WANT TO *KNOW...*

...WHAT *HAPPENED* TO THE OTHER BRIDES WHO WERE SACRIFICED AS OFFERINGS TO HABAEK?
?!

ARGHHH... IT'S TOO HOT. TODAY IS ESPECIALLY HOTTER THAN USUAL.
OH, YEAH?
I THINK IT'S JUST PERFECT TODAY.
IF SUGUK IS THIS HOT, THEN...
THE FIRE GOD.
?
....
I JUST HATE HIM FOR SOME REASON.

......
콰콰아
FSHHAAAA
HABAEK ?!

HABAEK, ARE YOU OKAY? WAKE UP! CAN YOU HEAR ME?
WHEW...
YES... I'M ALL RIGHT.
DON'T WORRY ABOUT ME, I'M FINE, YUK-OH.
IT'S SOAH!
WAKE UP!

DON'T WORRY YOURSELF. HE WAS JUST LIGHT-HEADED.
HABAEK IS THE WATER GOD, SO HE IS WEAK IN STRONG SUNLIGHT.
YOU MUST'VE BEEN FRIGHTENED, TOO, SO WHY DON'T YOU RELAX A LITTLE WHILE YOU DRINK TEA?
BY THE WAY, I HEARD THAT YOU STILL GET LOST OFTEN, HUH? HEH HEH...
SUGUK IS A VERY BIG PLACE. BE CAREFUL SO YOU DON'T SUDDENLY DISAPPEAR.

WELL... WHO TOLD YOU SUCH A THING ...?
LIKE HABAEK'S OTHER BRIDES?
THE GODDESS MURAH DIDN'T TELL ME ANY MORE THAN THAT, BUT YOU KNOW--DON'T YOU, TAE-EUL-JIN-IN-NIM?
WHEW! WELL... YOU'RE PUT-TING ME IN A TOUGH SPOT.
I DON'T KNOW MANY DETAILS, SINCE I'M NEW HERE MYSELF.
WHAT I KNOW IS THAT HABAEK'S FIRST BRIDE'S NAME WAS NAKBIN.

"HABAEK LOVED HER VERY MUCH, BUT UNFORTUNATELY SHE DIED TOO SOON."
WHY SHE DIED OR...
...WHAT HAPPENED TO THE OTHER BRIDES OF HABAEK, I DON'T KNOW.
SO, I ONLY KNOW ABOUT THAT ONE BRIDE.
BUT THERE'S ONE THING FOR SURE THAT I *CAN* TELL YOU.

MANY MIS-UNDERSTAND HIM SINCE HE'S SO IRRITABLE...
...BUT HABAEK IS NOT A *BAD GUY.* SO YOU DON'T NEED TO FEEL UNSAFE.
WELL... I'M ALREADY AWARE OF THAT.
HE GAVE US *RAIN*... BUT...
IF YOU ARE *STILL* NOT SURE, I CAN HAVE A LOOK AT YOUR PALM LINE.
MAYBE YOU WILL FEEL SAFER IF YOU KNOW YOUR FUTURE.
HMMM...
WHAT? IS SOME-THING *WRONG?*

NO, YOU WILL LIVE HAPPILY EVER AFTER FOR A *LONG, LONG* TIME.
WHILE YOU ARE AT IT, WOULD YOU LIKE TO BUY SOME SCROLLS? I'LL GIVE YOU A DISCOUNT.
NO!
HABAEK! HABAEK!
NO.
I WAS *WORRIED* TO DEATH ABOUT YOU WHEN I HEARD YOU COLLAPSED. SO TAE-EUL-JIN-IN TOLD YOU THAT YOU SHOULD GO TO THE FOREST TO RELAX AND REST, HUH?
I'LL GO, TOO, SINCE I'M WORRIED ABOUT YOU.
YOU ARE A PAIN.
YOHEE, I'M NOT GOING THERE TO *PLAY*.
......
PAIN...

촤아아아
FSHHSHHHH
THIS IS YOUR FIRST TIME TO THE FOREST, RIGHT? SUGUK HAS LOTS OF WATER, SO TREES GROW REALLY WELL HERE. THERE ARE SO MANY BEAUTIFUL TREES.
HEY, AREN'T YOU GUYS SUPPOSED TO BE HERE FOR MY REST?
IT'LL BE SO MUCH FUN.
RIGHT? HEE!
첨벙
SPSH PLISH

PLANTS ARE VERY HONEST... THEY DON'T LIE, AND THEY RETURN AS MUCH LOVE AS THEY RECEIVE.
BEAUTIFUL...
YES... THEY ARE! HEH HEH!

JUDONG, YOU ARE THE FIRE GOD. WHY ARE YOU COMING TO SUGUK SO OFTEN?
HUMPH! MIND YOUR OWN BUSINESS!
I'M NOT HERE TO SEE YOU.
첨벙..
SPSH PLISH
ARF!
ARF!

WOW! HOW DID *YOU* GET HERE?
ARE YOU *ALONE?* WHERE'S YOUR FAMILY?
YOU AND I ARE KIND OF ALIKE...
I AM ALONE, TOO...
FWSH
HUH?

SLLITTCH
WHAT?
SOAH! NO!!!
THOKK
IT'S TOO LATE...
KRRAAARGG

KRAK
SHHINNG

KSPTTCH
PHEW! HUYE'S THE BEST. NO DOUBT, HE IS THE ***BEST ARCHER*** IN THE GODS' REALMS.
BUT WHY IS A ***CHE*** AROUND HERE?
CHE: A MONSTER THAT IS SIMILAR TO A TIGER, BUT HAS AN OX'S TAIL. BARKS LIKE A DOG. EATS HUMANS.
YOU IDIOT!!!
FLINCH

ARE YOU GOING TO GROW BRAINS AFTER YOU DIE? WHY AREN'T YOU MORE CAREFUL?!
FOO! HE DIDN'T EVEN HELP, BUT NOW HE'S ALL TALK...
스윽
FWSH
ARGH!
OUCH ...!
털썩
THUMP
WHAT SHOULD WE DO? I THINK SHE SPRAINED HER ANKLE. WE DON'T EVEN HAVE TAE-EUL-JIN-IN WITH US...
AH, I'LL--
I'LL CARRY HER.

WOOSH
WOW! I ENVY YOU, SOAH!
NOW THAT I'M LOOKING AT THEM, THEY LOOK *GOOD* TOGETHER, HUH?
WOULD YOU LIKE TO GO BACK TOO, HABAEK?
......
WSH
KRNCH

FLICKER
I JUST... CAN'T SLEEP.
WHERE IS HABAEK, ANYWAY?

I HEARD FROM THE OTHERS THAT THERE WAS AN ACCIDENT THIS AFTERNOON?
IF HUYE WAS NOT THERE, IT WOULD'VE BEEN A DISASTER.
HABAEK, YOU SHOULD ALWAYS BE CAREFUL, SINCE YOU'RE POWERLESS DURING THE DAY.
SHE DOESN'T KNOW ABOUT THIS YET, RIGHT?
YOUR FORM RIGHT NOW?
......
YES.

WHY DID YOU HIDE IT?
I *DIDN'T MEAN* TO HIDE IT ON PURPOSE, BUT IT JUST WORKED OUT THAT WAY.
WHEN DO YOU THINK YOU'LL TELL HER? DON'T YOU FEEL *BAD* FOR YOUR BRIDE?
WELL...
...WHEN THE TIME COMES FOR ME TO TELL HER, THEN I WILL.
'LEAP
I'M HAVING FUN WITH ALL THIS, SO IT REALLY DOESN'T MATTER TO ME ANYWAY, BUT...

SHE MUST BE SLEEPING NOW...
탁
LEAP
휘익
SHWISH

철썩
THUMMP
WHAT THE-- ?!

WHOA...!

BRIDE of the WATER GOD

WOBBLE
?!
WUMP

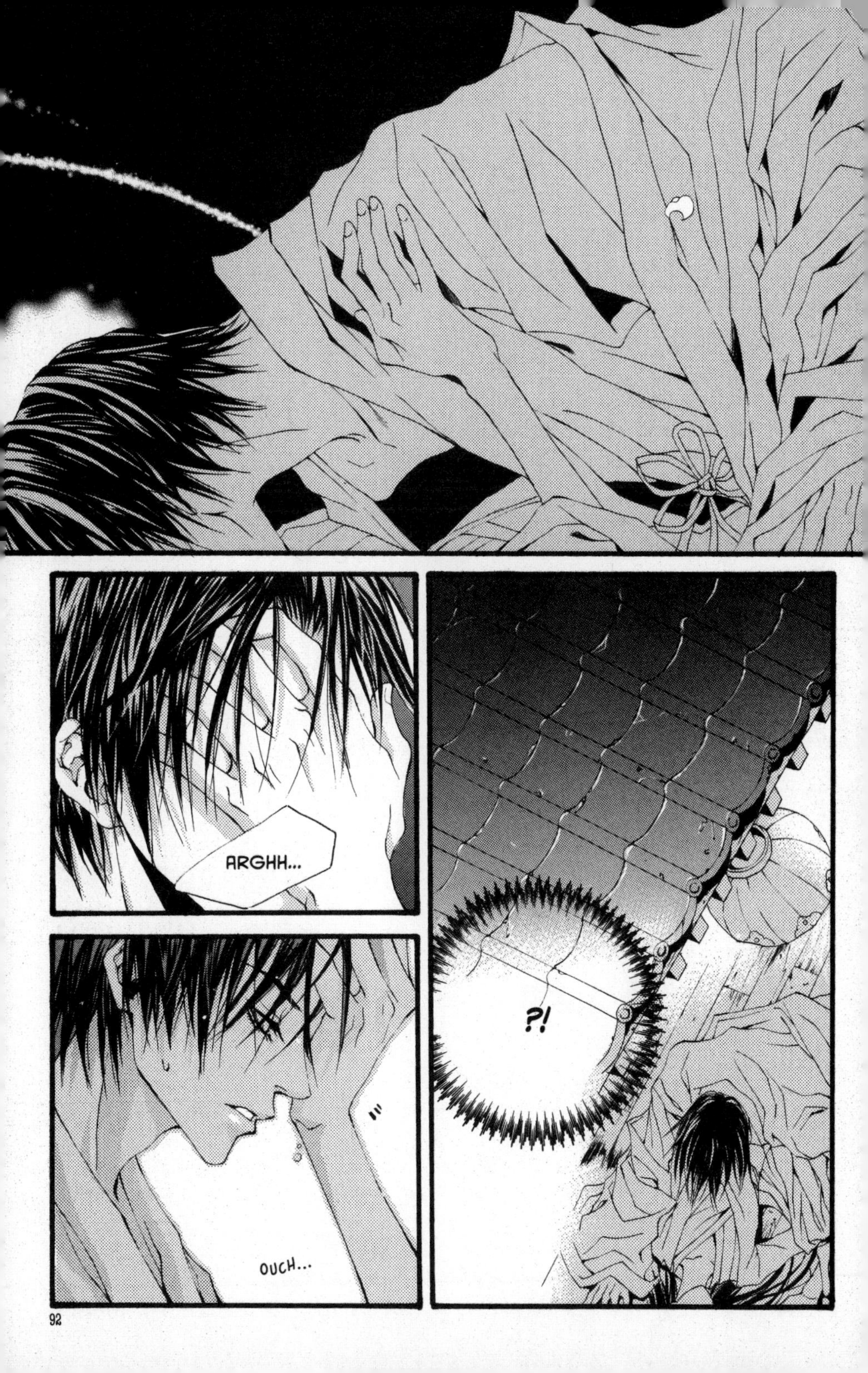
?!
ARGHH...
OUCH...

AH...
AH...
YAAAAH!
HNNG!
MFF!

I DON'T WANT TO MAKE A BIG FUSS, SO IF YOU *PROMISE* ME THAT YOU WON'T SCREAM, I WILL LET YOU GO.
PROMISE?
WELL, NOT THAT YOU LOOK REALLY TRUSTWORTHY, BUT...
NOD NOD
WSH

I WAS GOING TELL HER ONE DAY, BUT I DIDN'T EXPECT IT TO HAPPEN THIS SOON...
...AND BESIDES THAT, HOW AM I SUPPOSED TO EXPLAIN TO HER THE SITUATION I'M IN?
THAT I'M A LITTLE KID DURING THE DAY, AND I ONLY GROW AT NIGHT? IT'S THE TRUTH, BUT SOMEHOW THE NUANCE IS JUST...
I PROBABLY SHOULD'VE HIT HER AND RUN OFF...
WHO... ARE YOU?
HNN?
HEY...
SHOULD I KNOCK HER OUT NOW?
I REALLY DON'T WANT THINGS TO GET OUT OF HAND.

...SHE REALLY
DOESN'T KNOW?
WELL, OF COURSE.
NOBODY WOULD THINK
I'M THE SAME PERSON.
I AM...

MY NAME IS MUI.
MUI...
SO, LIKE...
...YOU'RE HABAEK'S COUSIN, RIGHT?
I'M MYSELF.
GUESS YOU'RE A FAR REMOVED COUSIN. YOU GUYS DON'T LOOK ALIKE AT ALL...
I LIED IN THE HEAT OF THE MOMENT, BUT IT'LL BE BETTER TO KEEP THE SITUATION LIKE THIS.

AH, BY THE WAY, I HAVE SOMETHING TO ASK YOU.
WHY DIDN'T YOU RUN AWAY?
WEREN'T YOU AFRAID OF HABAEK?
I'M SURE THAT THERE WERE MANY WAYS YOU COULD'VE ESCAPED BEING OFFERED AS A BRIDE.
LIKE... YOU COULD'VE BRIBED MUNYEO OR YOU COULD'VE RUN AWAY SOMEWHERE AND TRIED TO HIDE...
......

I DON'T RECALL EXACTLY, BUT...
...ONE DAY I WAS PLAYING AROUND THE POND WHEN I WAS YOUNG, AND I ALMOST DROWNED IN THE WATER.
풍덩
SPLOOOSH
I CAN'T BREATHE...

HELP ME...
MOMMY...
덥썩
SNNCH
SHWOOOSH
WHO?
HHHFOO!
HOFF!
HOFF!
SOAH!
SOAH, ARE YOU OKAY?

LATER I LEARNED THAT IT WASN'T A PERSON WHO GRABBED MY HAND...
...IT WAS THE STEM OF A WATER LILY.
HABAEK-NIM MUST'VE HELPED YOU.
THE WATER LILY IS THE FLOWER OF HABAEK.

IS THE WATER LILY DIFFERENT FROM THE LOTUS?
THE WATER LILY BLOSSOMS DURING THE DAY-TIME, CLOSES AT NIGHT, THEN BLOS-SOMS AGAIN THE NEXT MORNING--SO THAT'S WHY IT IS CALLED THE "SLEEPING LOTUS."
AND PEOPLE CALL IT THE WATER LILY, TOO.
A LONG, LONG TIME AGO, HABAEK WAS LAMENTING FOR A PERSON WHO DROWNED IN THE WATER. HE NEVER WANTED SUCH A THING TO HAPPEN AGAIN, SO...
...USING HUGE LEAVES, HE TURNED THE PERSON INTO A WATER LILY.
"YOU, TOO. HABAEK-NIM PROTECTED YOU."
THAT'S WHY I WASN'T SCARED.
ANYBODY WHO CAN GRIEVE SO MUCH FOR SOMEONE'S DEATH...
...CANNOT BE A BAD PERSON, DON'T YOU THINK?

AND LIKE MY GRANDMA TOLD ME, THAT REALLY MIGHT'VE BEEN *HABAEK.*
THERE IS SOMETHING THAT GRANDMA *LEFT OUT.*
THERE ARE SOME WATER LILIES THAT BLOSSOM *"ONLY AT NIGHT,"* TOO.

?

쏴아아아
WSSHWAAA

I MET HABAEK'S OLDER COUSIN LAST NIGHT.
?
AN OLDER COUSIN?
THE ONE NAMED MUI.
AH HAH... MUI...

AN OLDER COUSIN?
YES, THERE REALLY IS A PERSON NAMED MUI. HEH HEH!
SO... HOW WAS THE FIRST MEETING?
GUESS IT WASN'T A LIE, THEN?
......
THE WATER LILY...
HE'S LIKE A WATER LILY.
?

피이--
PIRREE
피피피---
PIPIRREE
HABAEK HAS A BRIDE NOW?
......
HMPH! WITHOUT TELLING ME A WORD?
MUI--THAT KID-- HE HASN'T CHANGED AT ALL...DOING WHATEVER HE PLEASES.
I CAN'T BELIEVE HE LET ANOTHER *PETTY HUMAN* INTO SUGUK AGAIN...

SEOWANGMO'S MESSENGER IS HERE!!
I'M GOING TO SUGUK MYSELF.

펄럭
FWWUPP
파닥
FWIP FWIP
파닥
FWIP FWIP
파닥
FWIP
파닥
FWIP
파닥
파닥
FWIP FWIP
철푸덕
KTMPP
THAT'S SUPPOSED TO BE A MESSENGER?
THEY ARE VERY CLOSE TO THE GODDESS. YOU SHOULD NEVER THINK LIGHTLY OF THEM.

I SHOULDN'T BE FOOLED BY APPEAR-ANCES.
BUT DARN! IT'S CUTE.
?
THIS IS--?!
THIS IS A BIG DEAL. SEOWANGMO IS COMING TO SUGUK.
REALLY? WHAT ARE WE GOING TO DO?
WHY NOW OF ALL TIMES?
AH...
WHO IS SEOWANGMO?
SHE IS...

...HABAEK'S MOTHER.
I GUESS SHE IS VERY STRICT?
IT SEEMS LIKE EVERYBODY'S SCARED OF HER...
IT'S NOT THAT SHE'S MERELY STRICT...

...THE REAL REASON SEOWANGMO IS *FEARED*...
...IS BECAUSE SHE'S THE GODDESS OF PUNISHMENT AND TORTURE!

WHY DID
EVERYTHING TURN
OUT THIS WAY?

IF I HAD KNOWN IT SOONER...
...THEN...

...THINGS
WOULDN'T HAVE
TO BE LIKE THIS...

NOBODY KNEW BEFORE.

IT'S NOT THAT SHE'S MERELY STRICT...
I GUESS SHE IS VERY STRICT?
IT SEEMS LIKE EVERY-BODY'S SCARED OF HER...
IT SEEMED THAT ALL THIS HAPPINESS WOULD JUST GO ON FOREVER.

...THE REAL REASON SEOWANGMO IS FEARED...
...IS BECAUSE SHE'S THE GODDESS OF PUNISHMENT AND TORTURE!
?!
BUT THEN AGAIN, YOU DON'T NEED TO BE ALL TENSE. SHE'S ALSO THE GODDESS OF LOVE AND BEAUTY.
WHEW!
BUT THEN AGAIN, YOU REALLY CAN'T LET YOUR GUARD DOWN BECAUSE SHE'S ALSO THE GODDESS OF DISEASE.
BY THE WAY...
...WHERE IS OUR MOST IMPORTANT HERO, ANWAY?

SHWOO
슈이-
휘이이!
HWWOOSH
휘이이!
HWWOOSH
HWOOO
슥
WSH
......

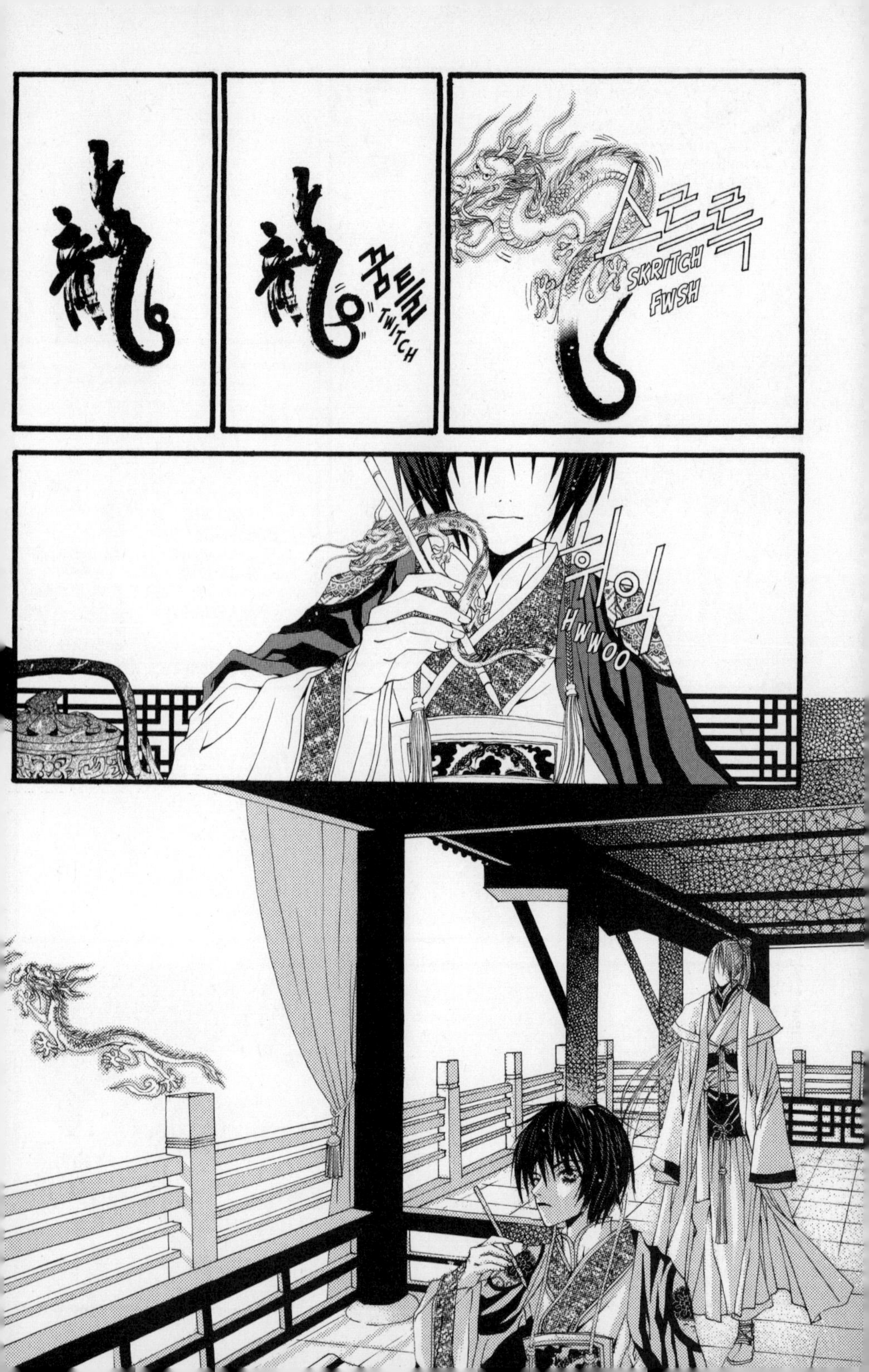

꿈틀
TWITCH
스르륵
SKRITCH
FWSH
HWWOO

THE WATER AND WIND ARE MAKING A BIG FUSS TODAY.
THEY ARE STIRRING BECAUSE OF AN UNKNOWN PRESENCE.
DID SOMEBODY COME?
YES, THE *CHUNGJO* OF SEOWANGMO HAS COME WITH A MESSAGE.
NEEDLESS TO SAY, JUDONG ALREADY OPENED IT.
WHAT DID IT SAY?
THAT SHE WILL VISIT SUGUK SHORTLY...

...BECAUSE OF SOAH.
BUT HOW DID SHE FIND OUT? SHE HASN'T BEEN IN SUGUK FOR A FEW HUNDRED YEARS...
WAS IT *YOU*, HUYE?
출렁
SPLSH
촤아아
SPSHOOO
I'M SORRY. I'LL ACCEPT ANY KIND OF PUNISHMENT.

HMPH! DON'T WORRY.
I KNOW YOU DIDN'T DO IT.
NO DOUBT, IT IS *YUK-OH*. HE WAS WITH HER ORIGINALLY
촤아악
SPSHWAAA
YOU KNEW IT FROM THE BEGINNING. HMPH! DON'T YOU KNOW THAT IT'S NO USE TRYING TO COVER UP FOR HIM?
I'M SORRY.
후두둑..
PLOOSH

DON'T *EVER* DO THAT AGAIN.
......
YOU'RE THE *LAST* ONE, AND IF *YOU* BETRAY ME...
...I'LL NEVER FORGIVE YOU.

NEVER...
...FORGIVE YOU...
YES...

BTAMM!
HABAEK!
DID YOU HEAR? SEOWANG-MO IS--!!
WHAT THE--?
WHAT ARE YOU DOING HOLDING EACH OTHER?
HRK!!

SOAH...
YOHEE?
WHAT ARE YOU DOING HERE *ALONE?*
I WAS JUST THINKING ABOUT SOME THINGS.

DON'T WORRY TOO MUCH. IF IT'S ABOUT SEOWANGMO-NIM...
...EVERYTHING WILL BE ALL RIGHT. CHEER UP, SOAH.
THANK YOU...
PFF! WHAT IS HE DOING? A HUSBAND SHOULD BE WITH HIS BRIDE AT A TIME LIKE THIS!
WHAT DID HABAEK SAY?
WELL, I DON'T KNOW...

AREN'T YOU GOING INSIDE, SOAH?
I'LL STAY OUT HERE FOR A LITTLE WHILE.
HUH?
IT'S REALLY LATE, YOHEE. YOU'D BETTER GET BACK.
OKAY, THEN. I'LL GO BACK FIRST.
OKAY...

WHERE HAS HABAEK BEEN ALL DAY LONG?

?
첨벙...
KASPLOOSH
첨벙
KASPLOOSH

출렁
KSPLISH
쏴아아
SPSSHHAAA

BRIDE of the WATER GOD

SPSH
SPLSH
바스락
WSHH
WHO'S THERE?!

AROUND GUHA WE WANDER ABOUT
THE WIND RISES TO CROSS THE WAVE
WITHIN THIS WAGON OF WATER, HOW CAN I TAKE SHELTER
WHILE RIDING THE TWO DRAGONS THAT FOLLOW ANOTHER?
--FROM "THE POEM OF HABAEK"
(GUGA POEM / CHOSA STYLE)

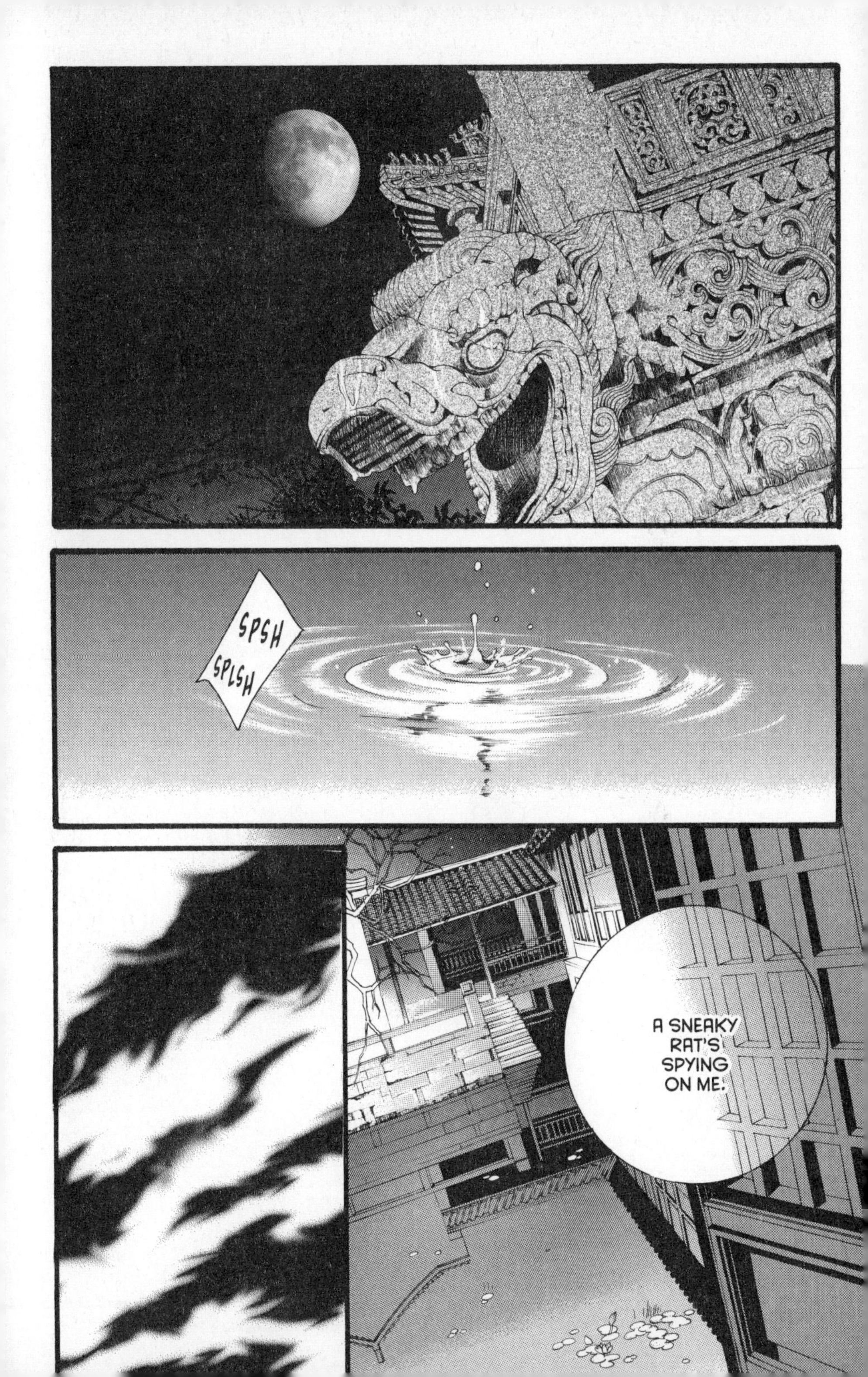
SPSH SPLSH
A SNEAKY RAT'S SPYING ON ME.

I KNOW YOU'RE THERE, SO COME OUT AT ONCE.
HRK!

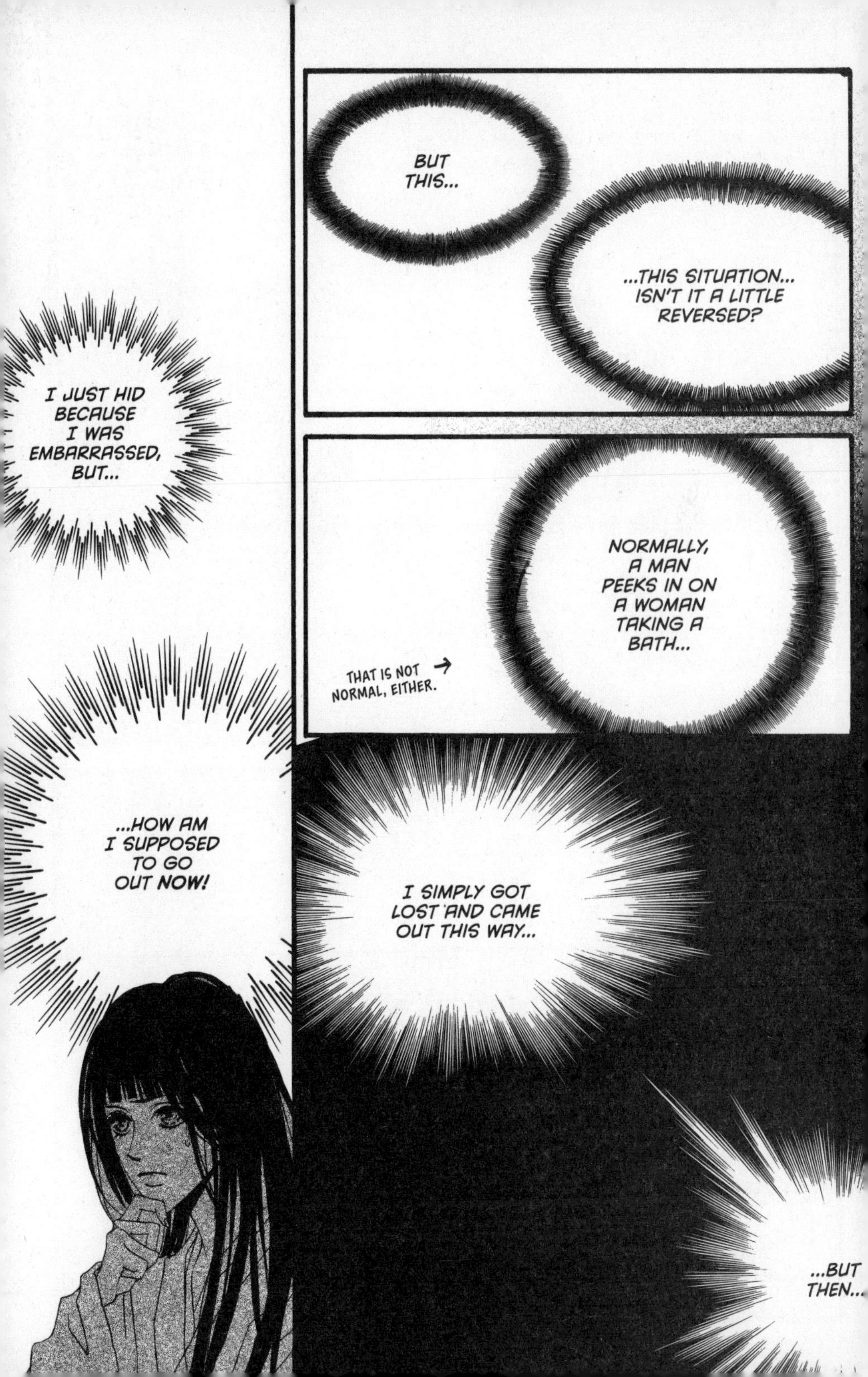
BUT THIS...
...THIS SITUATION... ISN'T IT A LITTLE REVERSED?
NORMALLY, A MAN PEEKS IN ON A WOMAN TAKING A BATH...
THAT IS NOT NORMAL, EITHER.
I SIMPLY GOT LOST AND CAME OUT THIS WAY...
...BUT THEN...
I JUST HID BECAUSE I WAS EMBARRASSED, BUT...
...HOW AM I SUPPOSED TO GO OUT NOW!

HEY, WHY DO I HAVE TO BE CALLED A SNEAKY RAT?!

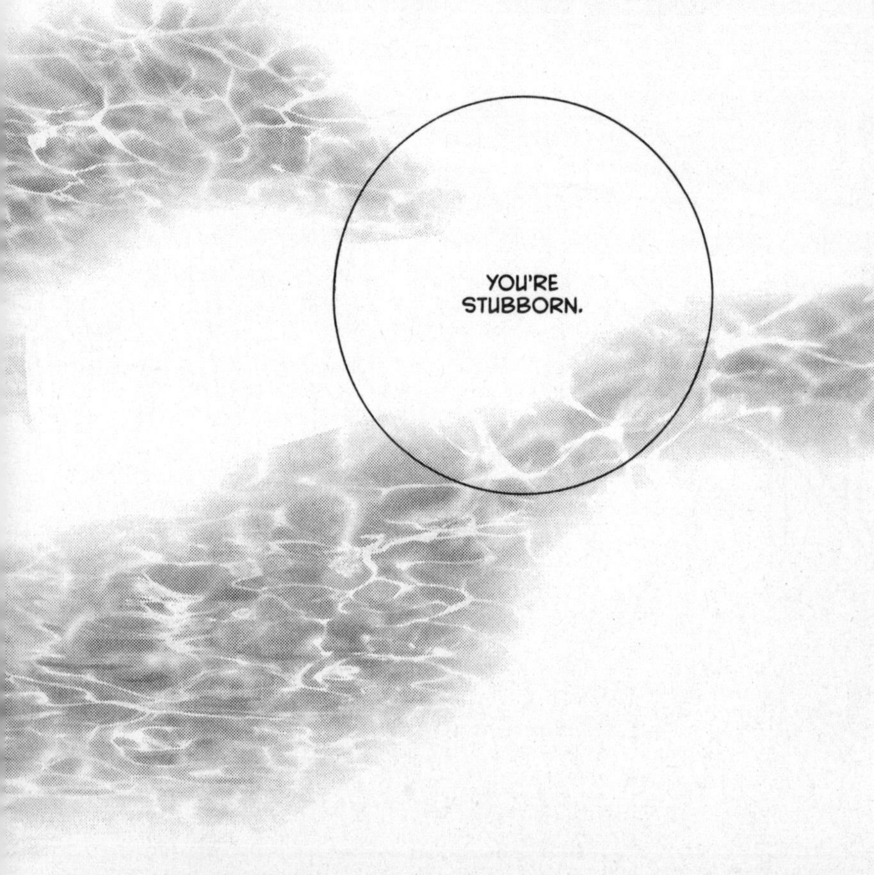
YOU'RE STUBBORN.

WELL, I CAN ALWAYS SEE WHO YOU ARE AFTER I KILL YOU.
SPSHAAA
GYAH.
콰콰콰아아
FSHHHHAAA

촤아아
SPSH
SHWAAA
콰아아아
FSHHHAAA
LIKE HABAEK, LIKE COUSIN!
THEY BOTH HAVE A SHORT TEMPER!!
WAIT--

WAIT!!
FWOOSH
WSHAAA

TNK
BANWANG... WAS THAT YOU?
LONG TIME NO SEE, LORD OF THE WATER.

YOUR QUICK TEMPER IS STILL THE SAME.
HRRF HRRF
SHUT UP. A PERVERTED DOG WHO SNEAKS A PEEK AT SOMEONE BATHING HAS NO ROOM TO TALK!
......
URK!
HMPH! WELL...IF YOU DON'T LIKE MY FORM, THEN...
KRAK
KAKRAK
KRAK
...I WILL TALK TO YOU IN THIS FORM.

THE *EMPEROR* TOLD ME TO FETCH THE LORD OF THE WATER.
I DON'T WANT TO HEAR ANYTHING ABOUT *HIM.*
SO-- BE GONE NOW! YOUR DOG HAIR IS EVERY-WHERE!
HFF! 휘이
......
HWIK 휙
HWIK 휙
IT'S ABOUT *NAKBIN...*
멈칫
FREEZE

HE TOLD ME YOU'D UNDERSTAND IF I SAID THAT.

I CAN ONLY SEE MUI FROM HERE.
WHO IS HE TALKING TO?
I THINK I'LL HEAR HIM BETTER IF I CAN JUST GET CLOSER.
SKFF
?!
투둑
KTTUK

YAA!!
HA HA! IS THERE ANOTHER RAT HERE?!
확
FWAP
?!

휘익
HWWIK
첨벙
SPLOOOSSH

HABAEK...
콰아아아
FSHHHAAA
HABAEK...
ARE YOU GOING TO PRETEND AS IF NOTHING'S HAPPENED AND JUST PLAY? WE'VE BEEN LOOKING ALL OVER FOR YOU.
GROAN
WHERE WERE YOU LAST NIGHT?
LEAVING SOAH ALL ALONE...

WELL...
FWSH SPSH
FMP
THU-THUMP
THU-THUMP
THU-THUMP
SHE MUST'VE FAINTED.

첨벙
SPLOOSH
THAT LADY IS...
스윽
FWSH
...SHE IS...
꽉
SNNCH
SHE'S *NOBODY--*
NOTHING.

......
VERY WELL...
SHK SHK SHK SHKAAAH

WHO IS
THIS?

A FAMILIAR SCENT.
...HABAEK?
끼익
KRIK KREEE
TAK

휘잉
HWSH
덜컥...
FWOOSH

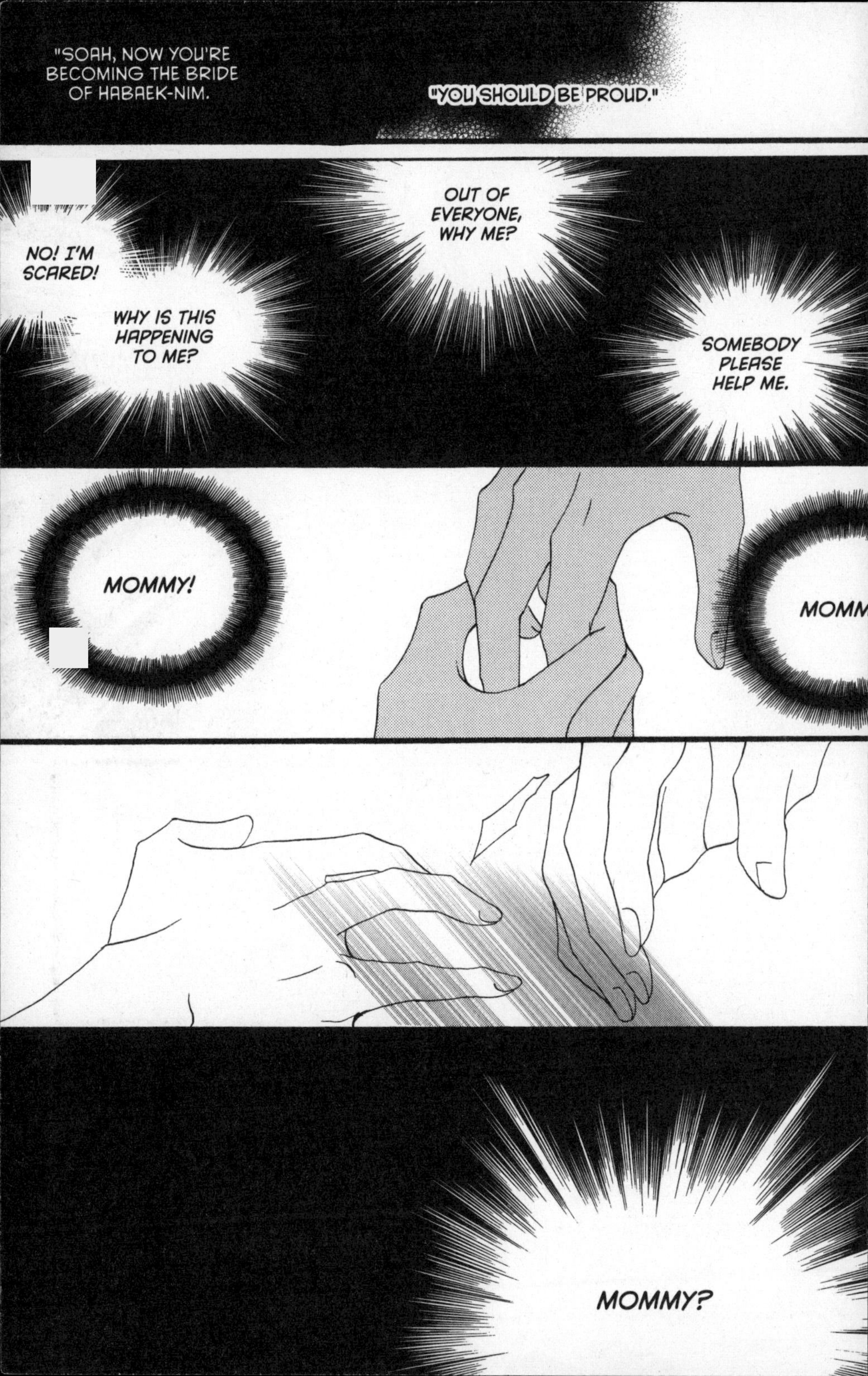
"SOAH, NOW YOU'RE BECOMING THE BRIDE OF HABAEK-NIM.
"YOU SHOULD BE PROUD."
OUT OF EVERYONE, WHY ME?
NO! I'M SCARED!
SOMEBODY PLEASE HELP ME.
WHY IS THIS HAPPENING TO ME?
MOMM
MOMMY!
MOMMY?

HAHH!
IS IT BECAUSE OF THE WAY I FEEL?
IT WAS... A DREAM...
WHEN DID I COME BACK?

IT FEELS LIKE... THE MOON FEELS A LOT BRIGHTER THAN USUAL...

TWO MOONS?
NO.
THAT IS NOT THE MOON.
THAT IS...
WHAT'S GOING ON?

...GONRYUN MOUNTAIN.
VOOM KOOM KOOM KOOM
SEOWANGMO'S HERE...

HER FACE IS SO BEAUTIFUL AND COLD. IT'S QUITE SCARY.

I CAN TELL WHO THIS IS WITHOUT ASKING ANYTHING...
스윽
FWSH
움찔
FLINCH
SO THIS IS THE *HUMAN GIRL* WHO IS SUPPOSED TO BE THE BRIDE...
SHE IS...

...HABAEK'S MOTHER!!
AND...
...SHE IS ALSO THE GODDESS OF PUNISHMENT AND TORTURE...
I JUST STOPPED BY FOR A WHILE TODAY TO SAY HELLO.

WE'LL TALK MORE WHEN THE DAY GETS BRIGHTER.
휴이이잉
HWWOOO
IT'S COLD...
IT'S NOT A DREAM...!!

콰아아아...
VOOM KOOM KOOM KOOM
탁
TAK
HEARD THAT YOUR MOTHER'S ARRIVED, HUH, HABAEK?
SHOULD YOU BE HERE PLAYING LEISURELY LIKE THIS?
......
ARHGHH! MOVING YOUR PIECE THERE...
탁
TAK

HA-
BAEK...
...ARE YOU GOING TO PRETEND AS IF NOTHING HAPPENED AND JUST PLAY? WE'VE BEEN LOOKING ALL OVER FOR YOU.
WHERE WERE YOU ALL LAST NIGHT?
......
WELL...
YOU CAN'T JUST SAY "WELL"... SOAH'S BEEN CALLED TO GO BEFORE SEOWANGMO!

IT'S BEEN A REALLY LONG TIME, JUDONG.
HAS IT BEEN ABOUT FOUR HUNDRED YEAR SINCE YOU STOLE A CHUNDO AND ATE IT AT SUNDOWON?
DARN! WHAT A GOOD MEMORY.
AHAH HA HA HA... THAT'S RIGHT.
HEH HEH!

WAS YOUR NAME SOAH?
GUHRK!
AH, YES--
큭 HEH!
DON'T BE SO AFRAID OF ME. I'M NOT REALLY ALL THAT HORRIBLE.
LIE!
HOW OLD DO YOU THINK I AM?
UH... WELL... ABOUT THIRTY...
BLAH! SHE IS ACTUALLY ABOUT TWENTY THOUSAND YEARS OLD...!
퍽 SPAKK
WHAT GOOD EYES YOU HAVE, JUST CALL ME "MOTHER" AS YOU WISH.
NO WONDER WHY HABAEK IS SO HANDSOME. YOU ARE SOOO BEAU-TIFUL.
← STRUGGLING FOR SURVIVAL.

IT DOESN'T MATTER HOW OLD YOUR CHILD IS, PARENTS ARE ALWAYS CONCERNED.
WHAT BROUGHT YOU TO SUGUK?
HABAEK...?

IS THAT ALL YOU CAN SAY TO A MOTHER YOU HAVEN'T SEEN IN SUCH A LONG TIME?
SOAH.
YOU GO BACK WITH YOHEE.
FUMP
?
WHAT ARE YOU WORRIED ABOUT?
YOU DON'T THINK *I* WILL DO ANYTHING TO HER, DO YOU?

RIGHT NOW!
AH... I...
FWAA
......
I'M DELIGHTED TO SEE YOU AFTER SUCH A LONG TIME, BUT YOU DON'T SEEM TO LIKE IT AT ALL.
HWIK
YOU SAY THAT YOU'RE GLAD TO SEE ME, BUT WHY HAVEN'T YOU VISITED IN SUCH A LONG TIME?

'T WAS JUST FOR A LITTLE WHILE, BUT SHE LOOKED LONELY...
YOU WERE SCARED, WEREN'T YOU SOAH?
SOAH?
HUH? I'M SORRY.
I WAS JUST THINKING ABOUT MY MOM...
ARE YOU HOMESICK?
IT'S NOT THAT...
"HONEY, I'M SO SORRY..."

WHY IN THE WORLD WAS HABAEK SO ANGRY LIKE THAT THIS AFTERNOON?
TOK
TOK
AT THIS HOUR? WHO COULD IT BE?
WHO IS IT?
?!
MUI?

FWAP
WHAT THE--?
WHAT IS THIS, ALL OF A SUDDEN ?!
FWSH
THU-THUMP
THU-THUMP
THU-THUMP
THU-THUMP

......
......
WHAT ...?

HWIK
WHAT...
...WHAT DID YOU SAY...?
GO BACK.

I'M TELLING YOU TO GO BACK HOME.
Bride of the Water God Volume One / END

EPILOGUE
THANK YOU SO MUCH FOR READING ALL THE WAY UP TO THIS POINT.
ACTUALLY, I'M REALLY SHY ABOUT TELLING MY STORIES TO OTHERS.
수줍
BLUSH
SO...WHEN I WAS YOUNG, I USED TO WRITE MY STORIES DOWN, FOLDING THE SHEETS OF PAPER ABOUT TWENTY-SEVEN TIMES. THEN I HID THEM SO THAT NOBODY COULD SEE THEM.
FOLD FOLD 꼬깃 꼬깃
SO "BRIDE OF THE WATER GOD" IS THE FIRST STORY I EVER TOLD TO OTHERS.

YOU ACTUALLY CANNOT FOLD PAPER MORE THAN ABOUT TEN TIMES.

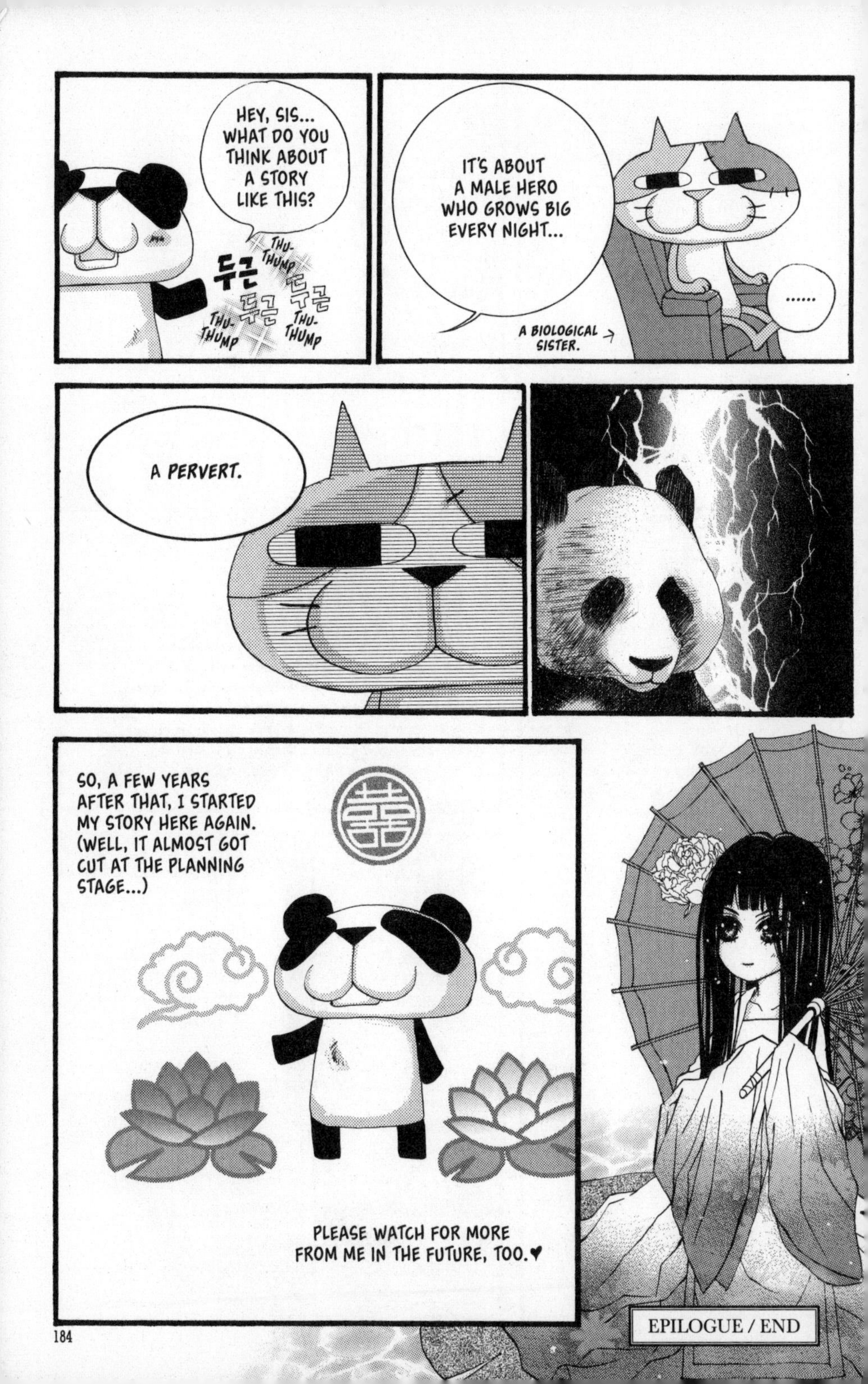
HEY, SIS... WHAT DO YOU THINK ABOUT A STORY LIKE THIS?
두근
THU-THUMP
두근
THU-THUMP
두근
THU-THUMP
IT'S ABOUT A MALE HERO WHO GROWS BIG EVERY NIGHT...
......
A BIOLOGICAL SISTER.
A PERVERT.
SO, A FEW YEARS AFTER THAT, I STARTED MY STORY HERE AGAIN. (WELL, IT ALMOST GOT CUT AT THE PLANNING STAGE...)
PLEASE WATCH FOR MORE FROM ME IN THE FUTURE, TOO.♥
EPILOGUE / END

publisher
Mike Richardson

digital production
Ryan Hill

collection designer
David Nestelle

art director
Lia Ribacchi

Special thanks to Tina Alessi, Davey Estrada, Michael Gombos, Julia Kwon, and Cara Niece.

English-language version produced by DARK HORSE COMICS.

BRIDE OF THE WATER GOD Volume 1

Dark Horse Manhwa
A division of Dark Horse Comics, Inc.
10956 SE Main Street
Milwaukie OR 97222

darkhorse.com

To find a comics shop in your area, call the
Comic Shop Locator Service toll-free at 1-888-266-4226

First edition: October 2007
ISBN: 978-1-59307-849-2

7 9 10 8 6
Printed in the United States of America

People say that one's creation comes to possess their soul when one pours their mind and hope into it.

I thank you so much for reading my stories, although I have a lot to work on. I will keep working harder.

—*Mi-Kyung Yun*

CREATOR PROFILE

Born on October 14, 1980. Majored in Animation at Mokwon University.

Received the silver medal for Seoul Media Group's "Shin-in-gong-mo-jeon" ("New Artist Debut Competition") for *Na-eu Ji-gu Bang-moon-gi* (*The Journey of My Earth Visit*) in 2003.

Received a "Shin-in-sang" ("Best New Artist") award from the Dokja-manhwa-daesang organization for *Railroad* in 2004.

Currently publishing *Bride of the Water God* serially in the Korean comics magazine *Wink*.

STORY NOTE: The poem that appears on page 136 is a Chinese poem. *Chosa* is one of the literary styles developed during China's "Cho" dynasty. Within this style, *guga* poetry was specially dedicated to singing about and worshipping gods such as Habaek (the water god), Judong (the fire god), and others.

Bestselling and award-winning author **Anita Higman** has thirty books published (several coauthored) for adults and children. She's been a Barnes & Noble "Author of the Month" for Houston and has a BA degree, combining speech communication, psychology, and art. Anita loves good movies, exotic teas, and brunch with her friends. Please visit Anita online at www.anitahigman.com.